THE
CANTERBURY
TALES

THE
CANTERBURY
TALES

by

Geoffrey Chaucer

Translated and Adapted by

PETER ACKROYD

Illustrated by NICK BANTOCK

PENGUIN CLASSICS
an imprint of
PENGUIN BOOKS

PENGUIN CLASSICS

Published by the Penguin Group
Penguin Books Ltd, 80 Strand, London WC2R ORL, England
Penguin Group (USA) Inc., 375 Hudson Street, New York, New York 10014, USA
Penguin Group (Canada), 90 Eglinton Avenue East, Suite 700, Toronto, Ontario, Canada M4P 2Y3
(a division of Pearson Penguin Canada Inc.)
Penguin Ireland, 25 St Stephen's Green, Dublin 2, Ireland (a division of Penguin Books Ltd)
Penguin Group (Australia), 250 Camberwell Road, Camberwell, Victoria 3124, Australia
(a division of Pearson Australia Group Pty Ltd)
Penguin Books India Pvt Ltd, 11 Community Centre, Panchsheel Park, New Delhi – 110 017, India
Penguin Group (NZ), 67 Apollo Drive, Rosedale, North Shore 0632, New Zealand
(a division of Pearson New Zealand Ltd)
Penguin Books (South Africa) (Pty) Ltd, 24 Sturdee Avenue,
Rosebank, Johannesburg 2196, South Africa

Penguin Books Ltd, Registered Offices: 80 Strand, London WC2R ORL, England

www.penguin.com

First published 2009
1

Set in 11.5/15 pt PostScript Adobe Sabon
Typeset by Rowland Phototypesetting Ltd, Bury St Edmunds, Suffolk
Printed in Great Britain by Clays Ltd, St Ives plc

A CIP catalogue record for this book is available from the British Library

ISBN: 978-1-846-14058-7

www.greenpenguin.co.uk

Penguin Books is committed to a sustainable future
for our business, our readers and our planet.
The book in your hands is made from paper
certified by the Forest Stewardship Council.

Contents

Introduction

Geoffrey Chaucer, the author of *The Canterbury Tales*, was fully representative of fourteenth-century London. Just as the individual tales themselves can be taken as a mirror for medieval society, so the life of Chaucer reflects the variously moving forces of the age. He was, for example, a familiar figure at the royal court, where he acted as a royal servant for no less than three kings and two princes. He was a customs official, collecting taxes at the Port of London. He was a diplomat and an official who supervised the building works of the king. He was, briefly, a soldier. He was also appointed to be a judge and a member of parliament. Somehow, within the interstices of all these tasks and duties, he was able to compose poetry that is the most accomplished and vigorous manifestation of medieval England.

He is best known of course for *The Canterbury Tales* but he wrote that work towards the end of a busy creative life. He had written, in previous years, fables and legends and dream poems; he had also composed *Troilus and Criseyde*, which has perhaps justly been described as the first modern English novel. No writer was more various or more complex. His character has proved as hard to define as his writing. In his verse he professes shyness and reserve, but a customs official cannot be shy. He liked to present himself as a bookish recluse, but he was sued for debt and accused of rape in the public courts. He remains most celebrated for his salacious humour and scabrous wit, but he was also possessed by a profoundly religious vision of the world.

Chaucer was born, somewhere between 1341 and 1343, as the son of a wealthy merchant family residing in London. His father, John Chaucer, was a successful vintner or wine-merchant whose house and office were beside the river in Thames Street; a few yards away lay Three Cranes Wharf, where the wines of Gascony were unloaded. All his life Chaucer lived within sight and sound of the river. As a child and young man he grew up in a noisy, crowded and busy world, the energetic spirit of which suffuses his writing. In the course of his often grand and elaborate verse we come upon the phrases of the London streets that were all around him – 'Come off, man ... lat see now ... namoore of this ... what sey ye ... take hede now ... Jakke fool!'

But although his real education derived from the streets, he was also given more formal instruction. He may have been taught at home by a resident tutor, or he may have attended Saint Paul's Almonry School a few hundred yards away. His knowledge of Latin, and of Latin authors such as Ovid and Virgil, can only have come from a thorough grounding in what was known as 'grammar'. He was also adept at French and Italian, but he may have mastered these languages by more worldly means. At the age of fourteen or fifteen, he was sent to the royal court.

His father had been appointed as deputy butler in the household of Edward III, and of course his ambitions for his son were best channelled through the great ones of the land. In 1357 Chaucer became a page in the service of King Edward's daughter-in-law, Princess Elizabeth, and began a career in royal service that would end only at his death. At court he was instructed in the arts of correspondence and of oratory. The study of rhetoric, in particular, is key to the understanding of *The Canterbury Tales*. He went to war, as a royal servant, and was captured by French forces just outside Rheims; four months later, he was ransomed for the sum of sixteen pounds.

He never went to war again, and it is safe to say that he had no taste for it. His was an art of peace. By his early twenties, in fact, he had entered the king's diplomatic service and was being dispatched on various missions to the princes of Europe. Yet the diplomat was now also a poet. By his own account he was writing 'many a song and many a lecherous lay'. He was a court poet, in other words, entertaining the ladies and gentlemen with elegant recitals of complaints and roundelays, ballades and envoyes. There are suggestions that this early work also became popular. His contemporary John Gower reports that Chaucer filled the whole land with his ditties and his songs.

On the death of his father Chaucer inherited part of a large estate; he promptly married Philippa de Roet, a royal servant in the household of the queen. It was in that sense a court marriage, but very little else is known about it. Chaucer was always reticent on private matters, and was so self-effacing that he sometimes seems invisible. We know only his wife's name and occupation. In later years they spent many months apart, but this does not seem to have troubled either party.

His connections with the court grew ever closer. He joined the retinue of John of Gaunt, one of King Edward's sons, and obtained an annual grant for services rendered. One of those services included the composition of suitable poetry for his new patron. On the death of John of Gaunt's wife, Chaucer wrote *The Book of the Duchess*, a dream vision in memory of the virtues of the dead woman. It seems to have been written for oral delivery, and Chaucer may have recited it at her memorial service held in Saint Paul's Cathedral.

It is also worth recording that the poem is composed in English. The royal court at Westminster was still pre-dominantly French, and therefore French-speaking, but the poetry of Chaucer is the best possible indication that the status of the English language was rising very rapidly. He was the first master of the language, rescuing it from its somewhat lowly role as the vernacular of a conquered race. It is no accident that within his lifetime English replaced French as the language of schoolteaching, and that in the reign of the next sovereign it became the language of the court. Everything conspired to render Chaucer the most representative, as well as the most authoritative, poet of his time. One definition of genius lies in its embodiment of the principles of the age.

Yet that genius did not thrive on wholly native principles. His duties as a royal envoy sent him to Italy on several separate occasions, where he engaged in trade negotiations with both Genoa and Florence. There was more than trade on his mind. While in Florence, for example, he had the opportunity of observing that city's cultural life at first hand. He was shown, and given, literary manuscripts. Florence was in particular the nurse and mother of contemporary Italian poetry, the exposure to which materially affected Chaucer's art. He read Dante, and Boccaccio, and Petrarch, in the original. Dante had of course written *Divina Commedia*, but he had also written a treatise, *De Vulgari Eloquentia*, extolling the virtues of the vernacular language. The lesson was not lost on the English poet.

At the time of Chaucer's visit to Florence, Petrarch was living a hundred miles away in Padua. But his influence was everywhere apparent; he was the master of eloquence, the prince of magnificence, who had raised the material and spiritual status of the poet. Chaucer could have surmised, from his example, that poetry was a vocation rather than simply employment or pastime. Without the overwhelming example of these two Italian writers, it is unlikely that Chaucer would have been tempted into writing a work as ambitious as *The Canterbury Tales*. The example of Boccaccio was also important. He wrote in various genres – romantic, mythological and historical – and in various styles. *The Canterbury Tales* itself owes much to *The Decameron*, being also a peripatetic feat of storytelling on an epic scale.

So Chaucer returned to England with his poetic ambitions clarified and heightened. Almost at once he began work on *The House of Fame*, another dream vision that seems to parody

Petrarch's 'high' style of discourse. One of the authorial
strategies of Chaucer was the use of wit and humour to convey
a vision of a world that is neither stable nor ideal. All things
are mixed under the moon. That is why the practical business
of life still had to be maintained. On 8 June 1374 he was
appointed controller of the wool custom, one of the most
important offices within the Port of London. It was hard, and
difficult, work. He was responsible for checking and weighing
the merchandise, counting the sacks of wool, and mediating
the disputes of merchants. He also collected the custom duties,
which, in the medieval period, also encompassed the taking of
bribes and various 'perks'. In *The House of Fame*, completed
after he had taken on the role of controllership, he describes
his working life:

> For when thy labour doon al ys,
> And hast mad alle thy rekenynges,
> In stede of reste and newe thynges
> Thou goost hom to thy house anoon,
> And, also domb as any stoon,
> Thou sittest at another book
> Tyl fully daswed ys thy look.

We can identify the 'hom' where he engaged in this laborious
study. The poet lived above Aldgate, one of the western gates
of the city, and from this lofty dwelling he could see the people
of London come and go in an endless parade of carts, wagons,
packhorses and pedestrians. He would have heard the confused
noise of their voices as they passed beneath; he would have
observed the details of their dress. He would have observed,
too, the figure of the solitary traveller. From the house above
Aldgate he would have become reacquainted with the idea of
life as an endless journey. On his way to his work in the Port of
London he would have walked through the busiest, noisiest
and most populous streets of the city. That great concourse of
people was the harbinger of *The Canterbury Tales*.

On 21 June 1377, Edward III was succeeded by an eleven-year-old boy who was crowned as Richard II. This transition did not disturb Chaucer in the least. The new court sustaining the majesty of the boy-king contained many friends and acquaintances of the poet, and he was dispatched on various embassies and missions over the next few years. His status may have helped him in one other respect. On 1 May 1380 Cecily Champain released Chaucer from all actions 'De raptu meo' – 'Concerning my rape'. She had accused him of rape, in other words, and she had been persuaded to settle out of court. Three of the witnesses to this declaration were important members of the royal household. And the fourth had been lord mayor of London. The existence of this document is itself enough to prove that Chaucer was not some amused or distant observer of events. He was at the heart of court and adminis-trative affairs. Of the 'rape' itself there is no contemporary evidence. It should only be emphasized that the ways of medieval law are tangled indeed, and that no single statement can be taken at face value. The rest is silence.

Chaucer had by this time acquired a considerable reputation as a poet as well as an officer of the crown. He had written another dream vision, *The Parliament of Fowls*, which repre-sents the essence of courtly poetry. It is crowded with minute and realistic detail, suffused with emotional symbolism, con-cerned with individual portraiture (birds, in Chaucer's works, are more than human), and filled with classical learning. But he was going beyond the confines of the court; he was addressing much of his poetry to the citizens, and in particular to the merchant class, of London. These affluent burghers made up a new, educated class.

In pursuit of a more broadly based audience, in fact, he was about to start work on a poem that would redefine the boundaries of English poetry. *Troilus and Criseyde* is a fiction of manners and a pantomime, a threnody and a philosophical enquiry, a farcical comedy and a lament upon the cruel wiles of fate. It is all of these things and more, and can be described as

the first modern work of literature in English. It is heterogen-
eous and various, in every way a fitting predecessor for
The Canterbury Tales. It is in part based upon Boccaccio's
Il Filostrato and narrates the story of Criseyde's unfaithfulness
to Troilus during the course of the Trojan War. But Chaucer
turns a romance into a human drama, an elaborate and artful
account of love and jealousy against the backdrop of eternity.
Yet it is also the work of a shrewd and practical man of affairs
who can see beneath the 'show' of things; Chaucer mocks
pretension and hypocrisy, false learning and false sentiment,
and in the course of this long poem he reveals his delight in low
humour and innuendo. The character of Pandarus, the human
catalyst between the lovers, is one of the greatest inventions of
the medieval imagination.

Even as Chaucer was completing *Troilus and Criseyde* he
was embarking work upon a miniature epic on the theme
of the two knights Palamon and Arcite competing for the
love of Emily. This became the first of the tales of Canterbury,
'The Knight's Tale'. He had left his lodging in Aldgate, on
relinquishing his post at the customs house, and had removed
himself to Kent. He became Justice of the Peace for that county
and then, a year later, he became one of the MPs for that
region. He also became steward of two royal palaces in Kent,
those of Eltham and of Sheen. It seems likely that he was living
in Greenwich, or in the neighbouring town of Deptford, when
he was composing *The Canterbury Tales*. Both localities are in
fact mentioned in the poem itself:

> Lo Depeford, and it is half-wey pryme!
> Lo Grenewych, ther many a shrewe is inne!
> It were al tyme thy tale to bigynne.

Did he have any particular 'shrewe' in mind?

So now, out of London and released from his more onerous
tasks, Chaucer had acquired a measure of time and freedom to
contemplate the nature of the long poem that stretched ahead

of him. 'The Knight's Tale' and 'The Second Nun's Tale' had already been completed, but it is likely that from the beginning he had in mind a great and open epic that would allow him to accommodate the most varied material. The poem was in fact never completed and exists in a number of stray manuscripts and groups of manuscripts that have been put together in more or less arbitrary patterns by later editors. There are connections between some of them, but there are not enough to convey any sense of a unified whole. That may in fact have been Chaucer's intention. He was working on the poem for the rest of his life, and perhaps believed it to be as quixotic and as unpredictable as life itself. He may have worked upon more than one tale at a time, leaving some of them unfinished. He revised prologues and epilogues to incorporate his changing thoughts; on occasions he took lines out of one tale and inserted them in another. Some of the tales are appropriate to their speakers, while others plainly are not. There are indications, for example, that 'The Shipman's Tale' was originally delivered by a woman. It was a great work in progress.

That is why certain characters grew in imaginative strength, as Chaucer seized upon their possibilities. The Wife of Bath, for example, took on a fresh access of life after her first appearance. Her prologue became the longest in the poem, and at a later date he added new lines about her. He introduced references to her in 'The Clerk's Tale' and 'The Merchant's Tale' as a way of reaffirming her identity. Characters like her have such naturalistic immediacy that it is hard to know where life ends and art begins. Chaucer also introduces 'real' people into the proceedings. The famous Host of the poem was based upon a real Harry Bailey, the proprietor of an inn in Southwark; the Cook derives from a famous cook of the period, Roger of Ware, known as 'Hogge of Ware'. And of course Geoffrey Chaucer appears as a bemused and bookish observer of human life, a trifle fat and a trifle obtuse. That is a measure of his own imaginative irony and indirection; it was a way of adverting to his authorial presence in the poem while at the same time disarming criticism.

Yet for all its naturalistic detail, *The Canterbury Tales* is not a realistic narrative in the modern sense. It is highly charged with rhetorical and stylistic devices, and is as close to a contemporary novel as Wells Cathedral is to an apartment block. He employs all the devices of *exclamatio*, *interrogatio* and *interpretatio*, even as he looks clearly into the secret recesses of human affairs. The human figures are all intensely conceived, vivid and vigorous; but their intensity comes from their formal status as types or tokens of the medieval world. They resemble the characters from the mystery plays and pageants that were then the stuff of popular entertainment. The poem opens with the Knight because he represents the apotheosis of military virtues in a society that is defined by warfare. In similar fashion Chaucer describes what were then called the 'estates' of the realm – those who fight, those who pray and those who labour. Each pilgrim is an allegory as well as a person. The Monk is 'ful fat and in good poynt' but he also represents the cupidity and corruption of the Church. The Wife of Bath is a formidable matron, but she also represents the corruption of the female sex after the disobedience of Eve in the Garden of Eden.

The Canterbury Tales is, then, a conflation of distinct and different narratives. Its 'General Prologue' and twenty-four separate tales cover every form from sermon to farce, from saint's life to animal fable, from heroic adventure to full-scale parody. Its twenty-eight characters furnish an assembly of fourteenth-century people in a medley of occupations and professions. The open form of the poem also allows Chaucer to introduce all the various styles of the age, from high chant to vernacular. The whole poem works by contrast – spiritual against secular, piety against buffoonery and salaciousness. That is why the high style of the first of the stories, 'The Knight's Tale', is followed by the broad sexual humour of 'The Miller's Tale'. 'The Miller's Tale' is in turn parodied by

'The Reeve's Tale', describing the cuckolding of a miller, which is followed by the short fragment of 'The Cook's Tale', concerning an apprentice and a prostitute. So this group of four tales represents a subtle gradation of love's joys from the chivalric romance of the Knight to the low pleasures of the urban poor. The Cook may not have the elaborate rhetorical skills of the Knight but he represents a broader if not richer tradition. The apparent naturalism of the poem is a product of its diversity; out of oppositions comes energy. Out of contrast arises beauty.

It has often been remarked that the poem does not concern itself with the events of the time; the Black Death and the Peasants' Revolt, both of which Chaucer experienced at first hand, are referred to only once in the entire course of *The Canterbury Tales*. But Chaucer deals with the world around him in a different way. It is possible through these pages to glimpse a great deal of medieval life as it was actually experienced. The pilgrims are in one sense caricatures, but they convey a great sense of the underlying reality of the time – the Cook who adds parsley sauce to disguise the old meat, the Miller who routinely and frequently exploits his monopoly in the district, the Reeve who manages to cheat his employer. We may note here also the casual misogyny and the equally casual anti-Semitism. All these were as characteristic of the time as the continual appeals to the Virgin and the constant invocations of Christ's name.

Geoffrey Chaucer's own life in the world continued as he worked on the long poem. He was engaged in royal business in the last decade of his life, and in 1394 was granted an annual pension of twenty pounds by Richard II. In 1398 he was given a document of 'safe conduct' for the pursuit of the king's 'arduous and urgent business'. That was also the year in which he left Kent and returned to London – or, more precisely, Westminster. In 1399 he took out a fifty-three-year lease on a tenement in the garden of the Lady Chapel of the Abbey there. He was now approaching sixty, a respectable age in a period when epidemic sickness and chronic illness were commonplace.

The cause of his death, however, is unknown. But he did expire in a year of plague, on a date generally accepted as 25 October 1400. This was the date inscribed upon his tombstone, albeit one erected one hundred and fifty years later. He was buried in Westminster Abbey itself. Now his tomb rests in Poets' Corner, but at the time it was placed in an obscure site generally left for monastic officials. He did not lie here because he was a great poet, only in recognition of his role as a royal servant.

Yet the poetry was neither ignored nor forgotten. There are more than eighty surviving manuscripts of Chaucer's long poem, gathered together after the poet's death. The number alone testifies to the extraordinary popularity of *The Canterbury Tales* in the early years of the fifteenth century. From the beginning it was seen as a great work of the imagination. William Caxton described Chaucer as 'the worshipfull father' of 'our englissh'. John Dryden also described him as 'the Father of *English* poetry'.

Why should we still read *The Canterbury Tales*? The immediate answer is also perhaps the most obvious. It is one of the greatest poems in all of English literature, one that will last as long as the language itself endures. It is also one of the most resourceful summaries of the sensibility of the Middle Ages, as rich and as complex as the stonework of the cathedrals. It represents the culmination of a culture that encompasses the Anglo-Saxon, as well as the medieval, world. It manifests a common European sensibility, too, with its adaptation of French and Italian literature within the broad English narrative.

It is in that sense also the first triumph of the vernacular, in an age when English was at last recognized as the official language of expression. It is the equivalent of Dante's *Divine Comedy*, the one poem that embodied the vernacular strength of the Italian language. Yet the differences between the two poems are instructive. *The Canterbury Tales* is a paradigm of a uniquely English sensibility, with its range of styles and tones that move easily from the most refined to the most vulgar. In some respects Chaucer can be considered the father of English humour; his portraits of the Wife of Bath and of the Summoner, for example, have influenced writers as diverse as Fielding and Dickens.

The Canterbury Tales moves between piety and farce, high and low styles easily accommodated within a flexible and fluent language that seems to spring forth effortlessly. He mingled the sacred and the secular, the romantic and the real, in the process invoking the great general drama of the human spirit. Successive generations of poets compared the poem to a fountain, ever fresh and ever renewed, and Edmund Spenser prayed

> But if on me some little drops would flowe,
> Of that the spring was in his learned hedde.

So Chaucer may be said to stand at the head, or source, of the great English tradition. G. K. Chesterton once wrote that he considered it extraordinary 'that Chaucer should have been so unmistakably English almost before the existence of England'. But it is perhaps not so extraordinary of a poet who seems to define or sum up the English genius, with his personal modesty and broadness of feeling, with his respect for tradition and his inventive diversity. Translating *The Canterbury Tales* into contemporary English is another way of affirming its centrality and its continuing life. It can be reborn in every generation.

A Note on the Text

There are no laws of translation. There are no general rules. Many theories of translation have been adumbrated over the centuries, but they are of limited value. Who can determine in advance how a certain word or phrase should be most finely rendered? In the case of *The Canterbury Tales*, for example, it would have been possible to follow the example of John Dryden, whose inventive and exuberant translation of 'The Knight's Tale' transformed that poem into an epitome of late seventeenth-century heroic epic complete with couplets. His was free translation of the very best. Or it would have been possible to follow the stricter and more faithful model of Nevill Coghill's translation of the entire *Canterbury Tales*; it was first published in 1951, and it remains the best verse translation in modern English.

I chose to follow neither example. Translation can be a form of liberation, releasing an older work into the contemporary world and thereby infusing it with new life. *The Canterbury Tales* has been endlessly reinterpreted – and indeed rewritten – over the centuries. It is a touchstone of the English imagination, and as such can be revisited and redefined amid changing circumstances and cultural styles. So I thought it best to approach my own task in the manner of Chaucer himself, whose translation of part of the *Roman de la Rose* (to give one of many examples) was faithful to the spirit if not always to the letter of the great original. He seems to have worked on the principle of inspired improvisation, guided by no other criterion than his own good sense. Sometimes he closely follows the text; on other occasions he will add his own gloss or interpretation in order to smooth the path of a difficult passage. He will add asides and moments of comedy as a way of connecting the reader with the life and momentum of the French poem. He lent the *Roman de la Rose* all the energy of the fourteenth-century imagination.

Of course I was writing prose rather than poetry. This was a daunting concession to the modern world, which does not love the long poem, but a necessary one. The transition from poetry to prose, however, need not necessarily be altogether harmful. It may be possible to intimate the nature of the poetry within the texture of the prose; it may be possible indirectly and almost subliminally to echo the euphonies and harmonies of Chaucerian verse. Thus, for example, the Prioress seeks divine guidance before beginning her tale to the pilgrims:

> My konnyng is so wayk, O blisful Queene,
> For to declare thy grete worthynesse
> That I ne may the weighte nat susteene;
> But as a child of twelf month oold, or lesse,
> That kan unnethes any word expresse,
> Right so fare I, and therfore I yow preye,
> Gydeth my song that I shal of yow seye.

In my translation her prayer is rendered thus:

> My learning and knowledge are so weak, holy Virgin, that I cannot express your mercy or your love. Your light is too bright for me to bear. I come to you as an infant, scarcely able to speak. Form my broken words uttered in praise of you. Guide my song.

The language of medieval devotion has long since gone but, in the search for an equivalent, it is possible that something of the poetry of the original can be preserved. That, at least, was my intention.

Of course Chaucer was not always writing in a pious spirit. *The Canterbury Tales* is perhaps best known for its bawdy and sometimes scatological humour. The modern translator can maintain the salacious energy of the original simply by transcribing Chaucer's words accurately. The language of sex, unlike the language of prayer, has not materially altered over the centuries. Chaucer is also justly praised for the directness and freshness of his vernacular style. That, too, may withstand the process of translation. Here is a representative passage from 'The Nun's Priest's Tale' concerning the adventures of a cock known as Chanticleer:

> And with that word he fley doun fro the beem,
> For it was day, and eke his hennes alle,
> And with a chuk he gan hem for to calle,
> For he hadde founde a corn, lay in the yerd.
> Real he was, he was namoore aferd.
> He fethered Pertelote twenty tyme,
> And trad hire eke as ofte, er it was pryme.
> He looketh as it were a grym leoun,
> And on his toos he rometh up and doun;
> Hym deigned nat to sette his foot to grounde.

I translated it thus:

And, with that, he flew down from his perch into the yard. It was dawn. With a crow and a cluck he woke up all of his wives, to feast on the corn scattered on the ground. He was manly. He was king of the yard. He put his wings around Pertelote, and fucked her, at least twenty times before the sun had risen much higher. He looked as strong as a lion. He did not strut in the yard like a common bird. He walked on tiptoe, as if he were about to rise in the air.

A contemporary reader, confronting Chaucer's words, might fail to realize that 'real' means royal, and that 'trad' is a euphemism for sexual intercourse. The meaning of 'pryme', or six o'clock in the morning, might also not be immediately obvious. The unfamiliarity of many of Chaucer's words will not deter the scholar; but it will certainly delay or confuse the lay reader. There are also more general aspects of the medieval world that are now irrecoverable. The genuine piety of the age, together with its appetite for doctrinal tracts, are reflected in two of the longest of Chaucer's tales. 'The Tale of Melibee' and 'The Parson's Tale' are standard narratives of pious exposition, the former being a didactic treatise on the value of patience and the latter an extended sermon on penitence and the seven deadly sins. I have not included them, in the belief that they will not be missed. 'The Parson's Tale' comes at the conclusion of *The Canterbury Tales* but, by following 'The Parson's Prologue' with 'Chaucer's Retractions', I have attempted to convey the sense of a fitting ending.

I believed that my task was essentially to facilitate the experience of the poem – to remove the obstacles to the under-standing and enjoyment of the tales, and by various means to intimate or express the true nature of the original. I hope that I have not failed in my purpose.

Peter Ackroyd

THE
CANTERBURY
TALES

The General Prologue

*Here bygynneth the Book of the
Tales of Caunterbury*

When the soft sweet showers of April reach the roots of all things, refreshing the parched earth, nourishing every sapling and every seedling, then humankind rises up in joy and expectation. The west wind blows away the stench of the city, and the crops flourish in the fields beyond the walls. After the waste of winter it is delightful to hear birdsong once more in the streets. The trees themselves are bathed in song. It is a time of renewal, of general restoration. The sun has passed midway through the sign of the Ram, a good time for the sinews and the heart. This is the best season of the year for travellers. That is why good folk then long to go on pilgrimage. They journey to strange shores and cities, seeking solace among the shrines of the saints. Here in England many make their way to Canterbury, and to the tomb of the holy blissful martyr Thomas. They come from every shire to find a cure for infirmity and care.

It so happened that in April I was lodging at Southwark. I was staying at the Tabard Inn, ready to take the way to Canterbury and to venerate the saint. There arrived one evening at the inn twenty-nine other travellers and, much to my delight, I discovered that they were all Canterbury pilgrims. They came from various places, and from various walks of life, but they all had the same destination. The inn was spacious and comfortable enough to accommodate us all, and we were soon at ease one with another. We shared some ale and wine, and agreed among ourselves that we would ride together. It would be a diversion, a merry journey made in good fellowship. Before the sun had gone down, we had determined to meet at dawn on the following day to make our way along the pilgrims' road.

Before we begin our travels, however, I want to introduce you to the men and women who made up our company. If I describe their rank, and their appearance, you may also acquire some inkling of their character. Dress, and degree, can be tokens of inward worth. I will begin with the Knight.

The KNIGHT, as you might expect, was a man of substance and of valour. From the start of his career as a warrior he had fought for truth and honour, for freedom and for dignity. He had proved himself in warfare in many lands; he had ridden through the territories of the Christians and the countries of the infidel, and had been universally praised for his military virtues. He had been present when Alexandria was won from the Turks; he had taken the palm of valour from all the knights of Prussia; he had mounted expeditions in Russia and Lithuania. He had proved himself in Granada and Morocco and Turkey. Where had he not travelled, and where had he not been victorious? He had fought fifteen battles, and taken part in three tournaments. These exploits were not for love of glory, however, but for love of Christ. Piety guided his sword. He considered himself no more than an instrument for God.

That is why he was, despite his reputation for bravery, modest and prudent. In appearance he was meek as any maid, and no oath or indecency ever passed his lips. He was never insolent or condescending. He was the very flower of chivalry, in this springtime of the year; he was a true and noble knight. Do you see him in front of you? He did not wear the robes of office but a tunic of coarse cloth that would have better suited a monk than a soldier; it was discoloured, too, by the rust from his coat of mail. He had a good horse but it was not festooned with bells or expensive cloths. It was the horse of a pilgrim. He told me that he had come from an expedition in order once more to pledge his faith. He asked me about myself then –

where I had come from, where I had been – but I quickly turned the conversation to another course.

He was travelling with his son, a young SQUIRE, a lusty and lively young man who also aspired to knighthood. He was of moderate height, but he was strong and agile. It is said that the hair is a token of vitality; the more virile a man is, the more hair he will have. His was knit in tight blond curls that flowed down his neck and across his shoulders. He was about twenty years of age, and had already taken part in cavalry expeditions in northern France. In that short time he had made a good impression on his comrades, but the only person he really wished to impress was a certain lady of his acquaintance. I did not discover her name. His tunic was embroidered with flowers, white and red and blue; it was as if he had gathered up a sweet meadow and placed it upon his shoulders. He wore a short gown, with wide sleeves, as suited his rank. He rode well and easily with the grace of a natural horseman. He was always singing, or playing the flute. He wrote songs, too, and I learned that he could joust, and write, and draw, and dance. All the finer human accomplishments came naturally to him. In his company it was always May-time. He had good cause for high spirits. He was so passionately in love that he could scarcely sleep at night; he enjoyed no more rest than a nightingale. Yet he never forgot his manners. He had been instructed in all the arts of courtesy, and carved the meat for his father at the table. When he spoke to me, he took off his hat; he did not glance down at the ground, but looked at me steadfastly in the face without moving his hands or feet. These are good manners.

The Knight in fact had only one servant with him, a YEOMAN, who was dressed in the customary hood and coat of green cloth. Green is the colour of faithfulness and service. He carried under his belt a sheaf of dainty peacock arrows, keen and bright, while in his hand he carried a bow. He knew how to take good care of his equipment, because the feathers were upright and the arrows flew to their target. His hair was closely cropped, and his visage was as brown as a smoked ham. On his arm he wore a glittering arm-guard, and by his right side hung a sword and small shield. On his left side was a dagger in its sheath, its handle richly ornamented and its blade exceedingly sharp. This was a young man ready for combat. Yet he had a silver badge of Saint Christopher, the saint of travellers as well as archers, shining on his tunic. I guessed that this Yeoman, when not dressed for battle, worked as a forester on the Knight's estates. He had a horn hanging at his hip from a broad belt of green. 'I have often seen such a horn,' I told him, 'in the woods and forests.' 'Yes,' he said, 'it rouses the buck.' Then he rode on. He was not a chatterer.

The PRIORESS, of course, rode before him. She was an exemplary nun who put on no airs of excessive piety. She was amiable and modest, and in the course of our pilgrimage she occasionally invoked the name of Saint Eligius; since he is the patron saint of horses and of smiths, she must have been wishing for good speed and a comfortable journey. I should have asked her. Her name was Madame Eglantine, and she was as fragrant as any sweetbriar or honeysuckle. She sang the divine service with perfect pitch, and intoned the sacred verses in a deft and sonorous manner. She spoke French elegantly enough, although her accent was closer to Bow than to Paris. What does it matter if we do not speak the exact language of the French? They are no longer our masters. English is even spoken in the parliament house now. The table manners of the Prioress were of the best. She never let any meat fall from her lips, and she did not dip her hands too deeply into the sauce; not a drop of it fell upon what I must call, if she will forgive me, her breasts. She wiped her lips so carefully that not one smudge of grease was to be found on the rim of her cup, after she had drunk from it, and she was careful never to grab at the food on the table. She knew that the manners of the table reflect the manner of a life. She deported herself very well, in other words, and was amiable and pleasant in all of her dealings. She tried very hard to imitate courtly manners, and remained very dignified on all occasions; she deemed herself to be worthy of respect and, as a result, came to deserve it.

Of her sensibility, there can be no doubt. She was so compassionate that she wept whenever she saw a mouse caught in a trap; even the sight of its blood made her lament. Against the rules of her order she had some small dogs that she fed with roasted meat and milk and fine white bread. She never let them out of her sight, in case one of them was trampled beneath the hooves of the horses or perhaps kicked by a fellow pilgrim. Then there would have been tears galore. You can be sure of that. She was all sympathy and tender heart. You have seen a prioress before, no doubt, but she was a very model of her kind. Her wimple was carefully arranged to show her features to their best advantage – her well-formed nose, her eyes as bright as the glass that comes from Venice, her little mouth as soft and red as a cherry. She was also eager to display the beautiful span of her forehead, that token of truthfulness. Her cloak was well made and finely embroidered, and about her arm she carried a rosary of coral with green beads. That was not her only decoration. She sported a bracelet of gold that was surmounted by the letter 'A' and then, beneath, the legend 'Amor vincit omnia'. Love conquers everything. I presume that she was referring to divine love. I did not ask her about that, either. In fact she seemed a little cautious of me, and I would sometimes catch her staring at me with a perplexed expression. Riding beside her was a nun who performed the duties of a chaplain, together with three priests about whom I could gather very little information. They were just priests.

And then there was a MONK, and a handsome one at that. He was one of those monks who do much business outside the monastery, arranging sales and contracts with the lay-people, and he had acquired lay tastes. He loved hunting, for example. He prided himself on being strong and firm of purpose; he would make a very good abbot. He had a stable of good horses as brown as autumn berries and, when he rode, you could hear his bridle jingling as loudly as the bell calling his fellows to chapel. He was supposed to follow the rule of Saint Benedict, in the small monastery over which he had authority, but he found the precepts antiquated and altogether too strict; he preferred to follow the modern fashions of good living and good drinking. He loved a fat swan on his table. He paid no heed to the injunction that huntsmen can never be holy men, and scorned the old saying that a monk without rules is like a fish without water. Who needs water, in any case, when there is ale and wine? Why should he study in the book room off the cloister, and make his head spin with words and texts? Why should he labour and work with his own hands, as Saint Augustine ordained? What good is that to the world? Let Augustine do the work! No, this monk was a sportive horseman. He owned greyhounds that were as swift as any bird in flight. He loved tracking down and killing the hares on the lands of the monastery. He looked the part, too. His sleeves were lined and trimmed with soft squirrel fur, the most expensive of its kind. He had a great gold pin, to fasten his hood under his chin, which blossomed into an intricate knot at its head. That could not have been cheap. His head was bald, and shone as if it were made of glass; his face glowed, too, as if it had been anointed with oil. He was a fine plump specimen of a monk, in excellent condition. His eyes were very bright and mobile, gleaming like the sudden spark from a furnace under a cauldron. He was all fire and life, a sanguinary man. He was the best kind of prelate, to my thinking, and not a tormented ghost of a cleric. He seemed to enjoy my company or, rather, he seemed to enjoy himself in my company; he did not enquire about my life or my occupation. I liked that.

And then there rode a FRIAR. He loved pleasure and any kind of merriment but, since he was obliged to beg for alms, he was still very resourceful. He was not importunate, but he was imposing. Of all the four orders, however, his was the most inclined to gossip and to flattery. He had arranged many marriages and sometimes, for reasons that I will not mention, he had to pay for them himself. Still, he was a pillar of the faith. He was well known to all the rich landowners of his neighbourhood and he was familiar, too, with the worthy women of his town. He had full power of confession, which, as he said himself, was superior to that of an ordinary curate; he could absolve the most awful sins. He heard the confessions very patiently, and pronounced the absolution very sweetly; he exacted the mildest of penances, especially if the penitent had something to give to his poor order. Bless me, father, for I have sinned and I have a large purse. That was the kind of thing he liked to hear. For, as he said, what is better proof of penitence than dispensing alms to the friars of God? There are many men who suffer from guilt and repentance, but are so hard of heart that they cannot weep for their sins. Therefore, instead of tears and prayers, these men must give silver to the friars. The tip of his hood, hanging down his back, was stuffed full of knives and pins which he gave away to pretty wives; whether he got anything in return, I could not say. I am only the narrator. I cannot be everywhere at once. I *can* say that the Friar had a very pleasant voice; he could sing well, and play on the gitern or lute. There was no one to beat him with a ballad. I heard him sing 'Grimalkin, our cat'. He was excellent. And when he played the harp, and sang an accompaniment, his eyes shone like the stars on a clear crisp night of frost. He had skin as white as a lily, but he was not lily-livered; he was as strong as a champion at the Shrovetide games. He knew the taverns in every town, as well as every landlord and barmaid; certainly he spent more time with them than with lepers or beggar-women. Who could blame him? 'My position as a confessor,' he told me, 'does not allow me to consort with the poorer sort. It would not be honourable. It would not be respectable. It would not be beneficial. I am more at my ease with the rich, and with the wealthier merchants. They are my congregation, sir.' So, wherever there was profit to be gained, he was modest and courteous and virtuous to a fault. No one was better at soliciting funds. Even a widow with no shoes to her name would have given him something. When he greeted a poor householder with 'In principio', he would end up with a farthing at least. In the beginning was the coin. His total income was higher than his projected income. I will say no more. He could frolic like a puppy and, on love days when conflicts are resolved, he was always on hand to reconcile opposing parties. On those occasions he did not behave like a cloistered cleric, wearing a threadbare gown like some poor scholar, but rather like a master or a pope. His cloak was made of expensive cloth, and it encircled him as round as a bell just out of the mould. He affected a slight lisp, so that his enunciation seemed all the sweeter. So, as he said to me on the first evening, 'God keep you in hith care.' Oh, one thing I forgot – this worthy friar was called Hubert.

Among our merry company was a MERCHANT with a forked beard. He was dressed in an outfit of many colours, just like the players in the Mysteries, and rode on a high saddle from which he looked down at me. He wore a Flemish hat of beaver, in the latest style, and a pair of elegant as well as expensive boots. When he expressed an opinion, he did so carefully and solemnly; he was always trying to weigh the likely profit to be gained from it. He commented, for example, that the sea between Holland and England should be defended at all costs. He was good at exchange dealings, as you would expect, and in fact this worthy gentleman was canny in every respect. He was so dignified in his business, in his buyings and in his sellings, in his barterings and in his tradings, that no one would ever know if he was in debt or not. What a notable man! Funnily enough, I did not discover his name. I never bothered to ask him.

A CLERK was there, from Oxford University. He was what you and I would describe as a scholar. He had studied logic for a long time, without progressing any further. He sat upon a withered horse that was almost as thin as its rider; he was grave and gaunt and hollow-cheeked. He had obtained no benefices, and he was too unworldly to seek for any profitable post; as a result his coat was as threadbare as his purse. He would rather have at his bedside twenty books of Aristotle, bound in red or black leather, than any amount of rich clothes or expensive musical instruments. He was a philosopher but he had not yet found the philosopher's stone; there was precious little gold in his coffers. Any money he could beg or borrow from his friends was immediately spent upon books and learning. He was a bookworm. He went down on his knees to pray for those who had paid for his education, which was not cheap, and he took the demands of scholarship very seriously indeed. He never talked more than was strictly necessary and, when he did speak, it was in careful and measured tones; he was brief and to the point, but full of elevated sentiment. He loved to discourse on problems of moral virtue. Like the lawyers he would begin 'Put the case that . . .'. But he learned from these debates, too, just as much as he contributed to them. 'A great friend is Aristotle,' he said to me, 'but a greater friend is truth.'

There was with us a SERGEANT OF THE LAW, as wise and as prudent as any in that exalted position. He consulted with his clients in the porch of Saint Paul's Cathedral, where he had acquired a reputation for judiciousness and discretion. No one was more revered than he. I am only reporting what I have heard, of course, but I do know that he often sat as a justice in the courts of assize that travelled around the country; he was appointed by the king, and in the letters patent he was granted full jurisdiction. He received an annual income, as well as private fees, for his exertions; his wealth allowed him to buy up land, and of course he purchased it on the principle of absolute possession or 'fee simple'. That is the lawyers' jargon. There was no one busier than this Man of Law, although in truth he seemed to be busier than he was. He was all bustle and hustle. He possessed all the year books, in legal French, so that he could consult cases from the time of William the Conqueror. By careful study of the precedents he was expert at drawing up the appropriate writs for each case; if he made any mistake then the prosecution would be deemed to be void. But he never made mistakes. He knew all the abridgements and statutes and registers of writs. How did he look? He looked the part, of course, as all men must. He wore a mantle of green cloth furred with black lamb and embroidered with stripes of mulberry and blue; he wore a round cap of white silk upon his head. He was dressed in the robes of authority. There is no more to say.

A FRANKLIN was in our company, a landowner free but not noble. The beard of this freeholder was as white as a daisy, and he was of red-cheeked sanguinary humour. That is to say, he was vigorous and cheerful. It was his custom, in the morning, to dip pieces of white bread into red wine; it may have been a tribute to his complexion. He was a true son of Epicurus, and thought no life more worthwhile than that of ease and pure delight. He held the opinion that sensual pleasure was the goal of every reasonable man. It was the secret of happiness itself. He was a lavish host in his neighbourhood, and worshipped at the shrine of Saint Julian, the patron saint of hospitality. His bread and his ale were always of the finest quality; he had a well-stocked wine-cellar, too. There was no shortage of roast meat at his table. There were baked pheasants, and geese, and wild fowl, and pullets, and pork. There was fish served in green sauce, partridges roasted in ginger, peacocks with pepper sauce, lobster in vinegar, fried eels in sugar and mackerel in mint sauce. The meals changed with the seasons, but they were always plentiful. The whole house snowed meat and drink. He even had a pen for his birds, and a pond for his fish. So the food was always fresh and always renewed. He would berate his cook if the sauces were not piquant and sharp and if the utensils – the flesh-hooks, the skimmers and skillets, the ladles and pestles – were not prepared. His table was always covered in the hall, ready for use. But he was not just a man of appetite. He presided at the sessions of the local court, and on many occasions represented the shire in the parliament house. He had been a sheriff, and a county auditor. Upon his girdle there hung a dagger, and a silk purse as white as morning milk. There had never been such a worthy freeholder. I told him so, and he laughed. 'Well, sir,' he said, 'I walk in the open way.'

There were some worthy citizens among our company. I saw a HABERDASHER, a CARPENTER, a WEAVER, a DYER and a MAKER OF TAPESTRIES, all in the livery of their parish fraternity. They were good guild folk, with their robes freshly turned out. Their knives were made of silver, not of brass, while their belts and purses were of the best manu-facture. These were the citizens you would see in the guildhall, sitting at the high table, greeting each other with 'God's speed' and 'God give you grace'. Any one of them could have been an alderman. Any one of them had the income, and the property, to attain civic office. Their wives would have agreed on that point, too, and would have blamed them if they failed to take advantage of the situation. These worthy women liked to be called 'ma dame'. They enjoyed leading the proces-sions to the parish church, on festal days, bearing themselves with all the dignity of royalty.

These worthy citizens had hired a COOK for the journey. I tasted one of his meals, a pudding of chicken, marrow bones, milk, hard-boiled eggs, ginger and other spices that he kept secret. It was delicious. He knew all about London beer, too, and he could roast or broil or fry or simmer with the best of them. He could prepare a stew, and bake a pie, with the same alacrity. There was just one problem. He had a large ulcer on his lower leg, which wept and was unsightly. Still, his chicken mousse was perfect. You can't have everything.

There was a SHIPMAN with us, hailing from the west country. I imagine that he came from Devon, judging by his accent, but I cannot be sure. He rode upon a carthorse as best he could, not being used to land transport. And he wore a robe of coarse woollen cloth, not being used to land fashion. He had a dagger hanging from a cord around his neck, as if he were about to encounter pirates. The hot summers at sea had weathered him. But he was a good enough fellow. He had tapped many barrels of fine Bordeaux wine, when the merchant was not looking, and had no scruples about it. A ship's cargo is not sacrosanct. The sea was the element in which he felt at home. He had acquired all the skills of observation and navigation; he had learned how to calculate the tides and the currents, and knew from long acquaintance the hidden perils of the deep. No one from Hull to Carthage knew more about natural harbours and anchorages; he could fix the position of the moon and the stars without the aid of an astrolabe. He knew all the havens, from Gotland to Cape Finistere, and every creek in Brittany and Spain. He told me of his voyages as far north as Iceland, and of his journeys to the Venetian colonies of Crete and of Corfu. He called his bed his 'berth' and his companions were his 'mates'. His beard had been shaken by many tempests, but he was a sturdy and courageous man. 'What is the broadest water,' he once asked me, 'and the least danger to walk over?' 'I have no notion.' 'The dew.' His boat, by the way, was called the *Magdalene*.

There was a DOCTOR OF PHYSIC also with us. No one on earth could have spoken more eloquently about medicine and surgery. He exemplified the old saying that a good physician is half an astronomer, and he could identify all the influences of the stars. He told me, for example, that Aries governs the head and all its contents; when the moon was in Aries, he felt able to operate upon the cheek or forehead. Taurus is the sign for neck and throat. The bollocks, or testicles, or cod, or yard, apparently lie in Scorpio. This was news to me. I thought that they lay in my mistress. But enough of that. I do not choose to display myself. Now this doctor knew the cause of every malady engendered in the bodily fluids. Some are hot, and some are cold; some are moist, and some are dry. But, alas, all things are mixed and mingled beneath the moon. And then he discoursed upon the humours. 'You,' he said to me, 'are melancolius. And a portion phlegmaticus.' I did not know whether to be alarmed or relieved. He was in any event an excellent physician. As soon as he knew the root and cause of any ailment, he could apply the appropriate remedy. He had his own chosen apothecaries to send him drugs and other medicines, from which both he and they made a great deal of money. The dung of doves was an excellent cure for sore feet. And what was his remedy for convulsions? Sage well mixed with the excrements of a sparrow, of a child, and of a dog that eats only bones. He was well versed in Asclepius and the other ancient texts; he could quote to you from Galen and Averroes and Avicenna and a score of others. He was in fact better versed in Galen than in the Bible. But he practised what he preached. He led a very temperate life, and had a very moderate diet. He told me that milk was good for melancholy, for example, and that green ginger quickened the memory. He wore the furred hood and robe of his profession; the robe, lined with silk, had the vertical red and purple stripes that proclaim the man of physic. Yet despite appearances he was not a big spender. He saved most of what he earned from his practice. The good doctor loved gold. Gold is the sovereign remedy, after all. It is the best medicine.

Among our company was a good WIFE OF BATH. She had such skill in making cloth that she easily surpassed the weavers of Ypres and of Ghent. It was a pity that she was a little deaf. She was also, perhaps, a little proud. Woe betide any woman in the parish who went up to the offertory rail with charitable alms before she did; she became so angry that all thoughts of charity were instantly forgotten. The linen scarves she wore about her head, on her way to Sunday mass, were of very fine texture; I dare say that some of them weighed at least ten pounds. Her stockings were of a vivid red and tightly laced; her leather shoes were supple and of the newest cut. Her face was red, too, and she had a very bold look. No wonder. She had been married in church five times but, in her youth, she had enjoyed any number of liaisons. There is no need to mention them now. She was, and is, a respectable woman. Everyone says so. She had made the pilgrimage to Jerusalem three times, after all, and had crossed many foreign seas in pursuit of her devotion. She had travelled to Rome, and to Boulogne; she had journeyed to Saint James of Compostella, and also to Cologne where the eleven thousand virgins were martyred. There was no need for any more. Yes she had wandered, and strayed, far enough. It is said that gap-toothed women like her have a propensity for lust, but I cannot vouch for that. She sat very easily upon her horse. She wore an exquisite wimple and a hat as broad as a practice target; she had hitched an overskirt about her fat hips, and she wore a sharp pair of spurs in case her horse despaired of her weight. She had an easy laugh, and was affable with everyone. She seemed to take a liking to me in particular, and was very fond of discussing stories of lost love and of forlorn lovers. She reached over and pressed my hand during the course of one affecting tale. She had performed in that game before. She knew, as they say, the ways of the dance. That was the Wife of Bath.

There was also riding with us a good man of religion, the poor PARSON of a small town. He was poor in wealth, perhaps, but rich in thought and holy works. He was also a learned man, a clerk, who preached Christ's gospel in the most faithful fashion and who taught his parishioners the lessons of devotion. He was gracious, and diligent; in adversity, as he proved many times, he was patient. He refused to excommuni- cate any of his flock for their failure to pay tithes to him; indeed he would rather give what little he possessed to the poor people of the parish. He did not earn a large income, or collect much from the offering plate, but he was content with what he had. He had a large parish, with the houses set far apart, but neither rain nor thunder would prevent him from visiting his parishioners in times of grief or dearth. He would pick up his sturdy staff, and take off to the furthest reaches of his parish where he would bless both rich and poor. He gave the best possible example to his flock. Perform before you preach. Good deeds are more fruitful than good words. He took this message from the gospel, but he added his own gloss – if gold may rust, then what will iron do? For if a priest be evil, what then might happen to the layman in his care? It would be a shame, as far as the priesthood is concerned, if the sheep were clean and the shepherd had the scab. A priest's life must be a sign, pointing the way to heaven. Only then will his parishioners follow his virtuous example. So he did not hire out his post as a benefice. He did not leave his sheep in the mire while he ran off to London, seeking sinecures in the guild or chantry business. No. He stayed at home, and protected his flock from the wolves of sin and greed that threatened it. He was a true shepherd, not a religious mercenary. But although he was a holy and virtuous man, he did not treat sinners with contempt or disgust; in conversation he was never disdainful or haughty, but properly benevolent and courteous. He wanted to draw people to God with kind words and good deeds. Do you think, he used to say, that you can simply hop into heaven? He was not so benign with men and women who were obstinate in sin. He would rebuke them with stern words, whatever their standing in the world. 'Barren corn,' he said to one of them, 'is known as deaf corn. A rotten nut is known as a deaf nut. You are a deaf man.' I do not believe that a better priest could be found. He never expected deference or reverence from those he met, and he did not affect an over-refined conscience. He simply taught, and followed, the law of Christ and the gospel of the apostles. He was God's darling. I was in such awe of him that I scarcely talked to him.

He had brought with him on pilgrimage his brother, a PLOUGHMAN, who had carted many wagons of dung in his time. He was a good and faithful workman who lived in peace and charity with his neighbours. He loved God before all things, even though his own life was sometimes rough and painful, and he loved his neighbour as himself. For the love of Christ he would thresh the hay, or dig the ditches, for a poor man who could not even afford to pay him. He paid his tithes in full and on time, in regard both to his labour and to his possessions. He wore a coarse workman's tunic, and rode on a mare.

The other pilgrims were a REEVE and a MILLER, a SUMMONER and a PARDONER, a MANCIPLE and then MYSELF. You will be glad to hear that there were no others. Otherwise this story would become too long.

The MILLER was a burly man. He had strong muscles and strong bones. I would have said that he was bigger of brawn than of brain. He was a bruiser, too, who always won the prize of the ram at wrestling competitions. He was broad and squat, with a thick neck; he could knock any door off its hinges, and would no doubt have excelled at that game the London apprentices play, known as 'breaking doors with our heads'. His beard was as red as a sow's tit or a fox's tail; it was broad enough, too, to pass as a shovel. There was a great wart on the top right of his nose, with a tuft of hairs growing from it as thick as from a pig's ear; his nostrils were wide, like two great pits, and his mouth was as big as a cauldron. He carried a sword and a small shield by his side. He seemed to distrust or dislike me, and narrowed his eyes when he looked at me. This was a trifle disconcerting. In any case I considered him to be a buffoon. He was always telling dirty stories about whores and other sinners. I trust that I will never be accused of that. He knew how to steal grain from the sacks, and charge three times the amount he should. In truth I do not think I have ever met an honest miller. He wore a white coat and a blue hood. He got out his bagpipes, as we passed the boundary of the city, and played a tune.

There was on our pilgrimage a MANCIPLE, a business agent who worked for the Inner Temple. I had studied there, for a short time, and we exchanged anecdotes about the wild apprentices of law. I soon discovered his acumen, however, in the buying of stores and provisions. He told me that cash or credit was good enough, as long as the purchaser looked ahead and waited for the right moment. 'The blacksmith always strikes,' he said to me, 'when the iron is hot.' I thought this was an excellent saying. I must remember it. Is it not an example of God's grace that such an unlearned man should outpace the wisdom of all the learned pates in the Inner Temple? He had thirty masters above him, all of them skilled in matters of law. More than a dozen of them had the expertise to run the lands and rents of any lord in England so that, unless they were out of their wits, they could live honourably and without debt. They had the knowledge to administer a whole shire, through any crisis or danger that might arise. But this was the funny thing. The unlearned manciple had always got the better of them. I will not say that he swindled them but many things, as they say, went under the thumb.

The REEVE was a slender and choleric man. His beard was closely shaved, and his hair was shorn around his ears like that of a priest. His legs were so long and so lean that he resembled a staff; you could not see his calves. But he was an excellent estate manager; he kept the granaries full, and the storage bins overflowing. No auditor could ever catch him out. He knew, from the intervals of rain and drought, how to calculate the harvests of seed and grain. This Reeve had complete control of the cattle and the sheep on his lord's estate, as well as the pigs, the horses, the livestock and the poultry. I dare say that he even managed the worms. He had kept the accounts, under the terms of his employment, since the time his lord turned twenty. He paid out promptly, too. He knew every trick used by the farm-managers, and every excuse offered by the herdsmen and the servants. They all feared him as they feared the plague. He had a pretty little house upon a heath, overshadowed by green trees. In fact he could probably have afforded to buy more property than his lord and master, for he had secretly amassed a lot of money. He had learned how to take his lord's possessions and then sell them back to him, so that he obtained both compliments and rewards equally. He could blear eyes better than any man in England. In his youth he had the sense to learn a good trade, and had become apprentice to a carpenter. Now he sat upon a sturdy horse. It was a dapple grey, and its name was Scot. He wore a long coat of dark blue cloth, which was hitched up around a girdle. By his side he carried a rusty sword. But he had no need to fight anyone. He was at peace with the world. He came from Norfolk, he told me, near a town called Baldeswell. I had never heard of it. He said that it was close to Norwich. But this did not enlighten me much. There is one other thing I forgot to mention. He was always the last rider in our little group.

There was a SUMMONER with us, unfortunately. He had the face of a fiery cherub, covered with pimples. He had swollen eyelids, adding to the unfortunate impression. He was as hot and lecherous as the proverbial London sparrow. His eyebrows were scabby, and the hair was falling out of his beard. You could understand why children were afraid of him. There was no medicine or ointment, no quicksilver or brimstone, no sulphur or cream of tartar, no white lead or borax, that could remove those unsightly pustules. They were like oyster shells on his cheeks. His diet may have had something to do with it. He loved onions, garlic and leeks, which are well known to nourish bitter humours; he drank the strongest red wine he could find and, in his cups, he would talk and cry out as if he were mad. 'You are all janglers and clatterers!' he said. He was looking at me at the time. When he was completely drunk he would speak only in Latin, and one evening he sang out the old rhyme:

> *Nos vagabunduli*
> *Laeti, jucunduli,*
> *Tara, tarantare, teino.*

He knew two or three Latin terms that he had learned from some ecclesiastical law-book. 'I will give you,' he said, '*dispositio, expositio* and *conclusio*.' This was the kind of language he used when he summoned the citizens to the Church courts and the local assize. He had learned it all by rote. But we all know that a parrot can say 'good-day' as well as any pope. If anyone ever tried to question him further, then his well of learning suddenly dried up. He would cry out, '*Questio quid juris?*', which is to say, 'What point of law are you trying to make?' And that was that. He was a bit of a buffoon, in other words, but some swore that he was kind-hearted. For the payment of a quart of wine, for example, he would allow some rascal to keep his mistress for a year; then he would excuse him completely. In secret he could pull a few swindles – and pull other things, too, if you know what I mean. If he came across any other scoundrel *in flagrante* he would counsel him to ignore any archdeacon's curse or threat of excommunication. If a man's soul was in his purse, only then would it be painful; only the purse was really punished. 'The purse,' he used to say, 'is the archdeacon's hell.' In that, of course, he was wholly wrong. Every guilty man should fear the consequences of excommunication, just as absolution is the only salvation for the human soul. The wicked man should beware, too, of the writ that consigns the excommunicated to the prison cell. This summoner had the young girls of his diocese under his control; he knew all their secrets, and he was their sole adviser. He had a green garland on his head, just like those you see outside taverns. And he had made himself a shield out of a loaf of bread. As I said, he was a buffoon.

Riding in company with him was a PARDONER, working for Saint Anthony's Hospital at Charing Cross. He had come straight from the papal court at Rome, where he had been granted his licence for the sale of pardons and indulgences. Now he could carry his staff wound with red cloth and sing out:

> Oh one that is so fair and bright,
> *Velut maris stella*
> Brighter than the day is light
> *Parens et puella.*

The Summoner joined in, with a strong bass voice, and their combined noise was louder than that of any trumpet. This Pardoner had hair as yellow as old wax, hanging down his back as limply as a bundle of flax and draped across his shoulders; it was very thin, and was gathered in tufts and clumps. He could have had rats' tails upon his head. They were all the more visible because he refused to wear any kind of hood. The hood was considered by him to be out of date, so he kept it in his knapsack. With head bare, except for a round felt hat, he considered himself to be in the height of fashion. He had the large and timid eyes of a hare. On his woollen robe he had sewn small wooden crosses as well as the image of the Saviour imprinted on the handkerchief of Saint Veronica. His knapsack, which he carried on his lap, was filled with papal pardons smoking hot from Rome. 'If any man full penitent come to me and pay for his sin,' he said to me, 'I will absolve him. If anyone gives seven shillings to Saint Anthony's, I will bestow on him an indulgence of seven hundred years.' I told him that I had scarcely enough money to pay my way. He had a voice as high as that of a nanny goat. He had no beard at all, nor was likely to grow one. His chin was as smooth as a girl's arse. He was either a eunuch or a homosexual, a nurrit or a will-jick, as the common people put it. I did not wish to investigate further. Yet, as pardoners go, he was effective enough. In his bag he had a pillowcase, which, he told us, was the veil of Our Lady. He had a piece of the sail from the boat of Saint Peter. He had a brass crucifix, set with pebbles, which he announced to be a precious ornament from Bruges. In a glass reliquary he carried pigs' bones, which, he claimed, were relics of the holy saints. If they were dipped into any well, the water from that well would cure all diseases. So he said. They did work in another sense. Whenever he came upon a foolish parson in the countryside, he would wheedle more money out of him than the priest himself earned in two whole months. So, with feigning and flattery and trickery, he made fools of the priest and the people. He had one virtue. It would be true to say that, in church, he was a notable performer. He was the very model of a modern ecclesiastic. He read out the liturgical texts during the mass and, best of all, he sang the offertories with gusto. He knew that, when the song was sung, he would have to preach and so modulate his voice that he might win more silver from the congregation. Therefore he took care to sing merrily and loudly. He was called 'the devil's rattlebag'.

Now I have completed – truly and, I hope, briefly – my description of the estate, rank and appearance of every pilgrim. You know how many there were. You know why they had come together in Southwark. You have been told that they all took lodgings for the night at that fine tavern known as the Tabard, which is close to the Bell. Every tavern in Southwark is close to another one. But now it is time for me to tell you how we all behaved that night, after we had arrived at the hostelry, and only after that will I describe to you the journey and the remainder of our pilgrimage. I will be your eyes and ears. I have no other purpose. But first I must ask you, out of consideration for my feelings, not to impute any malice or villainy to me if I describe plainly how they spoke and how they looked. Do not hold it against me if I report their words in full. For you know this as well as I do – if I intend to repeat the tale of another man, I must write it down precisely as I heard it word for word. I have a good example. Christ spoke out plainly in the gospels, and no one has ever accused him of rudeness. To the best of my ability I will record accurately all of the tales and conversations of the pilgrims, however obscene or absurd they may turn out to be. Otherwise my work will be inaccurate. It will be mere fiction. I will not spare my characters, even if one of them happens to be my brother. Characters? No. People. Living people. The words of living people will be preserved by me. I want you to hear their voices, just as if you were riding with us. Those who have read Plato will know well enough his apothegm, 'The word must be cousin to the deed.' I have another request to make. I hope you will forgive me if I do not introduce people precisely in their order of rank. Put it down to my general stupidity. Well. Enough of this rambling.

Our HOST gave us all good cheer, and set down a tasty supper for us on the table. In the tavern itself there were cries of 'Tapster, fill the bowl!' and 'One pot more!' He served us good fish and flesh; the wine was strong and potable. We all agreed, after our leather cups were filled, that the landlord was an attractive man. He could have acted as master of ceremonies at any public feast. He was a large fellow with bright eyes. You could not find a fairer citizen in the whole of Cheapside. He was forthright in speech, but he was also shrewd and apparently well educated. I did not find out what school he attended. Anyway, he possessed all the characteristics of a proper man. He was merry enough and, after supper, he began to amuse us with several stories. He trusted that we would enjoy ourselves on this journey and, after we had all paid our bills, he addressed us with these words. 'Now, good ladies and gentlemen, I would like to bid you all welcome to my inn. I must say that I have not come across a more joyful group of people under my roof. If I could entertain you more, then I would. Gladly. In fact I have hit upon one scheme to make your journey easier and more agreeable. Hear me out. It will cost you nothing. We all know that you are on your way to Canterbury where Saint Thomas, God bless him, will no doubt reward you for your devotion. And I fully expect that you will pass the time in telling stories and other amusements. That is only natural. There is no comfort or entertainment to be had in riding silently together, as dumb as any stone. That is why I have this plan of my own to put to you. It will keep you merry. So if you all agree to abide by my judgement, and play the game I have invented, I promise on my father's soul that you will be mightily entertained in the course of your journey tomorrow. Please, without more ado, hold up your hands in assent to my proposal!'

It did not take us long to decide. There was no point, in any case, in long deliberations. Without any real discussion, then, we all put up our hands in agreement with him. We had to ask, of course, what his actual plan was. 'Well, gentle ladies and gentle men,' he replied, 'I have a proposal. Take it in good spirit. Don't mock me. It is unusual, I admit, but it is not unprecedented.'

'Do tell us,' the Manciple said. 'We are on tenterhooks until we hear you.'

'Well, to be brief, I suggest this. On our way to Canterbury each of you will tell two stories. As every traveller knows, tales shorten journeys. Then on the way back to London, each pilgrim will tell two more.'

'Tales of what kind?' The Prioress was very demure.

'Anything you like, ma dame. Tales of saints. Tales of battles and adventures from long ago. And here comes my other proposal. The pilgrim who tells the best story, by common consent, will be awarded a free supper paid for by the rest. Here. In the Tabard on our return. What do you think?'

'What do you mean by best?' the Miller asked him. The Miller had a menacing face. I expected trouble from him in the future.

'It could be the most serious story. It could be the funniest. It could be the most pleasant. Let us see what happens. In fact the idea is such a good one that I can't resist coming along myself. I will ride with you tomorrow morning. I will make the journey at my own cost, and I will also be your guide. None of you are familiar with the way. Anyone who challenges, or disputes with, me will have to pay a penalty. He or she will be responsible for all the costs incurred on our travels. Is that reasonable? Let me know now. Then I can get ready for the feast of words.'

We agreed with his suggestion, and swore an oath that we would all perform as promised. Then we asked him if he would become our governor as well as our guide. He was the one who could best judge the quality of the stories, but he could also be the arbitrator in less important matters like the price of our suppers. We would all be ruled by his decisions. So by acclamation we decided to follow our leader. Then the wine was brought out and, after a cup or two, we went off to bed without any prompting. We were cheerful, though. Tomorrow, as they say, was still untouched.

Then the morrow came. At the first stirring of dawn our Host sprang out of his chamber and awakened us all. He called us together in the yard of the inn, and led us at a slow pace out of Southwark; after a mile or two we reached the little brook known as Saint Thomas a Watering, which is the boundary of the City liberties. He reined in his horse here, and addressed us. 'Ladies and gentlemen, or should I say fellow pilgrims, I hope you all remember our agreement. I recall it vividly myself. I take it for granted that none of you have changed your minds. Is that not so? Good. Well, who do you think should tell the first story? We agreed that you would all be bound by my decision. Any man or woman who dissents will be obliged to pay all of our expenses. If I am mistaken, then I swear that I will never drink again. The best plan is to draw sticks, before we go any further, and he that picks the shortest will begin.' We got down from our horses and formed a circle. The Host stood in the middle, with the bundle of sticks in his hand. 'Sir Knight,' he said, 'my lord and master, you will be the first to draw the lot.' The Knight stepped forward, gracefully accepting his authority, and took a stick. 'Now, my lady Prioress,' the Host said, 'will it please you to come closer to me? And you, sir Clerk, put aside any embarrassment. You do not need to be learned to draw a stick. As for the rest of you, take it in turns.'

And so we all chose our stick. Whether it was by destiny, or providence, or just chance, it turned out that the Knight had chosen the shortest stick. We were all pleased with this piece of luck. It gave us more time to compose our own stories. The first must be the boldest. The Knight would have to tell his tale. That was the agreement. In any case he was not the kind of man to break a promise. 'So,' he said, 'I have been chosen to begin the game. I welcome the challenge, in God's name, as I welcome all noble challenges. Will it please you to ride forth, and listen to my story?'

So we mounted our horses and crossed the stream. It was called, in those parts, 'going over the water'. Then the Knight, with a steady and cheerful countenance, began to tell his tale. This is what he said.

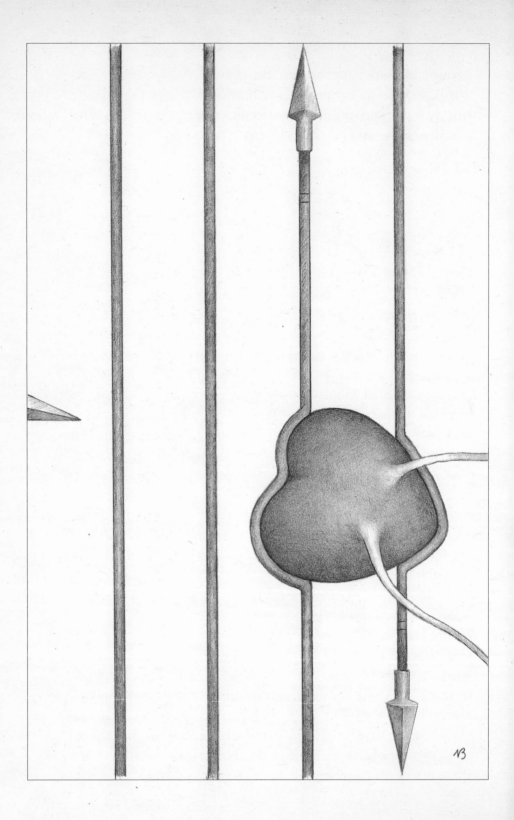

The Knight's Tale

Heere bigynneth the Knyghtes Tale

PART ONE

Once upon a time, as the old stories tell us, there was a duke named Theseus. He was the lord and governor of fabled Athens, and in his day he had won an unrivalled reputation as a conqueror. No one was more splendid under the sun. He had taken many rich kingdoms. By wise generalship and force of arms he had conquered the land of the Amazons, formerly known as Scythia, and wedded there its queen, Hippolita. He brought home his prize, his bride, with great celebrations and rejoicings. He also brought back with him her younger sister, Emily, who will be the heroine of this story. So for the time being I will leave Theseus at his victory parade. You can imagine the scene. The armies march in rank. POMP. MUSIC. HURRAHS. The wagons bring up the rear, stuffed with booty. It was glorious stuff.

Of course, if I had more time, I would like to tell you all about the victory of Theseus over the Amazons. Knights like to speak of war. And what a fight that was! I wish I could tell you about the pitched battle between the Athenians and the Amazon women. I wish I could tell you how Theseus laid siege, in more than one sense, to the beautiful and fiery Hippolita. I would like to have described the glorious wedding feast, and then I might have added the detail of the tempest that threatened to overwhelm their ships on their return to Athens. But there we are. It cannot be done in the time allotted to me. God knows I have ahead of me a large field to furrow, and the oxen at my plough are not the strongest beasts I have known. The remains of my story are long enough. I will not hinder any of this fair company. Let every man and woman here tell their tale in turn. Then we shall know who has won the supper. Where was I?

Oh yes. Duke Theseus. Well. When he had come close to Athens with his new bride, in all his glory, he noticed that there were some women kneeling in the highway; they kneeled in rows beside each other, two by two, and they were all clothed in black. They were screeching and crying and beating their breasts. I doubt that anyone has heard such bitter lamentation. They did not cease their cries until they had managed to get hold of the reins of the duke's horse. Of course he was very angry. 'What kind of women are you,' he asked, 'that ruin my triumphant homecoming with your tears and wails? Are you so envious of my honour that you cry out like scalded cats? Who has offended you? Who has done you hurt? I will do my best to help you, if I can. And then why on earth are you all wearing black? Answer me.'

The eldest of all the ladies then fainted; she looked so pale that even Theseus took pity on her. But she recovered from her swoon gracefully, stood upright, and answered him. 'My good lord,' she said, 'upon whom Dame Fortune has smiled, we do not grieve at your victories or lament your success. Far from it. But we do beseech your mercy and your aid. Have shame on our woe and our distress. Shed some tears of compassion upon us, poor women that we are. Show us your kindness. We do perhaps deserve your consideration. There is not one of us that was not previously a duchess or a queen. Now we are miserable, worn down by grief. Dame Fortune has thrown us aside. Well, it is the wheel. There is no joy that may not turn to sorrow. That is why we have been waiting for you here, in the temple of the goddess of pity, for the last two weeks. Please help us, noble duke. Give us your strength.'

'Who are you, ma dame?'

'Wretched woman that I now am, I was once the wife of the king known as Capaneus. He was one of the seven who stormed the city of Thebes. But there at the gate of the city he died, struck down by the thunderbolt of Zeus. It was the most cursed day of my life. You may know my name. Evadne. All of these women with me, flowing in tears, also lost husbands at the siege of Thebes. Yet the old man Creon, now alas king of Thebes, is filled with anger and evil. No, he is not king. He is tyrant of Thebes. With malice in his heart, this tyrant has defiled the bodies of our dead husbands. He has stripped them and piled them in a heap. He will not allow the corpses to be burned or buried. Instead they have become the prey of dogs and other scavengers.' At that the women set up another wail and beat their breasts. 'Have mercy on us,' one of them cried out. 'We wretched women beg for succour. Let our sorrow enter your heart.'

The noble lord Theseus dismounted. His heart was indeed filled with grief at the bitterness of their woes. To see women of such high rank reduced to this level of suffering and indignity – well, he feared that his heart might break. To leave the dead unburied was pure blasphemy. So great then was the respect given to the conventions of war. He embraced them all, one by one, and did his best to comfort them. Then he swore an oath, as a knight good and true –

'Just as you,' our Host interjected.

The Knight pretended not to hear the remark.

Theseus swore an oath that he would wreak such fatal vengeance on Creon that all the people of Greece would concur that the tyrant had met a prompt and welcome death at the hands of the ruler of Athens. This was his pledge. All at once, without any delay, he mounted his steed; then he unfurled his banner and led his army towards the city of Thebes. He vowed that he would not return to Athens, or linger for even half a day, until he had defeated Creon. He took the precaution of sending Hippolita, his new bride, and her beautiful younger sister, Emily, to take up residence in Athens. Meanwhile he spent his first night on the road rather than in his marital bed. There is no more to say.

The weapons of his army glittered in the fields about Thebes. On the great white banner of Theseus was embroidered the red image of Mars, god of war and king of combat, with his spear and shield held aloft. Beside the banner was the pennant of Theseus, curiously wrought of gold; it depicted the head of the Minotaur, whom he had killed in the labyrinth of Crete. Death to all monsters! So rode the duke, so travelled the conqueror, with the flower of chivalry all around him. In majesty he came up to the gates of Thebes and alighted there; then he arrayed his troops in the field where he expected to do battle.

I do not want to embarrass the ladies with accounts of the fighting. I will be brief. In combat Theseus killed Creon, according to the knightly book of arms, and put his army to flight. Then he stormed the town, and tore down its walls; not a beam or rafter was left in place. It was a just punishment. He restored to the ladies the corpses of their husbands, although little was left of them except the bones. Still they could now be dispatched with due form and order. It would be too harrowing to report all the tears and cries and laments of the ladies when they saw the remains of their husbands burning on the funeral pyres. It is enough to say that Theseus, the illustrious conqueror, paid great honour and courtesy to them before they left for their respective cities.

After Theseus had killed Creon and captured Thebes, he stayed with his troops in the field. They still had work to accomplish in the conquered kingdom. There was pillaging to do. The dead soldiers of Thebes lay in heaps upon the ground, and the Athenians began systematically to strip them of their armour and their clothing. The pillagers did their work with diligence, searching all those defeated in battle for anything of value. There is now a turn in the tale. Among the piles of the dead the Athenians found two young knights, lying side by side, as if they had fought valiantly together. They were both bearing the same heraldic device, and they were both richly clad in ornamented armour. And they were both badly wounded. They were neither alive nor dead, but in some uncertain state between. One of the knights was named Arcite. The name of the other knight was Palamon. You will have heard of them, I am sure.

When the Athenian heralds examined their coats of arms they declared that these two young men were cousins of royal blood and true aristocrats of Thebes. So the soldiers carefully extracted them from the morass of the dead, and carried them gently to the tent of Theseus. The noble duke then pronounced that they should be consigned to an Athenian prison, where they would remain for the rest of their lives without the possibility of freedom. No ransom would be sought or accepted. Now that Theseus had finished his glorious work, he led his army from the scene of battle and rode home to Athens bearing the laurel wreath of victory. There he still lives, in honour and in comfort. Happy ever after. What is left to say? Yet turn your eyes towards a dark tower. There, in anguish and in woe, lie Palamon and Arcite. They will suffer there for the rest of their lives. However large the ransom offered, they will never be released.

So the world whirled on, day by day and year by year, until on one May morning everything changed. On that spring morning Emily left her bed – Emily, the sister of the queen, lovelier than the lily on its stalk of green, fresher than the new flowers of May, prettier than the rose whose hue is not so fair as hers – I say that Emily left her bed before dawn and was prepared for the day before the sun ever rose. The month of May will brook no sluggishness at night. The season stirs every noble heart and awakes the spirit with the words, 'Arise. And do homage to spring.' So Emily paid her obeisance to the season of rebirth. She dressed in yellow and in green. Her blonde hair, waist length, was braided in tresses behind her back. At the rising of the sun she strolled through the garden of the castle, gathering red and white and particoloured flowers to make an intricate garland for her head. She was singing like an angel as she picked the lilac and the violet. Yet beside this garden, separated by the garden wall, was the dark tower where Palamon and Arcite were confined. It was the principal dungeon of the castle, as thick and strong as any prison in the world. So, with Emily singing and the two knights languishing, heaven and hell were close together.

Bright was the sun, and the air most clear, when Palamon had risen from his pallet bed. By permission of his gaoler this woeful prisoner had the use of an upper cell, from which he could see the city of Athens. He could also see the garden beneath him, clad in the green vesture of spring, where radiant Emily was still walking. Palamon, however, had not yet seen her. He was pacing to and fro, measuring the strict confines of his chamber and lamenting his fate. 'Alas,' he whispered to himself, 'I wish that I had never been born!' But then just by chance he happened to look through the thick iron bars covering his window. He cast a glance upon Emily sauntering below. Then immediately he turned pale and cried out, 'Ah!', as if some barb had caught at his heart. At the sound of his cry Arcite started up from sleep and asked what had upset him. 'Cousin,' he said, 'you have gone as pale as the dead. What troubles you now? You look so ill suddenly. Why did you cry out? Who has offended you? For God's sake do not rail so much against our imprisonment. We must have patience. This is our fate. We have no choice in the matter. We are subject to the bad aspects of Saturn, in the turning of the spheres, and cannot escape our destiny. What is the saying? "He must need swim that is borne up to the chin." So stood the heavens on the day that we were born. We must endure.'

Palamon answered him, shaking his head. 'Cousin, you have received the wrong impression of my woe. It was not our confinement that made me cry out. My new torment entered my heart through my eye, where very likely it will kill me. I am woeful because of her. With the flowers. Below us.' He went over to the window again, and looked down at Emily. 'The fairness of this lady that I see, walking to and fro through the castle garden, is the cause of all my pain and lamentation. I cannot tell whether she is a woman or a goddess. My guess is that she is Venus, come to earth.' Thereupon he fell to his knees and prayed aloud. 'Venus, great goddess, if it be your will to reveal yourself in this garden before me, a wretched and sorrowful creature, I beseech you to deliver us from this dark prison. Yet if it be my destiny to remain in durance vile, imprisoned by divine decree, then turn your piteous eye upon my family that has been brought so low by tyranny.' And as he prayed Arcite walked over to the window and beheld Emily wandering in the garden. The sight of her beauty affected him so greatly that, if Palamon had been wounded, Arcite almost expired. He sighed deeply, and could not refrain from speaking out. 'This perfect beauty, this vision of her that walks within the garden, has slain me suddenly. Unless I obtain her mercy and her grace, unless at the very least I am permitted to see her, I am as good as dead. There is nothing else to say.'

When Palamon heard his complaint, he became angry. 'Are you serious? Or is this a joke?'

'I am in deadly earnest. God help me, I have no reason to play.'

'It does not reflect well on your honour, you know, to be false and treacherous to your cousin.' He was frowning at Arcite as he spoke. 'We have both sworn deep oaths that we would never cross each other in love, and would each seek our common good. We have both sworn that we would rather die under torture than oppose or hinder one another. We would remain true till death do us part. That was my oath. I presume that it was yours. I don't think you will deny it. But now what has happened? You are aware of my love for the lady in the garden, but you have decided that you also wish to be her lover. No chance. I will love and serve this lady until the day of my death. That will not be your fate, Arcite, I swear it! I loved her first. I took you into my confidence, and told you all my woe. As my sworn brother, you are bound by oath to help me. Otherwise you will be judged a false and perjured knight.'

Arcite, in pride of spirit, answered him with disdain. 'You will be judged the faithless knight, Palamon. I was the one who loved her first.'

'What are you saying?'

'Look at you. You still do not know whether she is a goddess or a woman! You are touched by love for a deity, while I am consumed by love for a mortal woman. That is why I confessed my feelings to you, as my cousin and brother. Put the case that you loved her first. What do all the learned clerks tell us? When love is strong, love knows no law. Love itself has greater dominion. Earthly rules are of no account. Lovers break them every day. A man must love, even if he strives against it; he cannot escape love, even at the cost of his own life. It may be love for a maid, for a widow, or for a married woman. It does not matter. Love is the law of life itself. In any case it is not likely that you or I will ever win her favour. You know well enough that we are both consigned to this cell perpetually, without hope of ransom. We are like the dogs in Aesop's fable, striving for the bone. They fought all day, without result, and then there came a kite that bore the prize away. Therefore we must behave like courtiers around the king. Each one for him-self. Do you agree? I tell you again that I will always love her. You can love her, too, if you wish. There is nothing more to say, nothing else to do. We will remain in this prison for the rest of our days, and endure whatever fate is visited upon us.'

If I had more time, I would tell you more about the continual strife and enmity between them. But let me be brief and to the point. It happened one day that the worthy duke Perotheus, king of the Lapiths, arrived in Athens. He had been the intimate of Theseus since earliest childhood, and had come to the city to resume their happy companionship; he loved no one in the world so much as his friend, and Theseus returned that love. Anyone who reads the old books will learn of it. The story is that when Theseus died, Perotheus went down to hell in order to rescue him. What was Theseus doing in hell? I do not know that part of the story. To resume my own tale, if I may, I should inform you that Perotheus had been the lover of Arcite. So at his friend's earnest desire and entreaty, Theseus decreed that Arcite should be released from prison without any ransom. Arcite would be free to go wherever he wished, but there was one condition to his liberty. It was agreed that, if Arcite were ever found and caught in Athenian territory, he would be instantly beheaded. Whatever the pretext and whatever the time of his incursion, he would die. What did Arcite do? What else but leave Athens at once and return to Thebes? There was no safer course. But he had best beware. He had left his head as his pledge.

Yet, in truth, he suffered more keenly than before. He felt all the pangs of death. He wept; he wailed; he groaned; he lamented. He secretly longed for an occasion to kill himself. 'Alas,' he cried, 'that I was ever born! My prison now is darker and more dreary than my cell. I am now forced to endure the torments of hell, not of purgatory as before. I wish that I had never known Perotheus. Then I could still lie imprisoned with Palamon. Then I would have been in bliss and not in woe. For then, even fettered and immured, I could have enjoyed the sight of the mistress I adore. I may never have enjoyed her favour, but at least I could have looked upon her. Oh Palamon, dear cousin, you have been awarded the palm of victory. You may endure the pain of imprisonment – endure, no, enjoy. Compared to me, you are in paradise. Fortune has turned the dice for you. You have the sight of her while I am rendered blind. And since you have the blessing of her presence near at hand it is possible that you, a worthy and a handsome knight, might one day attain that goal you so fervently desire. Fortune is ever turning like the wheel. But I, living in barren exile, have no such expectation of grace. I am deprived of all hope, in such despair that no creature on earth can comfort me. There is nothing made of fire, of earth, or water, or of air, that can console me. So I must live, and die, in misery and distress. I must say farewell to joy and happiness.'

He broke down weeping, before he once more resumed his

lament. 'Why do so many people complain of the actions of providence, or the decisions of God Himself, when their eventual fate is better than any they could possibly have imagined? Some men long for riches, but at the expense of their health and even of their lives. Some men desire to escape from prison, as I once did, only to be murdered in the households of their kin. In hope and ambition there lie infinite harms. We do not know the answers to our prayers. We fare as one who wanders drunk through the streets; he knows that he has a house, somewhere, but he cannot remember the name of the street. His is a long and wayward journey. So do we fare in this fallen world. We search for felicity down every lane and alley, but often enough we take the wrong path. All will agree. And I especially know the truth of this – I, who believed that release from prison would be the highest good! I should have known better. Now I am exiled from all hope of happiness. Since I can no longer see you, Emily, I am as good as dead. Who can give more heat to the fire, or joy to heaven, or pain to hell? There is no more to say.' He sat in silence, and bowed his head.

Let us return to the cell where Palamon still lay. After the sudden departure of Arcite, he cried out in a paroxysm of anguish and despair. The dark tower rang with his laments. The fetters that held his legs were wet and shining with his salt and bitter tears. 'Alas, Arcite,' he cried, 'in our contest you have the victory! You now enjoy your freedom in our home city. Why should you give a thought to my suffering here? I know that you are valiant. I know that you are shrewd. It is possible that you will call together the members of our affinity, and prosecute so bold a war against Athens that by some chance – or even by some treaty with Theseus – you will obtain the hand of my lady Emily. I would rather lose my life than lose her. But you are free to roam. You have been delivered from our prison. And you are a great lord. My case is different. I am confined. I must weep and wail, for the rest of my life, with all the woes that prison life can give. Yet there is no woe so deep as that of unrequited love. So I must endure a double torment upon this earth.' As he lay upon the stone floor of his prison, lamenting, he was seized by a fit of jealousy so strong and so sudden that he felt his heart contract within him. It enveloped him like madness. He turned as pale as milk – no, worse – as pale as the bark of a dead ash tree.

Once more he began to cry out loud. 'Oh cruel gods that govern this world, binding it with your eternal decrees inscribed on sheets of adamantine steel, what is humankind to you? Do men mean more to you than the sheep that cower in the fold? Men must die, too, like any beast of the field. Men also dwell in confinement and restraint. Men suffer great sickness and adversity, even when they are guilty of no sin. What glory can there be for you in treating humankind so ungenerously? What is the good of your foreknowledge, if it only torments the innocent and punishes the just? What is the purpose of your providence? One other matter, too, outrages me. Men must perform their duty and, for the sake of the gods, refrain from indulging their desires. They must uphold certain principles, for the salvation of their souls, whereas the silly sheep goes into the darkness of non-being. No beast suffers pain in the hereafter. But after death we all may still weep and wail, even though our life on earth was also one of suffering. Is this just? Is this commendable? I suppose I must leave the answer to theologians, but I know this for a fact. The world is full of grief. I have seen a serpent sting an unwary traveller and then glide away. I have seen the thief murder his prey, and then wander forth unchecked and unharmed. But I must linger here in prison. Truly the gods, in their jealous rage against my race, have all but destroyed my family and razed the walls of Thebes. Now Venus herself has decided to slay me, too, by poisoning me with jealousy for Arcite. Where can I turn?'

I will now leave Palamon in his sad plight for a moment, and tell you what has been happening to Arcite. The summer has passed, and the long nights have merely increased the duration of his pain. In truth I do not know who has endured the most suffering, the freed lover or the prisoner. Let me summarize their situation. Here is Palamon. He is condemned to perpetual imprisonment, consigned to chains and shackles until the day of his death. Here is Arcite. On pain of death by beheading he is exiled from the territory of Athens, forever excluded from the sight of fair Emily. I will ask you lovers the question. Who is worse off? One of them can glimpse his gracious lady, day by day, but will never be able to approach her. The other is as free as air, able to journey wherever he wishes, but he will never see Emily again. Consider it. Judge the matter as best you can. Put the two characters before you, as if they were upon a gaming board. Meanwhile I will carry on with the story, just to see what happens next.

PART TWO

When Arcite eventually returned to Thebes, he grew faint and sick. His one word, endlessly repeated, was 'Alas!' We know the reason. I will add only that no other creature upon the earth has ever suffered, or will ever suffer, so painfully. He could not sleep. He did not eat or drink. He became lean and emaciated, as dry and brittle as a stick; his eyes were hollow, and his complexion turned a sickly yellow as if he had the jaundice. He looked truly frightful. And he was alone. He sought out solitude like a wounded animal. He spent his nights in tears and, if ever he heard the music of a lyre or lute, he wept openly and without pause. His spirits were so feeble, and his demeanour so changed, that no one recognized him or knew his voice. He behaved madly, wildly. He did not seem to be suffering from lovesickness, but rather from despair engendered by the melancholy humour; he had been touched in the foremost ventricle of the brain, which is the proper home of the imagination. So, in the fantasy of Arcite, everything was turned upside down. All was on a totter. There is no point in recalling every detail of his despair.

After two years of sorrow, while he lived and suffered in

Thebes, as he lay sleeping one night, he had a vision or dream of Mercury. The winged god stood by his bedside, holding his wand of sleep, and bid him to be of good cheer. Now this great god wore a silver helmet, ornamented with wings, upon his golden hair. In just such a guise he had lulled Argos of the hundred eyes, when he came to steal Io. He spoke, or seemed to speak, to Arcite. 'You must journey now to Athens,' he said. 'In that city there will be an end of all your woe.' At that, Arcite woke up with a start. 'Whatever the consequences,' he said, 'even on pain of death itself, I will follow my dream and travel to Athens. Right away. I will not be deterred by anything or anyone. I will see my lady again. I will be with her, even if I have to die in her sight. Death then will be delightful.' Then he took up a great mirror, and saw the reflection of his altered looks. He was so wan and ravaged that he was scarcely recognizable even to himself. And then inspiration came to him. Whether he was inspired by Mercury, I cannot say. He realized that he was so disfigured, by suffering and sickness, that he could remain quite unknown in Athens. If he was cautious and prudent he could live there for the rest of his life without being discovered by the authorities. And then he could see Emily every day. What a wonderful prospect! So he threw himself into joyful activity. He changed his clothes, and dressed himself in the garb of a poor labouring man. His only companion was his squire. This young man knew everything, from first to last. But he was happy to follow Arcite. He, too, dressed in the garb of a poor man.

On the following day the two of them set off for Athens. As soon as Arcite arrived he went to the court of Theseus, and at the great gate there he offered his services to those who passed him. He offered to drudge, to draw water, to carry goods – anything that might help him to get closer to Emily. Eventually, and by great good fortune, he was offered a job in the household of the chamberlain who looked after the fair lady. He watched and waited, taking advantage of any opening to gain access to her. He was expert at cutting wood, and tireless

at carrying barrels of water. He was strong, with fine sinews
and big bones. He did any kind of work that was required.
He was zealous and indefatigable. So by degrees he became a
personal servant to fair Emily herself. What name did he give
himself? He was known to everyone as Philostratus.

There never was a more well-respected man. He was so
gentlemanly, so modest in demeanour, that his reputation
spread throughout the royal court. Everyone said that it would
be an act of charity on the part of Theseus to give him more
honourable employment, in a post where his particular virtues
might be nourished and displayed. So his good deeds and
eloquence were spread abroad. Theseus himself came to hear
of them. What was his response? He made him squire of the
chamber, and gave him enough gold to maintain his new
position. But Arcite also had another source of gold. He
received rental income from his lands in Thebes. It was
brought to him privately and secretly, by agents from his home
city, and they were so discreet that no one in Athens ever
guessed the truth. He spent it wisely, too, and avoided gossip.
In this manner he spent the next three years of his life. He
worked so well, both in peace and war, that Theseus held no
man in higher regard. Now I will leave Arcite for a little while,
and turn my attention to Palamon.

Oh dear. What a difference. While Arcite dwelled in bliss,
Palamon lived in hell. For seven years he had lain in darkness
and despair, fettered in the dark tower, wasted by suffering
and suffused with woe. He endured double distress, with his
unfulfilled love for Emily increasing his burden of imprisonment. He would never leave his cell. He would never kneel
before her or address her. He was close to madness. Who could
describe, in plain English, his suffering? I am not the man. So,
if you don't mind, I will pass on.

'Take your time,' our Host told him, 'for this day has been a
green day. It will stay fresh in our imaginations.'

'I thank you. But I must move on.'

In the seventh year of his imprisonment – on 3 May, to be

exact – the wheel turned for Palamon. That is the date given in the old books, at least, which are more to be trusted than I am. I have no skill at narration. Whether by fortune or by destiny – if there is any difference, actually – when something is meant to be it is meant to be – at least that is what I think. It was fated, anyway, that soon after midnight on 3 May Palamon escaped from his prison cell with the assistance of a friend. This is how he did it. He had given his gaoler a glass of sweet, spiced wine in which he had mingled some narcotics and the best Theban opium; they had the required effect, and the gaoler slept so soundly that no one could wake him. And so Palamon fled the city. Full speed ahead. Yet the spring night was short, and at break of day he decided to conceal himself in a neighbouring wood; he crept there, fearful of discovery. It was his plan to spend the rest of the day in hiding, shaded by the dark trees, and then to resume his flight to Thebes that night. Once he had arrived there, he planned to ask his friends to join him in making war upon Theseus. He would either die in combat or win Emily to be his wife. There was no third course.

Now, if I may, I will turn back to Arcite. The poor man little knew what was in store for him. Fortune was his foe. Fortune set a trap. And we all know that an hour's cold can suck out seven years of heat.

The busy lark, the messenger of day, saluted in her song the break of day. The mighty sun rose up, with beams so bright that all the east was laughing in the light; his welcome rays the land receives, and all the dewdrops perish on the leaves. This is the poetry of the morning that greeted Arcite, the squire of the royal chamber, as he rose up from his bed. He decided to pay homage to May, inspired by his desire for Emily; so forth he went upon his fiery steed, and rode some two or three miles beyond the city. Here were the open fields where he could find exercise and recreation. Quite by chance he had ridden towards the wood where Palamon lay concealed. Here he wove for himself a garland of branches, made from the leaves of the woodbine and the hawthorn, and thus crowned he sang out in the sunlight this happy greeting. 'May, with all your flowers and your green livery, welcome to you! Welcome to the fairest and freshest month! May I deserve this green garland!' He dismounted from his horse and in lively mood explored a path that led into the wood itself. Where did the path take him? It led him directly to the thicket of trees where Palamon, in fear of his life, had taken refuge. He had no idea that Arcite was close to him. God knows it would have seemed an unlikely coincidence. But there is an old saying, proven many times, that 'Fields have eyes and woods have ears.' It behoves all of you to behave wisely, because you never know whom you are going to meet. The course of life is unexpected. So Palamon little knew that the voice he heard was that of Arcite. He just lay very still in the obscure grove.

Meanwhile Arcite was singing his heart out, wandering among the trees and bushes of the wood. Then he stopped suddenly and fell to musing, as lovers will often do. One minute the lover dallies among flowers and the next he is thrust upon thorns. He goes up and down, just like a bucket in a well. Venus, like her day, can change her countenance – Friday can be sunny and then filled with clouds. Friday is unlike any other day of the week. In the same way Venus is quixotic and unpredictable with her votaries.

So after Arcite had sung, he sighed. He sat down upon the trunk of an upturned tree, and began to mourn. 'Alas,' he cried, 'I wish that I had never been born! How long, cruel and pitiless Juno, will you continue to wage war upon Thebes? The royal blood of Cadmus and Amphion, the founders of Thebes, has been sprinkled and spilled. Cadmus was the first king of Thebes. I am of his direct lineage. Yet what has become of me? I am now no better than a slave, or a captive, serving as a squire in the court of the most bitter enemy of our city. Yet Juno heaps ever more shame upon me. I dare not acknowledge my own name. I cannot proclaim myself as noble Arcite. I must hide under the name of the insignificant Philostratus. Oh Juno, and your ruthless son, Mars, you two have destroyed my kith and kin. The only survivors are myself and Palamon, who is now consigned by Theseus to the martyrdom of endless prison. And then, above all else, I am also a martyr. I am a martyr to love. Love has fired its arrow into my heart. My heart is gone before my life is done. I believe that I was destined to this fate before I was born. The eyes of Emily have slain me utterly. They are the warrant of my death. Nothing else in the world is of any consequence to me. Nothing else has meaning for me. Oh Emily, if only I could serve you!' And, with this, he fell down in a trance. He lay face down for a long time before getting to his feet again.

Palamon, concealed close by, had heard every word of Arcite's love lament. He felt that a sword, as cold as ice, had been plunged into his heart. He shook with anger. He could no longer stay in hiding. So, like a madman, pale as death, he jumped out of the thicket shouting, 'Arcite! Arcite! Wicked Arcite! False traitor, Arcite! I have caught you! You proclaim yourself the lover of my lady, Emily, for whom I have suffered so much pain and woe. You are of my blood and allegiance, as I have told you many times, and yet what have you done? You have deceived Theseus. You have lived at his court under a false name. But you will not deal falsely with Emily. I am the only one who can, or will, ever love her. So. One of us will have to die. Look upon Palamon as your mortal enemy. And although I have no weapon in my possession, since by great good fortune I have just escaped from my prison, it makes no difference. Either you will die or else you will renounce your love for Emily. Choose which one you will. Otherwise you will never leave this wood.'

Then Arcite, with anger in his heart, unsheathed his sword. He was as ferocious as a lion close to a kill. 'By God above us,' he said. 'If you were not sick with fever, and made lunatic by love, you would not walk out of this grove alive. If you had a weapon, you would surely die at my hand today. I deny the covenant, and I defy the bond, that you say I pledged to you.

What? Do you think, like a fool, that love is negotiable? That it can be tied down? I will love Emily despite all your threats.' He stopped for a moment, and wiped his brow. 'Since you are a knight of high degree, I take it that you will decide the right to her by mortal combat. So here I pledge my faith to meet you in battle tomorrow. Without the knowledge of anyone in Athens, I will bring you armour and weapons. You choose the very best, and leave the worst for me. Tonight I will bring you food and drink, too, as well as blankets for your bedding here. And if it so happens that you win my lady, and slay me in this wood where now we stand, then you may possess her with as firm a right as I.' And Palamon answered, 'I accept your terms.' So they parted from each other, both of them pledging their knightly duty to fight the next day.

Oh Cupid, god of love, you are devoid of charity. You are the youngest of the gods, but you will permit no other to share your power. It has been said, with truth, that neither love nor lordship will allow a rival. Arcite and Palamon are, as yet, living examples. So Arcite rode back to Athens and, before daybreak on the following morning, he quietly and secretly prepared two suits of armour; they were both sturdy enough to decide that day's battle between the two noble kinsmen. Then, on his horse, as alone as he was born, he carried all this gear to the place of combat.

In the wood, at the time and place appointed, Arcite and Palamon confronted one another. They both tried to gain their composure, and master their countenance, just like the hunters of Thrace who stand waiting for the lion or the bear to be flushed out. When they hear the beast come rushing through the branches and the leaves, they think to themselves, 'Here comes my mortal enemy. One of us must die. Either I will slay it when it comes rushing forward or, if fortune is against me, it will kill me.' Palamon knew the strength of Arcite, and Arcite was well aware of the might of Palamon. They did not greet or salute each other, but without any words they helped one another to put on his armour. They were so courteous that they might have been brothers. But then they sailed out in deadly combat, their swords and lances at the ready. How could they maintain their contest for so long? Well, as you may imagine, Palamon fought like a ferocious lion while Arcite attacked him with all the savagery of a tiger. No. They were more beastly than that. They fought like wild boars, their jaws frothing with white foam. They fought up to their ankles in blood. CRASH. BANG. OUCH. There I will leave them, fighting, to their destinies.

Destiny is the administrator, the general surveyor, of God's plan. Providence lies in the mind of God. Destiny is the means whereby it is worked out in the world. It is so powerful that it overrules all contradiction. That which is deemed impossible may be determined by destiny, even if it happens only once in a thousand years. All our instincts and appetites on earth – whether for war or peace, for love or hate – are ruled by destiny.

So in that spirit I turn to Theseus, lord of Athens, whose instinct and appetite were for hunting. In May, particularly, he was eager to chase and kill the royal hart. The day did not dawn when he was not dressed and ready to mount his horse, accompanied by huntsmen and hounds and horns. He loved the chase, and he loved the kill. He cried out, in the pursuit, 'So ho!' and 'Ware! Ware!' He worshipped the god of war, of course; but after Mars he venerated Diana, the goddess of the hunt.

Clear was the day, and bright the trembling air, when Theseus rode out. He was in the highest spirits, accompanied as he was by his queen, Hippolita, and by fair Emily dressed all in green. He had been told by his men that there was a hart lurking in a nearby wood, and with all speed he rode up to the spot; he knew well enough that this was the place where the beast might break cover, and fly across the stream to make its escape. So he slipped the leashes of the hounds in preparation for pursuit. Yet wait. Call off the dogs. Where, under the sun, was this wood? You have guessed it. No sooner did Theseus ride up among the trees than he saw Palamon and Arcite, the two wild boars, still in ferocious battle. They wielded their bright swords with such power that the least stroke from one of them might have felled an oak. He had no idea, as yet, who they were. But he spurred on his horse and, riding between the two combatants, he unsheathed his sword and called out to them, 'Hoo! Stop this, on pain of losing your head! By mighty Mars, I will slay the next man who raises his sword! Now tell me, what rank or estate are you? How do you dare to fight in my land without judge or officer, as you must do in a legal duel?'

Palamon answered directly. 'Sire, there is nothing we can say. Both of us deserve the punishment of death. We are two woeful wretches, two slaves of destiny already overburdened by our own lives; as you are a rightful lord and judge, show us neither mercy nor refuge. Yet show some charity to me. Kill me first. But then kill him as well. On second thoughts, you might as well kill him first. It makes no difference. Shall I tell you who he is? Here stands Arcite, your mortal enemy, who was banished from Athens on pain of death. Surely, now, death is the fate that he deserves. You may know him by another name. This is the man that came to your court and called himself Philostratus. Do you recognize him? He has fooled you for many years. You even made him your principal squire. This is the man, also, who declares himself to be the lover of Emily! Well. Enough of that. Since the day has come when I must die, I will make a full confession to you. I am woeful Palamon, the man who unlawfully escaped from your prison. I am your mortal enemy, too, and I also profess myself to be the lover of fair Emily. Let me die before her now. That is all I wish. So I ask for the sentence of death to be carried out on me and my companion. Both of us have deserved our fate.'

Then the worthy duke Theseus replied to him. 'There is nothing much to say. Out of your own mouth comes your confession. You have condemned yourself. It only falls to me to pronounce judgment. There is no need to apply the rack or thumbscrew. You will simply die. I swear this by the patron of my life, great Mars.'

Yet now his queen, Hippolita, out of sympathy and pity, began to weep. Then Emily started to cry. And then, of course, all the ladies of the company joined in the lament. They bewailed the fact that two knights of such noble deportment should meet such a fate. The argument between them both was all for love. The women beheld the great and bloody wounds upon their fair bodies, and cried out in chorus, 'Have mercy, lord, upon all of us women!' They fell down upon the ground on their bare knees, and would have kissed his feet in entreaty. But then the anger of Theseus passed. Pity soon enters a gentle heart. He had at first been enraged at their abuse of his power but now, on considering the matter, he realized that their crimes were not so heinous. They had some reason to act in the way they had. His wrath was the accuser, but his judgment was the defender. He understood well enough that any man in love will try to help his cause, and that any man in prison will wish to escape. That was natural. That was human. He also felt some compassion for the women, still weeping all around him.

He contemplated the matter and then spoke softly to himself. 'There is a curse upon a merciless ruler who upholds only the law of the lion, who is pitiless to the humble and haughty alike, who does not distinguish between the unrepentant and the penitent. Shame on him who weighs all men alike.'

So his anger was mollified. He looked up with bright eyes, and spoke aloud to the assembled company. 'May the god of love,' he said, 'bless me and bless you all! How mighty and how great a lord is he! No one can withstand his power. He overcomes all obstacles. His miracles themselves proclaim his divinity for he can move the human heart in any direction that he wishes. Look here at Arcite and Palamon. They both escaped from imprisonment in the dark tower, and might have lived royally in Thebes. They both knew that I was their mortal enemy, and that it lay in my power to slaughter them. And yet the god of love has brought them here, where they may die. Consider it. Is it not the height of folly? Yet folly is the mark of the true lover. Look at them, for God's sake. Do you see how they bleed? Do you see in what condition they are? So has their lord and master, the god of love, repaid them for their loyalty to him! Yet of course they consider themselves to be wise men, and virtuous in their service, whatever may happen to them. And do you want to know the best joke of all? The lady who has provoked all their passion knew no more of it than I did. Emily was as unaware of their rash valour as the birds in the trees above us. Yet we have all to be tempered in the fire of love, whether we are hot or cold, young or old. I know it well enough myself. I was a servant of the god many years ago. And since I know all about the pain of love, and know how sore a wound it can inflict when the lover is caught in its meshes, then I fully forgive the trespasses of these two knights. I will accede to the petition both of my queen, who kneels here before me, and of my dear sister, Emily. There is one condition. Both of you must swear that you will never again invade my territories. You must never threaten war against me but, on the contrary, you must pledge yourselves to be my friends and allies. On that condition, you are forgiven.'

Palamon and Arcite humbly and gratefully assented to his terms. They asked him in turn to become their lord and protector, to which he graciously agreed. 'In terms of royal lineage and wealth,' he said, 'either one of you is worthy to marry a princess or even a queen. That is obvious. If I may speak for my sister, Emily, over whom you have suffered so much strife and jealousy – well, you yourselves know well enough that she cannot marry both of you at once. You can fight for eternity but, like it or not, only one of you can be betrothed to her. The other can go whistle in the wind. Be as jealous, or as angry, as you may. That is the truth. So listen while I explain to you my plan, to find whose destiny is shaped for Emily and whose is turned the other way. This is what I have devised. It is my will, and you must make the best of it. I will listen to no argument or objection. I stipulate that both of you should go your separate ways, without ransom or hindrance, and in a year's time that both of you should return with a company of one hundred knights fully armed and equipped for a tournament. Your men should be ready to decide the hand of Emily by dint of battle. Upon my honour, as a knight, I promise you this. I will reward whichever of you has the most strength. Whether you slay your adversary, or with your hundred companions drive him from the joust, I will give you the hand of fair Emily. Thus fortune will favour the brave. The tournament will take place here and, as God have mercy on my soul, I will be a fair and true judge of the contest. And I will allow only one conclusion. One of you will be killed or made captive. If both of you agree, then assent now and hold yourselves well served.'

Who could be more cheerful now than Palamon? Who could be more joyful than Arcite? I cannot begin to describe the rejoicing of the whole company at the decision of Theseus. He had behaved so graciously that all of them went down on their knees and thanked him. The two Thebans, in particular, expressed their gratefulness. So with heads high, and hope in their hearts, Palamon and Arcite made their way back to the ancient city of Thebes. They had a year to prepare themselves for battle.

PART THREE

I am sure that you would accuse me of negligence if I failed to tell you of the expense and trouble that Theseus went to in preparing the royal tournament. I dare say that there was no greater amphitheatre in the whole world. It was a mile in circumference, the shape of a circle, environed with great walls and moats. The seats rose in tiers some sixty feet, and were so well arranged that everyone had a full view of the arena. On the eastern side there stood a gate of white marble, balanced in harmony with its counterpart on the western side. It was a dream of stone. Nothing of this style had ever been built so well or so quickly. Theseus enquired throughout his land and enlisted the services of every craftsman skilled in arithmetic or in geometry; he hired the best artists, and the most renowned sculptors, in the construction of this glorious theatre. And then, for the purposes of worship and ceremonial, he caused to be built an altar and a shrine to Venus in a room above the eastern gate. Above the western gate there was constructed a temple to Mars. They cost a wagon-load of gold. And then on the northern side, within a turret on the wall, Theseus built an exquisite temple to the goddess of chastity, Diana, elaborately wrought out of white alabaster and red coral.

I had almost forgotten to describe to you the noble carvings and paintings that adorned these three temples, displaying all the most delicate skills of expression and action. On the walls of the temple of Venus, for example, were depicted images of the broken sleep and pitiful sighs of the servants of love; here also were pictures of the sacred tears and lamentations of lovers, together with the fiery strokes of their desires. Here were the oaths they passed. Here were the figures of Pleasure and of Hope, of Desire and of Foolishness, of Beauty and of Youth, of Mirth and of Costliness, of Luxury and Care and Jealousy. Jealousy wore a garland of golden marigolds, the token of cruelty and despair; on her hand was perched a cuckoo, bright bird of infidelity. On the walls, too, were painted frescoes of all the feasts, concerts, songs and dances devoted to love. Here were images of desire and display, all the circumstances of love that ever have been and ever will be celebrated. I cannot mention them all. Suffice it to say that the whole island of Cytherea, the dwelling and domain of Venus, was floating upon the walls of the temple.

In its gardens could be seen the figure of Idleness, the keeper of love's gates. Here was Narcissus, of ancient times, together with lecherous King Solomon. There were other martyrs to love. There was Hercules, betrayed by goddesses and mortal women. There was Turnus, who lost all for love. There was Croesus, wretched in captivity. On another wall were the two enchantresses Medea and Circe, holding out their potions of love. There is no force on earth that can withstand Venus – not wisdom, not wealth, not beauty, not cunning, not strength or endurance. All will fail. She rules the world. I have given you one or two examples of her mastery. There are a thousand more. She captured all these lovers in her net, and all they could do was let slip the word 'alas'.

The image of Venus, in this temple, was glorious to see. She was naked, floating on a limitless ocean of green; from the navel down she was environed by waves as glittering as any glass. She held a lute in her right hand, ready to play upon its strings, and on her head she wore a garland of fresh roses; their perfume rose into the air above her, where fluttered turtle-doves. Beside her stood her son, young winged Cupid; he was blind, as the legend tells us, but he bore a bow with arrows bright and keen.

Why should I not also tell you about the frescoes within the temple of red Mars? The walls were all painted from top to bottom, just as if they were the interior apartments of his desolate temple in Thrace. It is a region of frost and snow, where the great god of war has his dominion. So on the wall was painted the image of a forest, forlorn and deserted, with black and knotted boughs and bare, ruined trees. Between these stumps and dead things there came a blast of wind, like a sigh from hell, as though a hideous tempest might whirl every-thing away. There on a bank, beside a hill, stood the temple of Mars omnipotent; it was wrought of burnished steel, its entrance long and narrow. Through this grim portal there rushed an endless wind that shook the hinges of the gates. An icy light from the north shone through the doors of this temple, for there were no windows in the edifice itself. The doors them-selves were adamantine and eternal, their frames plated with sheets of thick iron. The pillars that supported the temple were as thick as barrels, cast out of cold glittering iron.

There on the walls I saw all the dark imaginings of the warring world. I saw the plans and schemes of Felony. I saw cruel Anger, glowing like a coal in a furnace. I saw the thief. I saw pale Fear itself. I saw the smiler with the knife under his coat. There was the farmhouse set on fire, wreathed in burning smoke. There were treason and secret murder, closely placed beside strife and conflict. I saw the wounds of war, pouring with blood, together with the dagger and the menacing blade that made them. This inferno was an echo chamber of groans. There was the suicide, the sharp nail driven through his temple, his hair clotted with his own blood. There was Death itself, lying upwards with its mouth agape. In the middle of this place lurked Misfortune, with the woeful countenance. Beside him was Madness, bellowing with wild laughter and with rage. And who else were there but Discontent, Alarm and Cruelty?

Painted on the wall was an image of the victim in the wood, his throat cut; of thousands dead, although untouched by plague; of the tyrant exulting over his prey; of the town razed and its inhabitants destroyed. I saw the burning ships tossed upon the waves; the hunter killed by the raging bears; the sow eating the child in the cradle; the cook scalded by the devil, despite his long spoon. All men and affairs are blighted by the evil aspect of Mars, even one so lowly as the poor carter. There he lies, his body broken under the wheel.

Here also were the trades favoured by Mars. Here were the barber and the butcher, wielding their blades; here was the smith, forging the bright steel. Above them was displayed the conquering general, sitting in triumph upon a tower, with a sword above his head hanging on a slender string. There were images of the death of Julius Caesar, of the notorious Nero, and of Anthony, who lost the world for love. Of course none of them was as yet born, yet their deaths were still foretold by thunderous Mars; he saw their fates fully shaped in the patterns of the stars. All the legends of great men come to the same conclusion. I cannot recite them now.

And there, pre-eminent, stood Mars in his chariot. The

glorious god of war, wrapped in his armour, looked grim. He was ferocious. Above his head shone two stars that have been named in the old books as the maid Puella and the warrior Rubeus; as the cunning men tell us, they are the tokens of the two constellations aligned with Mars himself. At the feet of the god lay a wolf, red-eyed, ready to devour a man. So stood Mars in splendour.

Now I hasten on to the temple of chaste Diana, which I shall describe to you as briefly as I may. On the walls of this edifice were painted all the devotion of this great goddess to hunting and to modest chastity. There was one of the nymphs of Diana, fallen Callisto in all her woe, whom the goddess in her wrath changed into a bear; then she relented and transformed her, and her son by Jupiter, into stars. So it was painted here. I know no more. There I saw Daphne, the daughter of Peneus, all changed into a laurel tree. Only thus could she preserve her virginity from lustful Apollo. There too was Actaeon, turned into a stag for the crime of observing Diana naked by the poolside. His own hounds pursued and devoured him, little knowing that he was their master. There was an image of Atalanta and Meleager, who with others pursued the Calydonian boar, for which crime Diana punished them both severely. I saw there depicted many other wonderful stories and legends. This is not the place to recall them all.

The goddess herself was depicted upright upon a hart, with small dogs playing about her feet; beneath her was the changing moon, ever about to wax or wane. She was clothed entirely in bright green; her bow was in her hand, her arrows in their quiver. Her eyes were cast down upon the ground, as if searching for Pluto's kingdom beneath the earth. Before her lay a woman in labour. The baby was so long in coming forth that the woman was crying out, 'Diana, goddess of childbirth, only you can help me endure!' The painter spared no expense with the colours of the work; it was a living piece of nature. These were the temples, then, that Duke Theseus had caused to be built at great cost within his amphitheatre. When he saw them completed, he was content. The work had gone well. Now I will return to Palamon and Arcite.

The day was fast approaching for their return to Athens, where, according to their agreement, they would bring with them one hundred knights armed for the battle. They were the flower of chivalry. I do not think that there were any better warriors in the world at that time. There were none more noble or more brave. All of them were devoted to the knightly virtues of modesty and honour. All of them wished to acquire a matchless reputation by dint of arms. What better opportunity than the joust for the hand of Emily? It could happen today. If there was a similar contest, in England or elsewhere, what knight would hesitate before coming forward as a champion? To fight for a fair lady – that is the height of bliss. It is, in my mind, the meaning of knighthood then and now.

So rode out the hundred in the company of Palamon. Some were armed with a coat of mail and armoured breastplate, covering a light tunic. Some were wearing sets of plate armour, heavy and strong. Others carried a Prussian shield and buckler, or were wearing leg armour. One brandished a battleaxe, and another wielded a steel mace. So it was, and so it will ever be.

Among the knights who followed Palamon was Lycurgus, king of Thrace. Black was his beard, and manly his appearance. His eyes were brilliant, flashing somewhere between yellow and red. His eyebrows were wide and shaggy, so that he looked half lion or like some mythical beast of strength. He had large limbs, and powerful muscles; his shoulders were broad, and his arms long. What more is there to say? As was the custom in his country he rode in a golden chariot, pulled by four pure-white bulls. Instead of a tunic over his armour (which was studded with bright nails, golden in the sun) he wore a bearskin black with age. His long hair, as black and lustrous as the feathers of a raven, was combed behind his back. Upon his head he wore a coronet of gold, its threads as thick as a man's arm; it was studded with precious stones, with rubies and with diamonds, and was of tremendous weight.

Beside his chariot ran a score or more of white wolfhounds, as large as any steer, used to hunting the lion and the stag. They followed him with their muzzles tightly bound, their leashes fastened to collars of gold. He had a hundred knights in his train, armed well, with hearts stout and defiant. So rode out Lycurgus.

According to the old stories, which I must use, the procession of Arcite was accompanied by the great Emetreus, king of India. He rode upon a bay horse; the noble beast had trappings of steel, and was covered in cloth of gold embroidered with curious devices. Truly Emetreus resembled Mars himself. His coat of arms was woven of rare silk and embroidered with large white pearls; his saddle was of newly beaten gold, and the mantle around his shoulders was studded with glowing rubies. His hair hung down in curls, carefully fashioned; it was as yellow, and as radiant, as the sun. He had an aquiline nose, and eyes that gave out a golden light; his lips were firm and well rounded, his face fresh and fair except for some freckles scattered here and there. He was a lion in appearance and in purpose. I guess his age to be twenty-five. He had the makings of a beard, and his voice was as stirring as the note of a trumpet. He had a wreath of laurel on his head, all garlanded with green. For his sport he carried on his hand a tame eagle, as purely white as a lily. He had brought with him, like Lycurgus, a hundred knights armed and equipped in every point. Only their heads were bare, in honour of the fact that they fought for love. You should know that in their company were dukes and earls and even other kings, assembled together for their delight in chivalry. Around them on all sides gambolled tame lions and leopards. So in this manner the noble group rode to Athens. They arrived in the city at nine o'clock in the morning, on a Sunday, and in the streets they dismounted.

The duke of Athens, renowned Theseus, greeted them and then led them through his city to their lodgings; each of them was given hospitality according to his rank. He ordered a great feast for them, too, and arranged everything so well that no one else could have equalled his munificence. You may expect me to comment on the music, and the service, at the feast – on the gifts that were given to high and low – on the rich furnishings of Theseus' palace – or on the order of guests on the dais – or on the ladies who were fairest or most expert at dancing – or who sang best – or who sang most passionately of love – but I am afraid you will be disappointed. You will not hear from me about the tame hawks that strutted on their perches, or about the mastiffs lying upon the floor of the hall. You may see these things in tapestries. I deem it more important to carry on with the story.

That Sunday night, before the dawn of day, just as the lark was beginning to sing – it was an hour or two before the end of darkness, and yet the lark still sang – Palamon rose from his bed and blessed himself. He was in high spirits, and was prepared to make a pilgrimage to Venus. He intended, in other words, to visit the shrine of the goddess erected in the amphitheatre. In her holy hour, the fifth hour of the day, he entered the temple and kneeled upon the marble floor where in all humility he prayed to her image.

'Fairest of fair, oh my lady Venus. Daughter of great Jove and spouse of mighty Vulcanus; joyful comfort of mount Cytharea by virtue of the love you had for Adonis, have pity on my bitter tears. Receive my humble prayer into your heart. Alas I do not have the words to tell the sorrows and the torments of my private hell. My heart cannot convey the grief I feel. I am so distracted and confused that I can only invoke your blessed name. Have mercy on me, fair lady. You see into my heart. You know my sorrow. Consider my plight. Have pity. And I promise you this. I will ever more be your servant, and combat the blight of barren chastity. That is my vow. I do not ask for fame in arms, or for a splendid victory on the field; I do not crave feats of vainglory or of martial prowess. I crave only the possession of Emily, so that I might live and die in your service. You may choose the means, as long as you inform me. I do not care if I win victory or suffer defeat, as long as I can hold my lady in my arms. Although I know that dread Mars is the god of battle, I also know that your power is so great in heaven that your wish is enough to bring me to bliss. Then I will worship in your temple, before your sacred image, for the rest of my life. I will bear sweet fire to your altar, in whatever place I am, and sprinkle incense on the sacrifice. If your will is against me, and you disregard my plea, then I wish to die tomorrow at the hand of Arcite. Guide his spear against me. When I have lost my life, I will not care if he gains the favour of Emily. Now that you have heard the purpose and the substance of my petition, great goddess, grant me her love.'

When the prayer of Palamon was ended, he performed the rite of sacrifice to Venus with all due diligence and solemnity. I cannot recount all of his words and gestures here, but I can tell you this. At the close of his devotions, the statue of Venus trembled and made a sign. It was a good omen. He believed, then, that his prayer had been accepted. The sign of the goddess had intimated some delay, but he understood well enough that his request would be fulfilled. So he returned home with a light heart.

Three hours after Palamon had set out for the temple, the bright sun began its pilgrimage across the sky. Whereupon Emily rose, too, and hastened to the temple of Diana. Her maidens escorted her, bearing the sacred fire, the incense and the vestments that would be used in the ritual sacrifice. The drinking horns were filled to the brim with mead, as was the custom; they had everything they needed for the holy ceremony. Emily washed herself in the water of a holy well before sprinkling the temple with incense; then she, of the gentle heart, robed herself modestly. I dare not tell you how she performed the sacred rites, except in the most general terms –

'What can be forbidden?' the Monk asked him. 'Those days are past. The pagan night is over.'

'Tell us all,' the Reeve urged him. 'It will entertain us.'

'It can do no harm,' the Miller said. 'Not if you mean well. We must be free and easy in this company.'

'If you permit me, then so will it be.'

Emily's bright hair was loose, combed behind her back. Upon her head was set a coronet twined from the leaves of the evergreen oak, sacred to Zeus. First she kindled two fires upon the altar, and then performed the ritual as it is outlined in the *Thebaid* of Statius and other ancient authorities. When the fires were fully lit she kneeled before the statue of Diana, and prayed to her.

'Oh chaste goddess of the green woods,' she murmured, 'to whom all things of heaven and earth are visible, queen of Plato's dark dominions, goddess of innocent maidens – you have seen into my heart for many years. You know my desire. I hope I never shall incur your wrath and vengeance, as Actaeon did when he was turned into a stag. But you understand, great goddess, that I seek only to remain a virgin. I never wish to be a mistress or a wife. I am a part of your order of maidens, devoted to hunting and not to love. I long to walk in the wild woods, never to marry and never to bear children. I have never wished to lie with any man. So help me now. As goddess of the chase, the moon and the underworld, cast your triune grace upon me. Cure Palamon, and also Arcite, of their passion for me. Restore love and peace between them, and turn their hearts away from me. Let all the flames of burning love and hot desire be quenched. Assuage their violent torment and put out their fire. Or, at the very least, send them other loves. But if you will not vouchsafe this favour to me, and if my destiny will not be as I wish, then I ask you this. If I must have Arcite or Palamon, grant me the one who loves me best. Yet let it not come to that. Behold, goddess of chaste purity, one who kneels before you weeping bitter tears. Since you are maid and preserver of us all, I pray you keep my maidenhead intact. As a virgin, I will serve you all my life.'

The bright flames lit up the altar, while Emily kneeled in prayer. But then to her amazement one of the fires was suddenly extinguished, only to flare up again; after that the other fire went out and, as it died away, there came a great crackling and roaring as of wet branches burning in a heap. From each of the branches of the fire there now dripped blood, drop upon drop falling to the floor of the temple. Emily was confused and terribly alarmed. What was this? In her fear she cried out like a mad woman. She broke down and wept. But at that moment she had a vision of Diana. The apparition of the goddess stood before her, with hunter's bow in hand, and spoke thus.

'Daughter, cast off your melancholy. The gods have decreed, and by eternal oath confirmed, that you must be wedded to one of these two noble knights who have suffered so much on your behalf. I may not tell you which of them. But one of them will be your lawful husband. Farewell. I must leave you now. But I can tell you this. The fires now burning on my altar have been a sign to you. You have seen your destiny.' Then the figure of Diana vanished, with the rattling of her arrows in the quiver.

Emily was amazed at this sudden vision. 'I do not know what the goddess meant,' she said. 'But, Diana, I put myself under your protection. Dispose of me as you will.' Thereupon she left the holy place and returned to the palace. There I will leave her.

The hour after this, in the planetary hour of Mars, Arcite walked to the temple of the god where he would make his sacrifice. He performed all of the sacred rites and then, with passion and devotion, he prayed to the god of battle.

'Oh powerful god, who holds dominion in the freezing land of Thrace – who holds the outcome of all wars, in all countries and kingdoms, in your hands – oh lord of all the fortunes of war – accept my sacrifice and hear my plea. If my youth deserves your sympathy, and if my strength is sufficient to serve you as one of your followers, I entreat you to have pity on my pain. You suffered the same anguish, the same hot flame of desire, when you took as your paramour the fair, young and fresh Venus. You possessed her at your will. Of course there was the occasion when lame Vulcan caught you in his net, just as you were lying with his wife, but let that pass. For the sake of all the pain you suffered, have pity upon my agonies. I am young and ignorant, as you know, but I believe that I am wounded by love more sorely than any other man in the wide world. Emily, the cause of all my woe, does not care whether I sink or swim. I know well enough that I must win her in the tournament before she will have mercy on me; I know well, too, that I will need your help and grace before I assay my strength. So assist me, lord, in the battle tomorrow. For the sake of the fire that once burned you, and for the sake of the fire that now burns me, ordain that the victory tomorrow will be mine. Let my portion be the labour, so that yours may be the glory. I will honour your sacred temple before any other place on earth. I will strive for your delight in all the arts and crafts of war. I will hang my banners, and all the arms of my company, above this hallowed altar. Here, too, I will light an everlasting flame where I will worship to the day of my death. And I make this vow to you. I will cut off my hair and beard, that have never yet felt the blade or razor, and offer them as a sacrifice to your might. I will be your true servant for the rest of my life. Now, great god, have pity on my sorrow. Grant me the victory. I ask no more.'

When Arcite had finished his prayer, the rings that hung upon the doors of the temple began to shake; the doors themselves trembled with some unearthly power. And Arcite became afraid. The fires upon the altar flared up, and the whole temple was filled with brightness. A sweet scent issued from the ground, and wafted through the trembling air. Arcite raised his hand and sprinkled more incense upon the flame. When he had finished all the rites of worship, he waited with head bowed. The statue of Mars began to move, and the god's coat of arms rattled. There was a sound as of low murmuring, and one word was whispered. 'Victory!' Arcite rejoiced and, having paid homage to Mars, returned to his lodgings with high hopes for the coming battle. He was as exultant as a lark ascending.

Yet now, as a result of these events upon the earth, there sprang up strife among the gods above. Venus and Mars were opposed, the goddess of love against the god of war. Jupiter attempted to resolve their dispute, but it was really Saturn who restored their harmony. Saturn is the pale and cold god, but he was experienced in all the foibles and adventures of the other divinities. He knew how to bring unity to the chambers of heaven. Age has its advantages, after all. It is a sign of wisdom and of long practice. You can outrun the old, but you cannot outwit them. It may not be in the nature of Saturn to quell strife and dispel terror, yet on this occasion he found the means to satisfy both parties.

'Venus, my granddaughter,' he said. 'My wide orbit extends much further than humankind can understand. Mine is the drowning in the dark sea. The prisoner in the dark cell is also mine. I am the lord of strangling and of hanging by the throat. I am the leader of revolt and rebellion. I provoke the loud groaning. I administer the secret poison. When I am in the sign of Leo, then I deal out vengeance and punishment. I stand in triumph above the ruined halls. I throw the walls down on masons and on carpenters. I slew Sampson as he shook the pillar. I am the master of shivering ague. I direct the treasons and the secret plots. I smile upon pestilence. So listen to me now. Weep no more. I will look after you. Your knight, Palamon, will win the lady just as you have promised to him. Mars will in turn help Arcite and save his honour. Nevertheless there must now be peace between the two of you. I know that you have different temperaments, and that as a result there is division between you, but enough of strife. I am your grand-father. I am ready, and willing, to help you. Dry your eyes.' So spoke dread Saturn.

Now I will leave the gods in heaven, and return to the events of earth. It is time for the tournament. Of arms, and the men, I sing.

PART FOUR

The festivities that day in Athens were glorious. The vigour of May entered every person, so that all were bold and playful. They danced and jousted all that Monday, or spent the day in the service of Venus. The night was for rest. All were eager to rise early and to witness the great fight. On that morning there was a great bustle and noise, in the inns and lodgings, as the horses and the suits of armour were prepared for the battle. The knights and the companies of nobles, mounted on stallions and fine steeds, rode out to the palace. If you had been there, you would have seen armour so ornate and so exotic that it seemed to be spun out of gold and steel. The spears, the head-armour, and the horse-armour, glittered in the morning sun while the golden mail and coats of arms glowed in the throng. In the saddle were lords wearing richly decorated robes, followed by the knights of their retinue and their squires; the squires themselves were busy fastening the heads to the shafts of the spears, buckling up the helmets and fitting the shields with leather straps. This was no time to be idle. The horses were foaming and champing on their golden bridles. The armourers were running here and there with file and hammer. There were yeomen in procession, and also many of the common people with thick staffs in their hands. All of them rode, or marched, to the notes of pipes, trumpets, bugles and kettledrums blaring out the sound of battle.

In the palace there were small groups of people in excited debate, all of them discussing the merits of the Theban knights. One had an opinion, which another contradicted. One said this, another said that. Some supported the knight with the black beard, while others commended the bald fellow. Yet others gave the palm to the knight with the shaggy hair. 'I tell you this,' one courtier said, 'he looks like a fighter. That axe of his must weight twenty pounds at least.' 'Never!' So, long after the sun had risen, the halls rang with gossip and speculation.

The noble lord, Theseus, had already been woken by the music of minstrels and by the noise of the crowd. Yet he remained in the privy chambers of his palace until Palamon and Arcite, equally honoured guests, were brought into the courtyard. Theseus appeared at a great window, where he sat in state as if he were a god enthroned. The crowd of people were allowed to enter, and pressed forward to see him and to do him reverence. They were also curious to hear what he had decided to say. So they grew silent when the herald called out, 'Oye! Oye!' When they were quite still, he proceeded to read out the duke's decree. 'The lord, Theseus,' he said, 'revolving the matter of this tournament in his noble mind, and deeming it little better than folly to risk the lives of these noble knights in mortal struggle, whereupon, what with one thing and another, with the intent that none of them shall die, he has changed his original plan. No man, therefore, on pain of his life, will bring any arrow or axe or knife into the jousts. No one will carry, or cause to be carried, or draw, or cause to be drawn, any short sword; no such weapon will be allowed. Only one charge will be allowed with a sharp spear against an opponent. If on foot, the combatant is allowed to thrust in self-defence. If by mischance he is taken, he is not to be slain but marched under guard to a post that will be set up on either side. There he must stay. If either Palamon or Arcite is captured, or if one of them dies, then the tournament comes to an end. God speed to all the fighters. Go forth now, and smite hard! Good luck with your maces and your long swords. Make your way to the list. This is the will of noble Theseus.'

The people cried aloud with one voice, and their approbation reached the gates of heaven. 'God bless you, great lord! In your goodness of heart, you are not willing to shed noble blood!' Then, as the trumpets blew and the drums began to beat, the whole company made its way to the amphitheatre of stone. The people of Athens proceeded according to their rank, through a city decked in cloth of gold. Leading them was Theseus himself, with Palamon and Arcite riding on either side;

after him rode his queen, Hippolita, and fair Emily herself, while all the rest followed. It was not yet nine o'clock when they arrived at the lists, but Theseus took his seat of state. When he was enthroned in majesty, Hippolita and Emily sat in their appointed places. Then all the others took their seats. They looked towards the western gate of Mars where Arcite, with a banner of red, entered with his hundred knights. At the same moment, through the eastern gate dedicated to Venus, Palamon rode out with his retinue; he had unfurled a banner of white, and carried it with spirit and dedication. There could not have been two sets of troops in the world who were so evenly matched in every respect, in courage, in nobility, and in age; they rode in two ranks, like beside like. When their names were called, to confirm their number, each one answered in turn. There was no attempt at treachery. After the muster was taken the gates were shut, and the cry rang out – 'Knights, fulfil your duty!' Then, as the trumpets blared, the heralds withdrew. The battle was set to begin on both sides.

In go the spears, held firmly for attack; in go the spurs, piercing the flanks of the horses. These were plainly men who could joust and ride. The shivering shafts then fell against the sturdy shields. One rider feels the thrust against his breast-bone. The spears spring up, some twenty feet in height; the gleaming swords are raised, as bright as silver. The helmets of the knights are smashed to smithereens. BLOOD BUBBLES. BONES BREAK. BREASTS BURST. One knight hurls himself through the thickest of the throng. One steed stumbles, and down come horse and rider, rolling under foot. Another knight stands his ground and fights with his spear, sending his opponent tumbling. Here is one wounded and taken; despite his protests he is led to the pillar of defeat, where he must remain for the duration of the tournament. Another fallen knight is escorted to the other side. From time to time Theseus ordains a pause, so that the knights may rest and with drink or other cordials refresh themselves.

There were many occasions when the two Thebans, Palamon

and Arcite, were engaged in single combat; they scarred and slashed one another, and were both unhorsed. There is no tiger in the woods of Greece, her whelp stolen by a hyena, who was more savage than Arcite stalking his foe. The Moroccan lion, hunted down and weak from hunger, was not more fierce than Palamon against his enemy in love. Enraged with jealousy they struck each other hard; their blood ran in streams upon the earth. Yet there is an end to everything. Before the day drew to a close the strong king, Emetreus, managed to get hold of Palamon while he was fighting Arcite; he plunged his sword into his flesh and with twenty men dragged him to the stake. Immediately the great king, Lycurgus, rode to the rescue of his champion, but he was knocked from his horse; Emetreus himself was wounded by Palamon, who, refusing to yield, had struck out at him with his sword and dislodged him from his saddle. Yet it was all for nothing. He was taken struggling to the stake. His brave heart could not assist him now. As the rules of Theseus had stated, he was obliged to remain where he was. He had been defeated. He was bowed in sorrow, knowing well enough that he could not fight again. When Theseus witnessed all this he cried out to the knights left in the field, 'No more! The fighting is over! I can now give my just and proper decision. Arcite of Thebes has gained the hand of Emily. He has won her in a fair contest. Fortune is on his side.' The people then exclaimed with joy, in cries and shouts so loud that it seemed the lists themselves might fall.

What can fair Venus, patron of Palamon, do now? What can she say? Of course, as women will, she broke down in tears. She wept at the thwarting of her will. 'I am disgraced,' she said. 'I have been put to shame.'

'Wait,' Saturn told her. 'Be calm. Mars has had his wish fulfilled, and his knight has gained the victory. But trust me. Your heart will soon be eased.'

Together they looked down upon the scene on earth, as the trumpets blared out and the heralds joyfully declared that Arcite had triumphed over Palamon. But do not join the general clamour. Listen to me first. I will relate to you a miracle. Fierce Arcite had removed his helmet so that the crowd might see his face. He rode in triumph on his charger, around the course, looking up at Emily. She returned his look with an affectionate glance, indicating to everyone that fortune's favourite was also her own. It seemed to Arcite that his heart might burst with love and tenderness.

But then something happened. A hellborn fury rose up from the ground, despatched from the dark world by Pluto at the request of Saturn. The horse started with fright at the apparition, reared up and then fell on its side. Before Arcite could leap from his saddle he was thrown off and pitched headlong on to the ground. He lay there as if he were already dead, his chest shattered by his own bow; the blood ran into his face, so that it seemed to turn black. Immediately he was taken up and carried to the palace of Theseus. He was cut out of his armour and gently laid in a bed. He was still alive and conscious, crying out all the time for Emily.

Meanwhile Duke Theseus returned to Athens with all of his company; he travelled in ceremonial state, and in festive guise, since he did not wish to dishearten the people by dwelling on the accident. It was widely reported that Arcite was not in danger of death, and that he would soon recover from his wounds. There was another reason for celebration, too, since not one of the combatants had been slain in the tournament. There were many who were badly injured, especially one whose breastbone was broken by a spear, but no one had died. Some of the knights had sweet-smelling ointment for their wounds, while others had magical charms to work on broken limbs and broken heads. Many of the fighters could be seen gulping down the fermentation of herbs, even sage, in order to heal themselves. Sage is good for convulsions. Hence the saying, 'Why should a man die when sage grows in the garden?'

Theseus also did his best to comfort and to cheer them and, according to the laws of good hospitality, he organized a revel that would last all night. He also issued a proclamation in which he stated that no one had been defeated or disgraced. It had been a noble tournament, an affair of honour to all concerned, subject only to the whim of fate. There was no shame in being captured and dragged to the stake by twenty armed men; Palamon had not surrendered but had been manhandled by knights, yeomen and servants. Even his horse had been beaten with staves. He had no reason to be ashamed or humiliated. His bravery was clear for all to see. So Theseus calmed both sides of the dispute, and prevented any outburst of anger or resentment. In fact they embraced one another like brothers. The duke gave them gifts, their worth determined by their rank, and organized a lavish feast that lasted for three days; then he escorted the two kings, Emetreus and Lycurgus, royally out of his lands. Every man went home well pleased by the adventure, and the final words among them all were 'Farewell! Good fortune!'

Now I will return to the two Thebans. The breast of Arcite was terribly swollen by his injury; the pressure on his heart increased, and the blood was clotted beyond the remedy of any physician. It was trapped, corrupted and seething in his body, and could not be released by cupping or bleeding or herbal cure. The animal spirits of the body were not powerful enough to expel the rotting matter. So all the vessels of his lungs began to swell, and all the muscles of his breast were paralysed by the venom. He could neither vomit nor excrete. That part of his body was thoroughly broken down. Life held no dominion there. And if there comes a time when the powers of nature no longer work, then the benefits of medicine are worthless. It is time for church. Arcite must surely die. That is the sum of it.

So on his deathbed he sent for Emily, and for Palamon, and whispered to them his dying words. 'The woeful spirit in my heart cannot begin to tell my grief to you, sweet lady, whom I love most. I am about to die. Now that my life is over I bequeath to you above all others, lady, the service of my spirit. What is this woe? What are the pains so strong that I have suffered for you? And for so long? What is this death that comes for me? Alas, Emily, from whom I must depart for ever! You are the queen of my heart, my wife, my sweetheart, and the ender of my life. What is this life? What do men know of it? We are in love and then we are in the cold grave; there we lie alone, without any company. Farewell my sweet enemy, my Emily! Yet before I leave you take me softly in your arms, for love of God, and listen to what I say. My dear cousin, Palamon, is with us. For a long time there was strife and anger between us. We fought each other for the right to claim you. But I pray to Jupiter now to give me the power to portray him properly; to depict, that is to say, his truth and honour; to celebrate his wisdom and humility; to applaud his nobility of character; to describe his noble lineage, and his devotion to all the knightly virtues. He is a servant, too, in the cause of love. So by the great gods I recommend him to you, Emily, to be your lover and your husband. There is no one on earth more worthy. He will serve you for the rest of his life. If you do decide to marry, do not forget this gentle man.' At this point the speech of Arcite began to fail. The cold of death had travelled from his feet to his chest; his limbs grew weak and pale from loss of vital strength. Only his intellect remained. But that, too, was dimmed when his heart grew feeble and felt the approach of death. His eyes began to close, and his breath was weak. Yet still he gazed at Emily. His last words were 'Have pity, Emily!' And then his soul changed house. I do not know where it travelled. I have never been to that distant country. I am not a theologian. I can say nothing. And why should I repeat the speculations of those who profess to know? There is nothing about souls in the volume where I found this old story. Arcite is dead. That is all I can tell you. May his god, Mars, guide his spirit.

And what of those left in life? Emily shrieked. Palamon howled. Theseus led his sister-in-law, swooning, from the deathbed. There is no point spending more time recounting how her night and morning were spent in tears. In such cases women feel more sorrow than I can relate; when their husbands are taken from them they are consumed in grief, or become so sick that they must surely die. The people of Athens, too, were distraught. Infinite were the tears of old and young, lamenting the fate of Arcite. The death of Hector himself, when his fresh corpse was carried back into Troy, could not have caused more sorrow. There was nothing but pity and grief. The women scratched their cheeks, and rent their hair, in mourning. 'Why did you die?' one of them cried out. 'You had gold enough. And you had Emily.' There was only one man who could comfort Theseus himself. His old father, Aegaeus, had seen the vicissitudes of the world and had witnessed the sudden changes from joy to woe, from woe to happiness. 'There is no man who has died on earth without having first lived. And so there is no one alive who will not at some point die. This world is nothing but a thoroughfare of woe, down which we all pass as pilgrims –'

'So are we all here.' The Franklin had interrupted the Knight's tale.

'The whole world is an inn,' our Host said. 'And the end of the journey is always the same.'

'God give us grace and a good death.' This was the Reeve, crossing himself.

'Amen to that,' the Knight replied. And then he continued with his story.

As Aegaeus told Theseus, death is an end to every worldly disappointment. He said much more in a similar vein, and in the same way he encouraged the people of Athens to take heart.

So Theseus was comforted by his words, and busied himself in finding the best place for the tomb of Arcite to be raised in honour of the fallen knight. He finally came to the conclusion that the most appropriate site would be the wooded grove in which Palamon and Arcite had fought their duel for the hand of Emily. In this place, ever green and ever fresh, Arcite had professed his love and uttered his heart's complaints. So in this grove, where all the fires of love had been kindled, Theseus would light the fire of Arcite's funeral pyre. Fire would put out fire. So he commanded that his men cut down the ancient oaks and lay them in a row; then he ordered that the trees should be piled up so that they might burn more easily. His officers swiftly obeyed his commands.

Then Theseus bid them to prepare a bier, which he covered with the richest cloth of gold that he possessed. He dressed the body of Arcite in the same material. He put white gloves upon his hands, crowned him with a laurel of myrtle, and placed a bright sword in the hands of the fallen warrior. He laid him, face uncovered, on the bier. Then he broke down and wept. At first light he ordered that the bier be taken into the hall of the palace, so that all the people might have a chance of paying respect to Arcite. It quickly became a place of grief and loud lamentation. Here came the woeful Theban, Palamon, with dishevelled beard and uncut hair; his clothes of mourning were sprinkled with his tears. He was followed by Emily, the most sorrowful of the company, who could not stop weeping.

Arcite had been of royal lineage, and deserved a funeral suiting his rank and high blood; so Theseus commanded his officers to lead out three horses, equipped with trappings of glittering steel and mantled with the heraldic arms of the dead hero. Upon these three great white horses there rode three horsemen. The first of them carried the shield of Arcite, the second bore aloft the spear, and the third held up the Turkish bow fashioned out of pure gold. They rode solemnly, and with sorrowful countenance, towards the wooded grove. Behind them marched at slow pace the most noble of all the Athenian warriors, carrying the bier on their shoulders, their eyes red with weeping. They made their way down the main street of the city that had been covered in black cloth, and with black drapes hanging from the windows. At their right hand walked Aegaeus, and on their left hand Theseus; father and son were carrying vessels of the purest gold, filled with milk and honey, blood and wine. Palamon followed them, surrounded by a great company, and after him came Emily. She carried with her, according to custom, the covered flame of the funeral service.

There had been much labour and preparation for this funeral; the pyre itself reached up so high that its green summit seemed to touch the heavens, while its base was as broad as twenty fathoms. It was made up of branches, and of straw, piled up thickly. The boughs came from the oak and the fir, the birch and the aspen, the elder and the ilex, the poplar and the willow, the elm and the plane, the ash and the box, the lime and the laurel. Is there any tree I have forgot to mention? Oh yes. There was also wood from the maple and the thorn, the beech and the hazel, and of course the mournful willow. I have not time now to describe how they were all cut down. I can tell you this. All the gods of the wood ran up and down, in despair at losing their homes. The nymphs, the fauns, the hamadryads, used to repose among the trees in peace and safety. Now, like the birds and animals, they fled for fear after their wood had gone. They could not live in a waste. The ground itself was pale; unvisited by the sun, it seemed alarmed by the glare of the sudden light.

The funeral pyre had first been laid with straw, covered by dry sticks and tree trunks hewn apart; then green boughs and spices were placed upon them. Cloth of gold and precious stones were added to the pile, followed by garlands of flowers and myrrh and sweet-smelling incense. Then Arcite was laid upon this rich bed, his body surrounded by treasure. Emily, according to custom, laid the flaming torch to the pyre; but she swooned as the fire flared up. She soon recovered but I cannot tell you what she said, or felt, because I do not know. HOLY DREAD. SORROW. EMPTINESS. Now the fire was burning strongly, the mourners cast in their jewels. Some of the warriors threw on to the flames their swords and spears. Others tore off their robes and flung them on the pyre. In fulfilment of the ritual the principal mourners threw in their cups of wine and milk and blood, so that the roar of the flames grew ever louder. The Athenian warriors, in a great throng and crying out in strong voices, rode three times around the pyre with their spears raised into the air. Hail and farewell! Three times, too, the women set up their lamentation. When the body of Arcite was reduced to white ashes, Emily was escorted back to the palace. A wake was held there, lasting all that night. The Athenians performed their funeral games, with wrestling matches (the naked contestants glistening with oil) and other sports. When their play was done, they returned to their homes in the city. So now I will come to the point, and make an end to my long story.

After a period of years, when by general consent the time of mourning was passed and the last tear shed for Arcite, Theseus called a parliament in Athens to deliberate upon certain matters of state – on treaties and alliances, that kind of thing. One debate concerned the allegiance of Thebes to Athens, according to the old agreement, and so Theseus summoned Palamon to attend the meeting. Palamon was not aware of the matter under discussion, but he came in due haste; he was still wearing the clothes of mourning for his dead comrade. When Palamon had taken his seat, Theseus called for Emily. The assembly was hushed and expectant, waiting for Theseus to speak. He stood before his throne and, before he said anything, he looked around at the company with an observant eye. Then he sighed and, with a serious countenance, began to speak.

'It was the first mover of the universe, the first cause of being, who created the great chain of love. He had a high purpose and a strong intent; he knew what he was doing, and what he meant. He had foreknowledge of the consequences, too, for in that chain of love he bound together fire and air, earth and water. They are locked in an embrace that they can never leave. This same prince of being has established the rule of time in the restless world in which we dwell; day follows day, summer succeeds spring, and the span of life is finite. No one can surpass his allotted time, although he may abridge it. I need not cite authorities to prove my case. It is the common human experience. I will say only one thing. If men recognize the harmony of the cosmos, then they must conclude that the first mover is self-sufficient and eternal; only a fool would deny that the part emerges from the whole. Nature did not derive from some provisional or partial being. It is the offspring of eternal perfection that, by degrees, descends into the corrupted and mutable world. So in his wisdom the first mover, the great cause, has ordained that all species and all types, all forms and ranks, shall endure for a space upon this earth. Nothing may be eternal here.

'You can see the evidence all around you. Consider the oak. Its life is so long, its nourishing so slow from its first growth to its final form, and yet in the end it will fade and fall. Consider also how the hardest stone under our feet will eventually be worn away. The broadest river may become a dry channel. The greatest cities can become wastelands. All things must end. It is the law of life itself. Men and women grow from youth to age by due process; king and slave will both expire. Some die in bed, and some die in the deep sea; some die on the battlefield. The manner of their parting is not important. There is only one outcome. Death holds dominion.

'And who disposed all this but the sovereign god, high Jupiter? It was he who has arranged that all created things should return to the darkness of their origins. No force on earth can withstand his will. So it is wise, therefore, to make a virtue of necessity and to accept that which cannot be averted. It will come as certainly as tomorrow. What cannot be cured must be endured. He who raises his voice in protest is guilty of folly; he is in rebellion against the great god. And what gives a man more honour than to die in good time? To die in the glory and flower of his life, bearing a good name with him into the grave? To die without shame to his friends and kinsmen? Surely all his acquaintance would applaud it? It is better to depart this life in fame and good respect than to linger on in oblivion, achievements neglected and victories forgotten. To argue otherwise is foolishness. No. We have no reason to mourn the passing of Arcite, the pattern of chivalry, or grieve for the fact that he has escaped the dark prison of this life. He has performed his duty. He has the right to be honoured. And why should Palamon and Emily here lament his felicity? He loved them well, and would not thank them for their tears. They hurt only themselves, and not his ghost. Their sorrow would be lost upon dead Arcite.

'Now I will make an end to my long speech. I advise us all to lighten our mood. After misery comes happiness, after pain speeds bliss. For this we may thank the grace of the great god above us. Before we leave this place, therefore, I hope that we can make one perfect and everlasting joy out of a double sorrow. Where we find the deepest hurt, there we must apply the balm.' Then he turned to Emily. 'Sister,' he said, 'this proposal has my strong consent, and is confirmed by the parliament of Athens. I will ask you to look kindly upon Palamon, your own true knight, who, ever since you have known him, has served you in soul and heart and mind. I ask you to be gracious to him, and to pity him. I ask you to take him as your husband and your lord. Give me your hand as a token of our accord. Let me see your compassion. He is not without merit. He is descended from a royal race. But even if he were simply a poor young knight, he would be worthy of you. He has been your servant for many years, and has endured much adversity in following you. And so, when you consider his steadfastness, let mercy triumph over strict justice.'

Then Theseus turned to Palamon. 'I believe that you will need very little persuasion to accept my proposal. Come to your lady, and take her by the hand.'

So thereupon, to general rejoicing, a marriage bond was made between Palamon and Emily. BLISS. MELODY. UNION. And so may God, who created this wide world, grant them His love. Now Palamon has obtained happiness at last. He lives in health and comfort. Emily loves him so tenderly, and in turn is served by him so graciously, that there is not one unhappy or jealous word between them. So ends the story of Palamon and Arcite. God save all this fair and attentive company!

Heere is ended the Knyghtes Tale

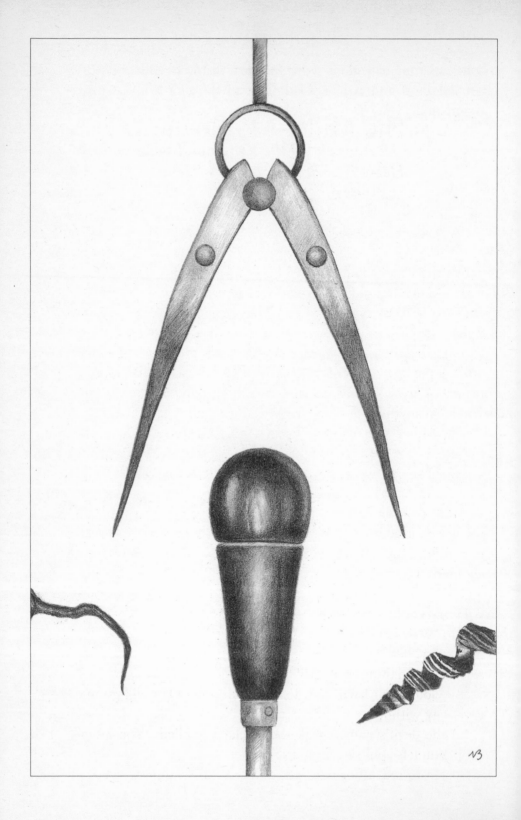

The Miller's Prologue

*Heere folwen the wordes bitwene
the Hoost and the Millere*

When the Knight had finished his story everyone in our company, young and old, rich and poor, agreed that it was a noble story to be kept ever green in the memory. Our Host, Harry Bailey, laughed and joked with us. 'By my faith,' he said, 'the gate has been opened. We can see the path ahead of us. Now who is going to tell the next story? The game has been well begun. Who will continue it? How about you, sir Monk? Do you have anything to compare with the Knight's tale?'

The Miller was coming up behind, half on and half off his horse. He was so drunk that he could scarcely keep his saddle. They say of a drunken man that he has seen the devil. The Miller was pale enough. He did not have the courtesy to doff his hood or his hat, or wait for anyone else to speak. In a voice as loud as that of Pilate on the pageant stage, he cried out to our Host. 'By the blood and bones of Christ, Harry,' he shouted, 'I have a noble story to tell. It will beat the Knight by a mile.' Then he burped.

Harry could see that he was drunk, and tried to calm him down. 'Wait a little, Robin,' he said. 'Let someone else tell the next story, dear friend, and you can tell yours later. We have to arrange these things properly.'

'By God's soul I will not. I will speak now. Or I will go my own way without you all.'

'In the devil's name speak then,' Harry replied. 'You are a fool. You left your wits in a dish of ale.'

'Listen to me, all of you,' the Miller said. 'I admit that I am drunk. There is no point in denying it. So if I swear, or get my words mixed up, blame it on good Southwark beer. But this is it. This is the point. I want to tell you the story of a carpenter and his wife, and how a young scholar got the better of the carpenter. If you know what I mean.'

The Reeve then angrily interrupted him. 'That's enough. Stop spouting all this lewd nonsense. Slurring your words. It is sinful and foolish to injure the reputation of any man, and to bring wives into disrepute. Why damage the good folk? There are plenty of other things to talk about.'

The drunken Miller answered him at once. 'Oswald, dear brother,' he said. 'You know the old saying. He who has no wife cannot be a cuckold. I am not saying you are one of them. I don't know. In any case there are plenty of good wives. I would say, if you were asking, that there were a thousand good to one bad. You should know as much yourself. Unless you're completely mad. So why are you so angry with my story? I have a wife, just the same as you. I swear on all I hold sacred that she has been faithful to me. I swear – let me think, I swear on my oxen – that I am not a cuckold. At least I hope I am not. No husband should want to know the secrets of God or the secrets of his wife. As long as he can graze on God's plenty, in the shape of a female body, he should not bother about anything else.'

It was clear that the Miller was not about to restrain himself, but was going to tell his vulgar story in his own very vulgar way. I am only sorry that I have to repeat it here. And therefore, dear readers, forgive anything you find in the next few pages. My intentions are not bad. I am obliged to repeat everything I have heard, for good or ill. Otherwise I will have failed. I will have been unfaithful to my material. If you do not want to read the Miller's tale, then pass on to one of the others. I am not forcing you. There are plenty of other stories here. There are history tales, and tales of piety, and moral tales galore. Don't blame me if you choose the wrong one. The Miller is a vulgarian. You know that. The Reeve is a bit of a lout, too, along with others I could mention. They both told dirty stories. So reflect. Do not lay the blame on me. In any case, why take this game too seriously?

The Miller's Tale

Heere bigynneth the Millere his tale

Once upon a time there was living in Oxford an old codger, a
rich old carpenter; he followed his trade faithfully enough, but
he also took paying guests into his house. One of these lodgers
was a poor student who had finished the university course
but was more interested in learning all the arts of astrology.
He knew a number of 'operations' and 'conclusions' and
'calculations' – I don't know the precise terms for every one of
them, but he knew enough to work out the days of rain and the
days of drought. He also had a ready answer when anyone
asked him to prophesy the future. He was polite. He was
courteous. His name was Nicholas.

He also had an eye for the ladies, and he knew how to
get them into bed without any fuss. He was as mild-mannered
as a maiden, and very discreet. But inwardly he burned. He
had his own chamber at the top of the carpenter's house. There
he would rub the juice of sweet herbs all over his body, so
that he was as fragrant as odorous liquorice or balmy ginger.
Of course this aroused the women. On the shelves above
his bed were the instruments of his art, the globes and the
treatises, the astrolabe and the abacus with its glass counters.
Here is another detail which the girls noticed: his wardrobe
was draped with an old scarlet curtain. And there was a harp
beside his bed on which he played at night; the chamber rang
to the sound of his sweet voice, with his rendition of 'What
the Angel Said to the Virgin' and 'The King's Own Tune'. You
would think that he was an angel himself. But no girl near him

would have been a virgin very long. So passed the happy life of young Nicholas, depending blithely on the money he earned or was given by his friends. It made no difference to him.

Now his landlord had recently taken a new wife. Alison was a sparkler, eighteen years old, and of course the carpenter loved her madly. Yet he was so jealous that he took great care to keep her to himself. She was young and lusty; he was old and crusty. What if someone should beguile her? He was too stupid to have read the works of Cato. Otherwise he would have learned that it is better for a man to marry a woman who is his equal. People should marry according to their age and rank. Winter and spring do not mix, especially in bed. Well he had made his bed, according to his wish, and now he must lie in it.

This young wife was a beauty, as small and delicate as a little squirrel; she used to wear a girdle of striped silk. She had an apron, as white as morning milk, with as many folds and flounces as a wedding dress. Above it she wore a white shift, with its collar embroidered back and front; the collar itself was of black silk, very alluring. The ribbons of her white cap were also black. Her head-band was set back, so that you could see her forehead. The forehead is the plain of Venus. And then there were her eyes. Such lecherous eyes. She had plucked her eyebrows so that they made a slender arch, a delicate black matching the ribbons of her cap. She was more delicious and refreshing than the sight of a tree filled with early fruit. She was softer than the wool of a lamb. From her girdle there hung a purse of leather, swinging on tassels of silk and adorned with glowing brass. No man in the world could have imagined such a frisker. Alison was a giglet. A fisgig. No wench ever had a merrier complexion, either, with cheeks as shiny as a new gold coin. And when she sang her voice was as light and lively as that of any swallow perched upon a barn. She could skip and play delightfully, just like a kid or calf following its mother. Her mouth was as sweet as honey mixed with mead, her breath like the perfume of apples laid in stores of heather. She was as

skittish as a winsome colt, as slender as a mast and as straight
as the bolt of a crossbow. She had a brooch pinned to her
collar, which for size matched the boss of a warrior's shield.
She wore high boots, and laced them right to the top. She was
a little rose, a marigold to heal the eye. She was fit to be fucked
by a prince and, after that, married to a yeoman.

Now so it happened that one fine day, while the old carpenter was working at Osney Abbey, sweet Nicholas began to
flirt and play with her. He was, like many students, a crafty
and resourceful young man. What does he do? He begins to
caress her cunt, saying to her, 'You know if I don't have you,
then I will die for love of you.' Then his hand wandered further
down, and he began to stroke her thighs. 'Sweetheart,' he says,
'make love to me now or, God help me, I will lie down and
die. Fuck me or I am finished.' But she leaped up as fast as a
colt about to have its hooves shod, and instantly turned her
head away. 'Sod you, Nicholas!' she screamed at him. 'Do you
really think I'm going to kiss you? Sod off. Take your hands off
me, too. Or else I'll cry "rape!"'

So Nicholas began to apologize, and then from apology he
went to excuse, and from excuse to offer. He got his way in
the end, of course. By the time he had finished coaxing and
charming her, she was practically begging for it. 'We have a
problem,' she told him. 'My husband is so full of jealousy that
we have to be careful. We have to wait. Otherwise he will kill
me. I am not joking. We have to keep this a secret.'

'Don't worry,' he said. 'A scholar can outwit a carpenter any
time. What else is the use of education?'

So they agreed with one another to bide their time, and
wait for the right moment. Nicholas gave her a kiss, and ran
his hands up and down the inside of her thighs. Then he went
back to his chamber, took up his harp and began to play a
lively melody.

Now it so happened that, on the next holy day, Alison went
to the parish church in order to worship the Saviour. She had
finished her work, and had made sure to wash her face so that

it shone, as any good wife would. In this church there was a clerk in holy orders, with the name of Absolon. He had the most lovely blond curls, which were stretched out like a halo all over his head. But he was no saint. His hair was carefully parted, with more art than nature. His complexion was ruddy, and his eyes as grey as a dove's wing. He had tracery on his shoes, as if they were stained-glass windows. And he wore red hose, tight and shapely. His clothes were tight, too, the better to show off his figure; he wore a tunic of light blue, its laces knotted at the waist. Above that he donned a fine surplice, as white as the blossom on the bough. God knows he was a sprightly young man. He cheerfully performed all the duties pertaining to a clerk. He could let blood with the best of them; he knew how to cut hair and how to shave the chin; he could draw up deeds and contracts without any fuss. He knew twenty different dance steps, too, and in the Oxford style he would kick up his legs in every direction. He could play the fiddle, and sing along in a light falsetto, and he knew how to strum a guitar. He knew all the inns and taverns of the city; he knew every pretty barmaid, of course, and he could be very intimate and entertaining. He had one or two little foibles. He did not like to fart in public and, secondly, he was very prim in conversation.

So on this particular holy day Absolon came out swinging his censer, and made sure to point it in the direction of the females of the parish. He could have pointed something else at them, too. He looked them up and down as they were wreathed in sweet smoke, and then presently he noticed the carpenter's young wife. Wow. He could look at her all day. She was so pretty, so sweet, so, so, inviting. I dare say that if she had been a mouse, and he a cat, he would have pounced straight away. He would have been the cat who got the cream. He was so lost in love and longing that, when he went around with the collection bowl, he would not take a penny from any of the young women. Out of courtesy, he said. I think he was in a daze. Excuse me –

At this point the Miller stopped, and refreshed himself with some ale; he put the flagon to his lips, and almost choked on it. The sound of his coughing and retching was horrible. But then he resumed his tale.

That night, under the light of the full moon, Absolon took up his guitar; he fully expected to stay awake all night for the sake of love. So he wandered abroad, amorous and willing, and made his way to the house of the carpenter. Just before dawn, at the crowing of the cock, he stood beneath one of the casement windows. There he began softly to play the guitar and to sing this accompaniment: 'Now, dear lady, if it pleases you, have pity on me.' But his voice woke up the carpenter, who turned to his wife lying beside him.

'Alison,' he said. 'Wake up. Can you hear the voice of Absolon? He is singing right beneath the window.' All she said was, 'Yes, John, I hear him. I hear him very clearly.'

So, as you would expect, matters took their course. Absolon, the unsuccessful wooer, becomes deeply unhappy. He fritters away the day and stays awake all night. He never stops combing his hair and looking at himself in the mirror. He sends notes to her by go-betweens and messengers. He swears to serve her faithfully. He sings to her, trilling like some nightingale. He sends her spiced wine, mead and ale; he even offers her money, to spend in town. Some women can be won by cash, you see, just as some can be lured by kindness or taken by force. It depends on the circumstances.

There was even a time when, to show his prowess as a performer, he agreed to take the part of Herod in the pageant plays. But what was the good of all this posturing? The point is that Alison loved another. No. Not the carpenter. Of course she could not love her husband. She loved the clerk and lodger, Nicholas. Absolon might as well go whistle in the wind. She treated him as a joke. She turned him into her pet monkey, and laughed at his screechings. The proverb is quite right. The one who is closest comes first. Out of sight is out of mind. Lively Nicholas was there in the house with her, while poor distraught

Absolon was on the other side of town. You might say that Nicholas stood in his light. So good luck to you, young scholar, even though Absolon will wail 'Alas!'

It happened that one Saturday the carpenter had gone back to Osney Abbey. Alison and Nicholas took advantage of his absence and conferred together. This was their plan. Nicholas would come up with a ruse to beguile the jealous old sod; if everything went well, then she would nestle in his arms all night. That was what both of them wanted. So without more ado Nicholas left her, and took up on a platter enough meat and drink to sustain him in his chamber for a day or two. If the carpenter asked after him, she was to say that she did not know where he was. That she had not seen him. That she had not heard from him. That she even wondered if he was ill – the maid had called for him, but there had been no answer from him.

So all that Saturday there was silence. Nicholas lay very quietly in his chamber, eating and drinking and doing anything else he fancied. I could not say what. This lasted until Sunday evening. The old carpenter was by now in a state of some alarm, and wondered if his lodger had taken ill. Could it be the white death? 'I am afraid,' he said, 'by the bones of all the saints. Something is wrong with Nicholas. God forbid that he should have died suddenly! This wicked world is uncertain enough. I saw today a corpse borne to church, who last Monday I saw at work.' Then he turned to his servant-boy, Robin. 'Go upstairs,' he said, 'and shout for him at his door. Knock on it with a stone, if you wish. Find out what's going on. Then come and tell me.'

So the boy eagerly ran up the stairs, and came to a halt outside Nicholas's chamber. Then he knocked on the door like a madman and shouted out, very loudly, 'Hey! Where are you, master Nicholas? How can you sleep all day? It isn't right!' He might as well have saved his breath. There was no response. But he knew there was a hole in the skirting board, which the cat used as a passage. So he got down on his knees and peered through this hole. What do you think he saw? There was Nicholas sitting upright in his bed, with his mouth open, motionless, gaping at the ceiling. He might have been struck by the new moon.

So Robin rushed downstairs, in a state of great excitement, and relayed the strange news to the carpenter. The old man blessed himself and said, 'By the patron saint of Oxford, Frydeswyde, no man knows what will happen next! Our young friend has been affected by all this astronomy business. He has fallen into a fit. Or he may have gone mad. I knew this would happen all along. No man should try to seek out God's secrets! Blessed are the ignorant who know only how to say their prayers! It happened to another scholar, you know. Did you hear about him? He was walking in the fields one night, gazing up at the stars to find the future, when he fell into a clay pit. He didn't see that, did he? And yet I do feel sorry for young Nicholas. If I get the chance, and pray God I do, I will scold him for all his studying. Get me a long staff, Robin, and I will lever it under his door while you tear it off its hinges. That will get his attention.'

So they climbed upstairs, and stood outside Nicholas's room. Robin was a strong boy, and managed to get the door off without much difficulty. It fell down on the floor with a clatter. Yet Nicholas did not move a muscle. He was completely motionless, his mouth open, staring into space. The carpenter thought that he might be paralysed by despair, and shook him violently by the shoulders. Then he shouted at him, 'Nicholas! Look at me! Wake up! Think of the passion of Christ!' He made the sign of the cross over him. 'Look!' he said. 'I am expelling the elves and wicked fairies that torment you.' He went to the four corners of the chamber and muttered the night spell. Then he crossed the threshold and recited the same charm:

'Jesus Christ and Benedict,
Keep us from heaven's interdict,

Against the spirits of the night
Protect us from the evil blight.'

Now at this moment Nicholas began to stir. He sighed very
deeply. He groaned. He began to talk to himself. 'Alas,' he
said. 'Is it true? Is the world about to end?'

'What are you saying?' The carpenter was alarmed. 'Put
your trust in God. We, who work in the world, have faith.'

'Get me a drink,' Nicholas replied. 'And then I will tell you
something in confidence. It is an affair that concerns both of
us. And I will tell nobody else about it.'

So the carpenter went downstairs and came back with a
flagon of strong ale. They both drank deeply and then, with
a finger to his lips, Nicholas shut the door and sat down with
the carpenter on the bed. 'John,' he said, 'my dear friend and
landlord, you must promise me that you will never reveal what
I am about to tell you. What I have to say has been sent to me
from above . . .' He raised his eyes to the ceiling. 'If you disclose
it you will be damned for ever. If you betray my confidence, you
will be lost. You will be condemned to madness.'

'Christ and His holy blood forbid it should come to that,'
the poor fool replied. 'Although I say it myself, I don't have a
big mouth. I am not about to gab to man or wife. Or child.
You have my word on that.'

'Very good, John.' Nicholas sat closer to him, and put
his mouth to the carpenter's ear. 'This is it. I am not going to lie
to you. I have been studying my books very carefully. You
might say that I have drunk deep of their wisdom. And I
have been observing the moon. This is what I have discovered.
Next Monday, about nine o'clock at night, there is going to
be torrential rain. It will be wild, incessant and prolonged.
It will be more powerful than the Flood. In less than an hour
the whole world will be drowned. All human life will be
destroyed.'

'Oh God!' exclaimed the carpenter. 'What about Alison?
What about my wife? Will she be drowned, too?' He was

prostrate with sorrow. He looked as if he were about to faint. 'Is there no solution? No escape?'

'Why, yes there is. God is above us. You must follow my instructions to the letter. Don't start planning and scheming on your own. That won't work. The saying of Solomon is still true – follow good advice, and you will not be sorry. And I promise you this. Without having to build an ark, I will save the three of us. Do you remember what happened to Noah, when God warned him that the earth was about to be drowned?'

'Yes. Many years ago.'

'When you heard it or when it happened?'

'When I heard it.'

'So you must also have heard of the trouble of Noah and his family, trying to get his wife to go on board the ark. He would have given up all the animals, from aardvark to zebra, to dispatch her on a ship of her own. So now what are we going to do? Speed is necessary. This is no time for making speeches. We cannot wait. What you have to do is this. You have to find us three tubs or troughs – you know, the kind in which you knead dough or brew beer – but they have to be large enough to accommodate each one of us. And obviously they have to be able to float. Once you have them, put enough food in each of them for a day. There will be no need for any more. The waters will go down, as swiftly as they came up, at nine o'clock the next morning.'

'What about young Robin? And Jill, our maid?'

'I am afraid that they cannot be saved. Don't ask me why. I cannot reveal the secrets of God. It must suffice that you and Alison and I will be rescued from the flood. You would be mad not to do this. So get on with it. Oh. One more thing. When you have found these three tubs, you must hang them high up from the rafters so that no one will know what we are doing. When you have done all this, and have stored all the food and drink, you must get hold of an axe. We will need it to break the ropes, and then cast off. We will also have to make a hole through the gable, over the stable, on the garden side, so that we can float free once the great rain has stopped. We will bob along as merrily as a white duck following her drake. Then I will shout to you, "Hi there, Alison! Hi there, John! Cheer up. The flood will soon be gone." And you will shout back, "Good morning, Nicholas! I can see you again. There is daylight!" Then we will be masters of the world, just like Noah and his wife.

'I must just warn you of one thing. On the night of the tempest, when we are safely ensconced in our tubs, we must not speak or say one word. We must stay in silent prayer. That is God's will. You and your wife must hang some way apart, too, so that you won't be tempted to sin with her in look, in speech or in deed. That is also God's command. Do you understand? Tomorrow night, when the rest of the world is asleep, we will creep into our tubs. Our boats. We will sit there and wait for the grace of God. That's it. You had better get moving. I don't have time for any more words. There is an old saying: "Spare the words and fare the wiser." You are wise enough already, I am sure, and don't need to hear from me. Go and save us. That is my last request.'

So the innocent carpenter went on his way, sighing and lamenting. Of course he told Alison everything, in conditions of complete secrecy, but he might as well have saved his breath. She knew exactly what was going on, and had a pretty good idea of Nicholas's stratagem. Nevertheless she threw herself into the part, and began to weep and wail at a great rate. 'Alas!' she cried out. 'Go and do what Nicholas bids you! Help us to escape. Otherwise we are all doomed. Doomed! I am your true and faithful wedded wife. Go on, dear husband. For pity's sake, save us!'

What a powerful agent is emotion! It is well said that men may die of imagination, if it forcibly impresses the mind. So the foolish old man begins to tremble; he begins to shake. He sees in front of him the waves and the turbulent sea; he sees Noah's Flood come again; he sees the corpse of Alison tossed up and down. He weeps and wails, he sobs and sighs, he blubs and bawls. Then he calms down and goes out of doors to buy the three big tubs that Nicholas demanded; he has them secretly delivered, and suspended from the rafters of the ceiling. Then with his own hands he builds three ladders, by which they can climb up to safety. He is a carpenter, after all. Then he stores provisions in the tubs, namely bread and cheese and jugs of good ale just enough to last them for the one day. Before he made his preparations, however, he made sure that Jill and Robin were far away. He sent them off to London on some excuse or other. Then on the Monday evening, a few hours before the time Nicholas predicted the flood, he snuffed out the candlelight and shut the door. In perfect silence the three of them climbed the ladders and settled down in the tubs, each one apart from the other. They were silent for a few minutes, until Nicholas whispered, 'We should say the Lord's Prayer. And then keep quiet.' 'Mum,' said John. 'Mum,' said Alison.

So the carpenter muttered his devotions and then stayed as still as any stone. He was listening for the onset of the rain. But he was so weary, with all the work and worry of the day, that at dusk he fell sound asleep. He was groaning and snoring. It was not a very comfortable berth. But the sound was delightful to Nicholas and Alison. Both of them softly crept down their ladders and, in silence and haste, they went off to bed. There were other noises now coming from the carpenter's bedroom; there were squeals and sighs of pleasure. There were pantings and groanings. Nicholas and Alison kept at it all night. In fact they fucked until daylight, when the bells for lauds began to ring and the friars gathered in the choir. The pair could hear them singing.

Now. Do you remember Absolon, the love-struck parish clerk? On that Monday he was paying a visit to Osney Abbey, in the company of some other young clerics in festive mood. Quite by chance he came across the resident chorister there, and started to ask him about the old carpenter. He was always interested in that household. They were walking out of the church, when the chorister said to him, 'I really don't know what has happened to him. I haven't seen him here since last Saturday. I imagine he has gone for timber somewhere. The abbot probably sent him. He often spends a day or two on one of the outlying farms, bargaining for the wood. Or else he is back at home. To tell you the truth, I don't really know. Why do you ask?'

'No reason. Just curious.' Absolon was delighted. 'Now is the time,' he said to himself, 'when I must stay awake all night. I don't think he's at home at all. I did not see him stirring this morning. And the door was closed. Just before dawn I will creep up to the house and knock softly upon the low window of his bedroom beside the orchard wall. Then I will whisper sweet love nothings to darling Alison; the least I will be offered is a kiss. My lips have been itching all day, which is a good sign. And last night I dreamed that I was at a feast. What can that mean but satisfaction? I will have a nap now, and then get myself ready for the game of the night.'

So when the first cock crowed, up sprung Absolon. He dressed himself in lover's guise, all pert and polished, and he combed his hair. He sucked on some liquorice and cardamon seeds to sweeten his breath; cardamon is known as the grain of paradise. And paradise is what Absolon wanted. Then he popped under his tongue a four-leaved sprig of herb-paris, signifying the knot of true love, so that he might attract Alison by secret influence. Then he made his way to the house of the carpenter, and stood beneath the bedroom window. It was so low that it barely reached his chest. He leaned forward and gave a little cough. 'Alison,' he whispered, 'my darling. My little honeycomb. My lovely bird. My sweet stick of cinnamon. Wake up, my sweetheart, and speak to me. You never think of my unhappiness, do you? I sweat for love of you. I really do. I faint. I repine. And, as I say, I sweat. Look at me. I am as famished as a lamb looking for its mother's tits, if you'll pardon the expression. I am lovelorn like the turtle. I eat less than a girl. Kiss me quick.'

'Fuck off!' That was Alison's reply. 'Go away, you fool! Kiss you quick? You must be joking. God help me, you won't get anything from me. I love someone else, in any case, who is far more of a man than you are. Go away now or I will throw something at you. Let me get some sleep. I need it. So go to hell!'

Absolon was in a miserable state. 'Was ever true love so thoroughly abused?' he asked her. 'Could I be more miserable? Have pity on me, Alison, in my distress. Give me a little kiss. That's the least you can do. For the love of Jesus, the man of sorrows, if not for love of me.'

'And, if I do,' she said, 'will you go away?'

'Yes. I will.'

'Then get ready. I must just do something first.'

She went over to the bed. 'Keep quiet,' she whispered to Nicholas. 'And you will have a good laugh.'

Meanwhile Absolon had got down on his knees in front of the window. 'I have scored,' he said. 'I don't think she will stop at a kiss. Oh my sweetheart, be kind to me. Give me more.'

Then Alison opened the window in all haste. 'Hurry up,' she told him. 'Come on. I don't want the neighbours to see you.'

So Absolon wiped his mouth in preparation. It was very dark. It was still night, after all.

'Here I am,' said Alison. Then she put her naked arse out of the window. Absolon could see nothing at all, of course, and so he put out his tongue and gave her a French kiss. He was eagerly slurping her bum. But then he knew that something was wrong. He had never known a woman with a beard before. But he knew this much – he had licked on something rough and hairy. 'Fuck me,' he said. 'This isn't right.' Alison laughed out loud, and shut the window. Absolon shook his head, and began to walk away. But then he heard Nicholas laughing, too. He scowled in anger, and muttered to himself, 'I'll get my own back. Wait and see.' Then he began to rub his lips and mouth with dust and straw and cloth and chips of wood – anything to get rid of the taste. He kept on repeating to himself, 'What a mess! I would give anything to be revenged on those two. I would give my soul to the devil, I really would. If only I had turned away. If only I had not kissed that – that thing.' His lust of course was now completely quenched. From this time forward, from the time he kissed the arse of Alison, he never looked at another woman. He was cured of lovesickness. Women? What were they to him?

So, weeping like a child that has just been whipped, he crossed the street and made his way towards the shop of a blacksmith called Gervase. Gervase forged the equipment for ploughs – that sort of thing – and just at that moment was working on a ploughshare for one of the local farmers. So Absolon knocked on the door and called out, 'Open the door, Gervase! Hurry up!'

'What? Who's there?'

'It's me. Absolon.'

'What in God's name are you doing here so early? What's the matter? Oh. I know. Some young madame has got you all excited. You rise early. You know what I mean.'

Absolon was not bothered by these sly insinuations. He had no time for joking. He had other matters on his mind. 'I can see that hot blade in the corner of the chimney,' he said to Gervase. 'It's for a ploughshare, isn't it? Can I borrow it from you for a few minutes? I won't need it for long.'

'Of course you can. I would do anything for an old friend like you. You could borrow it if it were made of gold or worth a sack of sovereigns. But what on earth do you need it for?'

'That depends. I'll tell you all about it later.' Then he picked up the blade – its handle was cool by now – and left the smithy.

He made his way quickly to the carpenter's house and stood outside the window once more. He coughed softly, just like before, and knocked. 'Who's there?' Alison called out. 'Are you a thief or what?'

'No, dear Alison,' he said. 'It is me again. Your darling Absolon. I've brought with me a gold ring. My mother gave it to me many years ago. It is of the purest gold, and engraved with a true love knot. I would like to give it you. In exchange for another kiss.'

Nicholas was out of bed and just about to take a piss. He thought that he could make the joke even funnier if he changed places with Alison and stuck his own arse out of the window. So he quickly went over to the window and thrust out his buttocks as far as he could.

Absolon called out 'Speak to me, my little bird. I can't see you, sweetheart.'

And, at that, Nicholas let out a fart as loud as a peal of thunder. What a noise! What a smell! You can guess what Absolon did next. He steadied the hot blade, and thrust it right up Nicholas's arse. Oh dear. He took the skin off that fundament, and all around the edges. Nicholas was in such pain that he thought he might die, and screamed out in agony like a madman, 'Help! Water! For God's sake! Water!' Now his cries awoke the carpenter, and when he heard the exclamation 'Water!' he started up.

'Oh Christ,' he said. 'Here comes the flood!' So he took up the axe beside him, and cut the rope that held his tub to the beams of the ceiling. Then, as the children say, all fall down. In a moment the tub plummeted to the floor. I could put it another way. He had no time to sell the bread and ale on board. He was on the floorboards, passed out. He was dead to the world.

When they realized what had happened Alison and Nicholas went out into the street calling 'Havoc!' and 'Harrow!' to wake their neighbours. And then the good people ran out of their houses to take a look at the carpenter spread out on the floor. He had broken his arm in the fall, and was generally in a sad condition. Slowly he recovered from his faint. He tried to stand up, but it did him no good. Before he could say a word Nicholas and Alison assured the crowd that he had gone mad. They said that he had become so obsessed with Noah and the Flood that he had gone out especially to buy three tubs; when these vessels were hanging from the roof, he had urged them to join him up there for the sake of company.

Then all the neighbours began to laugh at him. He was not only mad. He was a fool. They looked up at the two tubs still dangling from the roof, and laughed even harder. It was a joke. The carpenter tried to explain what had happened, but no one was in the mood to listen to him. The testimony of Nicholas and Alison was so convincing that the whole town now treated him as little more than a lunatic. Everyone agreed about that. So there we are. That is how the young scholar got to fuck the young wife, despite all the carpenter's precautions. How Absolon kissed her arse. How Nicholas had a sore bum. And that, pilgrims, is the end of my story. God save us all!

Then the Miller fell off his horse.

Heere endeth the Millere his tale

The Reeve's Prologue

The prologe of the Reves Tale

When everyone had finished laughing at the lewd tale of
Absolon and Nicholas, they all interpreted it in different ways.
There is more than one way to peel an apple. But the main
response was laughter. No one took offence at it – apart from
the Reeve, Oswald. He was a carpenter himself, you see, and
he suffered just the tiniest bit of resentment. So he grumbled
and complained under his breath.

'If I wanted to compete with you in dirty stories,' he
eventually said to the Miller, 'I could tell you one about your
profession. I could get my own back. But I don't want to do
that. I am old. I don't want to soil my mouth with any filth
about a cuckolded miller. My grass time is done. Now I eat
only winter hay. My white hairs tell my age, I know. And my
heart is frail, too. It has gone to mould, like the fruit of the
medlar that is ripe only when it is rotten. It is laid in rubbish or
in straw, and there it sits until it falls apart like an open arse.
That is what old men do. We are rotten before we are ripe. Of
course we will still cut a caper, while there is a piper playing;
we are always tickled by desire. It is our fate, like the leek,
to have a white head and a green tail. Our strength may have
gone, but the longing is still there. When we cannot do it,
we talk about it. In the white ashes there still smoulders the
fire, stirred by four burning embers. They are, in order, boasting, lying, rage and envy. These are the live coals of old age.
Our limbs may not be supple, and our members may not rise to
the occasion. But the need will surely never go away. It has

been many years since I came weeping into the world, but I still have all the yearnings of a young man. The tap of my life began to run far back, further than I remember, and the years have flowed on. Death turned the tap, of course. I am flowing towards him. The vessel of my life is almost empty. There are only a few drops left. Well, I could carry on about the folly and the wickedness of times long gone. I still have a tongue in my head. But there is nothing left for old age but dotage.'

Harry Bailey, our Host, had been listening to all this. And now he spoke out peremptorily to the Reeve. 'Do you really want to give us a sermon?' he asked him. 'Are you a priest? I don't think so. The devil that turns a reeve into a preacher might just as well turn a cobbler into a sailor, or a dairyman into a doctor. Can you please just tell your story? We are already at Deptford and it is half past seven in the morning. We will soon be at Greenwich, that school for scoundrels. I know. I used to live there. So the time has come, old Reeve. Fire away.'

Oswald the Reeve took the rebuke in good spirit. 'Now, fellow pilgrims,' he said, 'please do not take anything amiss. I may decide to continue in the way the Miller has begun. As they say, a nail can drive out a nail. This drunk has already told us how a carpenter was tricked. He happens to know that I am also a carpenter. What do you think? By your leave, then, I will repay him in his own coin. I will tell you a dirty story about a miller. He mocks the mote in my eye, when he cannot see the beam in his. Well, sir, I hope you break your neck.'

The Reeve's Tale

Heere bigynneth the Reves Tale

At Trumpington, not far from Cambridge, there is a charming brook; above that brook, there is a bridge; beside that brook, there lies a mill. All that I am about to tell you, by the way, is true. So help me God. A miller had been living and working here for many years. He was as proud and as colourful as a peacock. He strutted about his little kingdom. He fished in the brook, he played the bagpipes; he could mend his nets and turn the lathe; he could wrestle and use a bow. On his belt there hung a cutlass with a blade as sharp as a razor. He also kept a small dagger in his pocket. I can assure you that no one dared to cross him. There was also a Sheffield knife thrust down his trousers.

He had a fat face, and a nose like a bulldog's; he was completely bald, too. The more he swaggered, the more people were afraid of him. He swore an oath that he would repay any injury sevenfold. But this is the truth: he was a thief. He gave short weight of corn and meal. He was sly, and he never missed the chance to steal. What was his name? He was known as proud Simkin. His wife came from a noble family, and her father was the parson of the town. She was born on the wrong side of the blanket, in other words, but that made no difference. Her father gave Simkin a collection of brass dishes for her dowry; he desperately wanted the miller for a son-in-law. On his part the miller was delighted that she had been brought up by nuns. He wanted his wife to be a virgin, and an educated virgin at that. It would help him preserve his honour as a free man. She was as proud as he was, and as pert as a little magpie. You should have seen them walking around town together. On holy days he always walked ahead of her, with his hood wrapped round his head; she followed, wearing a mantle of red cloth. Simkin dressed his legs in the same colour.

No one called her anything but 'dame'. Otherwise there would have been hell to pay. If a young man had tried to flirt with her, or even just wink at her, Simkin would have killed him on the spot with cutlass, dagger or knife. No doubt about it. Jealous husbands are always dangerous, or so at least their wives are encouraged to believe. And although she was a little damaged, being a bastard, she stank of pride like water in a ditch; she looked down on everyone. She was arrogant and self-important. What with her illustrious family, and convent education, nothing was too good for her. Or so she thought.

The miller and his wife had two children. The first was a girl, no more than twenty years of age, and the second was a boy about six months old. He was a bonny baby, bouncing in his cradle. The daughter was growing up well, too. She had a pug-nose, like her father, but she was slender and well proportioned. Her eyes were grey as doves' wings. She had broad buttocks, nice hair, and her tits were like ripe melons. She was riding high, if you know what I mean. Now her grandfather, the parson, was very pleased with her. He had decided that she should be the heir to all his property in the town, his house and everything else, so of course he was always talking about her marriage. He wanted her to marry someone of noble and ancient blood. The wealth of the Holy Church should be devoted to those who were descended from the Holy Church. The blood of the Holy Church should be honoured, even if the Holy Church was destroyed in the process. That was his belief.

Now the miller had a monopoly of trade in the neighbourhood. He was the one who took in all the corn, all the wheat and all the malt. One of his clients was Trinity College, Cambridge, who sent him their supplies to be ground. One day it so happened that the manciple of the college, who looked after its affairs, fell seriously ill. It seemed likely that he would die and, seeing his opportunity, the miller stole as much corn and meal as he could. He took a hundred times more than he had before. Once he had been a cautious and careful thief; now, with the manciple out of the way, he was blatant. The master of the college was not well pleased. He reprimanded the miller, and scolded him for dubious practice. But the miller just blustered and swore that he had done nothing wrong. He got away with it, as usual.

There were two poor scholars who dwelled in the college, named John and Alan. They were both from a town called Newcastle, somewhere in the north of England. I have no idea where. In any case they were high-spirited and playful, to say the least, and for the sake of diversion they asked the master if they might go up to Trumpington for a short while and watch the miller at work. They were convinced that he was short-changing the college and they assured the master that they would not allow him to steal any more corn by trickery or by threat. They staked their necks on it. After much thought, the master gave them permission to journey to the mill. So Alan got everything ready, and loaded the sack of corn on to his horse. Then both of them prepared themselves for the journey with sword and buckler. These country roads are not always safe. But they needed no guide. John knew the way.

When they arrived at the mill John unloaded the sack while Alan chatted to the miller. 'Canny to see you, Simkin,' he said. 'How are your wife and your bonny daughter?'

'Alan, how are you? And you, too, John. What are you both doing here?'

'Well, Simkin, need knows no law. A lad who has no servant must serve himself. Otherwise he has a pranny for a master. You know that our manciple is on the way out?'

'I have heard.'

'Even his teeth hurt. It's that bad. So me and Alan have come here to grind our corn and take it back to college. Will ye give us a hand?'

'Of course I will. Better than that. I'll do it for you. But what do you want to do while it is grinding?'

'Well, I think I'll stand awa' there by the hopper when the corn flows in. I have never watched that happen. I wouldn't mind seein' it.'

'And I'll stand awa' there,' Alan said, 'and watch the meal gannin' doon into the trough. That'll keep me happy. You and I are just the same, John. We kna' nowt about mills or millers.'

The miller was smiling at their stupidity. 'They are trying to trick me,' he said to himself. 'They think that nobody can fool them. Well, well. I'll pull the wool over their eyes just the same. Their logic or philosophy – whatever it is they study – is not worth a bean. The more tricks they pull, the more I will return. Instead of flour, I'll give them bran. As the wolf said to the mare, the greatest scholars are not the wisest men. That was a shrewd wolf. And so will I be.'

So, when he saw his opportunity, he left the mill very quietly and went down into the yard. He looked about him, and finally found the clerks' horse tied to a tree behind the mill. The miller goes up to it, unties it, and takes off its bridle. When the horse was loose it started sniffing the air and then with a 'Weehee' galloped off towards the fen where the wild mares roam. Well pleased, the miller returned to John and Alan. He said nothing about the horse, of course, but laughed and joked with them as he got on with the job. At last the corn was finely ground, and the meal put in a sack, all above board. Then John went out into the yard. He looked around for the horse. And then –

'Oh fuck! The horse is gone! Alan, for fuck's sake get oot here! We've lost the master's horse!'

Alan forgot all about the meal and corn, forgot all about watching the miller, and rushed out of the mill. 'Which way did it gan?' he cried out to John.

'How am I supposed to kna'?'

Then out ran the miller's wife in a state of great excitement. 'That horse of yours,' she said, 'has gone off to find the mares in the fen. Somebody didn't tie him up properly. Somebody should have known better.'

'Let's put our swords doon,' John said, 'and gan after it. I'm strong enough to tek hold of it. It can't get away from both of us. Why didn't you put him in the barn, you clown?' So the two of them sped off towards the fen.

As soon as they had gone the miller took half a bushel of flour from their sack and told his wife to bake a loaf of bread with it. 'They won't be back for a while,' he said. 'A miller can still outwit a scholar. Well, let them go. Let the children play.' He started laughing. 'They'll have a hard time finding that horse.'

So the two scholars ran up and down the fen, trying to catch hold of their horse. They called out, 'Stay! Stay!' and 'Here, boy! Here!' And they called out to each other, 'Wait! Go back a bit!' and 'Whistle to him. Gan on.' However hard they tried, the animal always managed to elude them. He was fast. It was not until nightfall, in fact, that they managed to catch him in a ditch. The horse was exhausted. And so were they. They were weary, and wet from the rain. 'I divn't believe it,' John said. 'Everyone'll be laughin' at us now. Our corn'll be gone. We're both ringin' wet. We've both been made to look like cocks. The master'll rip the shit out of us. So will the scholars. And, as it happens, so will the miller. You just wait and see.'

So they walked back to the mill, leading their horse along the way. The miller was sitting by the fire. It was pitch black outside now, and they could travel no further. So they asked him to provide them with food and lodging for the night. They offered to pay, of course. 'If there be any room in my poor dwelling,' the miller said, 'then you shall have it. My house is small but you scholars know how to argue and dispute. You can prove anything with your rhetoric. See if you can prove that twenty square feet of space equals a square mile.'

'Well, Simkin,' John replied, 'that's a fair comment. I divn't kna' how to answer you. There's a sayin' up north – that a man has only two options. He can tek things as he finds them, or bring things of his own. But to be honest with you, Simkin, we're knackered and hungry. We need food and drink. Bring us some bread and meat – or anythin' – and we're happy to pay for them. Look. I've got silver here. I kna' that the hawk will not fly to an empty hand.'

So the miller sent his daughter into town to buy bread and beer. He roasted them a goose, too. And he made sure that the horse was tethered so that it would not escape again. Then he made up a bed for them in his own chamber, complete with clean sheets and blankets. It was only ten feet away from his own bed, but where else could John and Alan lie? There was no other room available. But this is the interesting point – the bed of his daughter was also in the same chamber.

So the miller and his guests ate and drank and talked and drank, until about midnight. Then they went up to their beds. The miller himself was by this time very drunk; his bald head was as red as a beetroot. And then at the next moment he had gone pale, as if he were about to vomit. He was sweating and belching, his voice croaking as if he had a bad cold or a fit of asthma. His wife had got into bed with him. She was also very far gone, but she was jolly and giggling. Their baby was in a cradle at the end of their bed, so that he could be easily rocked or given the teat. When they had drained the last drop of drink, it was time for sleep. The young daughter got beneath the sheets. So did Alan and John. What do you think happened next?

The miller and his wife needed no sleeping draught. That's for sure. He had drunk so much ale that he was gurgling and belching in his sleep like a horse; he kept on farting, too. His wife kept up the same peal of farts, the treble to his bass. And both of them snored. God, did they snore. They could have taken the roof off.

Alan could not sleep with all the noise, and poked John in the back. 'John,' he said. 'Are you kippin'?'

'I was.'

'Have you ever heard a noise like it? Worse than a frickin' earthquake. I suppose this is called the song of the night. Curse them with all diseases. Whoever heard such a disgustin' din. Yet I'll pay them back for their snores and their mingin' farts. I may not get any kip tonight, but I will get someik else. I tell you what, John. I am goin' to fuck their daughter. I even have a case in law, you know. Have you read the edict that states if in one point a man is aggrieved, in another point he may be relieved. I am sure that we have been screwed out of our corn, leavin' aside the other bollocks. We have been offered no compensation, so I will take my own from the miller's goods. I'll distrain the girl.'

'Think about it,' John replied. 'This miller's a dangerous man. If he should wake up when you're doin' it, he will not hold back. He'll attack both of us.'

'I don't give a flyin' fart. There are enough farts flyin' around in any case.'

So up he got, quietly and slowly, and crept towards the young girl lying in her bed. She was fast asleep, and he got so close to her that she had no time to cry out. She hardly had time to open her eyes. But she did not say 'oh no'. Oh no. They were at it in a moment. You have a good time, Alan, while I turn back to John.

He was lying there, listening to them. After five minutes or so he got tired of their moaning and squealing. 'This is miserable,' he said to himself. 'What am I doin' here, all on me tod, when he has got his cock up? He took a risk, and now he gets the reward. I am just lyin' here like a spare sack of shit. When he tells the story at college, I'll look a real knob. So here I go. I am goin' to follow his example. Fortune favours the brave.'

So he rose quietly, and went up to the baby's cradle. He lifted it very carefully, and put it at the end of his own bed. Then he waited. After a couple of minutes the miller's wife stopped snoring and got up to take a piss. When she returned to the bedroom she groped her way around and, just before she got back into bed, she realized that there was no cradle at its foot. 'God,' she said to herself, 'that would have been a joke. I almost went into the students' bed. Anything could have happened.' So she felt around until she found the cradle; then she got hold of the bed, and thought that it must be the right one. The cradle was there, wasn't it? It was dark, of course, and she was still a little fuddled. So she gets into bed next to the clerk, and lays herself down to sleep. But John was not about to let that happen. He got himself ready, wriggled on top of her, and then shafted her. He went for it, hard and deep. He was like a madman. She had not enjoyed herself so much for years. The two northern boys had the time of their lives, too, until they heard the crow of the cock. Dawn would not be far behind.

Alan was, to say the least of it, fatigued. He had fucked all night. So he whispered to the miller's daughter, 'Goodbye, sweet chuck. The sun is risin'. I can't stay any longer. But I'll tell you this much. Wherever I go, whatever I do, I swear to God that you will be me lass.'

'Well, lover,' she replied, 'I wish you well. But before you go I must tell you one thing. When you go past the mill, look in the right-hand corner behind the door. There you'll find a half-bushel loaf. Mum and I baked it together, with the meal Dad stole from you. I swear to God, too, that I am sorry.' She almost broke down in tears.

Alan got up, and then thought to himself, 'I'll get back into bed with John, for a quick kip.' So he crept about in the dark, until he found the cradle. 'I must still be arseholed. Or my head is spinning with all that shaggin',' he said to himself. 'I've got the wrong bed. This one has the cradle. I don't want to lie down with the miller and his wife. It must be the other one.' So he crept up to the other bed, where the miller was still sleeping on his own. He thought that he was getting in beside John, but of course he was getting close to the miller. It got worse. He threw his arm around the miller's neck and whispered to him, 'John, John, you fuck-face, wake up! You'll never believe it!

I fucked the miller's daughter three times tonight! God, she loved it. She was beggin' for more. Beggin' for it. What a game! I suppose you were just lyin' here with your hand on your cock.'

The miller was by now fully awake. 'You cunt!' he shouted at him. 'What have you been up to? Bastard! I'll kill you! How dare you touch my daughter? She's of noble blood!' Then he took hold of Alan by the neck and tried to throttle the life out of him; he kicked him hard and punched him on the nose. Alan hit him back, and the blood ran down the miller's chest; then they fell out of the bed, and struggled with one another on the floor like two ferrets in a sack. They rose and fell together, fists flying, until the miller stumbled; he tripped on something, and fell backwards right on top of his wife. She was fast asleep next to John, so exhausted by all the lovemaking that even the noise of the brawl had not woken her. Now the weight of the miller did.

'Oh my God!' she screamed. 'Lord help me! What is going on? Wake up, Simkin! I'm going to have a heart attack. The two boys are fighting! One's on my belly, and the other's on my head! For God's sake do something!'

John got up so fast. Greased lightning is slow by comparison. It was still dark, and so he groped around the chamber looking for a stick. The wife was looking for one, too, and she knew where to find it. There was a staff lying in the corner. The moonlight was coming through a hole in the wall, and in the light she could see the two men once again struggling on the floor. But she could not tell who was who. She saw something white, gleaming in the moonlight, and guessed that it was a nightcap worn by one of the clerks. So she picked up the staff and, thinking that she was about to strike Alan or John, she landed a hefty blow on the bald head of her husband. He collapsed on the floor, of course, screaming and crying. The two scholars gave him a few more kicks. Then they dressed themselves quickly, picked up their sack of flour, and rode off on the horse. But not before Alan had opened the door of the mill, found the loaf of bread in the corner and taken it away.

So that is the story. The miller was beaten up. He lost all the corn he had ground. He had even provided the scholars' supper. Oh. And his wife had been fucked. So had his daughter. That is what happens to deceitful millers. They never learn their lesson. Do you know the old saying? 'Evil to him that evil doeth.' A fraudster is often defrauded. May God, who sits above us in majesty, bless all of us pilgrims great and small. And as for you, sir Miller, I have paid you in kind.

Heere is ended the Reves Tale

The Cook's Prologue

The prologe of the Cokes Tale

The Cook of London was so pleased with the Reeve's tale that he sat on his horse with a silly smile on his face, just as if his back was being scratched. His name was Roger of Ware. 'Well,' he said, 'as God is my judge, that was a very intriguing little story. The miller certainly got paid back for giving the scholars lodging. He should have known the saying of Solomon: "Don't bring every man into your house." That especially applies at night. You have to be careful about your invitations. The bosoms of the family, if I can put it that way, have to be protected. I swear to God, I never heard of a miller so well requited. He had a taste of malice in the dark. But God forbid that we should stop there. I am a poor man but, if you will condescend to listen to me, I will tell you a story. It is an adventure set in London.'

'Of course,' our Host said. 'Tell us the story, Roger. You had better make sure that it is a good one. I know you. I know your tricks. You take the gravy out of the meat pasties so that they will last longer. You sell your fish pies warmed over from the day before – and from the day before that. I have heard many customers complaining about your parsley sauce. You stuff it in the goose to disguise the taste. And your cookshop is full of flies. God may send a man good meat, but the devil may send an evil cook to destroy it. Is that not so, Roger? No. Seriously. Tell your story. I'm only joking, of course. But sometimes the truth just slips out.'

'Oh does it?' said Roger. 'I suppose you are right, Harry

Bailey, as always. But, as the Dutch say, a true joke is a bad joke. Now that I think about it, I do know a very funny story about a Southwark innkeeper. Don't worry. I won't tell it now. I will save it for later. Before the end of our journey, I will give you all a good laugh.' Then he laughed himself and, with a cheerful expression, he told the pilgrims this story.

The Cook's Tale

Heere bigynneth the Cookes Tale

There was a London apprentice, bound to the victuallers' trade. I am in the same guild. That's how I heard about him. He was as merry as a goldfinch in a hedge; he was very good looking with a dark complexion and short dark curls. He was a little short, but that did not matter. He was, to put it in a phrase, well groomed. He could dance so nimbly that he was known as Peter the Performer. He was as full of love and lust as the hive is full of sweet honey. Any girl who met him was sure to have a good time. He would sing and dance at every wedding party, and he preferred the tavern to his shop. If there was any procession going down Cheapside, he would leap from behind the counter and stay in the street until he had seen everything. He would jump up and down and cheer as if his life depended on it. His fellow apprentices used to join him, and become very boisterous. You know how apprentices are. Anything for a laugh. A song and dance are better than work.

They also used to make appointments to meet in a certain secret place and play at dice. Peter was easily the best dice-player in the city and, in these out-of-the-way dives, he spent his money very freely. It was not exactly *his* money, however, as his employer discovered. The cash box was often mysteriously empty. A master will suffer for the sins of a wayward apprentice. He may have no part in the love games, or the revelry, or the gambling, yet he will pay for them in the end. That is sure. Peter might play well on the guitar and the fiddle but, as far as I am concerned, a debauched apprentice is nothing better than a thief. In a man of low degree, honesty and high living can never come together.

In any event the apprentice stayed with his master until he had finished his seven years' indenture. His employer scolded him and shouted at him. There were even times when Peter was led off in shame to Newgate prison, with the minstrels parading before him. But nothing seemed to do any good. At the end of the seven years, when Peter asked for his certificate of release, his employer remembered the old saying: 'It is better to get rid of a rotten apple before it infects the rest of the barrel.' It is exactly the same with a dissolute servant. Better to dismiss him before he corrupts the others. So the master gave Peter his release, wished him bad luck, and sent him on his way. Peter went off in high spirits, ready to begin a life of freedom and debauchery wherever he could find it. There is no thief without an accomplice, someone who can help him waste and spend any money there is to be found by good or evil means. In fact Peter had already sent his bed and his belongings to a companion in sin. Now this companion had a wife. She pretended to own a shop, but in fact she was a prostitute –

'Oh,' exclaimed the Prioress. 'Please. No more.'

'That's enough,' Harry Bailey said. 'I don't mind dirty stories. But I draw the line at whores. Whatever are you thinking of, man? There are nuns among us.'

Roger was a little abashed. 'I didn't mean to offend –'

'Well, you have offended. Sit on your saddle and stay silent. Someone else will have to tell a story.'

Heere endeth the Cookes Tale

The Man of Law's Prologue

The wordes of the Hoost to the compaignye

Our Host saw that the sun had risen high into the sky, and reckoned that it was already mid-morning. Although he was not deeply learned in matters of astronomy he knew from the shadows of the trees, equal in length to the trees themselves, that mighty Phoebus, the great globe of fire, the nurse of life, the sovereign of the heavens, had reached forty-five degrees in altitude. It was the 18th of April. It was ten o'clock. So he turned his horse about and addressed the pilgrims.

'Lords and ladies,' he said, 'I must tell you that a quarter of the sun's day has already passed. Look how he has climbed the steep heavenly hill. So for the love of God let's try to lose no more time. Time does not stay and wait for us. When we sleep, or daydream, it runs on like the motion of a stream, never turning and never slowing, forever running from the mountain to the plain. That is why true philosophers lament the loss of time more than the loss of gold. Seneca put it this way: "Belongings can be restored, but time cannot be retrieved." It cannot be recovered. It would be easier to turn a pregnant girl into a virgin. So let us not moulder now in idleness.'

Then he turned to the Man of Law, who was riding just behind him. 'Can I ask you, sir, if you would be so kind as to tell a story to us? You agreed by your free consent to furnish a tale, and to adhere to my judgement and choice. So will you now fulfil your promise? Then you will have done your duty.'

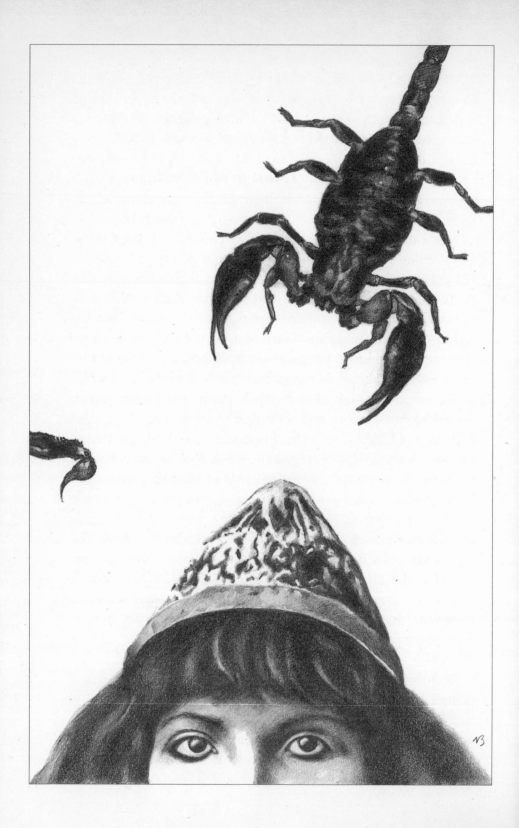

'My good Host,' the sergeant replied. 'I agree, of course. I have no intention of breaking my pledge to you and the others. A promise is an obligation, and I always fulfil my obligations. I am one who lays down the law to others. So to law I will be bound. But in truth I must say this to you all. I really do not know a tale that Geoffrey Chaucer has not already told. I admit that he knows very little about poetry, and is hopeless at rhyming, but he has recounted all the stories in such English as he could muster. He may not be very good, but I don't think there is one old fable he has not written down. If he hasn't put it in one book, he has put it in another. He has narrated the adventures of more lovers than are mentioned in Ovid's *Epistles*. Do you know that ancient volume?

'In his youth Chaucer wrote about Ceyx and Alcion. Ceyx was lost at sea, and Alcion threw herself into the waves in grief. Since he has written about so many star-crossed lovers, so many noble women and their paramours, why repeat him now? If anyone should open that hefty volume of his, *The Legend of Good Women*, he will come across Lucretia, who was raped, and Thisbe, who died for love. He loves sad stories. You can read in that book of poor Dido, who fell upon her sword after the treachery of Aeneas, and of Phyllis, who hanged herself from the branches of a tree. You can follow the laments of Dianire and Hermyon, of Adriana and Isiphilee. It is, as I said, a very long book. You can read about the barren island in the middle of the sea, and how Leander drowned himself for love of Hero. What else is there? I could mention the tears of lovely Helen and the woes of false Cressida. I could relate the cruelty of wicked Queen Medea, who hanged her own children for revenge when Jason abandoned her. It is not all doom and gloom, though. Geoffrey Chaucer does manage to praise the faithfulness of Penelope and Alceste.

'There is one story that he does not tell. He refuses to mention the wicked love of Canacee for her own brother. Well, incest is no fit matter. That is why he does not write about Tyro Appollonius and King Antioch. That cursed monarch took the virginity of his own daughter. Can you believe it? It is too horrible to talk about, especially that moment when he threw her down on the floor and began to –. Excuse me. Chaucer thought about including these stories, but then decided against them. I know that John Gower narrates them, but Gower is not known for his good taste. Chaucer would never sully his writings with such abominations. How do I know? I just know. I will follow his example, in any case, and say no more about them.

'How shall I begin my own story? I will not repeat Chaucer. I have said that already. I don't want to be compared to those braggarts who thought that they could rival the Muses and were turned into magpies for their insolence. I will become no bird. And I don't really care if I fall far short of him. Better a dull dish than no dish at all. Let him stick to his poetry. I will use plain prose.' So the Man of Law, with a solemn countenance, began the story that you are about to hear.

The prologe of the Mannes Tale of Lawe

Oh, oh, oh, oh. Oh hate and harm, the conditions of poverty! The thirst, the cold, the hunger and the hurt! If you are a poor man, then you are hard pressed on all sides. If you do not ask for your meat, you die of hunger. If you do ask for it, you die of shame. Your need is known to all. You must beg, or borrow, or steal, and all against your will. But how else will you stay alive?

Will you blame Christ himself, lamenting bitterly that He has falsely distributed the riches of the world? Will you accuse your neighbour of sinfulness? He has everything, while you have nothing. 'There will come a time,' you say, 'when he will burn in hell. He has turned the poor man from his door.'

Listen to a lesson from the wise: 'It is better to die than to be poor. It is better to leave this life than to be despised by your neighbour.' If you are poor, then all respect for you is gone.

Here is another saying from the wise: 'All the days of poor men are sorrowful.' Beware!

If you are poor, your own brother hates you. If you are poor, your friends all leave you. How different for you rich merchants, who are swimming in coin! What nobility! What prudence! You have cast the winning dice, and now scoop up the pool. Who dances most gaily at Christmas time? You do.

You search the land and sail the sea to find your fortune. You predict the rise and fall of kingdoms. You know the secrets of kings concerning peace and war. I said a minute ago that I knew no stories. But now I remember one told me by – guess who – a rich merchant. This is it.

The Man of Law's Tale

Heere begynneth the Man of Lawe his tale

PART ONE

Once upon a time there dwelled a company of wealthy merchants in Syria. They were serious and responsible people. They traded in spices all over the world, as well as in satin and in cloth of gold. Their merchandise was so excellent and luxurious that every broker and dealer wanted to do business with them; there were as many sellers as there were buyers.

Now it so happened that some of these merchants decided to visit Rome. I do not know whether they were going for business, or for pleasure, but they decided that they wanted to travel to that city in person. They did not want to deal with agents. So they journeyed there and took up residence in that quarter of the city where they felt most comfortable.

They stayed in Rome for some time, visiting all the sites and enjoying all the pleasures of the city. So it happened that they got to hear of the emperor's daughter, Lady Constance. Every day they heard more about her. The common report was that the daughter of the emperor (God save him!) was the most beautiful woman that ever was or ever will be in the world. Her honour was spotless.

'If only,' one man told them, 'she could be queen of all Europe. She has beauty without pride. She possesses the blessings, and none of the vices, of youth. She is not impetuous or foolish. She follows the promptings of virtue in everything she does. Modesty is her guide. She is a paragon of courtesy and gentleness. Holiness is in her heart. Bounty to the poor is in her hand.' All of this was true.

But let me return to the story. The merchants declared that they would not return home until they had seen Constance for themselves. Once they had seen her, they were in truth content. They loaded their ships with merchandise and travelled back to Syria where they conducted their business as before. They prospered. There is nothing more to say.

Now it so happened that these men were much favoured by the sultan of Syria. He was very courteous and gracious to them. Whenever they came back from any foreign country, for example, he invited them into his presence and questioned them about all the wonders they had seen or heard of. He loved to hear news of strange lands.

So the merchants told him, among other things, about Lady Constance. They told him of her beauty and her virtue. They praised her gentleness and her nobility. They extolled her so much, in fact, that the sultan began to imagine her in his arms. He wanted to love her and to cherish her for the rest of his life.

In the book of the heavens, the great dark sky above us, the stars will have written that his love was to end in his death. There can be no doubt about it. In the patterns of the stars can be seen, as if in a glass, the death of every man. Yet who can interpret them properly?

In ancient times the stars had foretold the death of Hector and of Achilles, of Caesar and of Pompey; their fates were decided before they were born. In the heavens could be seen the siege of Thebes. The stars prefigured the death of Socrates, the adventures of Hercules and the misfortunes of Sampson. Yet the wit of man is dull. He cannot see what is above him.

The sultan consulted his privy council and – to cut this story short – he told them of his intention to possess Constance by any means he could. If he could not have her, he said, then he was as good as dead. So he charged them with the task of discovering a way his wish might be granted. How could he get hold of her?

Diverse courtiers said diverse things. They argued between themselves and canvassed many opinions. They had plenty of ideas, of course. Some advised the use of magic, while others suggested even more deceitful methods. And yet finally they concluded that the only way to win her was to marry her. It was the best and simplest solution.

But then they realized the difficulties. To be quite plain about it, there was such a difference between the laws of East and West that it would be very difficult to find any accommodation. 'No Christian ruler,' they said to the sultan, 'would dream of marrying his daughter to one who professed the sweet teaching of Mahomet. Blessed be the prophet.'

The sultan gave a firm reply. 'Rather than lose Constance, then, I will be baptized as a Christian. She must be mine. There is nothing else to be said. No. Please. There can be no argument about this. Either I have her or I will die. So go on your way without delay. Travel to Rome. Bring back the woman who has plunged me into such distress.'

What else need I say? There were negotiations and embassies between the two realms. The pope was obliged to mediate between them, too. The princes of the Church, and the princes of the Roman court, were all involved. The Romans themselves were agreed that this was a good opportunity for augmenting the Christian communion. It represented a triumph against idolatry.

So these were the terms of the treaty. The sultan and all his kin, as well as the members of his court and government, would be baptized as Christians. After that ceremony was performed, the sultan was free to marry Constance. A great sum of gold was also to be paid to Rome, in surety of his good intentions. The pact was duly signed by both parties. Oh Constance, God help you!

Some people would now expect me to describe the feasts and celebrations arranged by the emperor for his daughter. But I do not have space to enumerate all the details of the festivities. I can only say that they were magnificent. It was, after all, a noble occasion.

It was agreed that Constance would be accompanied on her journey by many bishops. Travelling with her would also be lords and ladies of renown. There were others with her, too, but I cannot remember them all. Then it was proclaimed throughout Rome that the citizens should pray for her, and invoke the blessing of Jesus Christ upon the marriage.

So the day came for her departure. That woeful day, that fatal day, could not be avoided. Everyone came out on to the streets. Constance herself was overcome with sorrow. She arose that morning, pale and trembling, and dressed herself for the journey. She knew that there was no other course.

Who can wonder at her tears? She was being sent to a strange land, far away from the friends she had loved. She was being placed under the dominion of a man about whom she knew nothing. Husbands, of course, are always good and considerate. Just ask their wives. I say no more.

'Father,' Constance said, 'take leave of your wretched daughter. And you, Mother, who has brought me up so tenderly. I have loved you both. You have been most precious to me – more precious than anything, except the Saviour on high. I commend myself to your prayers, now that I am about to depart for Syria. I will never see you again.

'It is your will that I travel to a barbarian nation. So be it. May Christ, who died for our sins, give me the strength to obey His commands. I am only a weak female. It is no matter if I die. Women are born to servitude and punishment. It is ordained that they should be ruled by men.'

There was never such weeping heard when Troy fell in flames, or when Thebes was taken, or when Rome was wounded by Hannibal. The tears and laments echoed through her chambers. But she had no choice. She was obliged to go.

Oh first mover, outer sphere of heaven, inflexible and cruel! You are the power that moves all things from east to west, that makes the stars revolve in their unnatural course. It was you who put Mars in the ascendant at the beginning of this dangerous voyage. It was you who cast a blight upon the marriage.

Inauspicious ascent, bleak and tortuous in effect! Unhappy Mars must fall out of his place into the darkest house of all, the house of Saturn. Oh feeble moon, of unfortunate fate! You move into a place where you are not welcomed. You are banished from your blessed haven. Such are the movements of the spheres.

And as for you, imprudent emperor of Rome, Constance's father, was there no wise man in the city? Is one time no better than another in Rome? Surely you had an astrologer in your court who could have determined the proper moment for such a voyage? Was there no one who could cast Constance's horoscope? Or are all the Romans stupid or slow-witted?

So the woeful maid is conducted to the ship with every formality and every ceremony. 'Jesus Christ be with you all,' she cried out from the deck. And the crowd shouted out, 'Farewell! Farewell Constance!' They had no more to say. She tried to maintain her composure, but it was difficult. Now I must leave her on the high seas and return once more to Syria.

The mother of the sultan, a woman who was a pit of vice, knew all about her son's intentions; the sultaness had heard that he was about to abandon his old religion. So she sent for her own privy council. They gathered in the palace according to her instructions, and when they were all assembled together she told them her plan.

'Lords,' she said, 'you all know well enough that my son is about to turn away from the laws of the Koran, vouchsafed to Mahomet by God Himself, and to do great dishonour to our holy religion. But I make my vow, before you all, that I would rather die than disobey the least one of our religious laws.

'What will happen to us if we accept this new dispensation? We will be the slaves of Rome. But that is not the worst of it. If we renounce Mahomet, we will be consigned to everlasting torment. No. It cannot be. But, my lords, I have a plan. Will you follow me in the enterprise I am about to reveal? Assuredly it will save us all.'

They assented, and swore an oath that they would all live or die by her side. They would persuade all of their friends and colleagues, too, to support and protect her. So, assured of their fealty, she began to describe to them the scheme that she had contrived.

'First of all,' she said, 'we will pretend to embrace the false religion. A little baptismal water will not affect us. I will then throw such a feast and festival that the sultan will be paid back in kind. This heathen girl may be as white as the day she was baptized but, by the time I have finished with her, she will need more than holy water to wash away the blood. A Christian font will not be enough.'

Oh sultaness, root of iniquity! You are a harpie, unnatural and accursed. You are a reptile with a woman's face, as wicked as the serpent who lies coiled in hell. You are false and fraudulent, confounding good and evil with your malice. You are a nest of vices.

Dreadful Satan, you have been watchful and malicious ever since you fell from heaven. You know how to entrap women. It was you who tempted Eve, the source of all our woe. Now you wish to destroy this Christian marriage. And what will be the instrument of your guile? Alas it will be another woman.

I will get on with the story. So the evil sultaness, having dismissed her council with an oath of secrecy, rode out to visit her son. She informed him that she was willing to renounce her faith, and receive baptism at the hands of the Christian priests. She was sorry, she said, that she had remained a heathen for such a long time!

Then she asked permission to organize a great feast for the visiting Christians. 'I will do everything in my power,' she said, 'to make them welcome.'

'It shall be done as you wish,' he replied. Then he kneeled

down before her and thanked her for her thoughtfulness. He was overcome.

She kissed her son, and went on her way.

PART TWO

So, after a long journey by sea and land, the Christian legation eventually arrived in Syria. They were an impressive gathering of dignitaries. As soon as the sultan heard of their approach he sent a message to his mother, telling her that his new wife had come and urging her to welcome Constance nobly for the honour of the realm. He also announced the news to the rest of the country.

The throng was great, and the show very splendid, when the Syrians and the Christians finally greeted each other. The sultaness could not have been more charming or more gracious in her greeting to them all. She was especially nice to Constance, whom she received as tenderly as any mother would receive her favourite child. So they proceeded slowly towards the city, riding side by side in perfect amity.

I know nothing about the triumphal processions of Julius Caesar, except for the description in Lucan's *Pharsalia*. But I do not suppose that they were any more rich, or more spectacular, than the procession of Constance into Damascus. Yet this was the time when the scorpion of Syria, the wicked demon of the royal family, was preparing herself. The sultaness, for all her smiles and gracious words, was getting ready to use her deadly sting.

The sultan himself then rode out to greet his bride with great fanfare and display. He welcomed her with joy, and wonder, at her beauty. So, for the time being, I will leave them to their happiness. I will come soon enough to the heart of the matter. The rest of the day was spent in revelry and sport, until the company agreed that it was time to rest.

Then the moment arrived for the banquet that the sultaness

had organized. All of the Christians, young and old alike, were invited to attend. All the guests would be able to enjoy royal luxury, and to feast upon the most rare and delicate foods in the world. And yet, alas, they soon paid too high a price for them.

Woe is always the consequence of bliss. Sorrow follows prosperity, and suffering succeeds joy. That is the way of the world. Follow this advice for the sake of your well-being. If you ever experience happiness, keep in mind the day when it will end. Nothing abides.

I will be brief. While they were at this feast all the guests, Syrian and Christian, were stabbed or cut to pieces. All of them were killed, with the exception of Constance herself. And who do you think had murdered them? The sultaness, of course, together with her henchmen. The old hag wanted to rule the country alone. She had even murdered her own son.

All of the converts to Christianity, who had changed their faith on the instructions of the sultan, were killed before they could escape. Constance herself was immediately dragged to the port, where she was put on a boat without sail or rudder. They told her that it was her chance to learn how to sail, and bid her to go back to Italy.

She had managed to take some of her possessions with her. The Syrians had also given her food and drink, as well as a change of clothing. So off she floated on to the salt sea. Oh dear Constance, dearest of the dear, young daughter of the emperor, may Christ the Saviour be your pilot!

So Constance blessed herself and, holding the crucifix before her, she wept and prayed. 'Oh sacred altar, holy cross, red with the blood of the Holy Lamb spilled in pity for this world of sin, keep me safe from the claws of the devil. Safeguard my soul when I drown in the deep.

'Tree of victory, holy rood, cross of truth, preserve me. Oh tree that bore the sweet weight of our wounded Saviour, guard me. Oh white Lamb, pierced by the spear, who drives away the evil spirits, cast your grace around me. Help me to amend my life and do penance for my sins.'

Her fortune carried her across the eastern Mediterranean, and into the Strait of Gibraltar. She ate only meagre meals as she drifted onward. The days became months, and the months became years. There were many occasions when she prepared herself for death. She did not know if the wild waves would take her to a shore or harbour.

Why was she not killed at the feast in Damascus? Who could have saved her? I will answer that question with another. Who saved Daniel in the lion's den? How did Daniel survive when every other man had been killed and eaten by the creature? God saved him. God was in his heart.

In the same way God has shown His wonderful providence in the life of Constance; in her survival we see the miracle of His power. Christ is the cure for every ill. The scholars know that He works by mysterious means, and that His intentions cannot be understood by us. Our wit is too weak.

Who saved Constance from drowning in the sea? Who saved Jonah in the belly of the whale? We know well enough that he was spewed out at Nineveh unharmed. Who saved the Israelites from the waves of the Red Sea, when they passed through the raging waters on a path of dry land? God saved them.

Who commanded the four angels of the tempest? They were given the power to direct the winds of the world from north and south, from east and west. But God said to them, 'Trouble not the smallest leaf that trembles. Trouble neither the land nor the sea.' The Lord protected Constance from the tempest, too, and the mantle of His care covered her by night and by day.

How can it be that Constance had meat and drink enough for three long years of voyaging? Who saved the holy hermit, Saint Mary of Egypt, when she dwelled in the wilderness? It was no one else but Christ the Saviour. It was a great miracle when the crowd of five thousand were fed by five loaves and two fishes. A greater miracle still is God's love. He sent His succour to Constance at her time of need.

So she floated across the wide world, until she came to our

own ocean and our own fierce northern seas. She was washed ashore on the coast of Northumberland, beneath the walls of a castle; when her ship was run aground, it stuck so fast in the sands that the rise and fall of the tide could not move it. It was Christ's wish that she should stay here.

The governor of the castle came down to the shore to view the wreckage; he searched the ship, and of course found the poor weary woman. He also found the treasure Constance had brought with her. Then in her own tongue she beseeched him for deliverance. 'Take my life from me,' she begged him. 'Release me from the misery I am suffering.'

She spoke a corrupt form of Latin, but it was good enough for the governor to understand her. When he saw that there was nothing else to find on the vessel, he conducted her on to dry land. She kneeled down and kissed the ground, thanking God for His mercy to her. But she would not tell anyone who she was or where she had come from. Nothing, good or ill, would make her speak.

She said that she was so bewildered by the wild waves that she had, in truth, lost her memory. The governor of the castle and his wife, Hermengyld, took pity on her. They wept at her condition. Constance herself was so gracious and courteous – she was so willing to please all the people about her – that she became universally loved.

The governor and his wife were both pagans, in this dark age of our country, but Hermengyld still loved her. Constance stayed so long in the castle, praying and weeping, that, through the grace of Christ, Hermengyld was converted to the true faith.

In this period, the Christians of Britain could not assemble in public places. Most of them had fled, menaced by pagan invasions from the north by land and sea. They had gone to Wales, which had become a haven for the old Britons and old Christianity. That was their refuge for the time being. I am talking about the sixth century of our era.

Some Britons had remained, however, and practised their

religion in secret. They venerated Christ far from the gaze of their pagan rulers. There were in fact three such Christians living near the castle. One of these was blind. He could see only by the light of his mind, now that his eyes were closed for ever.

It so happened that on one bright summer morning the governor and his wife, together with Constance, decided to ride out to the shore where they could refresh themselves with the bracing sea air. It was only a short journey. In the course of it, however, they met the blind man. He was old and bent, leaning heavily upon his staff.

But then he straightened up when they passed him, and turned his face towards the governor's wife. 'In the name of Christ,' he shouted out, 'Dame Hermengyld! Give me back my sight!' Now Hermengyld was astonished by this outburst. She was terrified, too, that her husband would kill her for renouncing the pagan faith. Constance, however, was calm and resolute. She urged Hermengyld, as a true daughter of the Church, to work the will of Christ.

The governor was inwardly troubled and amazed. He asked the two women, 'What does this mean? What is going on?' 'It is the power of Christ,' Constance replied. 'He is the Saviour who rescues us from Satan.' Thereupon she explained to him the doctrines of the true faith with such sweetness and grace that, before evening, the governor was converted.

He was not himself the ruler of this territory, but he kept it by force of arms in the name of Aella, king of Northumberland. He was a wise king who had proved himself stern in battle against the Scots. You probably know all about this. So let me return to the story.

The arch-enemy Satan, always ready to deceive us, had observed the goodness of Constance. He could not endure it. He determined to harm her in any way he could. So he cast his net upon a young knight who lived in the neighbourhood of the castle, and filled his heart with foul lust for Constance. If he could not lie with her and have her, he was willing to die.

He wooed her earnestly, but without success. She would not commit sin. There was no more to say. So, out of revenge and humiliation, he decided to ensure that she suffered a shameful death. He waited until the governor was absent from the castle, and then secretly found his way to the chamber of Dame Hermengyld.

Here Constance also slept. Both women had spent much of the night in prayer, and were very weary. The young knight, under the influence of the demon, crept up to the bed and cut the throat of Hermengyld. He placed the bloody knife beside Constance, and then left the castle. May God curse him!

Shortly afterwards the governor, in company with the king, Aella, returned to the castle. What greeted him there, but the sight of his wife with her throat cut? You can imagine his horror and grief. He also found the bloody knife lying in Constance's bed. What could she say? She was nearly out of her mind with the horror of it.

The king soon knew all about it. He questioned the governor about Constance, and learned her whole unhappy story – when and where she had been found on the ship, how she had conducted herself, and so on. He was touched by pity for her plight. She seemed too gracious a lady to be overwhelmed by distress and misfortune.

So the innocent woman stood before the king, like a lamb bound for the slaughter. The young knight came forward and swore falsely that she had committed the murder. Yet there was clamour and dissent among the people, who said that they could not believe Constance was guilty of so heinous a crime.

They said that they had seen her virtues every day, and that she had loved Hermengyld like a sister. All of them bore witness to this – except, of course, the young knight who was actually guilty. King Aella himself was deeply impressed with the bearing of Constance, and decided that he would enquire deeper into the matter in order to learn the truth.

Alas, Constance, you have no champion. You have no one

to fight your corner. So may Jesus Christ Himself come forward to protect you. It was He who bound Satan, so that the fiend still lies in the darkness where he first fell. It was He who saved humankind. May He now save you! If He does not work a miracle on your behalf, you will be slain as certainly as the coming of tomorrow.

In front of them all Constance fell down on her knees and began to pray. 'Immortal God, who saved Susannah from her false accusers, protect me! Holy Virgin, lady of mercy, before whose blessed child the archangels sing orisons, look kindly on me. If I am innocent of this crime, then come to my aid. Otherwise I will die.'

Have you not sometimes seen a pale face, among a crowd of those being led to their deaths? Have you not seen the dread and loneliness upon that face? Have you not seen the overwhelming misery? So looked Constance as she stood among the press.

All you queens who live in prosperity, all you duchesses and other ladies, have some pity on the plight of Dame Constance. She is the daughter of an emperor, but she must stand alone. She has no one to advise her or console her. Her royal blood is in danger of being spilled, yet she has no friends to protect her.

King Aella was so full of pity and compassion for her that the tears ran down his cheeks. He was a pagan, but he had a gentle heart. 'Now someone fetch a holy book,' he said, 'and we will see if the knight will swear an oath upon it that Constance murdered Hermengyld. Only then will I mete out justice.'

So a British book of gospels was brought forward. The knight placed his hand upon it and in a confident tone swore that Constance was guilty of the crime. But then all of a sudden a giant hand struck him on the neck so strongly that he fell forward on the floor; the blow had been so overwhelming that, in sight of all those around, his eyes burst out of their sockets.

Then a voice could be heard by all. 'Foul knight. You have slandered an innocent woman. In the sight of God Almighty, you have defamed a daughter of the Holy Church. You have shamed her. And shall I hold my peace?'

The crowd of people was of course amazed and terrified by the apparition. Those who had harboured suspicions of Constance were deeply repentant. And there was one other consequence of this miracle. Through the intercession of the innocent young woman, Aella and many of his courtiers were converted to the true faith.

The king made sure that the false knight was executed immediately, even as Constance lamented his death out of pity for him. By the guidance of our Saviour, too, Aella took her to be his bride in solemn ceremony. So at last this holy maid, this jewel of virtue, became a queen. Christ be praised.

There was one who did not join in the general chorus of adulation. This was the mother of the king, named Donegild, whose heart was full of malice and treachery. She thought her cursed heart would break in two. She considered it dishonourable for her son to take a foreign wife.

I will now remove the chaff and the straw from this story, and leave you with the shining corn. Why should I describe to you all the pageants and festivities that surrounded the marriage? Why should I sing to you the songs and melodies of the players? Enough is enough. They ate and they drank; they danced and they sang. There is nothing to add.

That night they were escorted to their royal bed, as was right and proper. Even the holiest virgin must do her duty in the darkness. I hope that Constance did hers patiently. There are certain necessary things to be done between man and wife. Saintliness must be put to one side on a solemn occasion such as this.

On that very night Aella begat a son. But soon he had other hot work to do. He had to fight the Scottish enemy, massing on the border, and so he left Constance in the care of a bishop and of the governor while he took his army to the north. Constance was so far gone with child that she kept to her chamber, as meek and as mild as ever. She lay very still, placing herself and her baby in the hands of Christ.

In due time she gave birth to her son, who was baptized with the name of Maurice. The governor of the castle called for a messenger and delivered to him a letter that he had written to Aella in which he gave the king the good news of the birth as well as other timely matters of state. So the messenger took the letter, bowed and went on his way.

This messenger thought that he would do himself a favour by visiting the king's mother. So he visited her quarters and paid her homage. 'Ma dame,' he said, 'I have some wonderful news. You will be so happy. My Lady Constance has given birth to a male child. There is no doubt about it. The whole realm will be delighted.

'Look. Here is the letter written by the governor. I have to take it to the king at once. But if you have any other message for your son, confide it to me. I will be your good servant.' Donegild needed time to think. 'I have no message for you as yet,' she said, 'but stay here overnight. I will write a letter in the morning.'

So the messenger settled down and drank some ale, followed by wine, followed by ale again. While he was sleeping off the drink the governor's letter was quietly taken from his bag, and a substitute placed there. This was a counterfeit letter, apparently from the governor, very subtly written.

It revealed horrors. The letter stated that Constance had been delivered of a fiend, an unnatural monster bred out of the devil. No one in the castle could endure the sight or sound or smell of it. It was agreed by all that its mother was a witch, sent to the castle by means of spells and sorcery. No one would go near her.

The king's grief, on reading this letter, was overwhelming. But he said nothing. He kept his sorrow secret, and wrote to the governor of the castle. 'Let the providence of Christ be my guide. I am now converted to His cause, and must abide

His will. Oh Lord, I will obey your commands in everything. Do with me as you wish.'

Then he added, to the governor, 'Keep this child safe, whether it be foul or fair. And safeguard my wife, too, until I return. Christ will grant me another child, fair and wholesome, when He deems it right.' Weeping, he sealed and dispatched this letter to the messenger. There was nothing else to be done.

Yet how false a messenger! You are a drunken sot. Your breath is foul, and your limbs are weak. You falter on your legs. You betray every secret entrusted to you. You have lost your mind. You chatter like a parrot. Your face is distorted and awry. Wherever there is a drunk, there is also a loud mouth. You can be sure of it.

Oh Donegild, evil queen mother, I have no words to describe the malice of your wickedness. I give you over to your companion, the foul fiend. Let him record your treachery. I defy you, unnatural creature – no, you are yourself a fiend. Wherever your body wanders, your spirit dwells in hell.

So the messenger left the presence of the king and returned to the court of Donegild. She was delighted to see him again, and offered him all the hospitality she could possibly provide. He drank himself close to bursting. Then he passed out, and spent the night snorting and farting like a swine in its sty.

In the meantime, of course, Donegild had stolen the letter from the king and forged one in its place. 'The king,' she wrote, 'commands the governor, on pain of death, to make sure that Constance is banished from the realm of Northumberland. She may remain only for three days. After that time, she must be gone.

'Place her in the same ship in which she arrived here. She must take her infant son and all her possessions. Then push the ship out to sea. And forbid her ever to return.' Oh Constance, well may your spirit tremble. Well may your dreams be sorrowful. Donegild intends to strike at you.

When the rising sun had roused the messenger, he took

the shortest route to the castle. He presented the letter to the governor of that place who, on reading its contents, burst into lamentation. 'Lord Christ,' he said, 'what is this world? It is a place of evil and of sin. Almighty God, why is it Your wish and will that the innocent should suffer? You are the judge of righteousness. Why do You allow the wicked to prosper? Oh Constance. I must now be your executioner or die a shameful death. There is no alternative.'

The old and the young of the castle wept at the news of Constance's banishment. They could not believe that the king had sent such a cursed letter. Yet Constance remained calm. She accepted the will of Christ. She went down to the ship, looking deathly pale, and kneeled upon the shore. 'Almighty Lord,' she prayed, 'I accept your command. He who saved me from false blame, when I lived in this land, will now protect me from harm. He will comfort me on the wild ocean. I do not know His means, but He is as strong now as He has always been. In Him I trust. Blessed be the Lord God and the Virgin Mother. They are my rudder and my sail.'

Her little child lay wailing in her arms. She cradled him and soothed him. 'Peace, my son,' she whispered to him. 'I will never harm you.' She took off the scarf she had been wearing and placed it over his eyes and hair. Then she rocked the child in her arms, praying softly all the while.

'Mother Mary, bright queen of heaven, it is true that human-kind fell through the sin of Eve. Through the fault of the first woman, your blessed son was nailed to the cross. Your own eyes witnessed His torment. Your woe was greater than the weight of all the world. There is no comparison between your suffering and my affliction.

'You saw your son tortured and slain before your eyes. My little son is yet in life. Now, blessed lady to whom all pray in this vale of tears, glory of womanhood and fairest maid. You are a haven of refuge, and the bright star of day. In your gentleness you take pity on all those in distress. Take pity on my infant son.

'Oh little child. You are innocent, without sin or guilt. Why does your cruel father wish to kill you?' Then she turned to the governor of the castle. 'Have mercy on him,' she said. 'Let my little son dwell with you here.' He shook his head. 'But if you dare not save him, for fear of punishment, then kiss him once in his father's name.'

She turned around and for the last time looked back at the land. 'Farewell,' she called. 'And farewell, cruel husband!' Then she rose up and walked along the shore towards the ship. She was caressing the child, as she went, and comforting him. Then at last she took her leave. She blessed herself and, with the child in her arms, stepped aboard the ship.

The ship was well stocked with provisions, and other necessary things for the long voyage ahead of her. God be thanked. And, dear God, grant her the winds and tides to steer her safely home. She must now make her way across the wild ocean.

PART THREE

Aella returned to the castle soon after her sad departure. He wanted to see, of course, his wife and newborn son. Where were they? The governor felt the cold creep into his heart. He told the king exactly what had occurred in his absence. He showed him the forged letter with the royal seal upon it.

'I did no more and no less than you asked, sir. You commanded me on pain of death. What else was I to do?' The messenger was summoned and put to the torture. He revealed every detail of his journey – where he had ridden, where he had supped, where he had spent the night. It all became plain. It did not take much enquiry or investigation to discover the guilty party in this wicked affair.

I do not know how they discovered that the queen mother had herself written those poisonous letters, but her fate was sealed soon after. All the chroniclers agree that Aella killed his own mother, blaming her for bringing dishonour and shame to his family. So ended the career of Donegild, a woman steeped in evil.

No one can adequately impart the grief that Aella suffered over the fate of his young wife and newborn son. I will leave it to one side, and return instead to the plight of Constance floating on the sea. By the will of Christ she spent five long years upon the waves, in pain and in woe, before finally she caught sight of land.

She came close to on a beach beneath a pagan castle – I do not have the name of it by me – where the sea delivered Constance and Maurice on to dry ground. Almighty God, I beseech you, preserve the fair maid and her child. Once more she has fallen into the hands of heathens, who might wish to kill her. Who can tell?

There came down from the castle a procession of people, eager to take a look at Constance and the foreign ship. But then, at nightfall, a steward of the castle came down secretly to the ship and told her that he would lie with her whether she liked it or not. God damn him for a rapist and a rogue.

Constance of course set up a great lamentation, in which her child joined. But then the Holy Virgin placed her mantle around her. In the course of his struggles with Constance the steward fell overboard and was instantly drowned. He had merited his punishment. So Christ kept Constance undefiled.

See the result of foul sensuality! It does not only darken the mind and mar the judgement. It can kill. The end of blind lust, the end of the dread deed itself, is misery. How many men have found that even the intention of committing that sin is enough to destroy them, whether they accomplish it or not?

How did this weak woman have the strength to defend herself against the wretch? How was it that the giant Goliath was slain by the young and untested David? How dared he even look upon that monster's dreadful face? His strength was derived from the grace of Christ. Who gave Judith the courage and endurance to murder Holofernes in his tent and to lift the chosen people out of their misery? I say that it was all God's work. And that same God instilled might and vigour within Constance herself.

So the ship sailed on through the narrow strait that separates Gibraltar from the tip of Africa. The wind came from the east and from the west, from the north and from the south, driving the vessel in all directions and in none. Constance was weary unto death when one day the Virgin Mary, blessed among women, brought an end to all her woe with an act of goodness.

Let us leave her for a moment, however, and turn to her father. The emperor of Rome had learned, from diplomatic correspondence out of Syria, that all of the Christians had been slain at the banquet in Damascus. Of course he had also discovered that the wicked mother of the sultan had dishonoured his daughter and cast her adrift.

So he decided to take revenge. He sent his principal senator, with royal authority, to Syria. He sent all of his lords and knights, too, with express orders to deliver condign vengeance. For a long time the Roman forces burned and pillaged and killed whatever and whomever they found in the capital. When they had meted out the punishment, they set sail again for Rome.

It so happened that the Roman senator, while making his progress across the sea, came upon the little ship in which Constance was marooned. He did not know who she was, or how she came to be there. And for her part Constance would not speak. She would rather die than reveal her condition.

He brought her back with him to Rome, and gave her into the keeping of his wife and young son. Constance spent the next part of her life in the senator's family. So did the Blessed Virgin rescue her from all her woe, as she has saved many others. Constance conducted herself in a devout and gentle way, doing good works wherever she could.

The wife of the senator was in fact her aunt, but neither one recognized the other. I can say no more about it. That was what happened. I will leave Constance with the family, and now I will return to the king of Northumberland, Aella, who still bitterly mourned and lamented his wife's absence.

The fact that he had killed his own mother now began to weigh on his conscience. He fell into such a mood of repentance, in fact, that he decided to travel to Rome in order to do penance. He would put himself under the authority of the pope, in all matters, and beseech Christ to forgive him his sins.

His ambassadors travelled ahead of him, announcing his arrival. It soon became known throughout the holy city that this high king was coming on a pilgrimage. So the senators of Rome rode out to greet him, according to custom, and to do reverence to his majesty. They also wanted to put on a good show.

One of these senators was of course the protector of Constance. He welcomed Aella, and paid him homage, and the king duly returned his courtesies. A day or two later the king invited him and his retinue to a banquet. Who do you think was among the guests? None other than Maurice, the son of Constance.

Some people would say, of course, that Constance herself persuaded the senator to take her son. I do not know the circumstances. All I know is that Maurice attended the feast. And I know this, too. Constance had told her son to stand before the king, during the meal, and look him steadfastly in the face.

Aella was struck with wonder on seeing the boy. He turned to the senator and asked him the identity of the handsome child standing before the table. 'I have no idea,' the senator replied. 'God be my witness. He has a mother but, as far as I know, he has no father.' And then he told the king the story of how mother and child were found.

'God knows,' he said, 'I have never seen a more virtuous woman in all my life. I have never heard of a woman – maid or married – who is her equal. She would rather be stabbed in the heart than perform a wicked deed. No man on earth could persuade her otherwise.'

This young boy was the image of his mother. There could not be a closer resemblance. So Aella was reminded of Constance herself, and wondered if it could possibly be that she – his dear wife – was indeed the mother of the child. He was troubled by this, naturally, and left the banquet as quickly as he could.

'What phantom or vision is in my head,' he asked himself, 'when I know well enough that my wife lies at the bottom of the sea?' But then he put to himself another question. 'But is it not possible that Christ the Saviour has brought Constance to this place, just as He once sent her to the coast of my own kingdom?'

On that same afternoon he decided to visit the home of the senator, and see for himself. Had there been another miracle? The senator greeted the king with reverence, and then summoned Constance. When she was told that she was about to meet Aella, she almost fainted. She could hardly stand, let alone dance for joy.

As soon as Aella caught sight of his wife he greeted her and began to weep piteously. He knew it was her. His wife stood before him. Constance herself was dumb with amazement, and was as rooted to the ground as a tree. She remembered all his unkindness (or so she thought), and she suffered double distress at the sight of him.

She swooned, and then recovered herself; then she swooned again. The king himself wept, and did his best to excuse himself. 'I swear by God and all the saints in heaven,' he said, 'that I am as guiltless of any crimes against you as your own son. *Our* own son, who so much resembles you. Let the devil take me if I am lying.'

So they wept together. They lamented the past. They lamented the evil done to them. Those around them were filled with pity, as their woes seemed to increase with their tears.

Will you excuse me from saying any more about their sorrow? It would take me until tomorrow to do full justice to it. And I am weary of describing nothing but pain.

Finally, when Constance understood that Aella had no part in her exile, the tears gave way to smiles. They must have kissed each other a hundred times. There was such bliss between them that no couple in the world have ever been, or could ever be, so happy. Only the joy of heaven is superior.

Then Constance begged of him one favour, to recompense for her life of woe. She asked him to send an invitation in the most gracious terms to her father, the emperor, and entreat him to attend a royal banquet. But she urged her husband not to say one word about her.

It has been said that Maurice was chosen to deliver the message to the emperor. I don't believe it. Aella would not have been so disrespectful as to send a mere child into the presence of the great ruler who has sovereign authority over all Christendom. It is better to suppose that the king himself visited the emperor's palace.

Nevertheless I have read that Maurice was indeed the ambassador. According to the story the emperor graciously accepted the invitation, while all the time studying Maurice intently. The child reminded him of his daughter. Aella, in the meantime, went back to his residence and prepared everything for the banquet in as magnificent a manner as he could. He spared no expense.

The day came for the feast. Aella and his dear wife prepared to meet their royal guest, and in joy and festivity rode out together. When Constance saw her father in the street she alighted from her horse and fell to her knees. 'Father,' she said, 'perhaps you have forgotten about your child, Constance. But I am here before you. I am the girl you sent to Syria. I am the one who was dispatched to die alone upon the wide ocean. Now, dear Father, have mercy upon me. Do not banish me to any more pagan lands. But thank my husband for his kindness to me.'

Who could portray the mingled joy and sorrow that now filled the hearts of Constance, Aella and the emperor? I cannot. In any case I must draw to a close. The day is fading fast. I won't delay. They sat down to dinner. That is all I will say. I won't begin to describe their happiness, which was hundreds and hundreds of times more joyous than I can possibly relate.

In later years the pope crowned Maurice as Holy Roman Emperor in succession to his grandfather. Maurice was a good and devout churchman, and ruled in Christian fashion. I will not tell you his story. I am more concerned with his mother. If you want to learn more about him, then consult the old Roman historians. They will enlighten you further. I am not so well informed.

When Aella realized that the time had come, he left Rome and with his beloved wife sailed back to England. In our nation they lived in bliss and comfort. But their happiness lasted for only a short time. The joys of this world do not endure. Life changes, like the tide. After the brightness of the day comes the darkness of the night.

Who can be happy even for one day without being moved by anger or by jealousy? Who has not been touched continually by guilt or ill will or resentment? Think about your own life. I tell you this only to reach my conclusion – that the happiness of Aella and Constance could not last for ever.

Death, who collects his tithes from high and low alike, could not be thwarted. Within a year of their return to England Aella was taken out of this world. Constance mourned him bitterly, of course. May God keep his soul safe! Then, after his burial she decided to go back to Rome.

On her return she found her friends and family safe and in good health. Now, at last, she felt that her adventures had come to an end. When she came into the presence of her father she kneeled before him and wept. Constance, of tender heart, sent up her orisons of praise to God a hundred thousand times.

And so they lived in virtue and in charity. They were never parted, except by death itself. And so farewell to you all. My story has come to an end. May Jesus Christ bring us joy after woe, and save us all on the last day. God preserve you, my fellow pilgrims.

Heere endeth the tale of the Man of Lawe

The Epilogue to the
Man of Law's Tale

Harry Bailey, our Host, stood up on his stirrups, and congratulated the Man of Law. 'That was a fine story,' he said. 'Very worthwhile. Don't you all agree?' And then he turned to the parish priest. 'Father,' he said, 'for the love of God tell us a story. You promised. I know well enough that learned men can be good storytellers. You know enough, for God's sake.'

The Parson reproved him. 'Bless us all. Why is this man blaspheming in front of us? Never take the name of God in vain.'

'Oh John Wyclif, have you come among us?' our Host replied. 'I smell a Lollard in the wind. I predict, fellow pilgrims, that before too long the priest will deliver a long sermon. That is what Lollards love to do.'

'On my father's soul, he will not.' The Shipman rode up to our Host. 'He is not going to preach. We won't allow it. This is not the place to teach the gospel. We all believe in God. We don't need the doctrines of Holy Mother Church interpreted or evaluated or revised. He will be sowing weeds in healthy ground. I'll tell you what, Harry. I will give you a good story. It will ring out loud and clear. It won't be full of philosophical terms, or learned quibbles. I don't have enough Latin for that –'

'Excuse me.' It was the good Wife of Bath, looking very majestic on her palfrey. 'Surely I take precedence over this seaman? It is a sad day when a good woman is refused her due. Come now, Mr Bailey. Do let me speak. I have a lot to say.' Then, without waiting for his assent, she began her story.

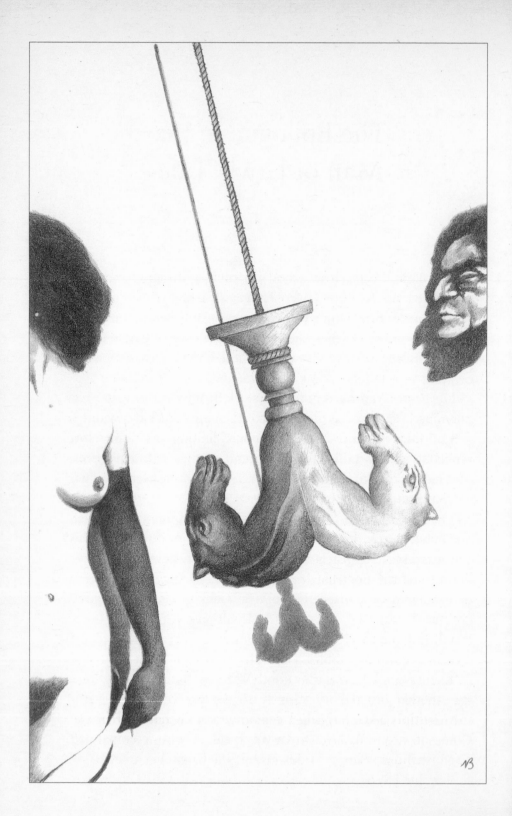

The Wife of Bath's Prologue

The prologe of the Wives Tale of Bathe

'I don't care what anyone says. Experience of the world is the best thing. It may not be the main authority but, in relationships, it is a good teacher. I know all about unhappiness in marriage. Goodness me. Oh yes. I was twelve years old when I first got a husband. I've had five altogether, thanks be to God. Five of them trooping up to the church door. That is a lot of men. By and large they were gentlemen, or so I was led to believe. Yet I was told quite recently – I forget by whom – that our Saviour attended only one wedding. It was in the town of Cana. So, the argument goes, I should only ever have been married once. And then there was the time when Jesus rebuked the Samaritan woman. They were standing beside a well, weren't they? "You have had five husbands," He said. "And the man you are living with is not your husband." He was God and man, so I suppose He knew what He was talking about. I don't understand what His point was, but I am sure He had one. Why was the fifth man not her husband? It doesn't make any sense. How many husbands had she actually had? How many husbands was she allowed? In all my life I never heard there was a limit. Have you?

'There will be ever so many experts telling us one thing and another. But I know this much. God told us to go forth and multiply. Am I right? I can understand that part of the Bible, at any rate. And wasn't it God who commanded my husband to "leave father and mother" and belong to me alone? But He never mentioned a number. It could be two. It could be eight. Who knows? There's nothing wrong with it, anyway.

'What about that Solomon? He was a clever man. Didn't he have more than one wife? I wish to God I had his luck. If I had half as many husbands as he had wives, I would be laughing. Think of it. I could be God's gift to men. And what about all those wedding nights? I bet that he did you-know-what as hard as a hammer with a nail. I bet he gave them a right pounding.

'Well, thank God, I have had five at least. Roll on number six. I don't care where or when, as long as he comes. I am not going to sew myself up. When my present husband goes the way of all flesh, I shall be looking for another. You can bet on it. What is the name of that apostle who said that was the best thing to do? "Better to marry than to burn." That's what he said. And he can say it again. I don't give a damn what people think. The father of Noah had two wives, didn't he? I saw them in the pageant play. It made no difference to him. And what about Abraham? What about Jacob? They were old holies, weren't they? And they had more than two wives. Plenty of these prophets did. Show me the passage where God forbids more than one marriage? Go on. Show me. You can't. Where is the part of the Bible that commands virginity? There isn't one. The apostle Paul says that he had no firm opinion on the matter. He may advise a woman to keep her virginity. That's fair enough. But he cannot order her. He leaves it up to her. If God Himself had wanted us all to be virgins He would not have invented marriage, would he? If we were never allowed to mate, then where would the next generation of virgins come from? Not even Paul dared to touch a subject that his master left alone. If there's a prize for virginity, I'm not going to compete for it. That's for sure. And I bet there won't be many runners.

'Not everyone will agree with me, of course. There are some people who stay virgins because they believe that they are per-forming God's will. Paul himself was a virgin, wasn't he? He may have wished that everyone else would follow his example, but he was just stating an opinion. He did not forbid me from marrying. How could he? So it is no sin to marry me, once the old man is dead. It will not count as bigamy. Of course it is always dangerous for a man to touch a woman, in bed at least. It is like putting a flame to dry wood. You know what I mean. But that is as far as I will go. Paul said only that he preferred the virgin to the married couple. The virgin is stronger.

'I grant you that. I have no quarrel with virgins. If they want to remain pure, in body and soul, I will not stop them. I can't criticize and, in any case, I make no great claims for myself. But let me put it this way. Not all the vessels in a house are necessarily made of gold. The wooden ones are good for certain purposes. A man can put his lips to wood as well as gold. Although it may not glitter, it serves its function. God calls men and women to different vocations. All of us have different talents – some can do *this*, others can do *that*. I can do *that*.

'I know that virginity is a form of perfection. Chastity is close to holiness. Christ Himself is perfection. But He did not tell people to surrender everything for the sake of the poor. He did not order them to give up their worldly goods and follow His footsteps. That was reserved for perfectionists, as I said. But, my lords, I am not one of those. I have a few years left in me yet, and I am going to devote them to the arts of married life. I will couple and thrive.

'And tell me this. Why does God give us those parts between our legs? Cunts are not made for nothing, are they? They are not unnecessary. Some will say that they have been created so that we can urinate. Others will say that they are just the marks to distinguish female from male. You know that isn't true. All experience tells us otherwise. I hope that none of you priests and nuns will be angry with me, but I must say this. We have been given our private parts for pleasure as well as necessity. We must procreate as well as pee, within the limits set by God. Why else is there the ruling that a wife must freely render her body to her husband? How is he going to receive it without using his you-know-what? I'll say it once again. Our parts are there for two purposes, for purging piss and for propagation.

'Now I am not claiming that every man and woman is bound to propagate. That would be absurd. That would be to deny the virtue of chastity. Christ was a virgin. And He had a male body, did He not? Many saints have been virginal, too. I expect that they had private parts. I will say nothing against them. They are loaves of the purest white bread, and we wives are buns of coarse barley. And yet Mark tells us that Christ Himself fed the multitude with barley bread. I am not fussy. I will fulfil the role that God gave me. I will use my hole, my instrument, my cunt, with as good a grace as He bequeathed it to me. If I am grudging about it, God will never forgive me. My husband can have it morning and night, whenever it pleases him. He can pay his debt any time. I want him to be my debtor and my slave. I will be troubling his flesh, as they put it, while I am married to him. I am given power over his body for the rest of my life. Is that not so? That is what Paul says. Paul also orders husbands to love their wives. I quite agree –'

The Pardoner suddenly rose from his saddle and interrupted her. 'Now, dame,' he said. 'By God and the cross you have been a noble orator in your cause. I was just about to get married myself but, hearing you, I am having second thoughts. Why should I put my flesh to so much trouble, as you put it? I don't think I will be wed at all.'

'Just wait a minute,' she said. 'I haven't begun my story yet. You may not find it a wholesome draught. It will not be as sweet as ale. But drink it down. I will tell you a story about unhappiness in marriage. I am old enough to be experienced in the subject – well, I was the one who held the whip. I know all about it. Do you still want to sip out of my barrel? I have given you fair warning. I will give you ten different examples of marital disaster. There may be more than ten. I am not sure. There is an old saying, "Forewarned is forearmed." I think those are the exact words of Ptolemy. Look it up. It's in one of his books.'

'Dame,' the Pardoner said to her, 'do begin. We are on tenterhooks until we hear you. Tell us the story, and spare no man in the process. Teach all the young men here your techniques.'

'Gladly,' she replied. 'If that is what you want. But yet I beg all of you to remember this. Don't get upset about anything I say. Don't take offence. I mean no harm. I just want to entertain you all.

'So now I will begin. I shall tell you the truth, so help me God. May I never taste wine or ale again if I deceive you. I have had, as I said, five husbands. Three of them were good, and two of them were bad. The three good ones were rich, and they were old. They were so old that they could hardly fulfil their duties. They could hardly rise to the occasion. You know what I mean. God help me, I can't help laughing when I remember how hard they tried. God, did they sweat. I set no store by them in any case. Once they had given me their land and their fortune, I wasn't bothered about the rest. I did not have to flatter or beguile them.

'They loved me so much that I took their love for granted. That is the truth of it. A wise woman will be busy looking for a lover only when she hasn't got one. But since I had them in the palm of my hand – and got all their money, too – why should I go to the trouble of pleasing them further? I could please myself instead. So I set them to work. Many nights they were exhausted and miserable. Were they unhappy with me? Well, let me put it like this. We would not have won many prizes for domestic bliss. Yet I got my way. I kept them sweet enough. They were always bringing me gifts from the local fair. And they were always happy when I spoke nicely to them. God alone knows that there were many times when I scolded them. Oh, did I nag them! Now, all you wives, listen to me carefully. Always be mistress in your household. If you need to, accuse your husbands of things they haven't done. That is the way to behave towards men. I tell you this much. Women are much better at lying and cheating than men. I am not telling this to experienced wives. They have no need of my advice. I am talking to those who are having trouble. A wise wife, if she knows what she is doing, can swear that fire is water. If a little bird whispers in her husband's ear, about something or other, she will call the little bird a liar. She will even get her maid to swear to her virtue. That's the way to do it.

'So this is the kind of thing I said: "Now, you old dotard, what have you got to tell me? Why is our neighbour's wife looking so pleased with herself? She is respected and flattered wherever she goes. And what about me? I am obliged to sit at home. I don't have any clothes to wear. And why are you always next door? Is that woman so good-looking? Or are you just randy? Why are you always whispering with my maid? Good God, man! Button up your trousers, you old lecher. And what if I do have a man friend? What's that to you? Why do you always complain if I just pop into his house for a minute or two? Then you come home rat-arsed, stinking of drink, and start lecturing me on my behaviour. What a load of nonsense. You go drivelling on about the curse of marriage. If you marry a poor woman, you say, then it costs a fortune. If you marry a rich woman, or a woman of high birth, you have to put up with her airs and graces. If she is good-looking, then you have to put up with her easy virtue. Oh yes, you say, any lecher can take her. Her virtue comes cheap. Everyone wants her, and everyone can have her. And all the while you are looking at me. How dare you?"

'I pause for breath and start again. "Then you start talking about women. Some men want them for their looks, and some for their money. Some men are only interested in their figures. Others are pleased if their women can sing or dance, or talk well, or are sociable. Some like slender hands and arms. Some like long legs. Oh, you say, no man can keep guard over these castles. The enemy is sure to get over the wall and make it inside.

'"An ugly woman lusts for any man she sees. According to you. She will leap on anyone with her tongue hanging out, like a spaniel, until she finds one who is willing to do it. There never was a goose so grey that it did not find its gander. Any itch can be scratched. This is your so-called philosophy. This is what you dole out to me when you come to bed. You say that no man needs to get married. No man who wants to get to heaven should consider it. Well, old man, may thunder and lightning strike you down! May your ancient withered neck be broken!

'"You tell me that there is an old proverb, 'The sight of a leaking roof, the smell of smoke, and the sound of wives, are enough to make a man flee from his home.' You silly old fool. What are you talking about? You say women will hide their vices until they are safely married. Only then will they show them. That is an idiot's opinion. They say that a good Englishman takes stock of his oxen and his cattle, his horses and his hounds, before he buys them. He tries out his bowls and his washbasins, his stools and his spoons, to make sure that they are sound. He even checks his chamber pots. Why does he not take the same precaution with his wife? You old dotard! You fool! How dare you say that we show our vices only when we are married?

'"And another thing. You say that I am only happy when you are praising my good looks. That I expect you to gaze lovingly upon me, and call me 'my most lovely wife' in public. I expect you to make my birthday a holy day, do I? And receive expensive presents? I never heard such nonsense in my life. You are supposed to receive my old nurse and my chambermaid in great state, and to entertain my father and all his relatives? Lies. All lies from the mouth of an old goat.

'"Oh yes. Then you make a fuss about our apprentice, Johnny. Just because he has lovely blond hair – it shines like gold, it really does – and just because he accompanies me on my shopping expeditions, you become suspicious. Johnny means nothing to me. If you died tomorrow, I would not give him a second look. And tell me this. Why do you hide the keys to your chest? It is as much mine as yours. Do you think you are going to make a fool out of me? You are not going to get my body and my goods. You must be mad even to consider it. You can have one or the other. But not both. Think about it, old man. What is the point of spying on me, and questioning the servants? If you had your way, I would be locked up in that damned chest as well. What you should be saying is this. 'Oh dear wife, please go wherever you like. Feel free. I won't listen to any rumours about you. I know you, Dame Alice, to be a true and faithful wife.' That is what you should say. We wives never like husbands who pry or who try to control us. We must be at liberty. That's the truth of it.

'"The best of all you men was that wise astrologer, Ptolemy. He was from Egypt, wasn't he? He wrote down a proverb in one of his books that sums it all up. 'The wisest man,' he said, 'is the one who minds his own business and does not worry about the conduct of the world.' You understand what he meant by that, I suppose? If you have enough, or more than enough, why should you bother about the pleasures of other people? Let me tell you this, you old goat. You will get cunt enough at night. Only a miser would stop a man lighting a candle with the flame from his lantern. Do you understand me? You will still be able to see in the dark. Don't worry. No one has stolen your flame.

'"I'm sick to death of hearing you say that we women should 'dress demurely and discreetly' just as if we were still virgins. You love to quote from the Bible, don't you? What is that text? 'No woman should be apparelled in precious stones or walk abroad with braided hair. No woman should dress herself in pearls or gold or fine fabrics.' What a load of nonsense. I can't even be bothered to argue with you about it.

'"What is that? I am like a cat, am I? You only have to singe my skin, and I will never roam from home? Is that what you think? But if the skin of a cat is sleek and shiny, then she will not stay in the house for half an hour. She will be on the tiles before daybreak, showing herself off and setting up such a caterwaul that every cat in the neighbourhood will know she's on heat. Do you get my drift? If I am in the mood, I will stray.

'"What good is it spying on me, you old fool? Argus was supposed to have a hundred eyes, but even he would not be able to stop me. Not unless I wanted him to lay his hands on me. Even so, I would still be able to fool him. You can count on it. You say that there are three types that torment the whole earth. They are – an upstart servant, a well-fed fool and a maid who is heir to her mistress. You tell me that the world cannot bear a fourth, namely a wife who is a shrew. You hateful old man. May God send you an early death. Why should you pick on wives, shrewish or not? Surely there are other candidates for that honour? Leave off your preaching.

'"And then you say that a woman's love is nothing but hell on earth, a piece of barren land without water. You compare it to wild fire; it burns out of control; the more it consumes in flame, the more it wishes to destroy. Then you change your metaphor. You compare the poor wife to a worm eating its way up a tree; she gets hold of her husband's vital parts, and eventually pulls him down. All husbands are supposed to know this, are they? Old dotard. Goat. Wait till I get my hands on you."

'And that, in a nutshell, is the way I talked to my five husbands. I really flattened them. I swore that they were drunk when they accused me of anything. I got dear Johnny and my maid to back me up. Oh Lord, the amount of trouble I caused them! And, to tell you the truth, they were quite innocent. I was like a filly. I could bite and whinny. I would scold them when I was really in the wrong. Otherwise I would have got the worst of it. That could not be allowed. The first one who comes to the mill is the first one to get bread. I called foul first. So I won the battle. They were quite ready to beg forgiveness for sins they had never committed. I accused them of having affairs with women, when they were so ill that they could hardly stand.

'Yet they put up with it. They really believed that I complained so much because, deep down, I loved them. Oh, I used to say, I go out at night because I want to check up on all the women you are screwing. With that excuse, I had quite a lot of fun myself. Women are born with these skills, you see. God gave us the gift of weeping and trimming and deceiving. I have been doing it all my life and, if I am allowed to boast, I must say that I managed to get the better of all of my husbands. Whether it was by trick or force, by nagging or complaining, I had the mastery. They got the worst of it in bed, of course. That's where I really gave them hell. If I felt their hands reaching out for me, I threatened to make a quick exit – unless, that is, they paid me some form of ransom. Once they had paid up, I let them do whatever they liked. I wasn't particular.

'So I tell you all this. You must pay for what you want. Everything in this world is for sale. An empty hand lures no hawk. You know that expression, I suppose. I would satisfy all their lusts, once my purse was full. Sometimes I even pretended to enjoy it. In fact I never really enjoyed the taste of tough old meat. That was probably the reason I gave them such a hard time. The pope himself could have been sitting right beside them, at table, and I would still have nagged them. I gave as good as I got. If I were making my last will and testament, I would still owe them nothing. I paid them word for word, so help me God. I was so smart and tricky that they gave up the fight. It was the best thing they could have done, believe me. Otherwise they would have had no rest. One or two of them may have looked at me like tigers, but they would never have got me in their jaws.

'This is what I said to one of them. "Oh look, sweetheart, at Willy." Willy was the name of our sheep. "Look at him. Look how meek and lovely he is. Come over to me now, dear, and let me give you a little kiss on your cheek. You should be like Willy. You should be patient and humble. You are always telling me about the patience of Job. Why not follow suit? You should practise what you preach. Is that not so? Otherwise I will have to teach you a harder lesson – that it is a good thing to keep a wife peaceful. One of us must give in. That's for sure. And it's not going to be me. A man is more reasonable than a woman, in any case, and must surely be able to bear more hardship. Why are you always moaning and complaining? Do you want to reserve my pussy for yourself? You can have it. Take it all. Go on. Take it. I know how much you love it. If I were able to sell it, I would be walking around in luxury. I can tell you that. But, no, I will keep it for you alone to graze on. But, by God, you do me wrong!" Those were my exact words to him.

'Let me tell you about my fourth husband. He was an old dog. He had a mistress, anyway. I was still young and full of life. I was a bit wanton, I admit, but I was strong and stubborn with it. I was as pert as a magpie. If anyone played the harp, I was up on my feet dancing. When I had drunk a glass of sweet white wine, I could sing like a nightingale in spring. Do you know the story of Metellius, who beat his wife to death because she liked her liquor? He would not have stopped me, even if I had been his wife. No one can keep me away from it. Once I have had a few, of course, I start thinking about you-know-what. Love is on my mind. Just as surely as cold weather makes hail or snow, so a greedy mouth makes for a greedy tail. A drunken woman is not going to be able to protect her virtue, is she? Every lecher knows that.

'Jesus, when I think about my youth, I can't help but laugh. All that fun. All that sex. The memories cheer me even now. I was on top of the world in those days. I was hot. Of course age poisons everything. It has taken my beauty. It has robbed me of strength. Well, let them go. Farewell to both of them. Let the devil take them. Now that the flour has gone, I have got to sell the bran. That's the sum of it. But I'm trying to keep up my spirits. Can't you tell?

'What was I saying about my fourth husband? Oh yes. I was furious when I imagined him in the arms of another woman. But I got my own back. My God. I made a cross for him out of the same wood. That's all I can say. I did not prostitute myself. Certainly not. But I was so friendly to other men, so approach-able, that I made him fry in his own fat. He simmered with anger and jealousy. I was his purgatory on earth. He suffered so much that his soul must have gone straight to heaven. When the shoe pinched, he cried out loudly enough. But no one, except God and my husband, knows how bitterly I tormented him. He died when I came back from my pilgrimage to Jerusalem. Now he lies buried before the main altar. I can't say that his tomb is as sumptuous as that of a king or emperor, but it will serve. It would have been a waste of money to build anything grand. Well goodbye, old man. May God give you rest in your coffin. Sweet dreams.

'Now I will tell you all about my fifth husband. I sincerely hope that he will not end in hell although, to tell you the truth, he was the worst behaved of all of them. God, he did beat me. I can still feel it in my ribs, and will do until my dying day. Ouch. Yet in bed he was so strong and supple that I have no complaints. He knew how to get the best out of me, especially when he grabbed hold of my fanny. I don't care how often he beat me. He knew how to kiss and make up. I loved him better than all the others. He played hard to get. He excited me. You know that we women have strange inclinations sometimes: we long most for the things we cannot have. It is perverse, isn't it? We will cry out and beg for the one thing forbidden to us. Deny us something, and we will desire it. Offer it to us, and we will run away. We spread out our wares and put on a show of indifference. You have seen it in the market. Nobody wants things that are sold too cheaply. A throng of buyers always puts up the price. Every woman knows this, if she knows anything.

'So I was talking about my fifth husband, Jankyn. God bless him. I took him for his looks and not for his money. He had been a student at Oxford but then he left university and took lodgings in the house of my old friend and townswoman Alison. God bless her, too. We used to gossip all the time. So she knew all my little secrets and desires better than our parish priest. I would not have told them to him in any case. But I told her everything. If my husband had pissed against the wall, she would have known about it. If he had done some dirty deed, I would have informed her straight away. I also used to whisper in the ear of my niece and another lady-friend, but I swear to you that otherwise I was very discreet. There were times when Jankyn got very hot and bothered about all this; he went red and grew short of breath. But, as I said to him, he only had himself to blame. He should not entrust his secrets to me, should he? It stands to reason.

'So it happened that one day, in the season of Lent, I was on my way to have an intimate chat with Alison. I did this all the time – March, April, May, whatever – since there is nothing I like more than hearing all the news of the town. You should see me darting from house to house! Well, on this day, in the company of dear Alison and of her new lodger, I decided to walk into the fields. My husband was in London for the whole of Lent. Thank God for that. I was not constantly looking over my shoulder. I had the chance of eyeing up some hunk. And I would be pretty visible, too. How did I know where luck might lead me? I did not really care what places we went to, as long as there were plenty of people around. So I went to vigils and to processions, to open-air preachings and to festivals. And of course I loved going on pilgrimages. You meet a better class of person, don't you think? Then I attended miracle plays and marriages. I always wore the same lovely red robes. There was no chance that the worms or moths would get at them, either. I put them on every day. They were gorgeous.

'Now I will tell you what happened next. I told you that the three of us were walking in the fields. I was having such a delicious conversation with Jankyn that, before I knew what I was saying, I told him that if I were a widow-woman he could have me. He could marry me there and then. Well, I did know what I was saying in actual fact. I am not boasting, but I do have a little bit of foresight left in me. I am prudent in marital matters, as in much else. If a mouse has only one hole, then it is asking for trouble; if that hole is blocked, then goodbye mouse. So I led him to believe that I had fallen madly in love with him (that's an old trick my mother taught me, by the way). I told him that I dreamed of him every night. I dreamed that he came into my bed and killed me, and that the sheets were drenched in blood. "But," I said to him, "this is a lucky dream. It is a good omen. Blood signifies gold, doesn't it?" Of course it was all a lie. I never dreamed of him at all. I always followed my mother's advice, though, in more ways than one. Now where was I? Oh yes!

'Fortunately my fourth husband was soon in his coffin. I wept buckets, as wives are supposed to do. Boo-hoo. I kept a sorrowful look upon my face and draped a black kerchief over my head. I followed the proper custom, in other words. But since I already had my eye on my next husband, you may believe that I mourned less in private. So my late husband was carried to the church, with all our neighbours following his bier. Jankyn was with them, too. What a great pair of legs he had! I had never seen a more handsome face in that church-yard. Even before I had entered the church, I had fallen for him. Do you blame me? He was only twenty years old. My age. No, I'm lying. I was forty by then, but I had the desires of a twenty-year-old. I had the hot blood of a colt. Venus was in my ascendant. What did I have to lose? I was fair, and rich, and well set up. And I wasn't that old. As my husbands always told me, I had the nicest pussy in England. I have got Mars in my heart, but Venus everywhere else. Venus gives me lust and lecherousness, but Mars grants me boldness. I was born under a good sign. So I ask you this. Why was love ever considered to be a sin? I have followed all my inclinations, by virtue of the constellations. I could no more withdraw my love from a handsome young man than I could disobey the stars. I will tell you something else. I have a red birthmark on my face, just where my hood hides it, and I have another one in a more private place.

'So God be my judge I have never been discreet. I have never been backward. I have always followed my appetites. I didn't mind if he was short or tall, black or white – if he liked me, I was on. I didn't care if he was rich or poor, noble or serf, as long as I had him.

'What else is there to say? At the end of the month, Jankyn was my new husband. We had a grand wedding. I gave him all my worldly goods, inherited from the previous four husbands. That is what marriage is all about. But, God, did I regret doing it! He was hard. He never let me do what I wanted. And he did beat me. Once I accidentally tore a page out of his book, and he went for me. He bashed me around the head so much that I became deaf in one ear. I still am. Yet I was stubborn. I was a lioness. And I had a loose tongue, too. He told me not to gossip in the neighbourhood, but I paid no attention to him. I still made my visits to Alison and the other dames. So then he began to preach at me, and cite all the ancient examples. There was one old Roman called Simplicius Gallus – I think that was his name – who left his wife for ever. What was her crime? One day he saw her standing on the doorstep with her head uncovered. Then there was another Roman who left his wife because she went to a midsummer revel without his permission. Can you believe it? Of course he quoted the Bible at me, too. He would recite that passage from Ecclesiastes which forbids men from letting their wives roam abroad. Then he would tell me this in a solemn voice: "A man cannot build a house with reeds. A man cannot ride a blind horse. It is even more foolish to have a wife that longs to go on pilgrimages. Such a man deserves to be hanged." What was I supposed to make of that? I made nothing of it. I ignored him. I despised his old sayings and proverbs. I was not going to be corrected by him. I hate anyone who tells me what my vices are. I'm sure that you all feel the same. This really made him mad, of course. But I was not going to put up with his whining.

'Let me tell you what happened about this book. I tore a page out of it, if you remember, and he beat me around the head. As I said, I am still deaf in one ear. He read this book all the time, night and day. He said that it was written by Valerius and Theophrastus, and that it was an attack upon women. He loved it. He lapped it up. There were other books bound up in the same volume. There was some cardinal at Rome, called Saint Jerome, who had written an attack on someone called Jovinian. Don't ask me what that was all about. Then there was a work by Tertullian, one by Chrysippus and one by Heloise who was an abbess near Paris. She was the one who ran after Abelard. I know all about her. Let me try to remember the other books. Oh yes. There was a copy of Solomon's proverbs and a book called *Ars Amatoria* by Ovid. There they all were, collected together.

'So he spent his time – when he wasn't working, that is – reading and rereading these old books. He loved to pore over the stories of wicked wives. He knew more stories about them than any scholar. He was not so interested in tales of good wives, even if they came from the Bible. I know for a fact, in any case, that no priest will ever speak well of wives or even of women. Unless they are saints, of course, when they don't really count as female. Who called the lion a savage beast? It certainly was not the lion itself. By God, if women had written the stories, instead of the monks in their cloisters, they would have made men so wicked that they would have been an accursed sex. Scholars and lovers are miles apart. Those under the sway of Mercury love study and learning, while those in the power of Venus love love itself. They love to party. That is why there is such a difference in temperament. When Venus rises, Mercury falls. When Mercury is in the ascendant, Venus is desolate. So no priest will ever praise a woman. When these pious men are old, and can no more make love than my old boot, then they will sit down and complain that women cannot keep their marriage vows. What old dolts!

'Let me get back to the point. I was about to tell you why Jankyn beat me up for meddling with his book. One evening the master of the house, as he liked to call himself, was sitting by the fire and reading. He read out to me the story of Eve, through whose wickedness all humankind was brought into woe. Only Jesus could save us, when He purchased our redemption with His holy blood. That is clear evidence, Jankyn told me, that a woman was responsible for the fall of mankind. It is an old argument. Then he read to me the tale of how Sampson lost his hair. It was cut off by his mistress, Delilah, while he slept. As a result, he was captured and blinded by the Philistines. Then he told me the story of Hercules and Deianira, and how the shirt she wove him consumed him in flames. Jankyn was thorough. He did not forget the trouble that the two wives of Socrates caused him. And how one of them, Xantippa, had thrown piss into his face. The poor innocent man stayed very still, as if he were dead, and then just wiped his face with a cloth. All he said was – "After the thunder comes the rain."

'As soon as he had finished that story, he told me all about Pasiphae, queen of Crete. He thought it was an excellent example of mad lechery and bestiality. I don't want to think about it. It was all too horrible. She must have been mad. And there was Clytemnestra, who, for the sake of her adulterous lusts, murdered her husband. He read out her history with great pleasure. He lectured me about the reason Amphiorax of Argos met his death. He knew the whole story. He was betrayed by his wife, Eriphily, who for a brooch of gold led the Greeks to the place where her husband was hiding. As a result, he died at the siege of Thebes. He was very indignant with Livia, wife of Sejanus, and with Lucia, wife of Lucretius. One killed her husband out of love, and the other out of hate. Livia poisoned her man, late one night, because he had become her enemy. Lucia, on the other hand, was so lecherous that she prepared an aphrodisiac for her husband. It was meant to ensure that he was besotted with her. But it was too powerful. He drank it and died before morning. Whatever way you look at it, the husbands come off worse. I am so sorry for them.

'That wasn't the end of it. Oh no. Jankyn told me about

another Roman of old times, Latumyus, who complained to a friend of his that in his garden there grew a tree of sorrow. Apparently, three of his wives had hanged themselves from its branches. Out of spite, I imagine. This friend, Arrius, clapped him on the back and said, "Listen, mate, let me have a cutting from that tree. It sounds great. I'd love to have one in my garden." Then Jankyn told me all about the wives that had killed their husbands in their beds. With the corpse lying on the floor, they would have sex in bed with another man. Other wives have driven nails into the brains of their husbands as they slept, while others have administered poison. He knew of more evil deeds than even I could imagine. And he knew more proverbs, too, than there are blades of grass or sands on the shore. "It is better," he said, "to live with a lion or a dragon rather than a nagging woman. It is better to live on the roof than share your bed with a shrewish wife. These women are so cantankerous and contrary that they hold in contempt what their husbands hold dear." That is what Jankyn said. You can imagine my reply. Then he told me another saying. "A woman casts off her shame when she takes off her dress." Oh, and here's another. "A good-looking women who has lost her virtue is like a gold ring in a sow's nose." Can you imagine how I felt? I was angry. I was in pain.

'When I realized that he was going to carry on reading that book – all bloody night, if necessary – I lost it. I grabbed the book from his hands and tore three pages out of it. Then I punched him in the face so hard that he toppled back into the fire. He got up like a wild animal and knocked me down with his fist; it was a powerful blow, and I lay on the floor as if I were dead. When he saw how still I was lying he got scared and would have run away. Men are like that. But then quick as a flash I came round. "Oh false thief," I whispered. "Have you finally killed me? Have you murdered me for the sake of my property? Oh Jankyn. Come to me. Let me kiss you before I die."

'That did it. He came over to me and kneeled down beside

me. "Oh sweet Alison," he said. "So help me God, I shall never strike you again! You know yourself what I have done. Forgive me, dearest. Have pity on me, I beseech you!"

'Then I got up and hit him again. "Now we are quits," I said. "I can die in peace. These are my last words." They were not, of course, and eventually we made up with much sighing and crying. I had won. He gave me the reins and I took control of my house and property. I also ruled over his tongue – and over his fists. What do you think I did with that book? I made him burn it. When I had taken charge of the household he came up to me and said, "My own true wife, my Alison, do as you please for the rest of your life. Just preserve my honour and my standing."

'From that day forward we never had an argument. I swear to God that I became the best wife in the world. I was loyal to him, and he was true to me. I hope his soul is now at peace in a better world. Shall I tell you my story now?'

Biholde the wordes bitwene the Somonour and the Frere

The Friar laughed when he heard all this. 'Now, ma dame,' he said, 'by God that was a long preamble to a tale!'

The Summoner was listening. 'What do you think?' he asked the other pilgrims. 'A friar will always be interfering. A friar is like a fly. He will alight on any dish and any meat. What is all this about preamble or perambulation, whatever you call it? Preamble yourself. Or trot, if you like. Or gallop ahead. You are spoiling our fun.'

'Is that all you have to say, sir Summoner?' the Friar replied. 'By God, before I leave you all, I will tell you a story about a summoner that will keep you in fits of laughter.'

'Fuck you, Friar. Before we get to Sittingbourne I will have told two or three tales about your profession that will reduce you to tears. I can see that you have already lost your temper.'

Harry Bailey intervened. 'Peace! No more squabbling. Let the woman begin her story. You two are behaving like drunks. Go on now, mistress, and tell us your tale.'

'I am ready, Mr Bailey. That is, if the worthy Friar here will let me continue.'

'Ma dame,' the Friar replied. 'Nothing would give me greater pleasure.'

The Wife of Bath's Tale

Heere bigynneth the Tale of the Wyf of Bathe

In the good old days, in the time of blessed King Arthur, this island was filled with spirits. It was a magical land. The queen of the fairies danced over green mead and meadow, with all her elves and pixies in attendance. That was what people believed, in any case. It must have been hundreds of years ago, by my reckoning. Now we live in the modern world. We no longer see fairies. Do you know why? They have been chased away by monks and friars who are forever purifying and sanctifying the different parts of the country. These clericals seek out woods and streams; they spread out over the land as thick as specks of dust in the sunbeam. They bless the halls, the chambers, the kitchens and the bedrooms; they bless cities, towns, boroughs, castles and high towers; they bless villages, barns, stables and dairies. That is why there are no more fairies. The friars now tread upon the elvish paths, morning and evening, saying their matins and their other holy offices; where there were once pixies there are now prayers. Of course a woman can feel much safer, knowing that there won't be an evil spirit beneath a bush or tree. She may meet a friar, of course. But he will take only her chastity, not her soul.

Once upon a time there was a knight at the court of King Arthur. One day this knight was riding by the riverside, without any company, when all at once he saw a young maid walking ahead of him. She was also alone. He took advantage of the situation, and raped her. She tried to fight him off, but she did not have the strength. This sinful deed caused such an uproar, and provoked such criticism at court, that the king ordered the knight to be executed. He would have been beheaded, according to the law, were it not for the fact that the queen and the other ladies of the court pleaded for his life. They cried, 'Mercy! Mercy!' so long and so loudly that the king eventually gave in and delegated the decision to his wife. She would decide whether the knight lived or died.

The queen thanked her lord for his graciousness and, as soon as she found the opportunity, she called the knight to her. 'Your fate is in the balance,' she said to him. 'You cannot be certain of your life. The day of your doom may be nearer than you think. I will save you, if you can tell me one thing. What is it that women most desire? Be careful! Think before you speak. That is the only way you will be able to rescue your neck from the executioner's blade. If you cannot give me the answer today, I will give you permission to leave the court. Seek out the answer far and wide. Then return here in a year and a day. Before you go, you must give me your solemn pledge that you will come back and surrender yourself to the court.'

The knight sighed, filled with doubt and perplexity. How could he answer such a question? Yet he had no real choice in the matter. In the end he decided that he would obey the queen's command. He would leave the court and return within a year and a day. He put his faith in God to find the right course for him, and jumped on to his horse. He tried every town and village, looking for enlightenment. 'What is it,' he said to one and all, 'that women desire most?' However hard he tried, he could not find a suitable answer. No two people agreed on the subject. Some said that women loved money the most; some said that they prized honour, and others pleasure. Some said that women wanted gorgeous clothes, but others chose sex as the main dish. Some said that women loved to be married, and widowed, often. Some said that they liked to be married and looked after in luxury. The knight was told that a man could win a woman with flattery. Or that any woman, young or old, rich or poor, could be caught by fuss and attention.

Of course there were others who claimed that us women really wanted our liberty. We wanted to do as we pleased, and not to be judged. I think there is a lot of truth in that. Who wants to be told that she is acting immodestly? I'll tell you one thing. If women are attacked on a sensitive point, then they will hit back. Try it, and you will see. Even if we are vicious on the inside, we need to appear virtuous and wholesome.

There were other arguments. Some people told the knight that, above all else, women wished to seem discreet and trust-worthy; they wanted to have a reputation for strength of mind, and for preserving secrets. That is rubbish, naturally. Women can never keep a secret. Have you heard the story of Midas?

According to Ovid and other learned writers, Midas had two great ass's ears concealed beneath his long hair. He was terrified lest anyone should find out about his deformity. That would be the end. So no one knew anything about it, except his wife. He loved her, and he trusted her. So he told her to keep quiet about this – this unfortunate development. Could she do that? Could she hell! Of course she swore to him that she would lose everything in the world rather than reveal his secret. It would be evil, she said, to besmirch the honour of her dear husband. It would shame her, too, beyond reckoning. Yet she almost died with the effort of suppressing the truth; she was sure that she would burst, that the words would make their way out somehow. Do you know that feeling? I do. She had promised to tell no one. So what was she to do? She ran down to some marshland near the house, her heart pounding, and put her mouth close to the reeds and the water just like a heron. 'Now,' she said to the water, 'don't betray me. Don't repeat this. I am going to tell you something that I will never tell anyone else. My husband has the ears of an ass! God. I feel so much better now that I've said it. I am so relieved that I have let go of the secret.' It just proves that we women cannot keep a confidence for very long. The words will pour out. If you want to learn the rest of the story, you will have to look it up in Ovid.

When the knight realized that he was never going to find an answer to the question – what do women love most – he felt ill at ease and unhappy. But the day for his return had come. He had to go home and attend the queen's court. On his way back, full of care, he happened to ride through a forest. There, by the side of the track, he saw a most amazing spectacle. There were twenty-four or more young maidens dancing in a ring among the trees. He was drawn to them, in the hope that he might acquire some secret wisdom from this circle of young women. Yet as he came up to them, they vanished into thin air. The dance had gone. He looked around in bewilderment. It was then that he saw an old crone, sitting on the upturned trunk of a dead tree. He had never come across an uglier woman. 'Sir knight,' she said, 'this is not the way for you. Tell me what you want here. What are you looking for? It may be that I can help you. Old women are sometimes wise women.'

'Dear mother,' the knight replied, 'I will die unless I find the answer to one question. What is it that women desire most? If you could tell me the solution, I will forever be in your debt.'

'Give me your word then. Take my hand and swear. If I provide you with the answer, then you must do whatever I require of you. Anything within your power. If you agree, then I will tell you the secret before nightfall.'

'I plight to you my oath as a knight,' he said.

'Then I am sure that your life is safe. Trust me. I have no doubt at all that the queen will agree with me about this. The proudest of all the great ladies, with all their jewels and fine headgear, will not dare to contradict me.' Then she whispered some words into his ear. 'Come now,' she added, more loudly. 'Be happy. Be confident. Let's travel on to the court without delay.'

When they arrived at the palace, the knight attended the queen as he had promised her. He announced that he had an answer to the burning question. You can imagine the excitement among all the women. The wives, the paramours, the maids, the widows, all came to the court. The queen was there, too, ready to give judgement before the assembly. Everyone was waiting to hear what he would say. The queen called for silence, and then ordered the knight to come forward. 'Tell us now, gentle knight,' she asked him, 'what is your answer? What do women desire most?'

The knight did not hang his head, like a beast in its stall. He stepped forward and, before them all, responded to her in a ringing voice. 'My liege, my lady, women desire to have sovereignty over their husbands and over their lovers. They wish to dominate them. Kill me if you wish. But that is the truth. I stand here before you. Do with me as you will.'

There was a general murmur of approval. Not a wife or widow or virgin disagreed with what he said. They all concurred that he had won his life. As soon as this was clear, the old crone came forward. 'Justice!' she called. 'Justice, sovereign queen! Before the court disperses, listen to my plea. I was the one who taught this answer to the knight. I made him swear an oath that, in return, he would grant me any wish that lay within his power. I vow to you that I am telling the truth. Now that I have saved his life, the time has come.' She turned to face him. 'Now, sir knight, I ask that you marry me without delay. I wish to be your wife.'

He looked at her in horror. 'Oh my God! Is that it? How can I? I admit that I did swear an oath to you. But for God's sake ask for something else. Take all my money. Anything. But don't take my body.'

'No way. I will not betray myself, or you. I may be foul and old and poor, but I don't want your money. I would not part with you for all the gold in the world. I only want your love.'

'My love? No. My ruin. My despair. I am to be degraded and disgraced.'

He complained in vain. It was determined that he must marry this old woman. He was also obliged to go to bed with her. I wish that I could tell you all about the happy festivities and the joyful ceremonies that accompanied the union. But I can't. There were none. There were no speeches of congratulation, no toasts, no wedding cake. There were, instead, expressions of sorrow and pity. He married her secretly the next morning, and then hid himself from the light of day like an owl. He could not look at her, ugly and dirty as she was. When eventually he got into bed with his new wife, he was disgusted and ashamed; he turned and twisted beneath the sheets, while she just lay there with a smile on her face. 'Oh husband dear,' she said. 'Bless me! Is this the way that knights treat their new brides? Is this the household law of King Arthur? Is everyone of your rank so shy? I am the love of your life, your own wife. I am the woman who saved you. I have never done you any harm. I know that much. So why are you behaving like this on our first night together? You are writhing like a madman. What is my crime? Tell me, for God's sake. If I can amend it, I will do so.'

'Amend it? I don't think so. There is nothing you can do about it. You are old. You are ugly. You come from such low stock that it is little wonder that I twist and turn. My lineage is besmirched! I wish to God that my heart would break!'

'Is that the only reason for your distress?'

'Only! What do you think?'

'Well, sir, I think I can cure it. I think I may do you a service, in a day or two if necessary. If you showed me a little bit more consideration, I might help you out. But please don't go on about your high rank. You get your lineage from old money. That is all. It isn't worth a damn. It is sheer conceit. You should be more concerned with human virtue. You should give more consideration to those who perform good works, in private and in public. They are the real gentlemen. Our Saviour tells us that true nobility comes from His example, not from the money bags of our rich ancestors. Although they may give us all of their worldly goods, from which we claim good breeding, they cannot bequeath to us the gift of holy living. An honest man is made by honest deeds. That is the only lesson your forefathers can impart to you.

'I suppose you know the high words of the Florentine poet,

Dante, who taught us this sentence – "A man cannot climb heavenward on his own slender branches. God wills us to claim from Him our strength and purpose." The only things we can inherit from our ancestors are material goods that in fact may harm or injure us. Everyone knows this as well as I do. If virtue were of natural growth in certain families, proceeding down the line from parent to child, then they could do nothing but good. It would be impossible for them to be caught in villainy or vice.

'Take a piece of fire. Carry it into the darkest house between here and the Caucasian mountains. Shut the doors upon it and depart. The fire will keep on burning, pure and unsullied, just as if twenty thousand people were observing it. It will perform its natural function until it expires. I stake my life upon it. So now you may understand what I have been telling you. Gentility cannot be borrowed or purchased. Fire is always and forever fire. Men are of more mixed natures, susceptible to change. God knows it happens often enough that the son of a nobleman behaves shamefully. There are some who make great play of their ancestry, and of their virtuous grandfathers and great-grandfathers, but who themselves are only notable as villains. They are not like their ancestors at all. A man may call himself a lord or an earl but, in reality, he is a sot and a churl. Nobility is the renown won by others who came before you. It does not belong to you by right of birth. God alone can grant you virtue. God alone is the source and spring of grace.

'Valerius Maximus was a Roman author. Have you heard of him? He praises the nobility of Tullius Hostilius, who rose from poverty to become the third king of Rome. That Hostilius was a real gentleman. Seneca, and Boethius, both teach us that gentle natures are seen in gentle deeds.

'And therefore, dear husband, I conclude as follows. Even if my ancestors were humble, I hope by the grace of God and by my own efforts to lead a virtuous life. When I choose virtue, and eschew sin, then I will be a gentlewoman. And do you blame me for my poverty? Did not the Saviour, the incarnate

God, choose a poor life on earth? Every man, woman and child will surely know that Jesus, king of heaven, would not have made a bad or sinful choice. Seneca and other philosophers tell us that cheerful and willing poverty is a great blessing. Whoever is satisfied with a slender purse, even though he does not have a shirt on his back, I hold rich indeed. He who is greedy is wretched; he longs for that which he cannot have. He that has nothing, and wants nothing, is a man of wealth; you may call him a knave, but I call him a spiritual knight. Poverty sings. You may know that quotation from Juvenal, to the effect that the poor man whistles and dances before thieves. Poverty may seem hateful but it is in truth a blessing. It encourages hard work. It teaches the wise man patience. It teaches the patient man wisdom. It may seem miserable. It may be a state no one wishes. But it brings us closer to God. It brings us self-knowledge. Poverty is the eyeglass through which we see our true friends. So therefore, dear husband, cease your complaining. I have done you no harm. Do not rebuke me for my poverty.

'But then you tell me that I am old. I don't know whether it is taught in any learned books, but I always believed that gentlemen were meant to reverence old age. You call an old man "father", do you not? I am sure that I could find many authors who say so. Why, then, do you call me "foul" and "ancient"? At least you will not be a cuckold. Age and ugliness are the best guardians of chastity in existence. Nevertheless I know that you have a good appetite. I will satisfy it as best I can. So choose now one of two things. You can have me old and ugly until I die, in which case I will be your humble and faithful wife obedient in everything. Or you can have me young and beautiful, in which case you can expect many visitors in the house; the crowd may flock to another warm place, too, but I leave that to your imagination. Which will it be? Choose now and forever hold your peace.'

The knight thought about this and could not make up his mind. He sighed, and shook his head, and sighed again. Finally he said, 'Dear wife, my lady and my love, I put myself in your hands. Choose whichever fate most pleases you. And choose the one most honourable to both of us. I don't care which way you decide. As long as you want it.'

'So am I in control?' she asked him. 'May I decide what is best for our marriage?'

'Sure,' he replied. 'That suits me.'

'Then kiss me. We no longer need to quarrel. By my oath I will now be both women for you. I will be beautiful and faithful, too. May I die a mad woman rather than let you down! I will be as good and true to you as any wife ever was or ever will be. And that's not all. In the morning I will be as fair as any lady, empress or queen in the whole world. Do with me what you will. But now just lift up the curtain and look at me.'

The knight was amazed to find her as young and as beautiful as she had promised. He took her up in his arms joyfully, and kissed her a thousand times. True to her word, she obeyed him in everything. She never once displeased him. And so they lived together in peace and harmony for the rest of their lives. God send us all gentle husbands – especially if they are young and good in bed. Pray to God, too, that we women outlive them. Cursed be the men who will not obey their wives. And double curses to mean husbands! That is all I have to say.

Heere endeth the Wyves Tale of Bathe

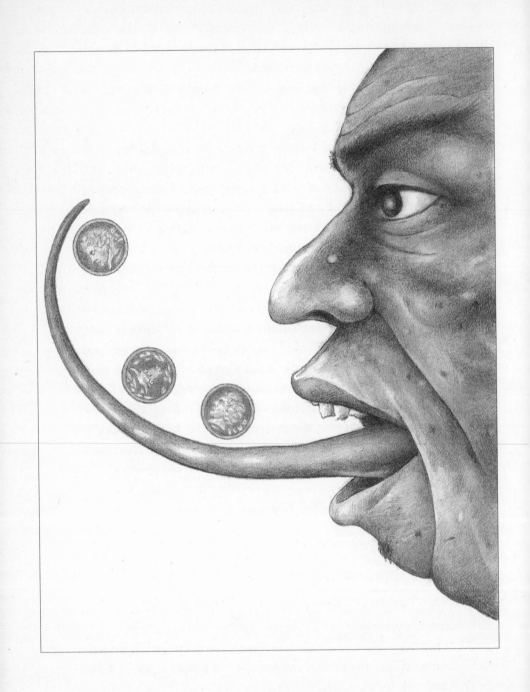

The Friar's Prologue

The Prologe of the Freres Tale

That worthy man, that Friar, had been frowning and glowering at the Summoner all the time that the Wife had been speaking. He had not forgotten their argument. But, for the sake of decency, he had not said anything vicious. Now he spoke up. 'Dame Alison,' he said, 'good Wife of Bath, God send you a long life! I swear that you have touched upon a matter for debate by scholars, and you have acquitted yourself very well. But, ma dame, while we are riding here together our only task is to entertain one another. There is no need to engage in moral discussion. Leave that to the priests in their pulpits. So, if the rest of the company are agreed, I will now tell you a funny story about a summoner. I think you will all admit that there is nothing good to be said about that profession. Summoners are the pits. Of course I am not referring to any individual here.' He glanced at the Summoner before continuing. 'A summoner is a jackal. He runs up and down with writs of arrest for fornication. And of course, consequently, he gets beaten up all the time.'

Harry Bailey, our Host, interrupted him. 'Good Friar,' he said, 'please be polite. A man of the cloth ought to be courteous to others. We will have no arguments between ourselves. Get on with your story. And leave the Summoner alone.'

'Let him say what he likes,' the Summoner replied. 'It doesn't worry me. When my turn comes, I will pay him back in kind. I will tell him all about friars, false flatterers as they are. I have a lot of dirty stories about them that I will keep in reserve. He will learn what it is to be a friar.'

'Peace. No more.' Our Host put up his hand. 'Now, good master Friar, will you please tell your story without more delay? It is getting late.'

The Friar cleared his throat.

The Friar's Tale

Heere bigynneth the Freres Tale

Once upon a time there was living in my district an archdeacon, a man of great position who sat in judgment on all
sorts of matters – fornication, witchcraft, bawdy, slander,
adultery. That kind of thing. He laid down the law on robbery,
violations of contract, making of wills, failure to take the
sacraments, usury and simony. He was tough, but he was
really hard on those caught in the act of lechery. He made them
pay for it. Did they sing! Then there were those who did
not pay the proper taxes to the Church. If any parish priest
complained about them, they were severely punished by the
archdeacon. They never escaped a very heavy fine. If anyone
gave a small offering in church, or a small tithe, he was in
trouble. He was in the archdeacon's black book before he
could be hooked by the bishop's staff. The archdeacon had
all the authority he needed; he represented Church justice,
after all.

Now among his officers there was a summoner. There
was no more crafty man in England. He had his own secret
network of spies, who told him exactly what was going on.
So he could go easy on one or two adulterers, as long as they
led him to a score of others. I can see that our Summoner here
is becoming angry. His nose is twitching like the snout on a
March hare. But I will not spare him on that account. I will
reveal all. He has no authority among us, does he? He cannot
punish us now or ever –

'That is what all the harlots say,' exclaimed the Summoner.

'You can't touch us. We are in the liberties. No wonder a harlot like you follows suit.'

'Stop this!' Our Host was very firm. 'God's punishment on you if you carry on like this! Continue with your story, sir Friar, and pay no attention to the Summoner. Don't spare his blushes.'

'Thank you, Mr Bailey. As I was saying –'

This false thief, this villain, this summoner, had any number of pimps ready to inform on their clients. They were like tame hawks in his hand. They had known most of these lechers a long time, and were quite happy to spill all their secrets. So they were the summoner's confidential agents. And he made a lot of money out of them. The archdeacon never knew the half of it. He never got the half of it, either. He had to be content with less. The men themselves were happy to bribe the summoner, of course. He could have called them to court, on pain of excommunication. Many of them could not even read his summons. So they filled his purse. They plied him with ale in the tavern. Just as Judas was a thief, taking the money given to him for safe-keeping by the apostles, so likewise was he. Let me give him his full title: he was a thief, a fraud, a lecher and a summoner. He had some women to service him. They were prostitutes, of course, and they whispered in his ear if Sir Robert, or Sir Hugh, or plain Jack, had fucked them. So he and the women were in league together. He would make up some false summons, bring them to judgment, fine the man and let off the woman.

'Friend,' he would say, 'I will strike the woman's name from the record for your sake. You don't want it known, do you? Don't worry. Everything is settled. I am your friend. I want to help you.' He knew of more ways to extort money than I could recount to you. It would take me years. There is no hunting dog that does not know a wounded deer from a healthy one. It was the same with him. He could smell a lecher, or an adulterer, or a whore, a mile away. Since that was the way he earned his living, he bounded after them with his tongue hanging out.

So it happened that, one day, this worthy summoner was after some new prey. He was about to pay a call on an elderly woman, an old trout from whom he was about to extort money on some trumped-up charge or other. It so happened that, as he was riding through the forest, he came upon a jolly yeoman; this young man was carrying his bow, with bright, sharp arrows. He was wearing a green jacket, and a smart black cap with tassels. 'Hail and well met!' called out the summoner.

'The same to you!' the yeoman replied. 'Where are you riding today beneath the greenwood trees? Are you going far?'

'No. Not really. I am travelling only a short distance. I have to collect the rent for the lord of my manor. And earn myself a little fee for the trouble.'

'Oh, so you are a bailiff?'

'That's right.' He would not admit, out of shame, that he was actually a summoner. He might as well pour shit on his head.

'Good God,' said the yeoman. 'What a coincidence. I am a bailiff, too. Isn't that something?' Then he grew more confidential. 'The trouble is that I don't know this area at all. So I would be very happy to make your acquaintance, brother with brother, and learn a thing or two. I have gold and silver in my box here. And if you should ever venture into my shire, in turn, I will be very happy to look after you.'

'That's very kind of you,' the summoner replied. He held out his hand. 'Put it here.' Then they shook hands, swore an oath that they would be true to each other until death, and rode on together in great good spirits. The summoner was as full of gossip as a carrion crow is full of worms. So he kept on questioning the yeoman about this and that. 'Now tell me this,' he asked him. 'Where exactly do you live? Where would I be able to find you?'

The yeoman answered him softly. 'I live far off in the north country. I hope very much to see you there. I will give you such directions, before we part, that you will never mistake my dwelling.'

'Now, dear brother,' the summoner went on. 'Tell me this as well. Just between the two of us, riding together. Since you are a bailiff like me, let me know some of your tricks. How I can make the most of my position? You know what I mean. Don't hold back for fear of offending me. You won't do that. We are all sinners. Just tell me. How do you do it?'

'I will tell you the truth, brother bailiff. I will be straight with you. My wages are low, and my lord is very demanding. I have a hard time of it, I can tell you, and so I am forced to live by bribery and extortion. I admit it. I take as much as I can. Sometimes I use low cunning, and sometimes I use force. That's the way I earn my living. There's nothing more to say.'

'Snap,' said the summoner. 'It's the same with me, too. I'll steal anything, God knows, as long as it is not too heavy or too hot. What I earn privately is my own business. I don't lose any sleep over it. If I didn't steal, I wouldn't live. It's as simple as that. And I'm not about to confess my sins to the priest. I have no pity. I have no conscience. These holy confessors can go fuck themselves. So there, sir, we are well mated and well met. Just one more thing. What do they call you?'

The yeoman began smiling, when he asked the question. 'Do you really want to know my name? To tell you the truth, I am a fiend. My dwelling is in hell. I ride about the world searching for gains. I like to find out if men like you will give me anything. That is the only profit I can earn. We are engaged in the same trade, you see. To get something, anything, is the sum of my endeavour. I will ride to the end of the world to find my prey. I am riding now.'

'God in heaven,' the summoner replied. 'What are you saying? I really thought that you were a yeoman. You have the shape of a man, just like mine. Do you have the same form in hell, where you chiefly dwell?'

'Certainly not. We have no shape in hell. But we can adopt whatever form we fancy, or else make it appear so. I can appear as a human being, or as an ape; I can even take on the form of a bright angel. Why are you surprised? A second-rate conjuror can deceive you easily enough. So why cannot I? I have more experience, after all.'

'So you are telling me that you can ride around in different shapes. You are only a yeoman for a short while?'

'Of course. I take whatever shape is necessary. To trap my prey.'

'Why, sir fiend, do you go to all this trouble?'

'There are many reasons, dear summoner. Now is not the time to explain them. The day is short. It is already past nine, and I have not yet found my quarry. I must attend to business, if you don't mind, and not spend the time revealing all my plans. Don't take this the wrong way, brother, but I doubt that you are capable of understanding them in any case. You asked me why we take such trouble. Well. Sometimes we are the instruments of God himself, fulfilling His commandment. He wreaks his will on humankind in various ways and for various reasons. We have no strength or purpose without Him. That is certain. Sometimes, if we ask kindly enough, we are allowed to afflict the body rather than the soul. Job is a case in point. We certainly punished him. There are occasions when we can do some harm to the soul as well as to the body. That's the fun part. There are other times when we can attack the soul, but not the body. It all depends. It works out well, in any case. I'll tell you why. If anybody can resist our temptations, then he or she will go to heaven. That was not our intention, of course. We want the soul to settle down with us. And there are even occasions when we act as servants to mankind. Take the case of Archbishop Dunstan. He used to be able to control us devils. I myself have served one of the apostles in a lowly way. But that's a long story.'

'Can you tell me this?' The summoner was now thoroughly absorbed in the conversation. 'Is it true that you make your new bodies out of the elements themselves? Out of the wind and the fire?'

'Not really. Sometimes we create the illusion of that. Yet there are other times when we reanimate the bodies of the dead and rise from their graves. Did you hear about the witch of Endor, who conjured up the spirit of Samuel before King Saul of Israel? Some people claim that it was not Samuel at all. I don't know. I am not a theologian. But I'll warn you of one thing. I won't deceive you. Soon enough you will find out about our changing shapes. You will not need to learn anything from me. You will know the truth from experience. You will be able to lecture on it, write books about it more learned than those of Virgil and of Dante. Come on. Let us ride. I enjoy being in your company. I'll stay with you until you tell me to piss off.'

'That's not going to happen,' the summoner replied. 'I am a yeoman, and widely respected. I am known to keep my word, and I would stick to it even if you were Satan himself. We are brothers, you and I, and we will be true to one another. We will help each other in our various trades. You take what you can, and I shall do the same. We are both businessmen, after all. But if one of us makes a killing, then he should share it with the other. That is fair, don't you think?'

'I grant you that,' the fiend said. 'On my honour.'

So they rode forth on their way. They passed through the forest and very soon came up to the village where the summoner hoped to exact some tribute. Here they happened to see a cart filled with hay, being driven with some difficulty by a carter. The road was deep in mud, and the wheels were lodged in it. They could not be moved. The carter was frantic, and kept on shouting at the horses. 'Come on, Brock!' he screamed. 'Come on, Scot! What are you stopping for? Get a move on! The devil take the lot of you, as whole as you were born! I have gone through hell today because of you. Well, you can go to the devil – hay, cart and horses!'

'This is going to be fun,' the summoner murmured to his companion. 'Did you hear what that oaf said? Did you hear the carter? He offered you the cart and the hay. And his three horses. What do you say to that?'

'Not much. He doesn't really mean it, you see. If you don't

believe me, go and ask him. Just wait for a moment. You will learn that I am right.'

The carter began to strike his horses on their hindquarters, all the while urging them on with the reins, until finally they began to move. They put their heads down and dragged the cart from the mire. 'That's good,' the carter exclaimed. 'Jesus Christ bless you! Well done, you dappled beauties! All the saints in heaven preserve you. You have got us free.'

'What did I tell you?' the fiend asked the summoner. 'This is a lesson for you, dear friend. The carter said one thing, but he thought another. Let's be on our way. I am going to earn nothing here. This is a waste of time.'

So they rode through the village. Just as they came to the edge of it, the summoner rode up to his companion and whispered in his ear again. 'There is an old woman living around here, who would sooner risk her neck than lose a penny. I'll get some money out of her, so help me. Otherwise she will end up in court. She hasn't done anything wrong, of course, but that doesn't matter. The important thing is to get her. You haven't had much luck so far, but I'll show you how it's done. Just watch.'

When they came up to the old widow's door, the summoner began beating on it. 'Come out, you old trout!' he shouted. 'Have you got some priest or friar with you? You old hag!'

'Who is knocking?' The old woman opened the door a fraction. 'God save us! What do you want, dear sir?' She knew that he was the summoner.

'I have a bill of summons here,' he said. 'On pain of excommunication I command you to attend the archdeacon's court tomorrow. There you will have to respond to certain charges made against you.'

'May God be my witness,' she said, 'I have done nothing wrong. I have been ill for a long time, in any case, and I cannot go very far. I can only hobble and, sir, I could no more get on a horse than on your back. The pain in my side is something dreadful. Can you not give me a written statement of the case?

Then I can get someone to answer the charges for me in open court.'

'If you pay up now, I'll consider it. Now let me see. Yes. Twelve pence should do it. If you pay me those twelve pence, I'll drop all charges. I shan't make much profit myself. It all goes to my lord and master. But for your sake I'll do it. Come on. Cough up. Where's the money?'

'Twelve pence!' she exclaimed. 'Mary, Mother of God save me from ruin! If I were to gain the whole world by it, I still haven't got the money. Twelve pence? I've never seen so much money in my life. You can see well enough, sir, what I am. Have pity on a poor old hag.'

'No way. If I let you off, may the devil take me! Pay up, even if it kills you.'

'In God's truth, I don't have any money.'

'Pay me now. Otherwise I will confiscate your brand-new frying pan. The one I can see lying in the corner. Don't you remember the debt you owe me for cheating on your husband? I paid your fine then to the archdeacon.'

'That's a lie! I swear to God that I have never once been summoned to your court, as a wife or as a widow-woman. I have always been honest.' She fell down on her knees in an attitude of prayer. 'May the black and smoking devil take you – and my frying pan, too, if he wants it!'

When the devil heard her curse, he said gently to her, 'Mother Mabel, is this what you really want? Are you saying this in earnest or in game?'

'In deadly earnest, sir. If this summoner does not repent his lies, may the devil carry him off. And he can take my frying pan with him.'

'Well, you old bitch,' the summoner replied. 'I don't repent anything I have ever had of you. I would take your smock, if I could. I would strip every stitch off your back.'

'Don't be angry, dear brother,' the fiend said. 'Your body and her frying pan are mine by right. You must descend to hell with me tonight, where I will teach you all of our secrets. You will become more learned than any theologian.' And, with that, the devil caught him in his arms and carried him off. The soul and body of the summoner were taken to the place where all summoners eventually retire. May God, who made us in His own image, grant us all salvation. May He even teach summoners to become good men.

I could have told you, gentlemen and gentle ladies – and, if I had time, I could have told this Summoner here – what Christ and the apostles have said about the pains of hell. That cursed house is filled with pain and suffering which I could not describe in the space of a thousand winters. No mind can conceive of it. No tongue can tell it. May Jesus our Saviour keep us from that evil place, and may He protect us from the wiles of Satan. Beware. Stay alert. Remember the old proverb: 'The lion is always poised to slay and eat the innocent, if ever he gets the chance. Dispose your hearts so fittingly that you will be able to withstand the snares of the devil.' The fiend cannot tempt you beyond your strength. Remember that. Christ will be your champion and your knight. Let us pray that all the summoners of this nation repent their misdeeds before they are taken down to hell. Amen.

Heere endeth the Freres Tale

The Summoner's Prologue

The Prologe of the Somonours Tale

The Summoner stood up in his stirrups and shook his fist at the Friar; he was so angry that he was shaking like an aspen leaf. He was as mad as hell. 'I want only one thing, fellow pilgrims,' he said. 'I ask you, out of courtesy to me, now that you have heard this false Friar lying through his teeth, to listen to my tale. This Friar boasts that he knows all about hell. I am not surprised. Friars and fiends are very closely related. You must have heard the story about the friar who was taken to hell in a vision. When the angel guided him through all the circles and pains of that inferno, the friar could see none of his brethren. There were plenty of other people in torment, but there were no friars. So he spoke up and asked the angel, "Tell me, sir, are friars so virtuous that none are damned?"

'"No indeed," the angel replied. "There are millions of them here." The spirit led him down to the body of Satan himself. "Do you see the demon's tail?" he asked the friar. "It is as broad as a sail on a great ship, is it not? Just look what is beneath it. Hold up your tail, Satan! Let us see your arse. Let the friar see where all his brethren are hiding."

'Satan did as he was told. A couple of minutes later the friars came out like a swarm of bees. They were pushed and prodded by junior fiends; they ran in all directions, here and there through the precincts of hell, till on one accord they fled back up Satan's fundament. Then the devil covered his arse with his tail, and settled down again.

'When the friar had thoroughly acquainted himself with all

the miseries and mysteries of hell, his spirit returned to his body. He awoke in his own bed, by God's mercy, but he was so fearful that he sweated and shook. He could not get the arse of the devil out of his thoughts. That was the place he was heading for.

'God save all of you gentlemen and ladies – all except the cursed Friar here. Now I will get on with my story.'

The Summoner's Tale

There is in Yorkshire, I believe, a marshy area known as Holderness. Or is it a town? I can't remember. Anyway, there was a friar who frequented the area, preaching and begging in the usual fashion of his breed. His name was Friar John. It so happened that one day he had given a sermon in one of the local churches. It was the same old story. Donate alms for the sake of masses for the dead. Donate alms so that we can build more friaries and honour God Almighty. Don't give money where it will only be wasted and misspent. Don't support those who are already living in luxury, thanks be to God, like the monks and the priests. 'Your alms,' he said, 'can release the souls of all folk, young and old, from the pains of purgatory. It does not matter if the prayers at the mass are sung hastily. I will not accuse any priest of being frivolous or wanton for saying only one mass a day. Far from it. These poor souls must be delivered from their torments as quickly as possible. It is hard for them to endure the flesh-hooks and the spikes. It is agony for them to be torn to pieces or burned or boiled. Can you imagine it? So give me your money quickly, for all their sakes.'

When the friar had finished his little sermon, he blessed the congregation and went on his way. But not before the folk in the church had given him their coins. As soon as that was settled, he was off. He was not going to stay around. With his satchel and his staff, tucked up in his belt, he went from house to house begging for bread or cheese or corn. He was always peering through the windows and putting his head around open doors. He had a companion with him, too, who carried with him a set of writing tablets and a long pointed pen. He told the people that this allowed him to note down the names of all those who gave him alms, so that he could pray for them later. 'Give us a little portion of wheat, malt or rye,' he would whine. 'Give us a piece of cake, or a morsel of cheese. Whatever you have, we will take. We are not fussy. A penny or a halfpenny will do. We would love some meat, of course, if you have any to spare. No? Well then give me the cloth blanket I see over there. Look, dear sister, we are ready to write down your name. How do you spell it? Are you sure that you don't have a morsel of bacon or of beef?' They were followed by a servant, who worked for the landlord of the inn where they were staying; he was carrying a sack. Whatever the people gave them, he added to the load on his back.

As soon as the friar had left the neighbourhood, however, he would take out the writing tablet and erase the names he had just put down. It was all a trick, an act, on his part.

'This is all lies!' The Friar was very indignant.

'Peace!' Harry Bailey called out. 'For the love of God go on with your story, sir Summoner. Go on till the end. Leave out nothing.'

'That's what I intend,' the Summoner replied. 'You can be sure of it.'

So Friar John went from house to house, until he came to one where he was accustomed to hospitality. He was sure of getting something here. But the good man who lived here was sick; he was lying upon a low couch, and could scarcely rise. 'God be with you,' the friar said. 'Good day to you, Thomas. And may God reward you, my friend. I have been very well fed at this table. I have enjoyed many meals, haven't I?' He shoved the cat from its favourite chair – put down his stick, his satchel and his hat – and then sat down at the table with a smile on his face. He was alone. His friend had already gone into town, with the servant, in order to book rooms in the inn for that night.

'Oh my dear master,' the sick man said, 'how have you been this last week or two? I haven't seen you for a while.'

'God knows, Thomas, I have been hard at work. I have been working for your salvation. You would never believe the number of prayers I have offered up for you and for my other friends in Jesus. I have just come from your parish church, as a matter of fact, where I delivered a sermon during mass. It was a poor thing, but it was my own. It was not entirely based on scriptures, of course, because I prefer to paraphrase and interpret in my own way. Holy writ is too hard for some to understand. So paraphrase is a good alternative. Do you know that phrase we friars use? The letter killeth. I simply told the congregation to be charitable, and give their money for a good cause. I saw your wife there, by the way. Where is she now?'

'She's in the backyard, I think. She'll be here in a minute.'

And then stepped in the good wife. 'Welcome, holy friar,' she said, 'in the name of Saint John. Are you keeping well?'

The friar rose to his feet very politely, put his arms around her very tightly, and kissed her on the lips. He was chirping like a sparrow. 'Never felt better in my life, good woman. I am yours to command in all things. I saw you in church today, you know. I have never seen a prettier wife, as God is my witness.'

'Alas I have my faults, good friar. I am a frail woman. But thank you. And welcome.'

'You have always been kind to me,' he replied. 'But can I beg your pardon in advance? I would like to have a quiet word with your husband. Do you mind leaving us for a moment? These parish priests are slow and negligent in their duties, particularly those of confession and absolution. I am a preacher, as you know. Preaching is my profession. I am well versed in the words of Peter and of Paul. Like them, I fish for men's souls. I render Christ Jesus His due. I spread abroad His message to the world.'

'Scold Thomas well then, my good sir. He deserves it. He gets as angry as a red ant, even though he has everything he could possibly want. Although I cover him at night and make him warm – although I give him a good cuddle – he still moans like the old boar in our sty. I don't get any enjoyment out of him at all. There's no pleasure in it.'

'Oh Thomas, Thomas,' Friar John said. 'Listen to me. This must be amended. This is the work of the devil himself. God forbad anger as a sin. I will have to have a word with you about this.'

'Before I leave you two alone,' his wife added, 'let me ask you something. What would you like for your dinner, good friar? I can prepare it while you talk.'

'Oh good woman, my wants are very simple. Just the merest taste of chicken's liver, perhaps, and some soft white bread to go with it. And then perhaps a pig's head? I don't want you to kill a pig on my behalf, of course. That would be sinful. But a head would suit me. I am a man of small appetite, as you know. I am nourished by the Bible. I am so used to mortification and penance that my appetite is all but destroyed.' He raised his eyes to heaven. 'Do not be annoyed with me, good wife. I am taking you into my confidence. I am baring my soul to you. There are very few people I can trust these days.'

'There is one last thing I must tell you,' she replied. 'My little child died two weeks ago, just after you had left the town.'

'I knew it! I saw his death in a vision! I was lying in the dormitory, when I saw him before me. It was probably less than a hour after he expired. I saw him being transported to heaven, so help me God! Our sacristan and our infirmarian saw him, too, and they have been holy friars for fifty years or more. They have reached the age when they may walk about in the world alone, God bless them. As soon as I saw your child in bliss, I got up from my bed. The tears were running down my cheeks. Lord. My eyes were waterspouts. The whole of our convent came out with me, with no bells and no noise at all, and we went into the chapel where we sang the *Te Deum*. Then I prayed to Christ, thanking Him for His revelation to me. Trust me, good wife and husband, when I tell you that the prayers of friars really do work. We know more about

the teachings of Christ than any layperson, kings included. We
live in poverty and abstinence. You lay folk indulge in luxury
and spendthrift ways. You love meat and drink and all the foul
temptations of the flesh. We friars, on the other hand, hold
the world in contempt.' The wife now left the room, in order
to prepare the pig's head for her guest. 'Do you know the
difference, Thomas,' he went on in the same even tone,
'between the poor man Lazar and the rich man Dives? One of
them came to a bad end. Which one do you think it was?
Those who wish to pray must fast and remain pure; they must
curb the body and attend to the soul. We follow the teaching of
the apostles. We are content with scraps of food and the merest
rags. So our penance and our abstinence give wings to our
prayers. They fly straight up to Christ in heaven.

'You recall, Thomas, that Moses fasted for forty days and
forty nights before he was permitted to converse with Almighty
God on the summit of Mount Sinai? Only after he had denied
himself food for all that time was he permitted to receive
the Ten Commandments, written with Jehovah's own finger of
fire. And do you remember Elijah on Mount Horeb? The
prophet fasted, too, and spent his days in contemplation before
God deemed it right to speak to him. Aaron and all the other
priests of the temple would never dare to approach the incense
altar without mortifying their flesh. They prayed only after
they had abstained from drink. How could they be drunk in
the holy place? It was unthinkable. God would have struck
them dead. Take warning from what I say, Thomas. The priest
who prays for your welfare and recovery must be sober – or
else . . . well, I will say no more. You catch my drift.

'Our own Saviour, as the New Testament tells us, gave us
many examples of fasting and of prayer. That is why simple
friars like myself are wedded to poverty and to celibacy. We
lead lives of charity, of pity and of purity. I myself am always
weeping. Yes I am. Of course sometimes we are persecuted for
our holiness. That is the world for you. Nevertheless I tell you
this. Our prayers are more acceptable to God. They rise higher

than those of you and your kind, who can think only of your sensual appetites. Adam and Eve were expelled from the Garden of Eden for the sin of gluttony. Is that not so? It was not for lechery. I know that much.

'Thomas, listen to me, I beseech you. I don't have the exact text about me at the moment, but I can remember the gist of it. These are the words of sweet Lord Jesus, when He was talking about us friars. "Blessed," He said, "are the poor in spirit." That's me! All the gospels sing our praises. Cleanliness is next to godliness. The eye of the needle. That kind of thing. Do you think they are referring to us or to those of you who wallow in your possessions? I pity those who are in thrall to gluttony. I spit on those who are addicted to lechery. I abjure them, Thomas. I renounce them. They are no better than that heretic Jovinian. He was as fat as a whale, and he waddled like a swan. He was as full of booze as a bottle in an alehouse. How can people like that pray? When they pray, they burp instead. Do you know that psalm of David when he says that his heart is issuing a great matter? All they issue is gas.

'No. We are the ones that humbly follow the path and example of Jesus. We are meek. We are poor. We are chaste. We are lowly, Thomas, ever so lowly. We do not just listen to God's word. We practise it. Just as the hawk in upward flight mounts to the firmament, so do our prayers and solicitations reach the gates of heaven. We aspire, Thomas. As I live and breathe, Thomas, you will not flourish unless you are part of our brotherhood. I swear that on all the saints. We friars are praying for you night and day, beseeching Christ to take pity on your sick flesh and restore your poor body to health.'

'God help me,' the invalid replied. 'I haven't felt the benefit. Over the last few years I have spent pounds and pounds on the various orders of friars. What good has it done me? None at all. I have got through most of my money, and now I might as well say goodbye to the rest.'

'Oh Thomas, Thomas, wash out your mouth. How can you talk like that? What is all this nonsense about "various orders" of friars? What is the point of seeking out "various orders" of specialists when you see before you the perfect doctor? Your fickleness will be the ruin of you. Mark my words. Do you really believe that my prayers, and those of my holy brothers, are not enough for you? That is ludicrous. If anything, you have given us too little. Give one convent a half-load of oats. Give another convent twenty-four pence. Give this friar a penny and let him go. Give that friar – well, you get the idea. No, no, Thomas, that is not right. That is not proper. What is a farthing worth if it is divided into twelve? A thing whole and complete is stronger than anything that is divided and scattered. That is common sense. I am not going to flatter you, Thomas. That is not my style. You want to get our prayers for nothing. Is that not so? But God Himself, great ruler of the universe –' and here the friar raised his eyes up to the ceiling '– He has declared that the labourer is worthy of his hire. I'm not interested in your money. For my part, I wouldn't touch any of it. But the fact is that the whole convent is praying for you. And we also need funds for the new church. I am reminded of the life of Saint Thomas of India. That blessed man built many churches that were very pleasing in the eyes of God. Oh Thomas, Thomas. You are lying here all eaten up by anger and impatience. The devil has inflamed you. That's what it is. That's why you are so foul to that lovely little woman, your wife. What an innocent she is! So meek. So patient. Listen to me, Thomas. Trust me. Leave your wife alone. Think about what I'm saying. It's not just me. It is the word of the wise: "Never have a lion in the house. Do not terrorize those who are subject to you. Don't make your friends afraid of you."

'Thomas, let me say one thing more for your benefit. Be careful of the anger that lies in your heart. It is like the serpent that glides through the grass with its poison hidden in its fangs. Listen to me. Don't be so restless. Twenty thousand men, to put it no higher, have lost their lives because they have become angry with their wives or their mistresses. What is the point of quarrelling with your sweet wife? You know that if you tread on the tail of a snake it strikes back in anger? That snake is not half so cruel as a wife who believes herself to be wronged. All she wants then is vengeance. "Vengeance is mine," said the Lord. But she is too fired up to listen. Revenge is one of the seven deadly sins. Revenge turns on the sinner, leading to destruction. Every common cleric – every parish priest – will tell you that anger leads to murder. Anger is at the mercy of pride. I could tell you so many stories of deadly anger that I would still be here tomorrow. No. All right. I won't. But I will pray for you. I will pray, day and night, that God curbs the might of all angry men. It does great harm to set up a man of ire and vengeance as a ruler.

'That noble gentleman Seneca has told the story of a magistrate of terrible temper. One day, during the course of his reign, two knights went out riding. It so befell that one of them came back. The other did not. The knight, returned home, was brought before the court where the judge pronounced sentence upon him. "You have murdered your comrade," he said. "So I sentence you to death." Then he turned to another knight in the court. "Take this man to the scaffold," he said. "At once." Now it so happened that, on their way to the executioner's block, the other knight suddenly appeared. He was meant to be dead, but he was very much alive. So everyone thought that the best thing was to return, with both knights, to the court. "Sir," said the knight who had accompanied the condemned man. "This knight has not killed his comrade. The dead man stands before you."

'"By God," the judge replied. "I will have the heads of all three of you." He addressed the first knight. "I have already condemned you to death. My word still stands. You will die." Then he addressed the second knight. "Since you are the cause of this man's death you, too, must be executed." Then he turned to the third knight. "Since you disobeyed my order, I sentence you to beheading." And that is what happened. All three men were executed.

'Do you know the case of Cambises, king of Persia? He was

a drunk, and a quarrelsome drunk at that. He was a bully. There was a lord in his household who was a proper and virtuous man. Now it happened one day that this good lord said to the king, "If a lord is vicious, then he is lost. Drunkenness is itself a blot on the name of any man, but especially on that of a ruler. A lot of people are watching him. He does not know all the eyes and ears that surround him. So, for God's love, sire, drink more temperately. Wine can affect the brain. It can affect the body, too."

'"Is that what you think?" Cambises replied. "I will prove to you how wrong you can be. The exact opposite is the case, as you will soon find out for yourself. No wine on earth is going to affect my eyesight, or my limbs, or my strength. Watch." So then he began to drink much more than he had ever done before – a hundred times more, I should say. When he was thoroughly pissed, he ordered the son of this courtier to be brought before him. He told the boy to stand upright in front of him. Then he took out his bow and arrow, and stretched the bow-string right back to his ear. Then he let go. The arrow killed the child, of course. "Don't you think," he asked the grieving father, "that I have a steady hand? Has my strength gone? Has my eyesight suffered? Has my judgement? I don't think so."

'What use was the answer of the courtier? His son was dead. There was nothing more to say. So beware, my friend, how you deal with kings and lords. Just say, "If it please you, sir" or "I will do whatever I can for you, sir." You can tell a poor man what you think of him, vices and all, but you cannot berate your master. Even if he seems to be going straight to hell, say nothing.

'Think of that other Persian king, Cyrus, who in his anger destroyed the river Gyndes because one of his sacred white horses had drowned in it on the way to Babylon. He drained the river by diverting it into various channels, so that in the end women could cross it without getting their skirts wet. What did wise Solomon tell us? "Never make friends with an angry man. Never walk in company with a madman. You will be sorry." I will say no more on that matter, Thomas.

'So swallow your anger. You will find me as straight and firm as a carpenter's square. Don't thrust the knife of the devil into your heart. Your anger will do you infinite harm. Come now, Thomas. Give me your full confession.'

'No way,' Thomas replied. 'I have already confessed to the curate this morning. I have told him everything. There is no need to repeat it all.'

'In any case, give me some of your money. Give us gold to build a cloister for the Lord. We friars have been forced to live off oysters and mussels while people like you have drunk and eaten well. Think of what we have suffered to raise that cloister. Yet God knows that we still have not completed the foundations. The pavement is not laid. Not a tile has been put in place. We owe forty pounds alone for building materials. Can you believe it? So help us, Thomas, in the name of He who harrowed hell! Otherwise we will have to sell our books. If we cannot preach, then the whole world will suffer. To take us from our pulpits and our preaching crosses will be to take the sun out of the sky. I am being serious. Who can preach and do good works as we can? We are not some novelty. There have been friars around since the time of Elijah. And that was a very long time ago. There are records mentioning us. I need your charity, Thomas! For God's sake, charity!' And at that the friar fell down upon his knees, and crossed himself.

Thomas himself was already in a very bad temper. He realized well enough that the friar was full of shit. He was a liar and a hypocrite. If he had had the strength, he would have tossed him into the fire. 'I can only give you,' he said, 'what I possess on my person now. Did you say that I had become a lay brother?'

'Yes. Of course. I have brought the letter of fraternity with me. I was going to give it to your wife for safe-keeping.'

'That is good. Thank you. I will make a donation to your convent, while I still live. You will hold it in your hand. I

promise you. But there is one condition. You have to swear to
me that every other friar in your convent has an equal share
of what I am about to give you. Swear to that, on your holy
brotherhood, without cavil or hesitation.'

'I swear it,' the friar replied, 'on the blood and bones of
Christ.' He shook hands with Thomas. 'You can have trust
in me.'

'All right then,' Thomas said. 'Just put your hand down my
back. Down there. If you grope just behind my buttocks, you
will find something that I have hidden away for your benefit.'

'Aha,' the friar thought. 'This is going with me. This is my
prize.'

So he plunged his hand under the sheets and started feeling
the man's arse to find some treasure. He put his fingers up
his cleft in case there was a small package. When Thomas felt
the fingers of the friar groping around his bum, he suddenly let
out a great fart. A farmhorse, pulling a cart, could not have
let out a greater fart. A ploughman's ox could not have made
a smellier one. The noise was terrific.

Friar John was so startled that he jumped up. 'You bastard!'
he shouted. 'You did that on purpose, didn't you! God help
you! You'll pay for that fart, I promise you! Just you wait!'

The servants of the house, hearing the uproar, came
scurrying into the room and chased out the friar. So he left
with a scowl on his face, and went in search of the comrade
who always followed him about. He looked like an old boar in
pain; he was grinding his teeth or, rather, his tusks. Then he set
out for the manor house of the village, where lived a gentleman
of great distinction to whom he sometimes gave confession.
This worthy man was, naturally, lord of the manor. He was
sitting at dinner, in his hall, when Friar John approached him
in a fearful rage. The friar was so angry that he could not get
his words out. Then he finally managed, 'God be with you!'

The lord looked up at him and greeted him. 'Friar John,' he
said, 'what on earth is the matter with you? I can see that
something has happened. You look as if the wood were full of

thieves. Sit down. Tell me all about it. If I can help you, I will.'

'I have been insulted,' the friar replied. 'Humiliated. In your village. There is no one so poor, so lowly, so despised, who would not feel that he had been degraded by the treatment I have received. Here. Just now. Of course I do not complain on my own account. I am a mere friar. But I do mind that this – this fool – this knave – this white-haired old clown – should blaspheme against my convent.'

'Now master friar –'

'No, sir, not master. Never master. I am a mere servant. I know that I have been made a master of divinity, but I never use the title. It is not modest. It is not seemly, here or anywhere else.'

'That's up to you. But please tell me what has happened.'

'Sir, today my order and myself have been dealt a shameful wrong. It is too dreadful to contemplate. The whole of the Holy Church – all its degrees from pope to priest – has been insulted. God help us all.'

'I am sure,' the lord of the manor said, 'that you know the best way to proceed. Don't get into a state about it. You are my confessor, after all. You are the salt of the earth. Be calm, for God's sake. And tell me what happened.'

So the friar sat down and told him the whole story. There is no need for me to repeat it to you. The lady of the house had come in, and heard what the friar had to say. 'Mother of God,' she said. 'Holy Virgin! Is there anything else? Tell me.'

'That's it,' Friar John replied. 'What do you think?'

'What do I think? God help me, I say that a common man has done a common deed. What else am I supposed to say? He will end up in trouble, I know that much. His sickness must be affecting him. He may be having some kind of seizure. He doesn't know what he is doing.'

'Ma dame,' the friar said. 'I will not lie to you. I will be revenged upon him one way or another. I will denounce him from the pulpit. I will defame him. I will shame him. How dare he tell me to divide a thing that cannot be divided? You know

what I am talking about. How can I give a portion of you-
know-what to all the friars? God damn him and his fart!'

The lord listened to all this in amazement, and asked himself
how it was possible for this wretched man to have the wit
to put such a problem to the friar? Who could solve such a
conundrum? 'I never heard anything like it,' he said out loud to
no one in particular. 'The devil must have put it in his mind.
I don't think that any master of arithmetic has ever asked the
question. Who could demonstrate the proper method by which
every friar should have a part of the sound, and the smell, of a
fart? Is this man, this invalid, fiendishly clever? Or what? He
is too clever for his own good. That's for sure. Who ever heard
of such a thing? One divisible part to every man alike? Tell
me how. It is impossible. It cannot be done. The rumbling of
a fart, well, it is just reverberation of the air. It is a hollow
sound, fading ever so slowly away. No man can judge if it
has been divided properly. Who would have thought that one
of my own villagers would come up with something so – so
problematic. And he put it to my confessor, too! He must be a
madman. Eat your supper, Friar John, and forget all about it.
Let the churl go hang himself!'

The wordes of the lordes squier and his kervere for departinge of the fart on twelve

Jack, the young squire of the lord, was standing by the table
and carving the roast meat. Of course he had heard everything.
'Sir,' he said, 'please don't be angry with me. If you gave me
enough cloth to make a new gown – as a reward, if you like – I
think I could tell the friar the solution to this riddle. I think
I could explain to him how to divide this man's fart among all
the members of his convent.'

'If you give us the answer,' the lord of the manor replied,
'you can have your cloth. God knows you will have earned it.'

'My lord,' the squire said, 'pick a day when the weather is

mild and favourable, when there is no wind or breeze to disturb the air. Then have a cartwheel with its usual twelve
spokes brought into the hall here. It has to be a complete
wheel.'

'Yes. And then?'

'Summon twelve friars into the hall. Thirteen make up a
convent, do they not? Well, your confessor here can be the
thirteenth. They all have to kneel down at the same time. Then
every friar has to put his nose against one of the spokes. Our
worthy friar here will place his nose against the hub in the
middle of the wheel. May God be with him. We will then bring
the churl among them. His belly will have to be as taut as a
drum, and ready to blow. He will bend down, on the other side
of the hub, and let loose a great fart. I swear to you, on my life,
that you will see the proof of my theory. The sound of the
fart will travel along all twelve of the spokes. So will the stink
of it. Of course your worthy confessor here will have the first
fruit, so to speak. He deserved the first offering. That is
only fair. Has he not said in the past that the worthiest friar
should be the first to receive alms? He deserves the best, does
he not? Only this morning I heard him preaching from the
pulpit. It did me good, it really did. I would let him savour
three farts, if I could. I am sure his whole convent agrees with
me about that. What a holy man he is.'

The lord and his lady were in full agreement with young
Jack. Everyone there said that he had explained himself as
subtly as Euclid or Ptolemy – everyone, that is, except the holy
friar. As for the churl who had started the whole business, they
all agreed that he was neither mad nor foolish; on the contrary,
he had all his wits about him. So Jack won his new gown. That
is the end of my story. And just in time. Look, we are coming
into a new town.

Heere endeth the Somonours Tale

The Clerk's Prologue

*Heere folweth the Prologe of the
Clerkes Tale of Oxenforde*

'Come now, master scholar from Oxford,' our Host exclaimed.
'You have been as coy and quiet as a young virgin waiting for
her first night in bed. You haven't said a word throughout the
journey. I suppose you are studying some great intellectual
problem. But you know what wise Solomon believed? "There
is a time for everything."

'For Christ's sake cheer up, man! This is not the occasion
to be serious. Tell us a funny story. Anyone who agrees to be
part of the game must play by its rules. Isn't that so? Don't
preach to us, in any case. That is for the friars. That is for Lent.
Don't start moaning about the sins of the world. And don't
tell us a tale that will bore us to death. Be jolly. Tell us about
fantastic adventures. And don't clothe everything with your
Oxford rhetoric. We don't want technical terms or figures of
speech. They are for the secretaries of kings. Speak plainly in
the language men use. Make sure that all of us here can understand you.'

The Oxford man answered him politely. 'Host,' he said,
'I am under your authority. You are in charge. I will obey you
in everything unless, of course, you become unreasonable. I
will tell you a story I first heard from a worthy scholar at the
university of Padua. He was a very learned man, and a good
one. Alas he is now dead and nailed in his coffin. God give
him rest.

'This scholar was also a great poet, Francis Petrarch by
name. Have you heard of him? His sweet rhetoric sugared the

poetry of Italy. His colleague at Padua, Giovani di Lignano, did the same for law and rhetoric. But you won't have heard of him. They have gone now. Death is no respecter of persons. It will not allow us to linger in the world. In an instant it had taken both of them. And we will all surely follow.

'Let me tell you more about Petrarch himself. Before he recited this tale to me, he explained that he had composed it in a high style fitting its matter. He also told me that he had written a prologue before starting on the substance of the story. In this prologue he had described the area of Piedmont and its region of Saluzzo, where the action is set. He described the Apennine mountains that make up the western border of Lombardy. In particular he portrayed Mount Viso, highest of the mountains, where the river Po has its source in a little spring among the rocks. From there the river goes eastward, increasing all the way, towards Ferrara and lovely Venice before entering the sea. But that's another story. It is irrelevant here, except as an introduction. Now that I have set the scene, I will get on with my tale.'

The Clerk's Tale

Heere bigynneth the Tale of the
Clerk of Oxenforde

PART ONE

On the western side of Italy, just beside the foot of chilly Mount Viso, there is a rich and fruitful plain dotted with towns and castles that were built up in ancient times. There are many other pleasant places to be seen here, in the region known as Saluzzo.

A marquis was the lord of this land, one of a long line of distinguished noblemen. All of his vassals, high and low, were diligent and obedient to his commands. So for many years he lived in peace and prosperity, the favoured son of Fortune, beloved and respected by the lords and by the common people.

He came from the stock of the most noble lineage in all of Lombardy. He was strong and courageous, young and fair, a very model of honour and of chivalry. He exercised his authority very well, except in certain affairs that I am about to mention to you. The name of this marquis, by the way, was Walter.

Walter was worthy of criticism in one respect. He never considered what might or might not happen in the future. His only concern was the present moment. He busied himself about hunting and hawking. That was all. Nothing else seemed to matter to him. He was not interested in marriage, for example. On no account would he take a bride.

This was the one thing for which his people blamed him. So a delegation asked to be admitted into his presence. Among them was a wise and worthy man. It was believed that the marquis would listen to him as a representative of the general opinion. So this man stood before the marquis and spoke thus.

'Noble marquis, your well-known benignity and humanity embolden us to speak to you plainly. It has become necessary for us to tell you of our distress. Listen to us, sir, in your usual merciful way. With piteous hearts we address you. Do not turn away from me, or condemn my words.

'I am no more able or more knowledgeable than any other man in this place but, in as much as I have found favour with you before, dear lord, I will be so bold as to put before you our request. It will then be up to you, of course, whether you accept or reject it.

'You know well enough that we have always admired your words and deeds. There is no way in which we could enjoy more peace and happiness – except, perhaps, in one matter. We would love to hear wedding bells. If you were to marry, sir, that would give us more pleasure than anything else.

'I plead with you to bow your neck and enter a new state of sovereignty, not service, which is called wedlock or matrimony. You are wise, sir, and will consider that our days flee like the wind. When we wake or sleep, when we ride or wander, time does not stand still. It abides for no man.

'You are still in your green time, but youth will one day give way to age. The years come as silent as a stone. Death is the enemy of all, young or old, high or low. No one can escape. But even if we are all certain that we will die, sir, none of us know when that day will come.

'Our intentions are good. You know that. We have never yet disobeyed you in anything. So very humbly we ask you to listen to our request. It concerns a marriage. If you agree, we will choose for you a wife in as short a time as possible. She will be of the utmost rank of the nobility, so that as your wife she will bring honour to you and to God.

'Free us from fear and trembling, dear lord. Take a wife, for God's sake. If it should happen – God forbid – that you should die and that your line came to an end, we might be ruled by some stranger from a strange land. We cannot think of anything more terrible. So we beg you to marry in all haste.'

Walter heard this humble and sorrowful request, and was moved by it. How could he be angry with such suppliants? 'You well know, my dear people,' he replied, 'that before this moment I have never thought of the sweet constraints of a wife. I enjoy my liberty, and know well enough that it is not to be found in marriage. Where once I was free, I would be in servitude.

'Nevertheless I understand your good intentions. I know your good will towards me. And I trust your judgement, as I have always done. So of my own free will I declare that I will be married as soon as I can. I know that you have promised today to find a wife for me, but I release you from that pledge. I wish to hear no more about it.

'God knows that children are often very different from their parents. Goodness comes from God and not from noble ancestors or a rich family. I will put my trust in God. I place my life and estate – and my marriage – in His care. Let Him do with me as He please.

'So allow me, please, to find a wife for myself. I will take the responsibility. But you must promise me this. I ask you to honour whatever wife I choose for as long as she may live. You must make the most solemn pledge to support her in word and deed, here and everywhere, just as if she were the daughter of an emperor.

'You must also swear another oath. You must swear not to complain or criticize. When I have chosen, I have chosen. You are asking me to give up my liberty, after all. So I must be allowed to follow my own inclination. Unless you assent to my proposals, I will have nothing more to do with the matter.'

So unanimously they agreed to all of the marquis's conditions. No one dissented. Before they departed, however, they begged their lord to name the day of the wedding as soon as possible. They feared, you see, that in the end he might not marry at all.

He did name a day, as they asked. On that particular day, he declared, he would be faithfully married in compliance to their wishes. They all kneeled down before him, and pledged their obedience. He thanked them for the respect and affection they had shown to him, and sent them on their way. They filed out of the hall, and went to their own homes.

Then Walter summoned the officers of his court and asked them to prepare a feast; he ordered the members of his private household to make all the arrangements for the bridal day. They busied themselves about the preparations with a good will, each of them wanting to make a success of the occasion.

PART TWO

Not far from this great palace, where the marquis was making ready for the feast, there was a hamlet nestling in very pleasant scenery. The poor folk of the neighbourhood lodged, and kept their cattle, here. They laboured in the fields, and the fields were often fruitful.

Among these poor people was one fellow who was reckoned to be the poorest of them all. Yet was not the Son of God born in a simple manger? God's grace can reach an ox's stall. The name of this poor man was Janiculus. He had a beautiful young daughter, whose name was Griselda.

To speak of virtue, and of beauty, she was in every sense one of the fairest in the world. She had been brought up in honest poverty, and there was no trace of greed or sensuality in her nature. She drank water more often than she drank wine. She embraced labour rather than idleness.

Griselda was still of a young age, and a virgin, but in her heart were genuine ardour and courage. She looked after her poor and elderly father with tenderness and affection. She watched the sheep in the pasture, and in the cottage was busy at the spinning-wheel. She did not stop working until she retired to bed.

When she came home from the fields she brought with her cabbages and other vegetables, which she cut up and cooked to make a modest meal. Her bed was hard. There were no feathers in her pillow. But she always cared for her father, and treated him with all the reverence and obedience he could possibly desire.

Walter, in the course of his many hunting expeditions, had often seen this maid. He had not looked upon her in lust. Far from it. He had gazed and gazed and sighed. He had contemplated her beauty.

He had recognized her to be the very image of a virtuous woman, passing all others of her age. He had seen feminine grace in her manner and appearance. It is true that many people have no insight into these things. But the marquis was an exception. He decided that he would marry Griselda and no other.

The day appointed for the wedding had come. But no one in the land knew who, if anyone, was to be the bride. Many of them wondered aloud. Others asked each other in private if the marquis had broken his promise. 'Is he not going to be married after all?' they complained. 'Is he going to make a fool of himself? And of us, as well?'

Yet secretly the marquis had already ordered rings and brooches and other precious gems, set in gold and azure, for the sake of Griselda. He had also found a young woman of the same stature, and had measured her for the dresses of his new bride. Griselda was sure to have a full trousseau as well as every adornment for her wedding day.

It was nine o'clock on the morning of the wedding day. All the palace had been decorated. Every hall, and every little chamber, had been made ready for the celebrations. The kitchens and storerooms had been stuffed with food and drink. You could not have seen better fare in the whole of Italy.

The marquis rode out in state, attended by all the company

of his lords and ladies who had been invited to the wedding feast. The knights in his service also accompanied him on the royal journey. To the sound of lutes and trumpets, then, the procession wound its way to the little hamlet where Janiculus and Griselda lived.

Griselda had of course no idea that all this magnificence and display were for her sake. She had gone to the well to fetch water, as usual, and was now hurrying back home to see the grand spectacle. She knew that the marquis was going to be married that day, and didn't want to miss it.

'I will stand with the other girls,' she said to herself, 'outside the door and take a look at the bride as she rides past. I will get through all the work at home as quickly as I can. Then I'll have time to catch a glimpse of her on the way to the palace. I hope she comes this way.'

She had just got up to her door, and was about to cross the threshold, when she heard a voice. The marquis had ridden towards her and was calling out to her! She put down the water-vessel in a little wicker enclosure, and fell upon her knees. She kneeled in front of her lord, waiting patiently to hear his will.

The marquis dismounted from his horse and walked over to her. She did not dare look up at him. He gazed at her thought-fully, and then in an earnest manner began to speak to her. 'Where is your father, Griselda?'

'He is here, sir. Inside the cottage.'

'Will you fetch him for me?'

So she rose to her feet and entered the cottage. When she brought out her father the marquis shook his hand and led him aside. 'Janiculus,' he said, 'I can't conceal my feelings any longer. I love your daughter and wish to marry her. If you give your permission to the match, I promise to love her and live with her until the day of my death.

'I know that you love me in turn and that you are my faith-ful subject. I am your liege lord. Whatever pleases me, I think, will also please you. Am I right? And, as I said, there is one thing that will please me more than anything else. Will you allow me to become your son-in-law?'

The old man was so astounded that his face turned scarlet. He was trembling, he was so nervous that he could hardly get the words out. Finally he managed to stammer an answer. 'My lord,' he said, 'please do whatever you like. I will agree to anything, so long as it pleases you. Anything at all.'

'Wait a moment, I think you and me, and Griselda, should have a conversation.' The marquis spoke very softly and politely. 'Don't you agree? I would like to ask her if she is willing to become my wife and to obey my wishes as her lawful husband. I want to talk to her in your presence. I will say nothing out of your hearing.'

So the three of them entered the cottage and began their discussion. I will tell you about that later. Meanwhile all manner of people began to gather outside the cottage, commenting loudly on how neat and clean it looked. Griselda herself was almost overcome with astonishment, as well she might, at the turn of events.

She had never seen before such lords and ladies, and such knights in gleaming armour. She had never experienced such magnificence. And to have the marquis sitting beside her – well, she had gone quite pale. Now I will tell you what the marquis said to this paragon, this cynosure, this true heart. Enough of that. These are his actual words.

'Griselda,' he said, 'you should know that your father and I have come to an understanding. We have agreed that you will be my bride and lawful wife. I don't suppose that you have any objection? But let me ask you this first. This is all being done at great speed, I admit. So I want to know whether you are happy to go along with it. Or do you want time to consider the matter further?

'I have another question. Are you willing to be ruled by me in everything, according to my pleasure? Will you remain true to me, whether I treat you for better or for worse? You must never complain. You must never contradict me with a "no" rather than a "yes". You must never frown or show any sign of displeasure. If you swear all this, I will swear to marry you.'

Griselda was afraid, and wondered at the meaning of his words. 'My lord,' she replied, 'I am unworthy of the honour you wish to pay to me. But if this is truly your will, then I will gladly accede to it. I swear to you now, in front of my father, that I will never disobey you in word or deed. I swear this on my life, even though life is dear to me.'

'You have said enough, Griselda. You will be mine.' He came out of the cottage, looking very grave, and Griselda followed him. As they stood together, the marquis addressed the crowd that had gathered there. 'Here is my wife,' he said. 'Honour her and love her, as you love and honour me. There is no more to say.'

He did not want anything from her old life to be brought into the palace, and so he ordered his ladies to undress her there and then. These ladies were reluctant to touch the scraps and tatters on her back, but they were obliged to obey orders even if they risked getting their hands dirty. Off came the rags. On came the new garments. And there was Griselda, radiant and resplendent in her natural beauty.

They combed hair that had hardly ever seen a comb before. They put a crown upon her head. They pinned on her brooches and precious jewels. What else can I say about her appearance? She had become so ornate and regal that she was scarcely recognizable.

Then the marquis gave her a ring especially bought for the occasion as a token of their union. He set her upon a snow-white palfrey, and with gentle pace they rode to the palace. They were greeted by well-wishers along the route and, after their arrival, they attended a great feast that continued until sunset.

I will not go on and on about her beauty and her virtue. It suffices to say that she had such natural grace that it did not seem possible that she had been brought up in poverty. She could not have come from a cottage or an ox-stall. She must have been educated in an emperor's palace!

Even the people who had come from the same village, and had seen her growing from year to year, could hardly believe that this was Griselda, the daughter of Janiculus. They could have sworn that this was a completely different person.

She was as virtuous as she had always been, but in her new eminence her virtues shone all the brighter. She was as fair as she was eloquent, as mild as she was bountiful. She became the princess of all the people. Whoever looked upon her, loved her.

So the fame of Griselda spread throughout the region of Saluzzo and was then conveyed further abroad; her virtues became known far and wide, and from all parts of Italy flocked men and women, young and old, to see her.

So Walter, the marquis, had not married one of low degree at all. He seemed to have married a noble woman, and he was so fortunate in his union that he lived at peace with himself and all others. He was highly regarded, too. He had proved that outward poverty may conceal virtue as well as grace. So the people deemed him to be a prudent man, a rare gift in one so favoured by Fortune.

Griselda's virtue was not confined to household tasks and duties. Far from it. When the occasion demanded it, she was able to nurture the common good and the welfare of the ordinary people. She could resolve any argument, appease any bitterness, and heal any division. She was the agent of peace and unity.

Even when her husband was abroad on business she could conciliate enemies and rivals, whether they were noble or otherwise. Her words were wise and succinct. Her judgements were models of equity. It was said that she had been sent by heaven to save the world and to amend all wrongs.

Then, nine months after her marriage, Griselda bore a child. Everyone had secretly wished for a male child, but in fact she gave birth to a daughter. Still the marquis was happy, and the people rejoiced with him. Even though a daughter had come first there was every reason to believe that in time she would bear a son. She was not barren, after all.

PART THREE

Then it happened. It has happened many times before. Soon after the birth of his daughter, Walter decided to test his wife. He wanted to see how constant, and how steadfast, she really was. He could not resist the thought of tempting Griselda. He wanted to frighten her even though, God knows, there was no need.

He had put her to the test before, and she had never disappointed him. She was always loyal, and always patient. What was the point of tempting her again and again? Some men might say that the marquis was a subtle fellow, but I say that it is evil to submit a wife to scrutiny without reason. It simply causes needless grief and anxiety.

This is what the marquis did. He came one night to her bedside with a serious face and a disturbed manner. They were alone. 'Griselda, do you remember that day when I lifted you out of poverty and placed you in an exalted rank? You haven't forgotten that, I hope?

'I hope you still recall the days when you lived with your father in that little cottage. I hope your present glory has not made you forgetful. You were in so wretched a position that you could scarcely have dreamed of your good fortune. So listen to every word that I am about to tell you. There is no one here but you and me.

'You know well enough the circumstances that led you here less than a year ago. Although I am of course mild and loving towards you, my noble courtiers are not so respectful. They tell me that it is shameful and humiliating for them to serve one of such humble estate as yourself. They do not wish to stoop so low.

'Ever since the birth of your daughter they have been

complaining more and more. She shares your blood, after all. My fervent will and wish is to live at peace with them. I must listen to what they say, and dispose of your daughter as I think best. It is not what I would, but what I must, do.

'God knows all this is distasteful to me. But believe me. I will do nothing without your knowledge. You must assent to all of my decisions. Show me your patience and your constancy. Be faithful to your promise to me on our wedding day.'

When she heard her husband she seemed to remain unmoved. She showed no fear, or alarm, or anger. She was calm and composed. 'Lord,' she said, 'you must do as you please. My daughter and I are your faithful servants. We will obey your commands, for better or for worse. We are wholly yours. Do as you wish.

'There is nothing in the world that will please me if it displeases you. I desire nothing. I dread nothing. I fear only to lose you, my husband. This is the truth rooted in my heart. It will remain there for ever, and will never fade. I will always be faithful to you.'

The marquis was happy with her answer. Yet he pretended otherwise. He looked at her gravely, almost angrily, and left the bedchamber. A short while later he confided in one of his servants, secretly told him what he intended, and dispatched him as a messenger to his wife.

This servant was a secret agent, or enforcer, very useful in matters of state. If there was any low or dishonest work to be done, he was the man. The marquis knew well enough that he loved and respected his master, and would ask no questions. He would obey orders. So without delay he went quietly into Griselda's chamber.

'Ma dame,' he said, 'you must forgive me for coming here. But I must do what my lord has demanded. You know well enough that his commands cannot be averted or evaded. They may cause grief and suffering, I know, but they cannot be challenged. He is our master. That is all there is to it.'

He took a step towards her. 'And he has ordered me to take

this child.' He said no more. He seized the infant girl and was about to carry her out of the room, with such an expression on his face – well, it seemed that he would murder her on the spot. Griselda was forced to endure all and to be patient. She was as meek, and as quiet, as a lamb. She witnessed the actions of the servant without remonstrance or complaint.

The bad reputation of this man preceded him everywhere. His appearance was threatening, his words ominous. Even the hour of his arrival was suspicious. Griselda truly believed that her little daughter was about to be killed before her eyes. But she did not cry out. She did not weep. She was obliged to fulfil the demands of her husband.

Yet in the end she was moved to speak. She pleaded with the servant, as if he were a good and noble man, to let her kiss her little girl before she died. She cradled the child on her lap and caressed her. She made the sign of the cross on her forehead, and then kissed her again.

She began to murmur to her in a soft voice, as if she were singing a lullaby. 'Farewell, my little child. I will never see you again. But since I have made the sign of the blessed Lord Jesus, who died for us on a wooden cross, I trust that He will take your soul to paradise. For my sake you will die tonight.'

I do not think that any nurse could have endured so much pain and sorrow, let alone a mother. What woman would not have broken down in tears? Yet Griselda stayed as firm and resolute as ever. Very quietly she said to the official, 'Here. Take back the child. The little girl is yours.'

As she gave the infant to him, she told him to go and obey his master's orders. 'There is just one thing I ask of you,' she said. 'Out of consideration to me and my child. Unless our lord absolutely forbids it, I would ask you to bury her little body in a place where the carrion birds and wild beasts will not get at it.' He made no answer to her, but left the chamber with the child in his arms.

He went back to the marquis, and presented him with his daughter. Then he told him everything that Griselda had done and said. He went through every detail. The marquis, on hearing this, was inclined to pity his wife. Nevertheless he decided to hold to his original purpose. That is the way with lords. They are always masterful.

He told his agent to convey the child to a secret place and to clothe her in the softest silks and linens; then he was to find a little box, or a shawl of linen, in which to hide her. Then on pain of his life he ordered him to remain silent about all these things, and to tell no one where he came from or where he was going.

He was in fact going to Bologna, where the marquis's sister was countess of the region; having explained the whole reason for the journey he was to leave the little girl with the countess, on the understanding that she would be properly brought up as a royal child. The countess was under no circumstances to tell anyone the identity of the infant. The servant obeyed his master's orders to the letter.

Let us return now to the marquis himself. Walter was eager to discover if his wife had changed in any way. He was alert to any alteration in her manner or her conversation. But there was none. She was as kind and as patient as ever.

She was as industrious and meek as she had always been, ever ready to smile and obey. She never said a word about her daughter. There was no sign of sorrow or blame. She would not so much as murmur her name in her dreams.

PART FOUR

Four years passed. Then, thanks be to God, Griselda bore a male child, a strong and handsome baby. As soon as Walter heard the news he was overjoyed. The whole country celebrated the birth with bells and church services.

When the child was two years old, and had finished with his wet nurse, the marquis was tempted to test his wife once more. There was no need for any of this, but men can become ruthless when they are married to patient and pliable wives. Griselda was at Walter's mercy.

'Wife,' he said, 'you have heard before that our marriage is unpopular with the people. Now that my son is born, the complaints and recriminations have grown ever louder. I am half dead with anxiety. The protests are making me ill. I can bear it no longer.

'Do you know what they are saying? When I am gone, I will be succeeded by an offspring of the peasant Janiculus. This low-born wretch will be our lord. That is what they whisper to one another. I have to listen to their grievances, Griselda. I cannot ignore them, even if they never mention them in my presence. What if they were to rebel against me?

'I want to live at peace with my subjects, as far as I am able. So this is what I propose. I propose to treat my son in the same way that I treated my daughter, under the cover of night and secrecy. I am telling you now so that you will not break out in passionate grief, or anything of that kind. I want you to be patient once again.'

'I have told you this before, sir,' she said. 'I will tell you again. I will do whatever you wish or request. If my son and daughter are killed – well, I will never grieve and never complain. I accept your commandments as my lord and master. I have had no part in my two children – except sickness and pain and sorrow.

'You are our lord. You must do with us as you please. There is no need to consult me. When I left my home I did not just leave my old clothing behind me. I left my will and my liberty, too. On that occasion I put on the clothes you chose for me. In everything else, your choice is my command. Do as you wish, sir. I will obey you.

'If I knew in advance what you wanted, I would hasten to perform it without even being told. Now I do know what you require of me. And I will not hesitate. If you ordered me to die in front of you, I would do so gladly. It would give me pleasure. Death is less powerful than my love for you.'

The marquis listened to his wife with averted eyes. He marvelled at her constancy, and wondered how it was possible for her to bear all the suffering he inflicted. He exulted inwardly, but he remained dour and grave in countenance.

So the secret agent was dispatched once more to Griselda's bedchamber where with even more brutality than before – if such a thing is possible – he snatched the pretty son as he had once snatched the daughter. Griselda was the model of forbearance. She did not lament or cry out. She kissed her little son, and made the sign of the cross upon his forehead.

She made the same request, too. She begged the agent to lay her son in a deep grave of earth, where the birds and beasts could not reach him. He made no reply to her. He did not care. Then, with the child, he rode on to Bologna.

Walter, the marquis, was more and more astonished by her endless patience. If he had not seen for himself her great love for her children, he would have thought that there was something wrong with her. He would have accused her of malice, or of coldness, or of hypocrisy, for bearing all this woe with an untroubled face.

But he knew well enough that Griselda dearly loved her children – next to himself, of course – and had always been tender towards them. I would like to ask all women here, whether he had not gone far enough in testing her? What more could any husband devise to challenge her patience and her fortitude? How cruel could he be?

But there are some people who will not be moved. Once they have devised a plan, they must follow it to the end. He was fettered to the stake of his intentions. He was caught fast. He had to continue torturing his wife, to see if she would break.

So he watched and waited. He wanted to see if Griselda would change in any way. But he saw no difference in her mood or manner. She was as patient and as loving as before. As the years passed she was more devoted to him, if such a thing were possible, and more attentive.

It was as if they were one person with one will and

understanding. They had their essence but in one. If Walter wished for anything, she wished for it, too. So, thanks be to God, all seemed to be for the best. She proved herself to be the model wife, happy to accept her husband's authority.

Yet there were now slanders spread abroad about Walter. It was widely rumoured that he was a wicked man who had secretly killed his two children, for the crime of being born to a wife of lowly estate. This was the opinion of the people, who had no reason to think otherwise. Who had any other theory? Where were the children?

So the marquis was no longer the well-beloved leader. He was now hated by his people. Who does not detest and despise a murderer? Yet he did not relent. He carried on with the cruel trial of his wife. He had no other purpose in life.

When his daughter was twelve years old he sent a secret message to the papal court in Rome. He asked his representatives there to counterfeit a papal bull, in which the pope gave him permission to remarry if he should so wish. Can you imagine such cruelty?

In the same edict the pope was supposed to state that the marquis had permission to divorce his first wife. The pontiff had given him this dispensation in order to resolve any conflict or misunderstanding between the marquis and his subjects. So the fake bull was widely published throughout Saluzzo.

The ignorant people obviously believed the edict to be genuine. Who would not? But when the news was brought to Griselda, she was bowed down with woe. Yet she remained calm. This humble woman was determined to endure all the adversities of Fortune. She had resolved to follow her husband's will and pleasure in everything. She had pledged her heart to him. He was the centre of her being. What more is there to say?

The marquis had meanwhile written a secret letter to Bologna, in which he explained his actions and his intentions. He addressed it to the husband of his sister, the earl of the

region, and asked this nobleman to bring the two children back
to Saluzzo in royal pomp and circumstance. But he begged him
not to reveal their true identity to anyone in the world.

He was supposed to say only that the young girl was
espoused to the marquis – that is, of course, Walter himself.
So the earl performed the duty given to him by the marquis.
On the following morning he set out in grand procession to
Saluzzo, with the lords of his court surrounding him; the young
girl rode out with him, in great state, and her younger brother
rode beside her.

The girl herself was arrayed with pearls and other precious
stones, in preparation for her bridal day, and the seven-year-
old boy was dressed as finely as a prince. He was a prince, after
all. So with grandeur and ceremony they made their way
slowly towards Saluzzo.

PART FIVE

The marquis there had abandoned none of his wicked ways.
He set out to test Griselda yet again, to find out if she was
really still as patient and as devoted to him as before. He
wanted to push her to the limit of her endurance. So at a public
audience he addressed her in a stern voice.

'It is true, Griselda,' he said, 'that I married you for your
virtue. I took you for my wife because of your piety and
your loyalty. I certainly did not marry you for your lineage
or your wealth. Far from it. But I have discovered from experience that power and lordship can be forms of servitude.

'I may not do what every humble ploughman may do. I am
not my own master. My subjects beg me to choose another
wife. They will not be denied. The pope himself has decreed
that I can divorce you, to restrain their anger, and marry again.
There is not much more to say to you. My new bride is already
on her way here.

'Be strong. Let her usurp your place. Take back the dowry you brought with you. I give you my permission. What was it, in any case? Return to your father's cottage. No man or woman can enjoy uninterrupted prosperity. With tranquil heart I urge you to endure the blows of chance and fickle Fortune.'

Griselda answered him in a clear, calm voice. 'My lord, I know and I have always known that there is no comparison between your wealth and magnificence and my poverty. There is no denying my low degree. I never believed myself worthy of being your chambermaid, let alone your wife.

'I swear, as God is my witness, that I never deemed myself to be the mistress of your household or to be a lady worthy of such a lord. I am your servant. I always have been, and I always will be. I have no other aim in life than to please you.

'God knows that you have treated me generously and nobly, when I never deserved such consideration. I thank you for your kindness to me. Now take it back. Renounce it. I will return gladly to my father, and live with him until the end of my life.

'I grew up in that little cottage, and am happy to remain there until my death. I will be a widow in mind and heart and deed. Ever since that time I yielded my virginity to you, I have been a true and faithful wife. That is how I will remain. I have been married to a prince among men. God forbid that I should ever take another man as a husband.

'I pray to God that your new wife brings you happiness and prosperity. I willingly give up to her my place, even though it was a source of bliss to me. You were, and are, my lord. Since you desire me to leave, I will leave whenever you wish.

'You asked me about the dowry I brought with me. I know well enough that all I possessed were rags and wretched scraps of clothes. I do not think that I will be able to find them again. Good God! When I think of your bounty to me on that day – how you looked at me, what you said to me – I still marvel.

'There is a saying that, for me at least, has proved to be true: "Love grown old is not the same as new love." But whatever happens to me, sir, even if it were death itself, I will never repent of my love for you. Never in this world.

'You know well enough, lord, that you took the poor clothes off my back and decked me in finery. I brought nothing to you but faith and modesty and maidenhead. I will give you back all of the rich clothing you presented to me. I will return my wedding ring.

'You will find the rest of the jewellery in my bedchamber, safely stored. I came naked out of my father's house, and naked I will return. I will follow your orders in everything. But may I ask you this, sir? Is it your intention that I should actually leave your palace without clothes?

'It would be a great dishonour to you, and to me, if the belly in which your children lay was paraded before the people. Let me not go as naked as a worm upon its way. Remember, sir, that, unworthy though I be, I was still once your wife.

'So in requital for the virginity I gave you, and which can never be restored to me, I plead with you to let me have as my reward a simple smock. Just like the smock I used to wear before I met you. I would then be able to cover up the womb of the woman who was once your wife. Now I will bid farewell to you, sir, in case I have angered you.'

'Keep the smock you are wearing now,' he said to her. 'Take it back with you.' That was all he said. He could say no more. Overwhelmed by sorrow and by pity, he went on his way. So Griselda removed her other garments, in front of the whole court, and then returned to her father's cottage in the simple smock.

She walked back with bare head and with bare feet, accompanied by many people bewailing her fate and cursing the misadventures of Fortune. But Griselda did not cry. She never shed a tear. And she never said a word. Her father, on the other hand, wept and cursed when he heard the news. He did not want to live a day longer.

In fact the poor old man had always harboured doubts about the marriage. He had always suspected that the marquis would get rid of his daughter as soon as he had had enough of her. He believed that the lord would regret having wed a poor woman, and would banish her from his court.

So he hastened out of doors to meet Griselda, alerted by the noise of the crowd, and covered her smock with an old coat that he had brought with him. He was weeping. Yet the coat did not fit her. It was old and coarse and out of date. She was not the same slim young girl she had been at the time of her marriage.

So for a while Griselda dwelled with her father. She was still a model of loyalty and patience, never complaining, never explaining, never lamenting. She did not show, to her father or to anyone else, any grief at her treatment. She did not mention her previous life as the wife of a great lord. She said nothing. She looked content.

What else would you expect? Even when she lived in great state she had always retained her deep humility. She had never been greedy or self-indulgent. She had never enjoyed pomp and circumstance. She had always been as modest and as kind as any young nun – except that she had a husband, whom she honoured above all others. Who could have been meeker or more obedient?

The patience and humility of Job are well known. Male clerks are all too ready to honour the achievements of other men. They rarely mention women but, in truth, women are far more faithful and patient than any man. Women are kinder. Women are more trustworthy, then and now. If someone has a different opinion, I will be astonished.

PART SIX

So the earl made his way from Bologna, as I have already described, with the two children of Griselda and Walter. The news of their arrival was soon spread abroad. It was rumoured that the earl was bringing with him the new wife of the marquis, and was surrounding her with more pomp and dignity than had ever before been seen in Italy.

The marquis, who had himself arranged all this, sent a message to Griselda before the arrival of the earl and his train. He ordered her to come to court, and of course she obeyed him. She arrived in her humble clothes, with no thought of herself, ready to fulfil whatever commands he gave her. She went down on her knees in his presence, and reverently greeted him.

'Griselda,' he said, 'I have determined that the young maiden – the young girl who is about to become my bride – must be received with as much ceremony as possible. It must be a royal occasion. All my courtiers and servants will be consigned to a place according to their rank, and in their proper role they will serve the new princess in every way I deem to be fit.

'It is true, however, that I do not have enough women to adorn and decorate the chambers in the luxury I desire. That is why I have called for you. You know how to spruce up the palace. You know my mind. You do not look very appealing, I admit, but the least you can do is your duty.'

'I will obey your command gladly, my lord,' Griselda replied. 'I long to be of service to you. I will do my best to please you in everything, without demur. Whatever happens, good or ill, I will never stop loving you with all my heart.'

Then she began to decorate the palace, setting the tables and making up the beds for the honoured guests. She did everything she could, and encouraged the chambermaids to finish their work as soon as possible. They were to sweep and to dust and to clean, while she busied herself about decorating the banqueting hall and the private chambers.

At about nine in the morning the earl and his charges finally arrived at the palace. The people ran over to see the two children, and to marvel at the richness of their retinue and their apparel. Then for the first time they said among themselves that Walter was no fool, after all, and that he had chosen his second wife well.

The young girl was much prettier than Griselda, according to common opinion, and a much better age for child-bearing. She and the marquis would have good progeny, especially since this young girl was – unlike Griselda – of proper lineage. The people also marvelled at the beauty of the young boy beside her; seeing sister and brother together, they all praised the marquis for his judgement.

Oh fickle people, people of the wind, unsteady and unfaithful! You are as ever changing as a weathervane. You delight only in novelty. You wax and wane as does the moon. You gape and chatter, much to your own cost. Your opinions are worthless, and your behaviour proves that you are never to be trusted. Only a fool would believe anything you say.

The more thoughtful knew this to be true, even as they watched the others running up and down and gawping at the fine dresses. The silly folk were so pleased with the novelty of this new maiden that they could speak, and think, about nothing else. Well, enough of this. I will turn now to Griselda, and see how she is coping with the situation.

She was as busy as ever. She was doing what was expected of her by Walter, and attending to all the details of the great feast. She did not care at all about the tattered state of her own clothing, but with cheerful spirit she hurried with the others towards the great gate where she could see the young bride advancing. Then she went back to work.

She greeted all the guests of the marquis with due deference and propriety. No one could fault her in anything and in fact she behaved with such decorum that everyone wondered who she might be. Who was this woman, dressed so unbecomingly, who was yet the soul of tact and cheerfulness? All of them commended her.

In the meantime Griselda praised the young brother and sister with such warmth and affection that no one could have equalled it. The time came when the whole company was about to sit down at the feast. At that moment, as she was supervising the preparations, the marquis called out to her.

'Griselda,' he said to her playfully, 'how do you like my new wife? Isn't she a beauty?'

'She is indeed, my lord. I have never seen a lovelier woman in my life. God send her good fortune. And I hope he will send both of you peace and prosperity until the end of your lives.

'I will say one thing, however, if I may. I would beg you not to test and torment this poor girl, as you once tested me. She has been brought up more tenderly. She is more delicate than me, I believe. She could not endure adversity in the same way as a girl born and brought up in poverty. You know who I mean.'

When Walter looked upon her cheerful face, when he saw that there was no malice in her heart towards him, he recalled the number of times he had grievously offended her. She was still as steady and as constant as a stone wall. So he began to take pity on her – yes, pity for her loyalty to him.

'Enough,' he said. 'You have suffered enough, Griselda. Fear no more. All things shall be well. I have tested your faith and kindness to the utmost. I have tested you in wealth and in poverty. No other woman in the world could have endured so much. Now I know, dear wife, the full measure of your truth and constancy.' With that he took her in his arms and kissed her.

She was so amazed that she did not know what was happening to her. She did not understand a word he said to her. It was as if she were walking in her sleep. Then suddenly she was wide awake. 'Griselda,' he said, 'I swear to God you have always been my true and faithful wife. I will have no other, as long as I live.

'This is your daughter. You believed her to be my new bride. But you yourself gave birth to her. This young man is your son. One day he will be my heir. They have been brought up secretly in Bologna, by my orders. Take them back again. You will never be able to say that you have lost your children.

'I know that the people think the worst of me. But I swear that I did not test you out of anger or out of cruelty. I merely wished to assay your patience and your womanly fidelity. I did not kill my children. God forbid! I merely wanted to keep them out of the way while I watched over you.'

When Griselda heard this, she almost fainted for joy. Then she called her two young children to her, and embraced them. She wept as she kissed them, her tears falling upon their cheeks and upon their hair.

All those around her were crying, too, as she spoke softly to her son and daughter. 'I give thanks to God,' she said, 'for saving my dear children. I give thanks to my lord and master, too. If I were to die now, I would know at least that I have found favour in your eyes. Now that I am restored to grace, I do not fear death. I do not fear anything.

'Oh my dear children – my little ones – your poor mother imagined that you were buried beneath the ground. She really believed that rats or dogs had eaten your bodies. But God has saved you. And your father has kept you safe.' Then she fainted upon the ground.

She had embraced her children so tightly, in fact, that it was difficult to prise them from their mother's loving arms. All those around her were still crying, of course. They could not bear to see her in her extremity of joy and bewilderment.

Walter kneeled beside her and tried to soothe her. After a while she stood up, a little disconcerted, and everyone cheered her and encouraged her until eventually she recovered her composure. Walter was the very soul of comfort and concern. Really, it was a delight to see them both together once again.

When the ladies of the court saw their opportunity, they led Griselda to her old chamber. There they removed her threadbare clothes and dressed her in a gown made of cloth of gold. They put a crown of many jewels upon her head before leading her into the principal hall, where the newly restored wife and mother was greeted with acclamation.

So this unhappy day had a happy ending. Every man and woman danced and feasted, as well they might, until the stars lit up the heavens with their blissful light. There was more joy, and more revelry – more expense, too – than the celebrations of the bridal day so many years before.

So for many years Griselda and Walter lived together in love and happiness. Their daughter was married to one of the richest and most noble lords in all of Italy. The marquis took good care of Griselda's father, too, who spent the rest of his days at ease in the palace.

Griselda's son, on the death of his father, took over the rule of Saluzzo. He married well, and happily, but he never put his wife to any test. It is said by some that this world is not so strong as it was in old times. I don't know about that. But listen to what our noble author, Petrarch, had to say in conclusion to his tale.

'I have not told this story to counsel wives into submission. They could not, and should not, copy the patience of Griselda. The real lesson is more simple. Every man and woman should, like her, try to be steadfast in adversity. That is enough.' And that is why Petrarch chose to narrate the story of Griselda in his most noble prose.

If a woman can be so submissive to a man, then how much more should we show our obedience to God Himself? He has every reason to test us all. He created us. But in his epistle Saint James tells us that God will never tempt us beyond our strength.

It is true that he tempts us every day. He disciplines us with seasons of adversity, since in misfortune we can exercise our virtue. He knows all our frailties, of course, and does not need to probe them further. He does everything for our own good. So be patient. Be of good cheer.

I will say one more thing to you, lords and ladies of the pilgrimage. It would be almost impossible to find another Griselda in modern England. If you put a wife or mother to the test, you would find more brass than gold. A woman nowadays is like a bad coin. She will break rather than bend.

Naturally I have nothing against the Wife of Bath. May God

give her, and those like her, a good life! Long may she rule over us!

Griselda is dead, and lies buried somewhere in the land of Italy. Her patience was in the end rewarded. But I beg you, all you husbands, never to test your wives as Walter tested her. Your efforts will not work. You will fail.

All you noble wives, take heed. Never let humility nail down your tongue. Do not allow some other writer to tell your story as Petrarch recounted that of kind and patient Griselda. Do you remember the story of Chichevache, who could feed only on humble housewives? That was why he was so lean. Please do not be fodder for his stomach.

You should follow the example of Echo, who always had an answer ready. Don't be naive. Don't be beaten down. Fight back. Keep the lesson of Griselda firmly in your mind. You can do nothing but profit from it.

Oh you mighty wives, defend yourselves. You can be as strong as elephants, I am sure of it. Don't allow men to get the better of you. Those of you who are not so mighty – well, I am sure you can still be fierce. You can rattle on and on, just like a windmill in a gale.

Have no fear of your husband. Even if he were clothed in full armour, the arrows of your eloquence would get through the chain-mail. Make him jealous. Or – better still – accuse him of something. Then he will be as still and frightened as a little bird.

If you are good-looking, make use of it. Show off your features, and your dress. If you are ugly, spend your money freely and make friends with everyone. Get them on your side. Be as light and playful as a leaf upon a linden tree. Let your husband do the wailing and lamenting. That is all I have to say.

Heere endeth the Tale of the Clerk of Oxenford

The Merchant's Prologue

The Prologe of the Marchantes Tale

'I know all about wailing and lamenting,' said the Merchant. 'I am acquainted with grief. Many married men can tell the same story, I am sure of it. I have learned by experience. I have the worst wife in the world, you see. If she were married to the devil, she would get the better of him. I won't bore you with all the details of her malice. Suffice to say that she is a complete bitch. There could not be a greater difference between her cruelty and the patience of Griselda. If I were free again, I would never fall into the same trap. A burned husband fears the fire. You know I am telling the truth. It may not be the case for all husbands. God forbid. But it is true of the majority.

'I have been married only for two months, I admit, but I have been tormented every day by my wife. No bachelor could possibly understand the pain I have endured. Even if he were knifed, or whipped, he would not suffer half as much as I have done. She is a wicked woman.'

Harry Bailey clapped him on the back. 'Well, sir Merchant,' he said, 'since you are such an expert on the woes of marriage, tell us all about them.'

'Willingly, sir. But I will say no more about my own plight. I am too depressed about it.'

And, heaving a sigh, he began his story.

The Merchant's Tale

Heere bigynneth the Marchantes Tale

Once upon a time there dwelled in Lombardy a worthy knight. He lived in Pavia, where he was prosperous and well respected. He had in fact been a bachelor for sixty years, but he enjoyed himself with any number of women. He was highly sexed, I believe, as are many unmarried men. His name was January. When he had just passed his sixtieth year he either went mad or he repented of his sinfulness. He decided to get married, in other words. He went around looking for a likely wife, beseeching the Lord God all the time that he might for once experience the bliss that lies in married life. I am not making this up. He was determined to live under that holy bond, that gracious union, that blessed state in which God determined that the first man and woman should dwell. 'No other life,' he announced, 'is worth anything. Wedlock is so pure. Wedlock is so easy. Wedlock is paradise on earth.' So said this wise and worthy knight.

He may have had a point, especially when the husband is old and infirm. Then a young wife is a regular treasure. She is a fruit to be plucked. He can enjoy her youth, and at the same time engender an heir. He can have a good time, while an old bachelor can only moan and groan. Confirmed bachelors always suffer for their calling. They are building on shifting ground. They think they have found stability, but it falls apart in their hands. They live like animals, without care or restraint. Married men, on the other hand, are happy and secure in the blissful state of matrimony. They have everything they could possibly need. Who could be so obedient as a wife? Who could be more true? Who could be more attentive, in sickness or in health? A wife will never leave her husband. She will never tire of caring for him, even if he became bedridden and close to death. Especially not then, of course.

Yet there are some wise men who beg to disagree with this. Take Theophrastus, for example, who wrote *The Golden Book on Marriage*. Marriage was not golden for him. But I suspect him of lying. 'Do not take a wife,' he said, 'for the sake of household economy. It is a false saving. A good servant will spare you expense, and will also look after you better than any wife. A wife will always demand her half share in everything. If you are sick you will be happier in the hands of your friends, or even of a serving-boy. Your wife, as always, will be thinking of your goods and chattels. I will tell you something else. If you marry, you are sure to be cuckolded. A woman is unfaithful by nature.'

No, no, Theophrastus! May God curse you for these words! You are telling nothing but lies and more lies! Pay no attention to him. Listen to me instead.

A wife is a gift from God. All other gifts are as nothing. Think of them. Lands. Rents. Pastures. Household goods. They are the gifts of Fortune, mutable and transitory. They are shadows on the wall. But be sure of this. A wife is for life. A wife can last a long time – longer, perhaps, than you might like.

That is why I hold marriage to be a great sacrament. He who is wifeless is cursed. He is helpless. He is desolate. I am not talking about monks or friars, of course. Let me tell you this, too. Women are born to be the servants of men. They are born to help us out. When God had made Adam, and saw him lying in the grass alone and naked, He took pity on him. In His goodness He thought to Himself, 'Let us now make a companion for this poor man who resembles him. That is the thing to do.' And He wrought Eve. So, you see, I have proved my point. A wife is a husband's comfort. She is his earthly paradise; she is his honey. She is so virtuous and obedient that the two of them are bound to live in harmony. They are one flesh. So of course they have one heart between them, both in sickness and in health.

A wife! Good God! How can a man suffer when he has a wife beside him? I cannot say. There is no way of describing or picturing the bliss between them. If he is poor, she will help him in his labours; she keeps house for him, and wastes nothing. She approves of everything her husband does. She will never say 'no' when he says 'yes'. 'Do this,' he says. 'Of course, sir,' she replies. That is the way it is. Oh happy sacrament of matrimony! You are so cordial, so delightful, so well loved and so well respected! Any man worth his salt will go down on his bended knees and thank God for the day he was married. Or else he will pray to God to send him a wife as quickly as possible. 'Oh God,' he says. 'Send me a woman to last me all my life. Then I will be content.' He will not be wrong in that, I can tell you, especially if he heeds his wife's advice. Then he will be able to hold up his head. Women are so truthful and so wise, as I am sure you all know, that men are duty bound to follow their commandments.

Do you remember how Jacob took the advice of Rebecca? His mother told him to wear the skin of a goat around his shoulders to trick his father and win his blessing. And do you remember the story of Judith, who slew Holofernes and thus saved the people of God? And then there was Abigail, who by her good counsel saved her husband, Nabal, when he was about to be slain by King David. What about Esther? She saved the people of God from a life of lamentation. She persuaded her husband, Ahasuerus, to advance the cause of Mordechai. You can look up the stories in the Bible, if you don't believe me.

Seneca, that wise man, tells us there is nothing more pleasing than a humble wife. Suffer your wife to speak, as Cato tells us, and fulfil her commands. Of course, if you are lucky, she may even obey you on occasions. That's only being polite. A wife must be the keeper of your worldly goods. Who is going to look after you when you are sick? Take my advice. Love your wife in the manner that Jesus Christ loves the Holy Church. If you love yourself, you must also love your wife. No man is an enemy of his own flesh, I am sure. He protects it. You must cherish your wife in the same way. Or you will never thrive. Whatever people say and joke – that was no lady, that was my wife – husband and wife are on the highway to happiness. They are bound so closely together that no harm can come to them. The wife, in particular, gets off lightly.

I will now return to my worthy knight named January. He had been considering all the matters I have put before you – the encroaching years, the physical bliss of marriage, the quiet and order of a settled home, the honey pot of a fair wife. Revolving these matters in his mind, he called together a group of his good friends in order to announce his decision. And with grave face he addressed them thus: 'I am growing old, dear comrades. I am getting closer and closer to the brink of the grave. I must think about the life to come. I have stupidly wasted my strength in pursuit of all sorts of folly. As God is my judge, I am going to change. I have decided to marry as quickly as possible. I need your help in finding a pretty young girl. I need a bride now. I don't think I can wait much longer. For my part I will look up and down the town. But you all must keep your eyes open, too. You must help me find a suitable wife.

'There is one thing I must tell you, though. I will not stomach an old bride. She must be below the age of twenty. I enjoy my fish, but not my flesh, mature. I like fresh meat. A pike is better than a pickerel, but a frisky calf is better than an old cow. I don't want or need a woman of thirty. Women of that age are nothing but bales of straw. They are beanbags. As for those old widows, God forbid I should come near any of them. They are nothing but trouble and strife. They are more wily than any scholar. They have been to the school of life, where they learned all the lessons. No. Give me a young thing. I will be able to mould her in my hands like a piece of warm wax. So there we are, friends. Throw out the old, and bring in the new. If I should by any chance be unlucky in love, and suffer an unhappy marriage, why, I would take up adultery for a living and go to the devil after my death. I would certainly never father any children on an old misery. I would rather be eaten by dogs than allow my inheritance to pass into strange hands. I am not kidding. I know all the reasons for marriage, although I suspect that there are many people who talk about it who haven't the faintest idea. So I will tell you this. If a man cannot live chastely, then he must marry. If a man wants to have children by lawful procreation, then he should take a wife. A mistress or a lover is not the same thing. That is mere lechery, in the eyes of God, and has nothing to do with the obligations of the marital bed.

'Husband and wife can also live together in perfect innocence, of course, just like brother and sister. I don't think that is the way for me. I can say, thank God, that all my limbs are in good working order. I can do the job of a man. I know where my strength lies. I may seem aged but I am like an old tree that still brings forth its leaves. I can feel my buds begin to swell. My blossoms will soon be poking out. I am not dried up or dead as yet. The only hoar frost is sprinkled on my head. In every other place I am as green and fresh as a laurel, year in and year out. Well, enough. Now that you have heard my proposal, let me know what you think.'

The company all had different opinions and different questions. Some of them praised marriage. Others criticized it. They all had stories and examples to confirm their points of view. They argued all of that day, in a good-humoured fashion, but in the end the main argument was between two of his closest friends. One of them was named Placebo, a pleasing sort of fellow, and the other was known as Justinus, or 'the just one'.

This was Placebo's point. 'Oh January, dear friend, you really have no need to ask any of us for our opinions. You are wise enough to know that it is best to follow the judgement of Solomon in this matter. Do you remember what he said?

"Work out what is the best advice. Then follow it. You will not regret it." That was the sum of his wisdom, I believe, and I agree with every word of it. Except on this occasion, dear brother, weighing one thing with another, I am inclined to believe that you should follow your instinct. Consult your heart, my friend. Let me tell you something. I have been a courtier all my life. God knows I am unworthy of the honour, but I have been privileged to serve some of the greatest lords of our land. Never once have I argued with them. I have never contradicted them. I knew well enough that they had more judgement than I could possibly claim. I agree with every word they say. I say the same, in fact, or something very similar. A courtier would be a great fool if he dared to presume that he had more wit than his lordship. He must not even think it! No. Our lords are not idiots. I will say that for them.

'This is my point, dear January. You have shown such eloquence and wisdom here today that I fully agree with every-thing you say. I would not change one word. There is not a man in all of Italy who could have spoken more nobly. Christ himself would concur. It is truly a courageous act for a man of your years to take on a young wife. It is bold. It is mag-nanimous. You are a good creature! So this is my opinion. Do whatever you think is best. I am sure that will be the right course.'

Justinus had been sitting quietly listening to Placebo. 'Dear friend,' he said to January. 'Be patient with me. I have heard everything that has been said. I will add a few words of my own. Seneca has told us that a man must be careful, and think twice, before giving away his lands or his cattle. Since it is important to be sure about the recipient of your worldly goods, surely there is even more reason to scrutinize the person to whom you are giving away your body? You will never get it back. Marriage is not child's play. You should never take a wife without very careful thought. You have to ask questions. You have to find out whether she is prudent or wasteful. You must know whether she is sober or a drunk. You do not want to marry a scold, do you, or a man-chaser? Or a bitch? It is important to discover, too, whether she is rich or poor. Don't tie yourself down with a shrew, in other words.

'Now I know that it will be impossible, in this fallen world, to find a woman who is perfect in every way. I give you that. Still you really ought to find out whether your wife-to-be has more good qualities than bad qualities. This will take time. But it is important. I should know. I have wept plentifully, and often, since I took a wife. Praise the married life all you like. But I personally have found it to be full of cost and care, of duties rather than pleasures. God knows that all my neighbours, especially the females, congratulate me on my choice of wife. They say that she is considerate and steady in the extreme. Yet I know where the shoe pinches. I know where it hurts. Of course, January, you must do as you please. But take my advice. You are a man of a certain age. Think very carefully before you take on a young and pretty wife. By Him who made heaven and earth, the youngest man among us would have trouble keeping on top of such a woman. Restraining her, I mean. Trust me. Within three years, she will be sick of you. You know what a wife needs, don't you? Do you think you have the strength to fulfil all her desires? A wife asks for a lot, you know. I just hope that you are not riding for a fall.'

'Well,' January replied. 'Is that all you have to say? I don't give a fuck for Seneca or for your own grave words. And as for your warnings, well, I dismiss them. They are a crock of shit. Wiser men than you, as you have heard, take quite a different view of my proposal. What do you say, Placebo?'

'I say, dear sir, that it is a serious matter – it is almost profane – to raise any impediment to holy matrimony.'

With that the whole company rose to their feet. They agreed, one and all, that January should be married when and where he wished. As for the bride, well, that was up to him.

And the bride was on his mind. He thought about her all the time. He had fantasies about her. Many beautiful bodies, and many pretty faces, went through his mind as he lay in bed at night. If you took a brightly polished mirror and placed it in the middle of a fair or a market, you would be bound to see the images of many people passing to and fro. January's imagination was the same. It was a mirror in which were reflected the shapes of all the prettiest young girls in his district. He was not sure which one to choose as yet. One had a beautiful face, while another had a good reputation for modesty and obedience. One came from a rich family, but had a bad character. Nevertheless, after much thought, he fixed on one above all others. Half in earnest and half in game, he dismissed thoughts of all the rest. Without consulting anyone else, he made his decision. Love is blind, after all.

When he got into bed every night, he imagined her in every state and every position. He gloated on her perfect body and on her youthfulness; he pictured her narrow waist, her long legs and her slender arms. Oh, of course he also reflected on her wifely virtues – on her modesty and her tenderness, her womanly bearing and her seriousness. When he had decided, then, he believed that he could not have made a better choice. Nothing and no one could have changed his mind. If anyone had been so brave as to try to do so, he would have dismissed him as a fool. He was living in a fantasy world. Once more he sent a message to all of his friends, asking them to assemble in his house as soon as possible. He would not detain them long, he said, and in any case he would spare them the labour of looking out for a young girl to be his mate. He had made his choice. He would not change his mind.

Placebo arrived first, of course, but he was soon followed by the others. January greeted them all, and then asked a favour of them. They would please not argue with him. He had made his decision. It would simply be foolish to oppose it. All his happiness depended on the choice he had made. He told them that there was a young girl in the town who was renowned for her good looks. She was of relatively humble stock, but her youth and beauty compensated for that. He said that he had determined to marry her, and to lead the rest of his life in perfect bliss and holiness. He would own all of her, and no one else would ever get a part of her.

So he asked his friends to assist him in this enterprise, and help him to succeed in securing his prize. His soul would then be at ease. 'There will,' he said, 'be nothing to mar my happiness. But I do have one thing on my conscience. Let me explain. Many years ago I heard that no man can enjoy the two kinds of bliss – the bliss of earth and the bliss of heaven. He can have one or the other. He cannot have both. I may not commit any of the seven deadly sins. I may not commit any of the little ones. But this is the trouble: I am about to get married to the perfect wife, with whom I will live in the utmost felicity. All will be calm. All will be sweet. So I will have heaven on earth. Do you see the problem? We are always taught that heaven itself is the reward of pain and purgation, of penance and tribulation. How can I, living in comfort and joy, attain my eternal reward? I am not alone, of course. All husbands live in comfort with their wives. Or so I believe. But give me your honest opinion on my problem.'

Justinus, despising January's total stupidity, responded straight away with a joke. He did not bother to quote authorities. He would give him a short answer. 'There is no obstacle on your path to heaven. God by some miracle will come to your aid. He will ensure that, before you are carried to the grave, you will have cause to repent your marriage. You say there is no woe or strife in marriage. By divine intervention He will prove you wrong. Did you not know that husbands always have more cause for repentance than single men? This is the best advice I can give you. Wait and see. Do not despair of heaven. It may turn out that your wife will be your purgatory. She may be God's instrument. His whip to scourge you. Then your soul will skip up to heaven faster than an arrow leaves a bow. I hope to God for your own sake, then, that you discover there is no great happiness to be found in marriage. There is nothing so pleasurable about it that will keep you from salvation. You still have to be moderate in all things, of course.

You must never fulfil all of your wife's desires, if you know what I mean. Do not be too amorous with her, and keep yourself free from other sins. Then you will reach heaven's gate. That is the only advice I can give to you. My cupboard is bare, as they say. Don't look so surprised, dear brother. Shall we forget we ever mentioned the subject? You have already heard the Wife of Bath discourse on the perils of marriage.'

'The Wife of Bath?'

'She made a lot of sense, didn't she? Well, enough. God keep you.'

And, with that, Justinus and Placebo took their leave of January. They knew that there was no alternative. So by secret negotiation and treaty they arranged that their friend should marry the young girl whom he admired as quickly as possible. Her name, by the way, was May. It would be too long a story to tell you of the marital arrangements – of the lands put in May's name, of the costly garments promised to her. The day came. May and January proceeded to the church in great array, where they received the holy sacrament of marriage. The priest came out before the altar, with the stole around his neck, and enjoined May to follow the example of Sarah and Rebecca; they were wise and faithful wives. Then he said a few prayers, made the sign of the cross over the couple, asked God to bless them, and performed every other holy rite he could think of. So they were joined with great solemnity. The pair of them sat at the feast, on the top table, with all the other noble guests. The house was filled with festival and music, with feasting and drinking, the like of which had never before been seen in Italy. The instruments were of such fineness and delicacy that they rivalled the harp of Orpheus and the golden lyre of Amphion. As every course was brought out the minstrels sounded their trumpets, making more clangour than Joab ever heard at Mount Zion or Theodomas at the siege of Thebes. Bacchus himself might have been pouring out the wine. And was that Venus laughing and smiling upon all the company? Yes, it was. January had become her devoted servant, after all. He was about to be tested in marriage as once he had been in his bachelor state. So the goddess, with a firebrand in each hand, danced before the bride and groom. I can tell you this much. The god of marriage, Hymen, never saw a more cheerful bridegroom than January. Say no more, Martianus Capella. You have written of the splendid marriage between Philology and Mercury, and extolled the songs the Muses sung for them. But your pen is too short, your tongue too small, to begin the description of the wedding day of January and May. This was the day when tender youth married halting age. Do you have enough ink for your quill? This cannot be told. The fun of it would not be believed. Find out for yourself. Then tell me whether I am lying or not.

It was a delight to look at the young bride, May, dressed in all her finery. She looked like a fairy queen. Queen Esther, who caught the eye of that Persian king, never looked half so lovely. I cannot explain her beauty. Words fail me. Suffice it to say that she lived up to her name; she was as fresh and lovely as a spring morning. Old January was ravished by her. Every time he looked at her, he went into a trance. In his imagination, of course, he was contemplating their first night. He would hold her in his arms more tightly than Paris held Helen. Yet he also felt sorry for her. She was going to be his victim, that very night, and he might have to hurt her. 'Alas,' he said to himself, 'you are such a tender creature. I hope God gives you the strength to bear up under me. I am on heat, to put it mildly. I am worried that I will be too much for you to handle. God forbid that I should injure you in any way. Do you know what I wish? I wish the night had come. I wish the night would last for ever. And, finally, I wish all these people would go away.' He did everything he could, by subtle means, to persuade the guests to finish quickly. He was, after all, an honourable man.

Eventually the time came for them all to rise from the table. The men began to dance and to drink deeply, while the women scattered spices about the house. Everyone was happy

– everyone, that is, except for a certain squire called Damian.
He carved January's meat for him every day, but now he had
an eye on tastier fare. He was so ravished at the sight of May
that he thought he would go out of his mind. Do you recall
Venus dancing with a firebrand in each hand? She put one of
those brands within Damian's heart. He could hardly stand.
He was about to faint. So he retired to his bed as quickly as he
could. There we will leave him to his tears and laments, until
such time as May will have pity on him.

Oh perilous fire that smoulders in the bedding! The enemy in
the household is the most dangerous of all. The traitorous servant is like an adder clasped to the bosom; he is treacherous
and sly. God keep him away from all good men. Oh January,
be careful. You are lost in pleasure now, but keep an eye on
Damian. Your own squire, your man, intends to do you harm.
I hope to God that you catch him in time. There is no worse
plague in the world than a dishonest and treacherous servant.

The sun had traced its arc of gold across the sky, and could
not linger on the horizon of that day. The night had fallen,
and darkness spread over the earth. The merry guests left the
marriage feast, giving thanks to January, and rode homewards
in cheerful mood. Were they going straight to bed? I don't
know. I do know, however, what January wanted to do. Bed
was the only thing on his mind. He was not going to wait any
longer. So he prepared himself a hot punch of spice and sweet-
ened wine, as an aphrodisiac. He also took some herbs and
simples recommended by the disgraceful monk, Constantinus
Africanus, who wrote that book *On Fucking*. He tried every
single ointment and concoction. Then he turned to the close
friends who were still in the house, telling them to leave
quickly and quietly 'for the love of God'. They did as they
were told. They drank up, and then they drew the curtains.
The priest blessed the bed, and May was brought to it. She
was as still and silent as any stone. Everyone filed out of the
bedchamber, leaving bride and bridegroom there alone.

January grabbed May as soon as they were gone. She was his

spring, his paradise, his wife. He petted her and clawed her, kissing her on the cheek and lips. His bristle was as tough as the skin of an old dogfish. His face was like a bed of briars, and he rubbed it all over her tender flesh. Then he started crooning to her. 'Oh dear, oh dear, I must trespass upon you, my sweetheart, and perhaps offend you. I may hurt you before I have finished with you. But consider this, my duckling. No labourer worth his hire can work hastily. It has to be done slowly and surely. It doesn't matter how long we play together. We are both coupled in holy matrimony, so we can take all the time we want. We have been blessed by the priest. Nothing we do will be considered sinful. A man cannot cut himself with his own knife. The law gives us permission to have some fun.'

So he fell upon her, thrusting and heaving all that night. He climbed off her, eventually, and refreshed himself with some bread soaked in fine red wine. Then he sat up in bed and began to sing loudly and clearly. He leered at her, and licked his lips. He was as frisky as a colt, as wanton as a monkey. When he started singing the slack skin about his neck began to shake. His voice gave out and he started croaking. God knows what May thought of all this. She stared at him as he sat there in his nightshirt and nightcap, with his scrawny neck and bony face. She did not praise his performance. That's for sure.

'I will take a rest now,' he said to her. 'It's already daylight. I need to sleep.' Then he laid his head upon the pillow, and fell into a sound slumber. When he woke up at nine o'clock, he sprang out of bed. May, however, stayed in the bedchamber for four days.

The labourer needs rest, you see. Otherwise he, or she, will not be able to survive. This is true of every creature under the sun, fish or bird, beast or man.

Now I will turn back to woeful Damian, who is languishing for love of May. This is what I should tell him. 'Oh foolish boy. You silly thing, Damian. Answer me this one question. How are you going to explain your plight to May? She will just turn you away. If you tell her how much you love her, she will simply betray you to her husband. God help you. I can say no more.'

So Damian is bathed in the fire of Venus, lost and helpless with desire, ready even to put his life at risk. He could stand it no longer. He borrowed a pen, and then wrote a letter in which he revealed all his sorrow. He wrote it in verse, a poetical complaint addressed to his fresh and lovely May. A lay is a lay in any language. He placed the manuscript in a little silk purse that he hung around his neck, close to his heart.

From the time of the wedding day, the moon had glided from the sign of Taurus into Cancer. That is how long May resided in her bedchamber. It was the custom of new brides. They must not eat in hall until three or four days have passed; after that time, she can sit at the feast. On the fourth day, therefore, January and May attended high mass before proceeding to dinner in the hall. She was as bright and lovely as a summer's day. Then the sight of the meat prompted her good husband to think of Damian. 'Mother of God,' he exclaimed, 'why isn't Damian here to wait on me? Is he sick or something? What has happened?' The other squires explained to him that Damian had indeed been taken ill and could not perform his duties. Only sickness would keep him away from the table.

'I am sorry for it,' January replied. 'Damian is a good and loyal servant. It would be a great pity if he were to die. He is as intelligent and as discreet as any young man of his rank; he has always been attentive and eager to please. After dinner my wife and I will visit him in his chamber, to see if we can offer him any comfort.' All the company blessed him for that. Out of sheer kindness this good knight was willing to visit his sick squire. It was very gracious of him. 'Dearest wife,' January said, 'listen to me. After we have finished the meal, I would like you and your women to attend to Damian. Try to cheer him up. He is a good boy. Tell him that I intend to visit him, too, after I have had a nap. Don't be gone too long, dear. I will not be content until you are back with me and lying by my side.' Then he called over one of the other squires, his master of ceremonies, and discussed some matters of business with him.

So May, accompanied by all her women, proceeded to the chamber of Damian. She sat down by the side of his bed, and comforted him as best she could. Then the young squire, as soon as he saw his opportunity, secretly put in her hand the little silk purse in which he had placed his lay of love. He sighed deeply as he did so, and then whispered to her, 'Have mercy on me, lady. Tell no one about this. If I am discovered, I am as good as dead.' So May hid the purse in her bosom, and went on her way. I shall say no more.

She came back to her husband, who was already in bed. He clasped her in his arms and kissed her. Then he laid himself down to sleep. May excused herself, saying that she had to visit the you-know-what – where everyone has to go. She took out Damian's verses and read them in the toilet; then she tore the paper into pieces and flushed them down the loo. May now had a lot to think about. She lay down beside January, who was fast asleep until he woke himself up with a coughing fit. As soon as he opened his eyes, he asked her to strip naked. He told her that her clothes got in his way. Whether she liked it or not, she was forced to obey her husband. I will not go into any more details, for fear of offending the more fastidious among you. Let me just add that he took his pleasure of her. Whether this was heaven, or hell, for her I cannot say. They were at their business until the time of evensong, when they rose from their bed.

I do not know whether it was chance or destiny. I am not sure if it was the work of grace or the work of nature. But it happened that, at this time, the pattern of the constellations worked in favour of lovers. This was the moment to submit a petition, a *billet-doux*, to Venus. The scholars tell us that all things have their season. This was the season for young women to find – who knows what? God alone knows all the causes within human affairs. I can tell you nothing about them. I do know this, however. May had taken such a liking to Damian that she could not stop thinking about him. His image was lodged in her heart. 'I don't care what anyone thinks about me,' she said. 'I love him. I love him more than anyone else in the world. If he had only his shirt to his name, I would still love him.' Do you see how pity soon suffuses a gentle heart?

You may perhaps now understand how generosity of spirit comes naturally to women. Consideration makes them bountiful. Of course certain women are as hard as adamant. They would rather starve a man to death than show him favour. They would not consider themselves murderers, oh no, they would congratulate themselves on their cruel virtue. Not so for May. She was full of pity for Damian. She wrote him a letter, in which she pledged to him her heart. All they needed to find was the time and place. Then she would be happy to satisfy all of his desires. Could he come up with a plan? This was the gist of her message.

When she found the opportunity she went to Damian's chamber, and surreptitiously slipped her note beneath his pillow. Would he find it? She squeezed his hand, without anyone else seeing, and begged him to get well soon. Then she returned to her husband, who was calling out for her.

Up rises Damian on the following morning. He had forgotten all about his sickness and his sorrow. There was a spring in his step. He combed his hair, cleaned himself and brushed down his clothes. He did everything to please a certain lady. Then he presented himself to January as humbly as a dog trained to hunt. He was so pleasant to everyone, in fact, that the household was full of praise for him. Craft is easy, for those who are crafty. Above all else he stood high in the favour of May. So I will leave Damian going about his business, and carry on with my story.

Some wise men suggest that human happiness is to be found in the pursuit of pleasure. Certainly the noble January was of this opinion; he looked for pleasure all the time, in the most virtuous possible way of course. He was an honest knight, after all. So his house, and all his other fine goods, were as fitting for his rank as are a king's. Among his treasured belongings was a delicious garden, walled all around with stone. I cannot begin to describe the beauty of it. There was nothing like it. The author of *The Romance of the Rose* could not do justice to it. The god of gardens, Priapus himself, would not be equal to the task of depicting the fairness of this place. There was a refreshing well, for example, under a laurel tree that was always green. It was said that Pluto and Proserpina, with their fairy band, sang and danced about that well; it was filled with music, not with water.

The noble knight took such pleasure in walking through these green arbours that he never allowed anyone else to enter the garden; he was the only one who held the key. It was a small silver latchkey that unlocked a wicket-gate. So he came and went as he pleased. In the summer he took his young wife with him, and there he had his way with her. He frisked and frolicked. Whatever he had not done in bed, he did on the grass. He did it, whatever it was, as often as he could. What fun. Can you imagine the happiness of January – and of May?

But wait. Worldly joy may not always endure for January, or for any other human being. Oh sudden chance! Oh unstable Fortune! You are as treacherous as the scorpion, who creeps towards his unsuspecting victim with a hidden sting. Its tail means death by sudden poisoning. Oh brittle happiness! Oh sweet and cunning poison! Oh Fortune! Let me cry out against you one more time! You are a monster who can paint your blessings with all the bright colours under the sun, as if they were to last for ever. But you are false to young and old, rich and poor! How could you deceive that honest and noble man, January, who placed such trust in you? Fie on you! What did you mean by taking away his sight?

Yes. That is what happened. Amidst all his joy and prosperity, January was suddenly struck blind. He wept and wailed. He wanted to die. And then another thing crossed his mind. He became inflamed with jealousy. He could no longer keep an eye, now gone, on young May. What if she were able to fool him? He was so heartbroken, so dejected, that he would willingly have paid someone to murder him and his wife. He hated the thought of her being the mistress of another man, or even the wife of someone else. He wanted her, after his death, to be clothed in perpetual black. He wanted her to be as solitary and sorrowful as the turtle-dove that has lost its mate.

After a month or two, however, he began to settle down. He became less miserable. He learned to adjust to his misfortune. What cannot be cured must be endured. But his jealousy had not abated. It burned as fiercely as ever. He had become so suspicious of his wife that he would not allow her to go anywhere without him. She could not go out for a ride. She could not visit friends. He even insisted that she stayed with him in the house. So May often wept. She loved Damian so truly that she believed she would die if she could not hold him in her arms. She believed that her heart would break.

Damian himself became the most sorrowful man that ever lived. He could not utter a word to May, night or day. If he had said anything to the purpose, January was bound to hear him. He never left her alone. His old hand was always upon her. Nevertheless they passed messages, and made certain private and silent signs so that one knew the mind and intentions of the other. Oh January, what good would it do you if you could see as far as the bounds of the ocean? What difference does it make to be blind and tricked, or to have sight and be tricked? Argus had a hundred eyes, looking into every corner; yet he was deceived. God knows how many other husbands have been fooled into thinking their wives are chaste. My position is simple. What you don't know can't hurt you.

Let us return to fresh and lovely May. She had taken some warm wax and made an impression of the little silver key to the garden that January always held. She gave it quietly to Damian, who then made a copy of it. I will not anticipate events. But listen to my story, and you will hear a wonder concerning this garden and its wicket-gate.

Ovid, my master, you know the truth of human life. You

have said that there is no subtlety, no deception, that lovers will not pursue for the sake of their passion. Nothing is too arduous. Nothing is too complicated for them. There was the case of Pyramus and Thisbe who, strictly watched and supervised, managed to hold converse through a wall. No man could have discovered their method.

Back to the story. On the morning of 7 June (I am not sure of the year), January, urged by his wife, conceived a great desire for some sportive tricks in the garden. He wanted to play with her. So on that morning he cooed to May, 'Rise up, my dearest, my lovely baby. The voice of the turtle-dove can be heard in the land, my dove, and the winter storms have gone. Rise up now. Open your dove-like eyes. Come forth with me. Oh, your breasts are sweeter than wine. The garden is walled. No one can see us. Walk out with me, white and fair as you are. You have captured my heart with your spotless beauty and virtue. Come. Let us go to play. I have chosen you for my pleasure.' These were the lecherous words of the old man.

May, meanwhile, had made a sign to Damian that he should go before them through the wicket-gate. So Damian took the counterfeit key, opened the gate, and silently made his way into the garden. No one saw or heard him. Once inside, he sat quietly beneath a bush. January, as blind as a stone, now entered the garden; he was holding May's hand. As soon as he had closed the gate behind him, with a great clatter, he turned to her.

'Now, wife,' he said, 'only the two of us are here. You are the creature I love best in all the world. As God is my witness I would rather cut my own throat than offend you. Do you remember how I chose you? Not out of greed, dear heart, but out of love for you. I may be old and blind, but I will explain to you the blessings of fidelity. It is a debt you owe to Jesus Christ, and to your own honour. And of course you will inherit everything – palace, money, everything. I will sign a contract to that effect before tomorrow evening. Now in return I will ask you for a little kiss. Your lips will seal the bargain. Don't blame me for being jealous, by the way. You are so deeply imprinted on my heart that, when I consider your beauty in contrast to my old age, I cannot bear to be out of your company. I must always have you beside me, precious one, for the love I feel for you. Now kiss me, dearest. Let's go for a stroll.'

May, hearing his words, began to weep very gently. Then she recovered herself, and replied to him. 'I have a soul to keep spotless, just like you, and of course I must guard my honour. The tender flower of my womanhood is in your hands. I gave it to you when the priest bound us together in holy matrimony. And I tell you this, my dear lord. I pray to God that the day never comes when I bring shame to my family or bring dishonour to my own name. I will never be unfaithful. I would rather die the most painful death in the world. If I prove false to you, then sew me in a sack and drop me in the nearest river. I am a gentlewoman, not a whore. Why do you talk to me this way? Well, men are ever untrue. They never stop reproaching their wives. They never stop being suspicious and distrustful.'

She caught sight of Damian sitting beneath the bush. She coughed lightly and then, using sign language, told him to climb a nearby pear tree full of fruit. He was on his feet and up the tree in a flash. He knew exactly what she intended, and could read her mind better than January ever could. She had written him a letter, in any case, where she had explained her plan. So for the time being I will leave him in the pear tree, with May and January strolling happily between the beds of flowers.

Bright was the day and through the trembling air the golden rays of Phoebus descended to the earth, warming all the flowers with their caress. He was at that time in Gemini, I suspect, close to the summer solstice. The bright sun would soon begin its decline. It so happened on this day that Pluto, king of the fairies, entered the garden on the farther side. He was accompanied by his wife, Proserpina, and all the ladies of her entourage. He had taken her from Etna, if you remember, when she was gathering wild flowers on the mountainside. You can read the story in Claudian's *The Rape of Proserpina*, where he describes the dark chariot in which she was driven away.

Pluto sat down upon a green sward of turf, in the middle of the walled garden, and addressed his queen. 'My wife, no one will disagree with me. Experience teaches us every day that women are treacherous towards men. I could tell you a million stories about their frailty and fickleness. Oh Solomon, wisest and wealthiest of all, winner of human glory, what reasonable person could fail to note and remember your words? He was praising the goodness of humankind, observing that "I have found one man among a thousand. But, among women, I have found none." So said King Solomon, knowing full well the wickedness of the female sex. Jesus of Syrak, author of Ecclesiasticus, rarely speaks of you with reverence. May wild fire cover you! May pestilence fall upon your bones! Do you see what is happening now? This honourable knight, old and blind as he is, is about to be cuckolded by his own servant. Look where the lecherous bastard is hiding in the pear tree. I now decree, of my majesty, that sight will be restored to this worthy old man. His eyes will open at the moment his wife betrays him. Then he will know her wickedness, to the great shame of her and of other harlots.'

'Oh will you?' Proserpina was very sharp. 'Is that what you intend to do? By the soul of my grandfather, great Saturn, I swear that I will give the woman a sufficient answer to him. I will help all other women, too, who are accused. If they are found in any sin, I will ensure that they put on a bold face and give a good excuse. They will bear down their accusers. None of them will die for lack of a retort. Even if the man sees the offence with his own eyes, yet the woman will face it out boldly. She will weep and swear and bully until she wins the argument. You men are as gullible as geese. What do your so-called authorities matter to me? I know well enough that this Jew, this Solomon, discovered plenty of fools among women. He may not have come across a good woman, but other men have found women to be true and faithful and virtuous. What about all those good Christian women who proved their constancy with martyrdom? The Roman annals are filled with stories of faithful wives. Keep your temper, dear husband. I will explain to you what Solomon meant when he said that he could find no good woman. I will interpret. He meant that supreme goodness lies only in God and that all flesh, male or female, is frail.

'Anyway, Solomon is only one man. Why do you make such a fuss of him? Who cares if he built a great temple to God? Who cares about his wealth and wisdom? He also built a temple to the pagan gods. There is no blasphemy worse than that. You may try and excuse his faults, but he was a lecher and an idolater. He abandoned God in his old age. The Bible tells us that God spared him only for the sake of his father, King David. If it had not been for David, Solomon would have lost his kingdom sooner than he would have expected. I don't give a damn for any of the slanders he and others have written against women. I am a woman, I must speak out, or else my heart will break. How dare he call us chatterers and worse? As long as I live I will attack him for his vicious opinions. I will never spare him.'

'Calm down, dear,' Pluto replied. 'Curb your anger. I give in! But since I swore an oath to restore his sight, I must keep it. My word must stand. I am a king. I cannot break oaths.'

'And I am a queen! This young woman will have her answer. I guarantee it. So. Let us not argue any more. I will not be at cross purposes with you.'

Let us leave the rulers of fairyland, and return to January. He was enjoying his stroll through the garden with May, and was chirping like a budgerigar. 'You know,' he said, 'I love you best. I always will.' They went up and down the walks, until eventually they returned to the pear tree in which Damian was concealed. He was sitting high among the green leaves. So May, glowing with health and energy, now piped up. 'Oh,' she said, 'I've got a terrible pain in my side. I must have one of those little green pears that I can see. I don't care about anything else. I must eat one. I must handle one of them. For the love of heaven, my husband, help me to the fruit. I might die otherwise. The fruit! The green fruit!'

'Oh God,' he replied, 'if only I had a servant here who could climb the tree. I am blind. I cannot help.'

'Yes you can. If you put both your arms around the tree – like so – then I could place my feet upon your back and climb up to the branches. Trust me. I can do it.'

'Of course I trust you. I would do anything for you, darling. Is this the right position?' So he stooped down on the ground beside her. She clambered on to his back and, grabbing a branch, hauled herself up into the tree.

Ladies, forgive the next bit. I am a rude man. I cannot gloss over the facts. As soon as she had mounted the tree, Damian pulled up her smock and fucked her.

When Pluto saw that this great wrong was being wreaked upon January, he gave back the old knight his sight. It was better than it had been before and, of course, the first thing he wanted to look upon was his lovely wife. So he glanced lovingly up at the tree. Whereupon he saw Damian thrusting away. I will say no more about it. It is not polite. I have already said enough. So January sets up a roaring and a crying, just like a mother who has lost her only child. 'Help!' he shouted. 'Harrow! Havoc! Alarm! What are you doing, you little whore?'

'What is the matter with you, sir?' May replied demurely. 'Have patience. Be reasonable. I have just cured your blindness. As God is my witness, I am not lying. I was told that there was one way to bring back your sight – if I were to struggle with a man up a tree, you would be healed. That's the truth. God knows my intentions were honest.'

'Struggle?' January replied. 'I saw his cock inside you! I hope to God that you both die of shame! He fucked you. I saw it with my own eyes. May I be hanged otherwise!'

'It seems that my medicine did not work,' May said. 'If you

really could see, you would not be using these words to me. You have a glimpse, or squint, and not perfect sight.'

'I can see as well as I ever could, thank God. Both of my eyes were open. I am sure – I thought – that he was fucking you.'

'You are still dazed, good husband. You are imagining things. And that is all the thanks I get for curing your blindness. I try to be kind, and then –' She burst into tears.

'Now, wife,' January said, 'let us forget all about it. Come down from the pear tree. If I have slandered you, then I am well punished for it by your tears. I really did believe that I saw Damian having sex with you. On my father's soul I believe that I saw your smock against his chest.'

'You may believe what you like,' May replied. 'But a man that is suddenly woken from sleep may not grasp a situation straight away. He has to be perfectly awake before he sees things clearly. You were asleep, in one sense. You were blind. Do you expect to see perfectly the very moment your eyes are opened? You have to wait a day or two. Until your eyesight has settled down, I am sure you will be deceived by other illusions. Be careful, dear husband. Men are fooled by their visions, or their fantasies, every day. He who misunderstands, misjudges.' And with these words she leaped down from the tree into his arms.

Who could be happier than January? He clasped her tight and kissed her all over. He ran his hand against her belly. Then, rejoicing, he walked with her back to the palace.

Now, good pilgrims, I hope that you are also content. So ends my story of May and January. God bless you all.

Heere is ended the Marchantes Tale of Januarie.

The Merchant's Epilogue

'God in heaven!' Harry Bailey exclaimed. 'Keep me away from a wife like that! Do you realize how many tricks and deceits a woman can use? They are busy as bees, morning and night, trying to fool us. The last thing they want is the truth. The Merchant's tale proves it. I will tell you plainly. My own wife is faithful to me. I know that. But she is a shrew. She may be poor, but she is rich in insults. She has plenty of other vices, too. Well, I can't do much about it now, can I? Forgive and forget. But do you know what? Between you and me, I wish that I were not wed to her. Of course I would be a fool to repeat all of her faults. Do you know why? It would get back to her. There would be gossip by one or two members of this company. I do not need to name names. You all know who I mean. Women have a way about them. They know the market for their wares. I haven't got the wit to carry on with a long story, in any case. Farewell to all that.'

Then he turned in his saddle and addressed another pilgrim.

The Squire's Prologue

'Squire, come nearer to me. Come. Do us a favour. Tell us a love story. I am sure you are an expert in that field.'

'I don't think so, sir,' the Squire replied. 'But I will do my best. I will not disobey your order. I will tell you a story. But don't think any the worse of me if I mess up. My intentions are good, in any case. Well. Here goes.'

The Squire's Tale

Here bigynneth the Squieres Tale

PART ONE

At the city of Tsarev, in the land of the Mongols, there lived a king who made continual war on Muscovy. It was a struggle in which many brave men were killed. The name of this king was Genghis Khan. He had achieved such glory by force of arms that there was no more renowned leader in the entire region. He lacked nothing that pertains to kingship. He faithfully observed all the laws of his religion; he was doughty, wise and rich. He was as pious as he was just. He kept his word in honour and in kindness. He was as stable as the centre of a circle. He was young, too, and full of life. Like any other bachelor knight, he prided himself on feats of arms. What else is there to say? He was a happy and a fortunate man, and maintained so royal an estate that no one else could hope for a better.

Now Genghis Khan had, by his wife, Elpheta, two sons. The oldest of them was named Algarsyf. And the younger one was called Cambalo. He also had a daughter, Canacee by name. I could not begin to describe her beauty to you all. It is beyond my abilities. I would not be able to stammer the words. My English is insufficient. It would take an excellent orator, knowing all the arts of his trade, even to attempt to portray Canacee. But I am no orator. I am a poor squire.

So it happened that, in the twentieth year of his reign, Genghis Khan proclaimed the feast of his nativity throughout the city of Tsarev. He celebrated that day every year. It was in the middle of March, I believe. The sun was powerful and strong in those climes. It was already in the first ten degrees of Aries, sign of heat and dryness, so that the weather was warm and refreshing. The little birds sang in the sunshine. Their notes rose up into the air, as if they were a protection against the keen frosts of winter.

So Genghis Khan, wearing the vestments of lord and king, was sitting on his throne in the royal palace. He was holding a feast to commemorate his birthday. There was so much of everything on the tables that I will not describe the array. It would take a summer's day to go through the entire menu. There is no point, either, in reciting the sequence of dishes brought from the kitchens. I will not mention the swans or the young herons, all boiled or roasted. I know that tastes vary. What is considered a delicacy in one country is scorned in another. In any case I cannot comment on everything. Time is running on. It is almost nine o'clock. I will resume the story where I left off.

The feast had come to the third course. The king and his courtiers were listening to the sweet music of the players, performing before the dais, when there was a sudden clatter. A knight appeared at the doors of the hall, sitting astride a horse of brass. In his hand he held a great glass mirror. He had a broad ring of gold on his thumb, and a gleaming sword hung down by his side. He rode up to the king's table. No one said a word. They were all astonished by the sight of this knight. Young and old looked on.

This knight was in full armour, except that he wore no helmet. He gracefully saluted all the company, king and queen, ladies and nobles, in order of rank. He seemed so full of reverence and modesty, in looks and speech, that Gawain himself (if he emerged from fairyland) could not have equalled him. Then, as he stood before the assembled company, he delivered his message in a calm clear voice, full of strength. He followed all the rules of discourse and enunciation, just as the orators teach us, fitting his gestures to his words. I cannot imitate his high style, of course. That would be too great a challenge. But I can give you the gist of what he said, if my memory doesn't fail me.

'The king of Arabia and India salutes you, great lord, and sends you greetings on this solemn day of festival. In honour of your birthday he presents you with this steed of brass. I, who am your willing servant, was asked to bring it into your presence. This horse can, in the course of a single night and day, carry you to any place on earth. Wind or rain does not deter it. Wherever you wish to go, there it will take you unharmed. If you want to soar through the air like an eagle, this horse will carry you. You can fall asleep on its back, and still come to no harm. Do you see this pin here behind his ear? If you twist it, the horse will return you to your starting place. The inventor who made this horse was a very cunning man. He waited until all the planets were in the right aspect before he began work. He knew all the secrets of his craft.

'Now let me tell you about the mirror I am holding. It has much power. When a man looks into it, he will see whatever misfortune awaits him. It will show you, sire, any harm that threatens you or your kingdom. Friend and foe will be reflected in the glass. If any gracious lady has set her heart on a man, she will see in this mirror if he is false to her; she will see his unfaithfulness as clear as day. Nothing will be concealed. On this auspicious spring day, my lord and master sends this mirror and this gold ring to your excellent daughter, Canacee.

'May I tell you about the virtues of the ring? If the noble lady cares to wear it on her thumb, or carry it in her purse, she will understand the language of the birds. She will be able to speak to them as they fly above her. She will also understand the language of every herb that grows upon the earth, and will know which of them heals or cures the most grievous wound.

'I will now explain the power of the sword that is hanging by my side. It has the ability to smite through the heaviest and greatest armour. It will cut through metal plates, thick as oak trees, as if they were made of butter. It has one other power. Any man who is wounded by this sword will never be whole again – unless you take up the blunt side of the weapon itself, and lay it upon his body in the place where he is hurt. Stroke the wound with the sword, and it will close up. I swear that all this is true. This sword will not fail you.'

As soon as he had finished speaking, the knight rode out of the hall and leaped from his horse. This animal, its brass shining as bright as the sun, stood absolutely still in the court-yard. The knight himself was led to a chamber, where he was carefully undressed and given meat. Meanwhile the gifts he had brought with him, the sword and the mirror, were taken by royal officers to the high tower of the palace. The ring itself was solemnly presented to Canacee as she sat at the high table. The horse of brass, however, could not be moved. It seemed to be glued to the ground. None of the courtiers or soldiers could dislodge it – not with pulley, or windlass, or mechanical engine of any kind. How could they? They did not know its secrets. So they left it in position until the knight in shining armour, as you shall hear later, told them the trick of shifting it.

Great was the crowd that swarmed about this horse. It was so tall, so broad, so strong and so well proportioned that it seemed like a steed out of Lombardy. It had all the qualities of a horse. It was the horsiest horse anyone had ever seen. It could have come from Apulia, in fact, rather than from northern Italy. From its tail to its ears, it was a model of its kind. Everyone agreed that neither art nor nature could have improved upon it. And of course everyone was astonished that it was made of brass. How could the knight ride it? Some said that it was a wonder of the fairy world. Some said that it was the work of magicians. Diverse people offered diverse opinions. There were as many theories propounded as there were heads. The people murmured like a swarm of bees. They came up with elaborate fancies, based upon the stories they had read. Some said that it resembled Pegasus, the horse that had wings. Others said that it was the twin of the wooden horse that brought destruction into Troy. They knew all about these animals from the old books.

'I am very afraid,' said one of them. 'I am sure that there is an army inside the belly of this beast, waiting to destroy this city. Why can't we find out? Why can't we know?'

'He's quite wrong,' another whispered softly to his companion. 'This is an apparition shaped by magic, just like the illusions created by conjurors at great feasts.'

So the company was besieged by various doubts and fears. This is the way of common people when confronted by something beyond their experience or understanding. They come to the wrong conclusion. They panic.

Others among them were wondering out loud about the mirror that had already been carried into the principal tower of the palace. They wanted to know how it worked. How could all these things be seen within it? One of them said that it might be a natural phenomenon. It was a question of perspectives and angles and reflections. There was one just like it in Rome. Then they all started talking about Alhazen and Vitello and Aristotle, who had written on the subject of mirrors and optics; they had heard of these authors, even if they had not actually read them.

And then again they wondered at the magic sword that could cut through anything. They talked about King Telephus, who was wounded and then healed by the wonderful spear of Achilles. It had exactly the same miraculous properties as this sword, as you have just heard. So the company talked about the ways in which metal could be hardened. They spoke of the especial solutions that could be used to temper steel. They debated all the whys and wherefores. I myself know nothing about them.

When they had satisfied themselves on that matter, they turned their attention to the gold ring given to Canacee. They all said that they had never heard of a ring like it. In all the history of rings they had never known one – except perhaps from the hand of Moses or Solomon, who were supposed to be masters of magic. They gathered in little groups and muttered to each other. Wasn't it queer to learn that glass was made from the ashes of fern? Glass doesn't look a bit like fern, does it? Or like ashes? Since it is a matter of fact that glass is made from the ashes of fern, they soon stopped asking stupid questions. They were like people who wonder all the time about the origins of thunder, or the causes of tides, or the webs of spiders, or the gathering of mist. They want to get to the bottom of everything. And so they questioned and debated and puzzled until the time that Genghis Khan rose from the high table.

The sun had left its meridian, and the lion was ascending, when the great king left the hall. It was two o'clock on 15 March, in other words. The minstrels walked before him, playing loudly on the gitern and the harp, as he made his way to the presence chamber. The music was so sweet and solemn that it might have issued from the halls of heaven. Venus was sitting in majesty, exalted in Pisces, and all her children on earth were dancing. She looked down at the revellers in the palace with a very friendly eye.

So the noble king is set upon his throne. Very soon the strange knight is brought before him. And, look, he is dancing with Canacee. All is joy. All is harmony. A dull-witted man like myself cannot describe the scene. It would need a love-struck genius, filled with the spirit of spring, to do justice to the occasion.

Who could explain to you the intricacies of the native dances, the subtle rhythms, the smiles, the devious looks and glances passing between the maids and the young men? Only Lancelot, the knight of love. And he is dead. So I pass over all the playfulness. They danced and flirted until it was time to dine.

Then, as the music played, the steward of the household called for the wine and spiced cakes to be brought in quickly. The ushers and the squires left the hall, while the revellers feasted on the food and drink. When they had finished they all trooped into the temple for a service. Once that was over, they fell upon their suppers. Why say any more about it? Every man knows that, at a king's banquet, there is enough and more than enough. No one goes hungry. There were more dainties there than I can describe. When the feast was complete, the king and his entourage walked out into the courtyard in order to view the miraculous horse.

There was more amazement at this animal than at any time since the siege of Troy. The Trojans were astonished at the appearance of a wooden horse; the lords and ladies at the court of Genghis Khan were even more astounded by a metallic one. Eventually the king asked the knight to explain the properties of this horse. He wanted to know how strong it was, and the best way to ride it. As soon as the knight put his hand upon the reins, the horse began to frisk and dance. 'Sir,' the knight said, 'there is nothing more to tell you. When you want to ride anywhere, you just twist this pin behind the ear. When we are alone, I will tell you how to do it. You simply mention to the horse the city or the country you wish to visit, and it will take you there. When you wish to stop and walk around, just twist this other pin. That is all there is to do. It will descend and wait for you until your return. Nothing in the world will move it. Or, if you want the horse to disappear, use this pin here. Then it will vanish out of men's sight, and will reappear only when you call him. I will give you the secret signal later on. So travel where you like. Ride the wind.'

The king listened carefully to everything the knight told him; as soon as he had understood the instructions, and the method of riding, he was delighted. He went back to the feast, and the horse's bridle was taken up to the tower. Thereupon the horse itself vanished. I don't know how. I can say no more about it. I know only that Genghis Khan stayed at the revels with his nobles until the following dawn.

PART TWO

The kind nurse of digestion and appetite, sleep, began to descend upon the party. Hypnos, the son of Night, let it be known that after much toil, and after much drink, it was time to rest. So he kissed them all. He yawned, and bid them all to lie down. Their blood was thick and heavy. 'Cherish your blood,' he said. 'It is nature's friend.' By now they were all yawning, too. They thanked him for his advice, and laid themselves down to rest. It was the best thing to do.

I shall not describe their dreams. They were filled with drink and, in that state, dreams have no meaning. They all slept until prime, nine o'clock – all of them, that is, except Canacee. She had been very sensible, as women are, and had gone to bed early after thanking and blessing her father. She did not want to look ill or pale on the following day; she wanted to look fresh and gay. So she slept a moderate amount, and then awoke. On opening her eyes she thought once more of the ring, and the magic mirror; she was so excited that she must have changed colour twenty times. Even in her sleep she had dreamed of that mirror. It had made such an impression on her. So just before the sun began to rise she called her governess to her bedside, telling her that she wanted to dress and get ready for the day. The old crone, who considered herself to be as wise as her mistress, readily answered. 'Where will you go, ma dame,' she asked her, 'when everyone else is still in bed?'

'I want to get up. I have had enough sleep. I want to walk about and take the air.'

So the governess clapped her hands and summoned the maidservants, a dozen or more, to attend their mistress. Then up rose Canacee, as bright and rosy as the sun itself. It was already warm, the sun having risen into Aries, and so the princess walked out blithely into the light. She was gaily dressed for the season and, with five or six of her attendants, she enjoyed the fragrance of the early morning. Together they made their way down a green avenue in the park.

The mist rising from the fresh earth made the sun seem roseate and large; it was so fair a sight that all of the ladies were glad at heart. It was a lovely season. It was a wonderful morning. All the birds began to sing. And, as they sang, Canacee understood them perfectly. She could follow their meaning note by note. I forgot to mention one thing, you see. She had put on the ring.

No one wants to hear a long story without a point, or a story in which the point is long delayed. All the fun goes. The patience wears thin. The narrative loses its savour. So, without more ado, I will put an end to this walk in the park.

Canacee was having a delightful time, when suddenly she came to a dry and withered tree as white as chalk. In its branches perched a falcon that set up such a shriek that the whole wood resounded with her cries. The bird had beaten herself so badly, with both of her wings, that her red blood ran down the white tree. She kept up her bitter lament all the time, stabbing her breast with her beak. There was no beast, no tiger, so cruel that it would not have pitied her. All the animals of wood and forest would have wept with her, if they had been capable of tears. There had never been a falcon so fair of shape and form, so beautiful of plumage, so noble of nature. She seemed to be a peregrine falcon from some foreign land; she was perched on the tree, but she had lost so much blood that several times she was close to swooning. She might have fallen out of the tree.

Now the fair princess, Canacee, who wore the ring, understood everything that the falcon had said. She could listen to her, and reply to her in her language. In fact she was so filled with pity for the bird that she might have died. So she hastened up to the tree, looking up through its branches at the falcon; then she spread wide the skirt of her dress, in case the bird fell through lack of blood. Canacee stood there for a long time, saying nothing, until eventually she spoke out loud.

'What is the cause of all this pain, if you can tell me? You are in hell, I know. What is the reason? Are you mourning a death? Or the loss of love? Those are the two reasons for sorrow such as yours. No other woe comes near to them. You are injuring yourself so grievously that fear or fury must be goading you. There is no one, as far as I can see, hunting you. Have pity on your own sufferings. For the love of God, tell me. How can I help you? I have never, in all the world, seen a bird or beast enduring so much self-inflicted pain. You are killing me with your sorrow. I feel such sympathy for you. I entreat you. Please come down from the tree. I am the daughter of a noble king. If I know the cause of your suffering, I will try to alleviate it as best as I can. As far as it lies within my power, so help me God, I will cure your woe before night comes. Here. Look. I will find herbs for you now, to cure the wounds you bear.'

On hearing the words of the princess, the falcon gave out a shriek more piteous than before. She toppled from the branches and fell down upon the ground, where she lay as still as any stone. Canacee took the bird into her lap, and caressed her gently until she had awoken from her faint. As the falcon recovered from her swoon, she began to speak to the princess in the language of the birds. 'It is true that pity runs freely in a gentle heart. It is only natural to feel another's woe as if it were your own. We have all experienced it. We have all read about it. A gentle heart manifests gentleness. I can see well enough, Canacee, that you have pity for my distress. Nature has given you compassion, fair princess, as one of the principles of your being. You are the paradigm of female kindness. I have no hope of getting better but, in honour of your kind heart, I will tell you everything. I will, perhaps, be able to set an example and act as a warning to others. You may beat the dog to warn off the lion. For that reason, while I still have breath in my little body, I will confess the whole truth.'

As the bird spoke the princess was bathed in tears; she was weeping so piteously that the falcon bid her to be still and stop her sobbing. Then with a sigh she began her tale. 'I was born –

God curse the day – and brought up on a rock of grey marble. I was raised so tenderly that nothing in the world ailed me. I knew nothing of adversity until the time when I first sailed high into the air. Close to me dwelled a tercelet, the male of my species. He seemed noble and honourable, but in fact he was filled with treachery and falseness. He seemed so cheerful and so humble that he fooled everyone; he was always so eager to please. Who could have known that it was all an act? As we birds say, he had dyed his feathers. He was like the snake who conceals himself beneath sweet-smelling flowers, the easier to bite and wound. He was the hypocrite of love, all smiles and bows, obeying all the rules and customs of courtly romance. A tomb is raised out of shining white marble, nicely carved, but there is a rotting corpse within; so did this hypo-crite display himself on every occasion. He was all front. Only the devil knew his true purpose. He was always crying on my feathers. He was always bewailing the miserable life of a lover. He courted me year after year until, finally, I relented. My heart was too soft. I was too gullible. I knew nothing of his malice, of course, and in fact I was afraid that he might die of love. So I made him utter a solemn oath. I would grant him my love on condition that my honour and good name were not tarnished; I wished to be blameless, both in private and in public. So I gave him all my heart, and all my hopes. I thought that he deserved them. When he agreed on oath to respect me, then I took him as my own true love.

'But there is a saying, as old as it is true, that "An honest man and a thief do not think alike." When this tercelet, this false bird, realized that he had snared me and had captured my loving heart, he fell down on his knees in gratitude. He was as faithless as a tiger. He vowed that he had never been so happy. He said that he was more joyful than Jason or Paris of Troy. Jason? Why do I mention him? This bird was more like Lamech, who, according to the old books, was the first bigamist. No man since the beginning of the world – no human being living or dead – could match the tricks of this tercelet. He

THE SQUIRE'S TALE   273

was the supreme counterfeiter. No other fraudster was fit to unbuckle his sandals! He was the prince of perjury. You should have seen the way he offered his thanks to me a thousand times. He was perfect in the part. The wisest woman would have fallen for it. The mask fitted his face. The paint was laid on thick. In looks and in words he was all charm. I loved him for the love he bore me, and for his true and honest heart. If anything troubled or upset him, I felt it so strongly that I might have died. So in time I became the supple instrument of his will; his will was the stronger, and I obeyed him in everything – within the bounds of reason and of modesty, of course. I never loved a bird more, or half as much, as I loved him. I never will again.

'So for a year or two I was convinced of his goodness. But nothing lasts for ever. Fortune turns the wheel. Eventually the time came when he was obliged to leave the land in which I lived. Of course I was distraught. I cannot describe my feelings. I can tell you one thing, though. I knew the pains of death. I was acquainted with grief, now that my love could no longer stay by my side.

'On the day of his departure he was so sorrowful that I believed he suffered as much as I did. When I heard him speak, and saw his pale countenance, I truly believed that he was also in despair. Nevertheless I was convinced that he would return to me as quickly as possible. I reassured myself that he would be back soon enough. He had to go away, for reasons of duty. So I made a virtue of necessity. I tried to stay cheerful. I concealed my pain, I took him by the hand and, calling on Saint John as a witness, told him that I would always be faithful to him. "I will be yours," I said, "for now and ever more. Please be loyal to me, too." There is no need to tell you his reply. Who could speak more nobly than him? Who could act more wickedly? "He who sups with the devil needs a long spoon." Is that not the saying? So, having made his little speech, he left and flew to his destination. I do not know where. But when he finally came to rest, I am sure that he had the following text in mind. "All creatures of the earth," wrote Boethius, "when they regain their proper nature, naturally rejoice." I think it was Boethius. Men love novelty. I know that much. Have you ever seen those birds that live in cages? They are fed on milk and honey, bread and sugar. Their cages are lined with straw as soft and smooth as silk. Yet as soon as the door of the cage is opened, what do they do? They fly away, of course. They leave the little cup and bells. They take wing to the wood where they can feed on worms and dirt. They need new meat. They need change and a new diet. Good breeding does not come into it.

'This is what happened to my tercelet. I could weep even now. Although he was of gentle birth, well mannered and well groomed, he happened to see a low-born kite sailing by. On that instant the sweet gentleman became infatuated with a scavenger bird. Can you believe it? Of course he forgot all about his love for me. He broke all his oaths and promises. So my so-called lover has fallen for a kite. And I am left behind without hope!' At that the falcon let out a scream, and fainted dead away in the lap of Canacee.

The princess and her entourage were greatly moved by the falcon's plight, but they did not know how to comfort her. Canacee decided to take the bird home, cradling her in her lap, and then she began to wrap up the self-inflicted wounds with bandages and plasters. The princess also took rare herbs from the garden of the palace, making ointments and other medicines from them; she tried everything in her power to heal the hawk. She even made a pen of wickerwork by the side of her bed, draped in blue velvet cloths, where the bird might rest. Blue, of course, is the colour of faithfulness. The outside of this cage was painted green, and on it were depicted the images of all the false birds of the world – the owls, the tercelets, the lecherous sparrows. There were also placed here, in derision, the portraits of those little chatterers known as magpies. How they scold and chide!

So I will leave Canacee in the company of her ailing hawk. I will say no more about her magic ring until a later occasion, when I will tell you how the poor bird regained her repentant lover. The old books relate how this reunion was accomplished by the son of Genghis Khan, Cambalus. I think I have mentioned him before. Anyway, he was the one who brought the birds together. Enough of that. I now want to proceed to tales of battle and adventure. I have many marvels to impart to you. I will tell you the history of Genghis Khan, the great conqueror. Then I will speak of Algarsif, the oldest son of the mighty warrior, who won his wife by magical means. He would have been in great danger, if he had not been saved by that wondrous horse of brass. Then I will narrate the adventures of another warrior who fought the two brothers for the hand of their sister, Canacee. There is so much to tell you! I will begin again where I left off.

PART THREE

Apollo was riding in his chariot so high that he entered the house of cunning Mercury – 'What's the matter? Why are you putting your finger to your lips?'

Here folwen the wordes of the Frankeleyn to the Squier, and the wordes of the Hoost to the Frankeleyn

'Great job. You have done very well, Squire,' the Franklin said to him. 'You have spoken nobly. I can only praise your wit and invention. Considering how young you are, you really got into the spirit of the story. I loved the falcon! In my judgement there is no one among us here who is your equal in eloquence. I hope you live a long life and continue to exercise your skill in words. What an orator you are. I have a son myself, about your age. I wish that he had half of your discretion. I would give twenty pounds of land to the person who could instil some common sense into him. What's the point of property, or possessions, if you have no good qualities in yourself? I have remonstrated with him time and time again. I have rebuked him for following the easy path to vice. He wants to play at dice all day, losing his money in the process. He would sooner gossip with a common serving-boy than converse with a gentleman, from whom he might learn some manners.'

'Enough of your manners,' called out our Host. 'You have a task to perform. You know well enough, sir Franklin, that each of the pilgrims must tell a tale or two on our journey. That was the solemn oath.'

'I know that, sir,' replied the Franklin. 'But am I not allowed to address a word or two to this worthy young man?'

'Just get on with your story.'

'Gladly. I will obey you to the letter, dear Host. Listen and I will tell you all. I will not go against your wishes. I will speak as far as my poor wit allows me. I pray to God that you enjoy my tale. If it pleases you, I will be rewarded.'

The Franklin's Prologue

The Prologe of the Frankeleyns Tale

The noble Bretons of ancient times sang lays about heroes and
adventures; they rhymed their words in the original Breton
tongue, and accompanied them with the harp or other instrument. Sometimes they wrote them down. I have memorized
one of them, in fact, and will now recite it to the best of my
ability. But, sirs and dames, I am an unlearned man. You will
have to excuse my unpolished speech. I was never taught the
rules of rhetoric, that's for sure. Whatever I say will have to be
plain and simple. I never slept on Mount Parnassus, or studied
under Cicero. I know nothing about flourishes or styles. The
only colours I know are those of the flowers in the field,
or those used by the dyer. I know nothing about chiasmus or
oxymoron. Those terms leave me cold. But here goes. This is
my story.

The Franklin's Tale

In Armorica, better known to us as Brittany, there dwelled a knight who loved and honoured a fair lady. He was wholly at her service. He performed many a great enterprise, and many a hard labour, before he earned her love. She was one of the fairest ladies under the sun, and came from such noble ancestry that he hardly dared to reveal to her his torment and distress. But in time she grew to admire him. She had such admiration for his modesty and his gentleness – such pity for his sufferings – that privately she agreed to take him as her husband. She would accept him as her lord, with all the obligations that implies. In turn he swore to her that, in order to preserve their happiness, he would never once assert his mastery. Nor would he ever show jealousy. He would obey her in everything, submitting to her will as gladly as any lover with his lady. For the sake of his honour, he would have to preserve his sovereignty in public. But that was all.

She thanked him for his promise. 'Sir,' she said, 'since you have so nobly afforded me such a large measure of freedom, I swear that I will never let anything come between us through my actions. I will not argue with you. I will not scold you. I will be your true and humble wife. Here. Take my hand. This is my pledge. If I break it, may my heart itself break!' So they were both reassured. They were happy, and at peace.

There is one thing I can say for certain, sirs and dames. If two lovers want to remain in love, they had better accede to each other's wishes. Love will not be constrained by domination. When mastery rears up, then the god of love beats his wings and flies away. Love should be as free as air. Women, of their nature, crave for liberty; they will not be ordered around like servants. Men are the same, of course. The one who is most patient and obedient is the one who triumphs in the end. Patience is a great virtue and, as the scholars tell us, will accomplish what the exercise of power never can achieve. People should not reply in kind to every complaint or attack. We must all learn to suffer and endure, whether we like it or not. Everyone in this world, at one time or another, will say or do an unwise thing. It might be out of anger or of sickness; it might be the influence of the stars or of the bodily humours; it might be drink or suffering. Whatever the cause, all of us will make mistakes. We cannot persecute every error, therefore. The best policy is mildness. It is the only way to retain self-control. That is why this knight agreed to be a devoted and obedient husband, and why the lady in turn promised that she would never hurt or offend him.

Here then we see a wise agreement, a pact of mutual respect. The lady has gained both a servant and a lord, a servant in love and a lord in marriage. He is both master and slave. Slave? No. He is pre-eminently a master, because he now has both his lady and his love. According to the law of love, his lady has become his wife. In this happy state he took her back to his own region of the country, where he had a house not far from the coast of Brittany. His name, by the way, was Arveragus. Her name was Dorigen.

Who could possibly describe their happiness? Only a married man. They lived together in peace and prosperity for a year or more, until that time when Arveragus decided to sail to England. Britain, as our nation was then called, was the home of chivalry and adventure. That is why he wanted to move here. He wanted to engage in feats of arms. The old story informs us that he lived in Britain for two years.

I will now turn from Arveragus to Dorigen. She loved her husband with her whole heart and, of course, she wept and sighed during his long absence. That is the way of noble ladies. She mourned; she stayed awake all night; she cried; she wailed out loud; she could not eat. She missed him so much that nothing else in the world mattered to her. Her friends tried to comfort her, knowing how greatly she suffered. They tried to reassure her and to reason with her. They told her, night and day, that she was tormenting herself unnecessarily. They tried every means of consoling her and of cheering her.

You all know well enough that, in time, water will wear down the hardest stone. If you scrape into flint, you will eventually create an image. So by degrees Dorigen was comforted. Little by little, she was persuaded to calm down. She could not remain in despair for ever, after all. Arveragus himself was writing her letters all the time, telling her he was well and that he was eager to return. Without these messages of love she would never have regained her composure. She would have died of sorrow, I am sure of it. As soon as they saw that she was beginning to recover, her friends got on their knees and begged her to go out and enjoy herself. She should spend time in their company, and in that way try to forget her cares. Perpetual woe is a dark burden. Eventually she agreed with them that this was for the best.

The castle of Dorigen was close to the sea, as I said, and there were many times when she would walk with her friends along the shore. From that vantage she could see all the ships and barges making their way over the waves, sailing to one port or another. But the sight of them of course renewed her suffering. Often she murmured to herself, 'Alas! If only one of these ships were bringing home my husband! Then all this pain would go away. Then would my heart be light again.' There were other times when she would stand by the side of the cliff, and look down upon the waves dashing against the black rocks. She would be filled with anxiety, so nervous and fearful that she could hardly stay upon her feet. She would sit down upon the short grass, and gaze out at the ocean. Then she would pray to God, her words mingled with sorrowful sighs.

'Almighty God, through whose will and foresight the whole world is governed, You create nothing without a purpose. Yet why, then, did You create these fearful rocks below me? They are so dark and so destructive. They seem more like a foul fault in creation than the work of a wise and benevolent deity. Why did You let them issue from Your hand? There is no living thing that cannot be harmed by them. Any man or bird or beast – from any point of the compass – can be broken against them. These sinister rocks do nothing but harm. Do You know, Lord, how many men and women have been shipwrecked? Of course You do. The rocks of the ocean have killed many hundreds of thousands of people, all of them lost and forgotten. It is said that You loved humankind so much that You fashioned it in Your own image. It seemed then that You were bestowing a great boon. How then is it possible that You should create these evil rocks that do nothing but provoke death and disaster? No possible good can come from them.

'I believe theologians argue that Your providence is such that all things turn out for the best. I myself cannot follow their arguments about destiny and free will. I say only this. May the God who made the winds blow, preserve my husband! That is all. The scholars can dispute as much as they like. I pray only that all the rocks in the world are consigned to hell for my husband's sake.' So Dorigen, in tears, would express her grief.

Her friends began to realize that these walks by the sea were not doing her any good. Quite the opposite. So they set about finding some other place to entertain her. They took her to cool rivers and to holy wells; they took her to dances and other celebrations; they taught her to play chess and backgammon. Then one morning, at the rising of the sun, they came into a garden where they had laid out food and drink to accompany their revels all that day. This was on 6 May, a fair morning when the sweet showers had brought forth the leaves and flowers of early spring; they had been arrayed so carefully throughout the garden that there was no other display like it in the world. It was like a garden in paradise. The scent and brightness of the flowers would have lightened any heart, except for one bowed down with sorrow or distress. It was a place of beauty and delight.

After they had eaten, the lords and ladies set out to sing and dance – all of them, that is, except for Dorigen, who still made her moan. There was no dancing for her if her husband was not part of the happy company. Still she sat on one side, not in solitary retreat, and hoped that her sorrow might lessen a little.

There was among the dancers a jolly young squire, handsome and fleet of foot; he was fresher than the spring day and, according to all reports, he could sing and dance better than any other man in the world. He was also one of the most good-looking. He was young and strong, virtuous and rich, wise and well respected. What else can I say? Oh, one more thing. Unknown to Dorigen and the others, this young squire, Aurelius by name, was in thrall to Venus; for the last two years he had secretly been enamoured of Dorigen. He loved her more than anyone else in the world, but of course he had not been able to disclose his love. He had drunk the bitter cup of misery down to the lees. He was in despair; but he was silent, save for the songs of woe that he sometimes sang. He did not sing of his own case but, rather, made general complaint about the pains of love in various chants and lyrics, roundels and virelays. He sang of a lover who was not beloved. He sang of a true heart beating in vain. He sang of a lover suffering all the pains of hell. Echo pined away for love of Narcissus. That will always be the fate of the star-struck lover.

So in all his pain Aurelius dared not reveal his feelings to Dorigen. Yet there were times, at dances where the young come together, when he looked upon her with such intentness that he seemed to be asking her for mercy. But she knew nothing about this. Nevertheless it happened on this day that, after the dance was over, they fell into conversation. There was nothing wrong with that. They were neighbours. They had known each for a long time. And he was an honourable man. Yet, as they talked, Aurelius came closer and closer towards the one theme that haunted him. When he saw the right time, he spoke out.

'Ma dame,' he said, 'I wish to God that I had gone over the seas like your husband. I wish I had set sail on the same day. If it would make you happy, I would gladly travel to a distant land from which I could never return. I know well enough that my service to you here is all in vain. My reward is a broken heart. Ma dame, have pity on my pain. You can cure me or kill me with one word. I wish that I lay buried here beneath your feet. I have no more to say. Have mercy on me, sweet Dorigen, or else I will die!'

She turned and looked at Aurelius. 'What are you saying to me? Can I believe what I am hearing? I never suspected this of you before. But now I know everything. By the God who gave me soul and life, I never shall be an unfaithful wife. In word and deed, to the utmost limit of my strength, I will be a true lady to my lord. Take that as my final answer.' But then, as if playing a game with him, she seemed to relent a little. 'Aurelius,' she said, 'I swear to the same god that I will bestow my love on you. I have taken pity on your tears. There is only one condition. On the day that you manage to clear all the rocks that deface the coast of Brittany – on the day that you remove, stone by stone, these cruel impediments to our ships and boats – I will promise to love you as no other man has ever been loved. When the coasts are clear, I will be yours. I swear it.'

'Is there no other way?' he asked her.

'None. I know that it is never going to happen. Don't dwell upon the possibilities. It just can't be done. In any case what kind of a person are you, to have designs upon another man's wife? My body is not for auction.'

Aurelius sighed very deeply. He was depressed by what he had heard, and with sorrowful countenance he replied to her. 'Ma dame,' he said, 'you have set me an impossible task. There is no choice for me now. I must die a piteous death.' And with these words he turned and walked away.

Now the rest of the company came and joined them, not realizing the conversation that had passed between them. They paraded through the garden walks, and soon began singing and dancing again until the setting of the sun. The horizon dimmed its light. The night came upon them. So they went back to their homes in peace and happiness – all except Aurelius, of course, who returned to a house of woe. He saw no remedy but in death. He felt his breast, and it was as cold as ice. He fell down on his knees and raised his hands to heaven. He prayed – he knew not what. He was out of his mind with grief. He did not know what to say or what to do, so instead he set up a long low complaint to the gods in heaven. He addressed the sun first of all.

'Fair Apollo,' he prayed, 'you are god and governor of every living thing on earth. You lend the time and give the season for every plant and flower and tree. Just as you take care of Nature, great god, will you take care of your poor servant Aurelius? Cast your eye upon the wretch who kneels before you. Oh god above! I am lost. My lady has condemned me to death, but I am innocent. Through your divine kindness have some pity on my plight. I know well enough, great Phoebus, that you could help me best – next to Dorigen, of course. I know that you can work all things to your will. Please tell me what I ought to do. Please give me hope.

'I know that your sister, Lucina, full of grace, is the mistress of the moon. She is also the principal goddess of the sea and the tides; she has dominion even over Neptune in the affairs of the deep. You know better than I do, Lord Phoebus, that she likes nothing better than to be lit by your fire. So she follows you through the firmament, and in turn the mighty seas follow her as their lawful protector and deity; she holds sway over every stream and brook. So this is my request to you, great lord. Perform this miracle for me, or I will die. When you and your sister are in opposition within the sign of Leo, when the tides are high, will you beseech her to send so great a flood along the coast that the highest rocks in Brittany are overwhelmed by five fathoms of water? That is my plea. And will you ask your sister to maintain the seas at that pitch for at least two years? Then I will be able to tell Dorigen that I have performed my part of the bargain and that she must fulfil hers.

'Perform this miracle for me, lord of the Sun. Ask your sister to travel in step with you, at your speed, for the next two years. Remain in opposition, one to another. Then there will be a full moon every night, and the spring tides will not abate one inch. But if glorious Lucina does not wish me to win my love in this way, then will you plead with her to take those dark rocks down with her to the realm of Pluto? Let them be buried leagues beneath the earth. Otherwise I will never gain my lady. I will journey in bare feet to your temple in Delphi, great lord. See the tears upon my cheeks. Take pity on my pain, sir.' And, with those words, he fell into a swoon. He did not recover for a long time. It was his brother who looked after him. When he heard of his distress, he took him up and brought him to his bed. So there will I leave poor grieving Aurelius to his painful thoughts. I do not know whether he will live or die.

In the meantime Arveragus, full of honour, has returned home! He came back with all the other knights, but there was none more renowned for chivalry. You are happy again, Dorigen, to have your loving husband safely in your arms! This noble knight, this famous man of arms, still loves you above all else. He is not a suspicious husband, either. He would not even have considered the possibility of a rival. The thought never crossed his mind. He just wanted to dance and joust and make good cheer. So I will leave them together in married bliss. It is time to return to sick Aurelius.

Oh dear. For two entire years he lay in woe and torment. He never left his bed. He could not have taken one step. He received comfort from no one except his brother, who was a scholar and very sympathetic to his plight. Of course Aurelius told no one else about it. He was silent and discreet. He kept the secret hidden deeply in his breast, just as Pamphilus once concealed his love for Galatea. His breast looked whole and healthy; but the arrow, unseen, had pierced his heart. Any surgeon will tell you that a wound healed only on the surface can be deadly. You must get at the arrow beneath. So his brother, the clerk, wept bitterly beside his bed.

But then this brother, learned in many things, happened to remember his time at the University of Orleans. While he was living there he fell into the company of other young students, all of them eager for learning. Above all else they were fascinated by the arts of the occult. They searched in every corner for secret lore. He remembered that one day he had come across a book of natural magic. It had been left on a desk by one of his companions, a student of law who was interested in more than legal matters. This book described the operations of the twenty-eight mansions, or stations, of the moon. It is all foolishness to us nowadays, of course, worth less than nothing. The faith of the Holy Church is all we need. We no longer put any trust in magic or necromancy.

But as soon as the clerk recalled the details of this book, his heart leaped. He said quietly to himself that his poor brother would soon be cured of his woe. 'I am sure,' he said, 'that there are ways and means of creating magical illusions. Conjurors can do it, after all. I have often heard it said that, at royal feasts, the magicians have summoned up lakes and rowing boats within the great hall. They have sailed up and down between the tables! They have conjured up fierce lions, about to spring. They have turned a hall into a meadow of sweet flowers. They have created fruitful vineyards, and stone castles. And then, in a puff, they have made them all vanish. That is how it seemed at the time.

'So this is my plan. I will return to Orleans and see if I can find some old scholar who is familiar with the mysteries of the moon and who knows how to practise natural magic. And, by these means, my brother will one day possess his wished-for love. I am sure that a good magician will be able to remove from human sight all of those dark rocks. Ships will be able to

come and go along the coast of Brittany, at least for a week or
so. Then my brother will be relieved of his suffering. Dorigen
will have to keep her promise to him, or else be dishonoured
for life.'

There is no need to make a long story out of this. He went
straight to his brother's bedside, and acquainted him with
the details of his plan. Aurelius was so heartened and excited
by the scheme that he rose immediately and took horse to
Orleans with his brother. All the way there he exulted at the
thought of being permanently cured of his pain.

They were two or three furlongs distant from the city when
they came upon a young scholar riding alone. They greeted
him in Latin, whereupon he astounded them with his first
words. 'I know why you have come here,' he told them. And,
without more ado, he informed them of their plans. The
brother of Aurelius asked him for news of the other scholars
at the university and, having learned that they had all died, he
broke down in tears.

Aurelius himself alighted from his horse and followed the
young magician to his house in the city. Here he and his
brother were nobly entertained, with all kinds of meat and
drink. Aurelius had never seen so comfortable and well-
stocked a house. Before they sat down to supper, their host
conjured into their sight extensive forests and parks filled with
wild deer. Aurelius saw, or thought he saw, stags with great
horns. He had never seen beasts so great. He saw one hundred
of them torn to pieces by mastiff dogs, and another hundred wounded to death with sharp arrows. When the wild deer
had disappeared, he saw falconers standing by the bank of a
great river; their birds had just killed a heron. And, look, there
were some knights jousting on a plain. And what is this?
There was Dorigen before him, dancing. Aurelius seemed to be
dancing with her, too. He could hear the music.

Yet at this point the young master clapped his hands, and
all the illusions vanished into thin air. Farewell. The revels all
were ended. They had seen such marvels as tongue could not

express, but they had not moved from his house. They were still in his study, surrounded by his books. They sat there, the three of them, in silence.

Then their host called out to his squire. 'Is our supper ready yet? I asked you to prepare it more than an hour ago, when I brought these gentlemen into my study.'

'Master,' the servant replied, 'it is ready whenever you want it. It is ready now.'

'We will go and eat at once then. These lovers, like my friend here, need to rest between dances.'

Then, after supper, they began to discuss the fee that the magician would require. He was supposed to remove all the rocks along the coast, from the mouth of the river Gironde to the mouth of the Seine. What would that cost? He said that it would be difficult, involving many problems. All things considered, he could not accept less than a thousand pounds. God knows, even at that price, he was working cheap.

Aurelius was too elated to argue with him. 'A thousand pounds is nothing! If I had the whole round world, I would give it away for such a blessing. We have a bargain, sir. We are in agreement. I swear to you that you will be paid in full. But let's get to work at once. Let us start tomorrow!'

'Certainly,' the magician replied. 'You have my word on it.'

So on that happy note Aurelius retired to his bed and slept soundly through the night. At last he had some hope for the future. He could see an end to his sorrow. On the following morning the three of them rode off to Brittany and arrived in good time at their destination. The old books tell me that their journey took place in the cold and frosty month of December. The sun had declined and grown old. In the summer it burns as brightly as polished gold, but in this season it is as thin and light as beaten silver. The frost and sleet had destroyed the flowers of the garden and the fruits of the field. The god of winter sat beside the fire, quaffing mead from his drinking horn and feasting on the flesh of the boar. All around him echoed the cries of 'Noel! Noel!'

In the days and weeks that followed, Aurelius did his best to
encourage, and defer to, the young magician. He begged him to
do everything in his power to work the miracle and deliver him
from grief. Otherwise, he said, he would take his sword and
kill himself. The clever young magician felt such pity for him
that he spent all of his time, night and day, trying to find
the answer. How was he to create such a grand illusion? It was
no easy matter to make it seem, to Dorigen and everyone
else, that the bleak rocks had disappeared or that they had
descended into the earth. This was high magic indeed. Yet at
last he thought that he had found the way. He took out his
astrological tables for the year, and calculated the proper time
for the deception. It was an act of diabolical wickedness, of
course, but he prepared for it assiduously. He drew up the
values for all the positions of the planets, and he measured
the paths they would take in the heavens. He devised charts for
the distances and the proportions involved. Then he set up
his astrolabe, and divided the sphere into the equal houses. He
followed the zodiac. I am no expert in astrology, so bear with
me. Then he singled out the eighth and ninth spheres, and
marked out the various mansions and degrees. He knew where
the moon would be, and where the fixed stars would shine.
He understood the pattern of the constellations. These were
pagan times. He knew all the tricks and japes of the heathen
astronomers. People were easily fooled in those days by such
an evil scheme.

But it worked! He hit upon the right formula and, for two
weeks, it seemed to the world that the dark rocks had disappeared. They were nowhere to be seen. Meanwhile Aurelius
had been in a state of panic and uncertainty. He did not know
whether he would win or lose his love. He was waiting for a
miracle. When he knew that it had occurred, and that the
ragged rocks had vanished from sight, he went immediately to
the magician and fell down at his feet. 'To you, my lord,' he
said, 'I owe everything. I was a woeful wretch, but you have
saved me. Thank you, master. Together with my Lady Venus

you have rescued me from a life of cold care.' Thereupon he went to the local temple, where he knew that he would see Dorigen. And there she was. With much trembling he approached her. He greeted her timidly, and then began to speak.

'My dear lady,' he said, 'whom I most love and fear in all this world. I would never do anything to hurt or displease you. But I cannot disguise my love for you. I could die here at your feet. I cannot begin to tell you of my misery. Yet I know that I must either express my feelings for you or perish on the spot. Even though you are innocent of any crime, you are killing me! But even if you have no pity for my plight, take care that you do not forfeit your honour. Relent. Keep your oath, for the sake of God in heaven, and save my life. You know well enough what you promised me. Understand that I claim nothing by right, and that I am entirely dependent on your grace. You know that, in a garden on a spring morning, you made an oath to me on a certain subject. You gave me your hand on it. If the rocks were gone, then you would grant me your love. I was, and still am, unworthy of it. I know that. But you should not renege on your promise. I am more concerned with your honour than my life. I swear it. I have done as you ordered. If you don't believe me, go to the shore and see for yourself. You must do as you like, of course, but once again I beg you. Do not forget your oath. Living or dead, I will be yours for ever. It lies in your power to decide my fate. I know only this. The dark rocks have gone.'

He took his leave of her, and she stood there astonished. All the blood drained from her face. She had never believed that it would come to this. She was trapped. 'How could this happen?' she asked herself. 'How could he have performed such a miracle? Or monstrosity? It is against the course of nature.' She returned to her home in sorrow and perplexity. She could hardly make her way back. For two days she wept and wailed. She cried aloud, and on occasions fainted away. It was pitiful to see her. She could confide in no one, of course.

And, as it happened, Arveragus was away from home. She could speak only to herself and, in the privacy of her own chamber, with pale and sorrowful face, she uttered her lament.

'Alas, Dame Fortune, I am caught upon your wheel. You have trapped me unawares, and there is no escape. There is no conclusion for me but death or dishonour. I must choose one or the other. The truth is that I would rather forfeit my life than my honour. Death would be preferable to the loss of virtue and the loss of name. I would be quiet and sinless in the grave. Have not many noble wives, and young maidens, killed themselves rather than sacrifice their bodies? I know many examples.

'When the thirty cursed tyrants of Athens slew Phidon at a feast, they ordered his daughters to be stripped naked and brought before them. They were forced to dance and perform like prostitutes, slipping in their father's blood, so that the foul lust of the tyrants could be satisfied. God curse the wicked men! The poor maidens were filled with shame and horror and, rather than lose their virginity, they broke away and rushed to a well in a nearby courtyard. They plunged in, and drowned themselves.

'Then the old books report the tale of the fifty Spartan virgins, captured by the people of Messene so that they might violate them. Of course the maidens all willingly chose to die rather than to assent. They would rather suffer death than dishonour. Why should I not join their company? The tyrant Aristoclides desired a young virgin, Stymphalides, and ordered her father to be killed one night; the maiden went at once to the temple of Diana, where she clung to the statue of the goddess and refused to move. No one could release her grip from the sacred image, and so she was killed on the spot. If these young girls died gladly for the sake of their chastity, why should not a wife follow their example? Why should I not defend myself from the foul desires of a man? Can I not learn from the example of the wife of Hasdrubal, who killed herself within the walls of Carthage? When she realized that the

Roman enemy were about to take the city, she took her children and walked willingly into the fire. She would rather be burned alive than ravished by Roman soldiers. Did not Lucrece kill herself after she was raped by Tarquin? She could not endure the loss of her good name. That was too great a shame for her. The seven virgins of Miletus sought self-slaughter rather than submit to the men of Galatia. I could repeat more than a thousand stories of this kind. Let me see. When Abradates was killed his beloved wife cut her wrists, letting her blood mingle with the blood and wounds of her husband; as she did so she called out, "I have made sure, at least, that my body will not be defiled."

'But why should I provide more examples, when it is obvious to me that many women decided to kill themselves rather than risk dishonour and degradation? There is only one conclusion. I will die like them. I will be true to my husband, Arveragus. I will embrace my fate with the courage of the daughter of Demotion. Do you remember her, Dame Fortune? And then there were the two daughters of Cedasus. That was another sad story. The Theban virgin killed herself when under threat from Nicanor. Oh yes, and another Theban maiden did the same thing. She was raped by a Macedonian soldier, and took her own life to redeem her virginity. It was not too high a price. What shall I say about the wife of Niceratus, who slit her wrists for the same reason? The lover of Alcibiades chose to endure death rather than to leave his body unburied. And what a wife was Alcestis! She agreed to die in order to save her husband's life. What does Homer say of Penelope, too? She was known throughout Greece for her chastity. I could go on and on.

'When Protheselaus was slain at Troy, his wife could not endure another day. Noble Portia could not live after the death of Brutus. She had given him her heart, and now she offered him her life. Artemisia, famous for her faithfulness, was honoured throughout the lands of Barbary. Oh Teuta, queen of Ilyrica, your married chastity is an example to all wives.

I could say the same thing of Billia, Rhodogune and Valeria.'

So Dorigen wept and lamented for a day or so, with the fixed intention of killing herself at the end. But then, on the third night, her husband came home unexpectedly. Of course he asked her why she was crying, at which point she cried all the more. 'Alas,' she replied, 'I wish that I had never been born! I have made a promise. I have sworn an oath.' Then she told him the whole story.

There is no need for me to repeat it here. He listened to her with good grace, and answered cheerfully. 'Is that all?' he asked her. 'Is there no more to tell me, Dorigen?'

'No. That's it. Isn't it enough?'

'Well, wife, you must know the old saying: "Let sleeping dogs lie." All may yet turn out well. Of course you must keep your promise to Aurelius. That goes without saying. So great is my love for you that I would rather die than allow you to break your word. Honour is the highest good of humankind.' But then he began openly to weep. 'Upon pain of death, Dorigen, I forbid you ever to mention one word of this to anyone. I will cope with my grief as well as I can. Don't show your feelings, either, to the world. A sad face will provoke comment and rumour.' Then he called for a squire and a servant-girl. 'Accompany your mistress,' he told them. 'You will soon find out where to go.' So they took their leave, and attended Dorigen. They did not know where they were going, and Arveragus himself said not a word about his intentions.

No doubt many of you would consider him to be a simpleton for placing his wife in such a compromising situation. But listen to the story before you come to any conclusion. She may have more luck than you imagine. Wait until the end.

It so happened that Aurelius, head over heels in love with Dorigen, happened to meet her in the busiest street of the town. She had to go that way in order to make her rendezvous with him in the garden. He happened to be going in the same direction. He had kept watch on her, and checked on her movements whenever she left the house. Whether by accident or design, therefore, they encountered one another in the high street. He greeted her warmly, as you would expect, and asked her where she was going. She replied, in a distracted and almost mad fashion, 'I am going to the garden. Where else? That's what my husband has told me to do. He has ordered me to keep my word.'

Aurelius was astonished by her reply. Yet he felt pity for her guilt and obvious grief. He also felt sorry for Arveragus, who believed so strongly in the sanctity of the oath that he was unwilling to allow his wife to break it. So he felt compassion, and perhaps shame. He weighed up the matter, and decided that it was far better for him to forgo his lust than to perform a wretched deed. Principle came before pleasure. So he addressed Dorigen with a few well-chosen words. 'Ma dame,' he said, 'send my greetings to your husband. Tell him from me that I recognize his graciousness towards you. I see your distress as well. I understand it. He would rather endure any shame than see your oath violated. In turn I would rather suffer any woe, however great, than come between you. I release you from your promise, ma dame. I renounce any claim I have upon you. I tear up any pledge or covenant there ever was between us. You have my word upon it. I will never take issue with you. I will never remonstrate with you, or rebuke you. And now I must say farewell to the noblest and truest wife in the world. Yet I will say this before I leave. Every wife must beware of large promises. Remember the plight of Dorigen. And I know this much. A lowly squire such as myself can be as honourable as the truest knight. Goodbye.'

She fell down on her knees, and thanked Aurelius for his generosity. Then she went back to her husband, and told him what had happened. You can be sure that he was pleased. He was so gratified that I cannot put it properly in words. What can I add, in any case? Only this. Arveragus and Dorigen spent the rest of their lives in married bliss. There was never a word of anger between them. He treated her like a queen. She was always loyal and faithful. I will say no more about them.

Yet what of poor Aurelius? He had lost everything. So he cursed the day he was born. 'Oh God,' he cried, 'I owe a thousand pounds of gold to the magician! What am I going to do? I am ruined. I will need to sell everything I own, and roam the streets as a beggar. I cannot stay here and be a source of perpetual shame to my family. My only hope is that he will be merciful towards me. I will suggest to him that I pay the debt by instalments, year by year, on a certain day. If he is kind enough to agree, I will never let him down.'

So with aching heart he went to his strongbox, unlocked it, and took out about five hundred pounds of gold. He presented the money to the magician, and asked him if he could pay the rest at a later date. 'I have never broken a promise in my life, sir,' he said. 'I will repay my debt to you. Even if I have to go begging in my bare tunic, you will get your money. I swear it. If you can give me two or three years, I would be very grateful. Otherwise I will have to sell my patrimony, house and all. There is nothing else I can tell you.'

The philosopher listened silently and solemnly. 'Did I not make an agreement with you?'

'Yes, sir, you did. Most certainly.'

'Did you not enjoy the lady, as you wished?'

'No. Alas, I did not.'

'Why not? Tell me the whole story.'

So Aurelius went through the entire sequence of events. There is no need for me to repeat them, is there? 'Arveragus,' he said, 'is such a worthy knight that he would rather die of shame and distress than allow his wife to break her oath.' Then he told the magician all about the anguish experienced by Dorigen at the thought of being unfaithful to her husband. She would rather have lost her life. She had made her original promise quite innocently. She had no knowledge of magic and illusion. 'So I felt sorry for her, sir. Arveragus sent her to me without conditions, and I freely returned her to him. That is the gist of it.'

The scholar answered him very gently. 'Dear brother, both

of you acted with honour and magnanimity. You are a squire. He is a knight. I hope to God that a scholar can act just as wisely. A magician can also be a gentleman, you know. So, sir, I acquit you of the thousand pounds. It will be as if we had never met or made an agreement. You are as new to me as that flower, rising out of the earth. I won't take a penny from you for my work. You have paid me for my meat and drink. That is enough. So farewell. Good day to you!' And, with that, he mounted his horse and went on his way.

Now, fellow pilgrims, answer this riddle. Which one of these gentlemen was the most generous? Let me know before we ride any further, will you?

Heere is ended the Frankeleyns Tale

The Physician's Tale

Heere folweth the Phisiciens Tale

There was, a Roman historian tells us, a knight called Virginius. He was a worthy and honourable man, with plenty of money and plenty of friends. He had only one daughter, however, a beautiful girl without equal in the whole world. Dame Nature had formed and moulded her with such care that it was as if she were ready to proclaim, 'Look at my work here. I, Nature, have created a perfect creature in exactly the manner I wished. Who could counterfeit this beauty? Who could possibly imitate it? Pygmalion himself could do no better, even though he laboured at his forge or at his easel. Apelles and Zeuxis would do a whole lot worse, however well they tried to use their pen or brush. No sculptor could match me, either. God above has given me the power to make and unmake all the creatures of the world. I am His representative on earth. I can paint and play just as I please. All things under the moon are susceptible to my sway. I ask nothing for my work, of course. I am in perfect agreement with my superior in heaven. I do all things in honour of Him above. That is why I made this perfect beauty.' That, I imagine, is what the dame would say.

This girl, in which Nature took such delight, was just fourteen years old. Just as the dame can paint the lily white, and bestow the blush of pink upon the rose, so did she apply her skill to the little limbs of the infant before she was born. The sun turned her hair golden, like the rays of the morning. Even so, she was a thousand times more virtuous than she was beautiful. There was nothing lacking in her, nothing I cannot praise. She was chaste in body and in soul. She was a virgin in spirit as well as in flesh; she was humble and patient, never straying from the path of virtue. She was always sober and respectful in conversation, too, and although she may have been as wise as Pallas Athene she was measured in her speech. She did not put on airs and graces. She never tried to be clever. She was the perfect female, in other words, always evincing modesty and grace. She busied herself with her womanly tasks, hating sloth and idleness before all else. She did not pay homage to Bacchus, either. She knew well enough that wine, as well as youth, can provoke excitement. You do not throw oil or fat upon the fire. There were times, in fact, when she feigned illness in order to escape vain company; she was uneasy at feasts and parties and dances, where there were bound to be intrigues and amours. Those are occasions when youths, little more than children, grow up too fast. It is dangerous for them, as all experience tells us. She will be mature enough when she becomes a woman and a wife. Not before then.

There may be some of a certain age among you here, who are governesses to young girls. Don't take anything amiss. I am only telling you the truth. You have been chosen to instruct the daughters of noble families for two reasons, as you well know. Either you have kept your chastity and set a good example, or you have fallen into sin and know all the signs of frailty. You know the old dance, and have forsaken it for ever. So, for God's sake, teach your charges to stay out of trouble. A poacher is the best gamekeeper, after all. A thief knows how to secure his own house. So keep them safe. You know best how to do it. Do not wink at any vice, lest you yourself be damned for wickedness. Then you would be a traitor to the whole household. Of all the sins in the world, the worst is the betrayal of innocence. It is unforgivable.

And listen, mothers and fathers, I am addressing you also. You must safeguard and defend all of the children in your care. Be careful not to give them a bad example. Make sure that you chastise them properly. Otherwise, they are lost. You will pay dearly for their sins, I can assure you of that. The careless shepherd loses many sheep; the wolf comes out of the wood, and destroys the lambs. I could think of other examples, but I must get on with my story.

This young maiden, Virginia, did not need any governess to teach her virtue. Her own life was itself a study in virtue, a book of goodness in which every page set an example to modest virgins. She was so honest and prudent that her fame spread throughout the country, where she was acclaimed for her beauty as well as her graciousness. All that loved virtue also loved her. Of course there were certain envious people who resented her happiness and wished her nothing but misfortune or tragedy. Saint Augustine has described those miscreants very well.

So Virginia went into town one day, with her mother, in order to visit one of the temples there. That was the custom. It so happened that the town magistrate, who was also the governor of the region, caught sight of her as she walked past him. He could not help but notice her. His heart beat faster. He was at once infatuated with her beauty. And he said to himself, 'I want her, and I will have her!'

So the foul fiend entered him, whispering to him that he might take this young girl by trickery and deceit. He would not get her by force, or with money. They would do no good. She had many friends, after all. She was also well defended by her own virtue that would never allow her to surrender to him. So, after much thought, he sent for a man of low degree living in the town; he knew this man to be a subtle and bold villain ready for anything. In the utmost secrecy he told this man the story of his lust, and confided in him his plans. 'If you repeat this to anyone,' he said, 'you will lose your head.' When the man agreed to help him, the judge was delighted. He showered gifts upon him.

So between them they hatched a conspiracy to take the virginity of the young girl. It was an elaborate plan, which I will explain to you in a moment. The judge's name was

Appius, by the way. He is well known in the history books. I am not making this up. The churl's name was Claudius. So Claudius went back to his humble home, and Appius returned full of anticipation for the delights in store. He could not wait.

A day or two later this false judge was sitting in his court-room, giving his verdict on various cases, when Claudius came before him and stood in the well of the court. 'I seek justice,' he said, 'I have a petition. I am filing a suit against Virginius.' He was the father of the girl, if you remember. 'If he denies the charge, then I will bring evidence against him. Do me justice, sir. I have truth on my side.'

The judge pretended to reflect upon the matter. 'In the absence of the defendant,' he said, 'I cannot come to a definitive judgment. Call him to the stand. Then you will get your justice.'

So Virginius was brought before the judge, and the following accusation was read out to him. 'Heretofore and hence-forward I will right aptly show you, sir judge, that the defen-dant has willingly and maliciously done wrong to your plaintiff Claudius. To wit, that against all equity and all law and all feeling this defendant stole from me under cover of night and darkness one of my servants, bound to me by duty and obliga-tion. She was very young at the time. I also declare that this defendant did willingly and maliciously claim this young girl to be his lawful daughter. I will bring forward witnesses to testify on my behalf, sir judge. Whatever he says, the young maid is not his daughter. Return her to me, sir, and uphold the law.'

Virginius looked with horror upon this villain. Of course he was ready to swear that Virginia was his child. He would have proved it in trial by battle, as suits a knight. He would have brought forward witnesses, too, to testify that the man was lying. But he did not get the chance. The judge refused to listen to any more evidence. He was an old man in a hurry. He cut Virginius short, and then delivered his verdict. 'I have decided that the plaintiff has suffered wrong, and can now claim back his servant. Wherefore, sir defendant, you no longer have the right to keep her in your house. Bring her forth and place her in my custody. Justice must prevail at all costs.'

That is what happened. The noble knight, Virginius, was forced by a false process of law to place his daughter in the hands of a lecher. The judge would soon be all over the young virgin. After the verdict was delivered Virginius returned home, and sat down in the hall. Then he called for his daughter. With ashen face, and piteous countenance, he looked upon her. He felt such pity for her that he could not express it. But he knew what he had to do.

'Daughter,' he said. 'Dearest Virginia. You must suffer one of two fates. You must choose between death and eternal shame. I wish that I had never been born! You have not deserved this. What have you done to warrant the knife or the blade? Oh dear daughter, ender of my life, I have tried to bring you up in peace and tenderness. You have never once been out of my thoughts. You were my first joy, but now you must be my last woe. You are a gem of chastity. Now, dearest one, you must suffer your death in patience. That is my sentence on you. I do it out of love for you, Virginia, not out of hate or anger. But you must die. I must cut off your head to save you from a far more terrible fate. I curse the day when that false judge, Appius, first saw you!' Then he explained to her what had happened in the courtroom. I need not repeat it.

'Oh dear father, have mercy!' These were the first words of Virginia as she wrapped her arms about his neck. Then she burst into tears. 'Dear father, shall I die? Is there no solution? No remedy?'

'None, dearest daughter. There is no escape.'

'Then give me time, at least, to lament my fate. Jeptha gave his daughter time to mourn before he killed her. God knows that she had committed no sin. Her fault was to be the first one to greet her father after he had returned victorious from war. He had vowed that, if he triumphed, he would slay the first person to come through the doors of his house. It was his own child.' Virginia then fainted on to the floor. When she had recovered, she looked up at her father. 'I thank God,' she said, 'that at least I will die a virgin. Kill me before I am polluted. In the name of God, do it now.'

So she begged him to take up his sword and slay her softly. Then once more she fainted away. With sorrowful heart Virginius picked up his sword and cut off her head with one stroke. Then, according to the story, he picked it up by the hair and took it to the courtoom. There he laid it on the judge's table. When Appius saw it, he ordered Virginius to be hanged immediately. But a thousand people gathered, in sorrow and pity for the knight. All of them knew, or suspected, that the judge had twisted and broken the law. They had noted the false demeanour of the churl Claudius, who had brought the charges. In any case, Appius was a notorious lecher. No one trusted him. So they marched against him, charged him, and threw him into prison; he killed himself in his cell. Claudius was sentenced to death by hanging, from the nearest tree, but Virginius pleaded his case so well that the churl was instead sent into exile. That is pity for you. Otherwise the villain would have died. All the other guilty parties were taken and executed immediately.

This is how sin is repaid. We must all take heed. No one knows the course of God's will. No one knows how, or where, He will strike. The worm of conscience may be nourished by a wicked life, and then bite. However secret, however well hidden, vice will get its reward. The simple man and the scholar have this in common: they do not know the time or the nature of their departure from this life. So be warned. Give up sin, before sin gives up you.

Heere endeth the Phisiciens Tale

The Pardoner's Prologue

Heere folweth the Prologe of the Pardoners Tale

Our Host began to swear as if he had gone crazy. 'My God!' he shouted. 'By the blood and body of Christ that judge was wicked! And so was the churl! They deserved to die, as do all false judges and plaintiffs. And the beautiful girl was murdered by her own father. Her beauty came at too high a price, that's for sure. I know one thing. I will say it over and over again. The so-called gifts of Fortune, and of Nature, can be fatal. Her beauty led her to the slaughter. It is a most sorrowful story. We are the darlings of Fortune and Nature, as I said just now, at our peril. They cause more harm than good.

'So, my good master, you have told us a sad tale. But let it be. It does not matter, sir Physician. I pray God to keep you alive and well. I pray that your glass vessels and urinals are sparkling clean, that your purges and ointments are efficacious, that your medicine bottles are well corked and that your old books are on the shelf. God bless them all! Then you are properly set up. You are a good-looking man, I must say, more like a bishop than a clerk. Did you notice how I enumerated all the items in your box? I don't know medical terminology, but I know about health and sickness. That story of yours almost gave me a heart attack. I need some medicine right away or, at least, a draught of strong ale. Then I will have to hear a merry tale, to drive away the sad image of Virginia.' He turned to the Pardoner. 'My good friend,' he said, 'tell us a funny story. I want some fun.'

'Of course I will,' the Pardoner replied. 'But first of all I need

a drink. Isn't that an alehouse over the way? I feel like a pie, too.'

But then others in the company began to remonstrate with the Host. 'We don't want any dirty stories. Let him give us a morality tale. Let him teach us a lesson or two.'

'If that's what you want,' the Pardoner said. 'But I must have a drink first. I need time to come up with something honest.'

When he came out of the alehouse he mounted his horse, and turned to them all. 'Lords and ladies,' he said, 'I am used to preaching in churches, as you all know. I take great pains with my delivery, so that my voice rings out like a bell. I know my theme off by heart, of course. It is always the same. Do you know what it is? Greed is the root of all evil. First I tell them from where I have come. It might be Rome or Jerusalem. They don't know the difference. Then I show them my papal indulgences. Oh. Before that I make sure that they all see the lord bishop's seal on my papers. That is just to protect myself from interfering clergy, who might try to prevent me doing Christ's holy work. They are so jealous, some of them. Then I really get going. I tell the congregation about the indulgences offered by cardinals and patriarchs and archbishops. I mutter a few words of Latin to spice up my sermon, and beg them to pray on their knees for their salvation. I get out of my sack the glass cases that hold the relics of the holy saints – a collar bone here and a wrist bone there.

'"Here, good sirs and dames," I might say, "is the shoulder bone of one of the sheep led by Jacob in the hills of Beersheba. Listen to my words. Wash this bone in any well, and the water from that well will cure your cattle of any murrain or blight. It will heal snakebites and kill intestinal worms. Bring your sheep to the well. When they drink from it, their scabs and sores will fall away from them. They will be uplifted. Listen to me carefully. If any one of you should drink a draught of the well water, once a week, just before dawn, your stock will thrive and multiply. There will be more lambs than you can count. That is what Genesis in the Holy Book tells us. You can read the passage for yourself. Chapter 39. Verses 37 to 39.

'"And I'll tell you something else. The water will heal suspicion and distrust. If a man should fall into a jealous rage, just let him mix it with his soup. He will feel the difference. He will never accuse his wife again – not even if he sees her in the company of a priest or two. Do you see this glove of knitted wool? If any man puts his hand in this glove, his harvest will be bountiful. It could be wheat or it could be oats. It makes no difference. Just make a small offering of silver to me. The crop will flourish. Mark my words.

'"There is one thing of which I must warn you, good ladies and gentlemen. If there is any man among you who has committed a mortal sin, too horrible to confess – if there is any woman among you, young or old, who has been unfaithful to her husband – such folks cannot come up and make an offering to my relics here. They do not have the grace. They do not have the power. But if the rest of you wish to make an offering, then come forward now. I will absolve you of your sins. I have the bishop's authority to shrive you."

'So by these deceits I have earned at least a hundred pounds as a pardoner. I stand like a priest in the pulpit. I preach to the dolts. I beseech them. I use every trick in the book. I can tell them a hundred lies, and never be found out. I lean forward and stretch out my neck, just like a dove perched on the rafter of a barn. My hands and tongue are working so hard that it is a joy to see me in action. I tell them to forsake the sin of avarice. I tell them to be charitable. Especially to me. I am only interested in their money, you see, not in the state of their souls. I don't care what happens to them once they are dead. They can pick blackberries, as far as I am concerned.

'I will tell you something else. Many sermons, and devotional homilies, spring from bad intentions. Some preachers just want to flatter or to entertain. Some are motivated by hypocrisy, or vainglory, or hate. If I cannot get at my enemy directly, I will sting him in a sermon. I will wound him in covert ways, so that he cannot fight back. "No," I say, "I will not name the enemies of us pardoners. That would be too low." But of course the congregation know exactly whom I am talking about. They can tell from my looks and gestures. That is how I retaliate against those who defame me. I spit out my venom under the cover of holiness. I seem virtuous, but seeming is not being.

'I will tell you the truth in one sentence. I preach only for money. I want their silver pence. That is why my theme has always been, and always will be, the same. "Greed is the root of all evil." It is suitable, don't you think? I preach against the very vices I practise! It saves time. And even though I may be guilty of that sin, I persuade other folk to repent with much wailing and lamenting. But that is really not my intention. I will say it one more time. I preach only for the cash. You have probably understood me by now.

'So I tell them tales of old times, taken out of books. The lewd people love a good story. That is the only way they can remember anything. Do you really think that I am going to live like a monk, when I can earn money so easily? I have never even considered the idea. Truly. I can preach and beg in all sorts of places. I never intend to work. I am not going to make baskets, or thresh wheat, for a living. I never beg in vain. I always get my reward. I am not going to imitate the example of the apostles, in other words. I want meat and fine clothes, and bread and cheese, and of course money. I will take it from the meanest servant or the poorest widow in the village, even though she has to deprive her children of food. I like to drink and make merry, too, and I make sure I have a whore in every town. Listen to me, ladies and gentlemen, in conclusion. You want me to recite a tale to you. I have had a draught of the landlord's best ale in that hostelry, and I am ready to tell you a story that will really entertain you. I may be a very wicked man, but I can relate a highly virtuous tale. It is one of the stories I use in my sermons, after all. So be silent. I will begin.'

The Pardoner's Tale

Heere bigynneth the Pardoners Tale

There were in Flanders three young people who loved to play around and amuse themselves. They used to dance and to fight, to haunt taverns and brothels. Everywhere they went came the sound of harps and lutes and guitars. They played dice night and day. They ate and drank to excess. So in the temples of the devil they sacrificed themselves to Satan. They rolled in the sty of abomination. Their oaths and blasphemies were terrible to hear. They swore on the crucified body of Our Lord, saying that the Jews had not tortured Him enough. They encouraged each other in every excess and sin. They paid for dancing girls, slim and shapely, as well as young street-sellers, singers, bawds, confectioners – any occupation designed to stir the fires of lechery and of gluttony. They are the officers in the army of the evil one. This is the first lesson. According to the Bible itself, lechery follows in the wake of wine and drunkenness.

Do you remember the case of Lot, who, in his cups, had intercourse with his two daughters? He was so drunk that he did not know what he was doing. And do you recall Herod? He drank so much wine at the table that he allowed his wife to cut off the head of John the Baptist. If he had been sober, would he have condemned an innocent man to death? Seneca has a word or two to say on the subject. As far as he is concerned, there is no difference at all between a madman and a drunkard. The only difference is that madness lasts longer.

Gluttony is a cursed vice. It is the cause of our confusion on earth. It was the reason for our damnation, until it was paid for by the blood of Christ upon the cross. Yet at what a high price! Gluttony has corrupted the whole world. Adam and Eve were driven out of Eden as a result of their greed, condemned to a life of labour and of woe. As long as Adam fasted, he was happy in paradise. There is no doubt about it. But as soon as he tasted the forbidden fruit he was cast into the lower world of shame and suffering. We all ought to cry out against gluttony. If you knew how many diseases and complaints afflict the greedy man, you would be more temperate. You would maintain a proper diet, and enjoy good health. Alas the open mouth and the eager appetite! Men must labour, north and west, east and south, on land and sea, and in the air, to satisfy the stomachs of greedy men who crave more meat, more wine, more everything. Saint Paul has summarized the matter very well. 'Meat is for the belly, and the belly is for meat. But in good time God will destroy them both.' No words can tell, no tongue can name, the horrors of gluttony. A man then turns his mouth into a public toilet, a sink into which is poured the filth of alcohol; then he spews it out again.

The apostle has recorded his lament. 'Many are walking on this earth,' he said, 'who are enemies of Christ crucified. I tell you this in sorrow. Their fate is death everlasting. If their belly is their god, they will be condemned.' Belly! Stomach! Words for a stinking bag of flesh, filled with shit and corrupted filth. From either end comes a foul wind. Sustenance is found for you at great cost and hard labour. The cooks have to grind and pound and mince, turning one dish into the likeness of another, just to satisfy you. They have to extract the marrow from the bones, just so that you can swallow the sweetest juices. They have to concoct spices out of herbs and leaves, so that they can make a sauce to stir your appetite. Yet you who live for such delights are as good as dead. Your vices have killed you.

Drunkenness is just as foul a sin. Alcohol provokes violence and creates misery. It sours the breath. It disfigures the features. Who would want to embrace a drunk? He snores loudly, and mutters broken words. Oh you drunkard, you fall down as heavily as a stuck pig. You have lost your tongue, as well as your self-respect. Drunkenness is the graveyard of intelligence and decency. Never trust a man who is lost in drink. Never confide in him. So, good people, keep away from the red and the white wines that are sold in Fish Street and Cheapside. Spanish wine is the cheapest and the worst. It seems to get mixed up with other wines, until it becomes quite over-powering. Its vapours go straight to the head. I do not blame the vintners for this, of course. God forbid. My father was a vintner. It must happen naturally somehow. Two or three glasses are enough. The drunkard may then think he is at home in London, but in fact he has been transported to a vineyard in Spain. He is lying among the grapes, burbling nonsense.

So, lords and ladies, listen to me. All of the great deeds and victories commemorated in the Old Testament were performed by men who practised abstinence. They never touched liquor. They prayed to Almighty God instead. Read all about it in the Holy Book.

In contrast, think of Attila. This great king and conqueror, to his manifest shame and dishonour, died in his sleep from too much drink; he was bleeding at the nose, in fact. A military man should live soberly. Remember what was commanded of Lamuel. Was it Samuel? No. Lamuel. It is in the Book of Proverbs. 'Give not to kings, Oh Lamuel, give not wine to kings. For there is no secret where drunkenness reigns.' There is no need to say more on that subject.

So let me turn to gambling. Next to drunkenness, gaming is the worst vice. Dice are the mothers of lies. They are the cause of deceit, of cursing, of perjury, of blasphemy, and even of manslaughter. They waste time and money. And, furthermore, to be known as a common gambler is deemed to be a great dishonour. The more exalted a man is in rank, as a gambler, the more infamous he will become. A gambling prince would be unfit to frame a policy. He would be considered incompetent in public life. Once upon a time the philosopher Stilbo was sent from Sparta as an ambassador to form an alliance with Corinth. He travelled in great state but, on his arrival, he happened to find all the greatest in the land grouped around a gaming table. As soon as he could, he returned to his own nation. 'I am not going to lose my reputation,' he said to his rulers, 'or bring shame to my own people, by making an alliance with gamblers. Send other wise envoys, if you wish, but on my honour I would rather die than negotiate with such wastrels. We Spartans are a glorious people. We cannot allow ourselves to be associated with them. I for one could not sign such a treaty.' So spoke the wise philosopher.

Take the case of King Demetrius. The king of Persia sent him a pair of golden dice to signify his scorn for him as a well-known gambler. Demetrius had no thought for his honour or his glory. As a result he had no reputation in the outside world. The great lords of the earth can surely think of better ways to spend their time than in dicing.

Now, dear pilgrims, I will turn to perjury and the swearing of false oaths. That is another subject treated by the old books. Cursing is a great sin in itself, of course, but perjury is greater still. God Almighty has forbidden swearing of every kind. We know that on the authority of Matthew. Jeremiah also touched upon the subject. 'Thou shalt swear in truth,' he wrote, 'in judgement and in righteousness.' Profanity is a wretched thing. Do you recall the three commandments concerning the duties owed to the Almighty? The third of them is this – 'Thou shalt not take the Lord's name in vain.' This is more important than the taking of life or any other enormity. In order of significance it lies third. Every schoolboy knows that. I tell you plainly that violence and vengeance will not be strangers in the house of a blasphemer who cries out, 'By Christ's passion!' or 'By the nails on Christ's cross!' When he plays at dice he calls out to his opponent, 'You have five and three. I need seven. By the blood of Christ, give me a seven!' And then he exclaims, 'By the bones of Christ, I will stab you to the heart if you play false with me!' This is the fruit of the cursed dice – curses, anger, perjury and murder. So for the love of Christ, who died for us, forsake all oaths. Now I will get on with my story.

These three young scoundrels, whom I mentioned at the beginning, were sitting in a low tavern long before daybreak. They were drinking together when suddenly they heard the chink of the handbell that announces the carriage of a coffin to the grave. One of them turned to his servant. 'Go outside,' he said, 'and find out whose corpse it is. Try to remember the name.'

'Sir,' the boy replied, 'that isn't necessary. I knew about it two hours ago. It is the body of an old comrade of yours. He was murdered last night, very suddenly, as he sat blind drunk upon the bench outside the tavern. A thief called Death sneaked up on him. Death is killing everyone around here. He took up his spear, pierced the drunk through the heart, and silently went on his way. He has killed another thousand during the recent plague. I think, master, that you should be careful not to come too close to him. It is better to beware such an adversary. That's what my mother taught me. Death is the constant enemy.'

'Mother of God!' the landlord said. 'The boy is right. Death has killed thousands of people this year. Why, he has slain an entire village a mile or so away from here, with every man and woman and child gone into the ground. I am sure that he lives there. It would be wise to be wary of him, sirs. Forewarned is forearmed.'

'By the blood of Jesus,' one of them exclaimed. 'Are we all so frightened of him? I will search out this fellow named Death in every street and every quarter. I swear that I will teach him a lesson. What do the two of you say? Are you with me? Let us hold up our hands together, and swear that we will act as brothers in the quest for Death. The slayer will become the slain, this very night, so help us God!'

So the three of them swore an oath to be true to one another, and to live or die in pursuit of their fraternal cause. So these newfound brothers jumped up from the tavern bench, as drunk as skunks, and made their way to the neighbouring village where Death was supposed to dwell. On the road they uttered many oaths, swearing by Christ's bones and blood, that they would tear Death to pieces once they had got their hands on him. They had walked about half a mile, and were just about to cross over a stile, when they were stopped by a poor old man. He saluted them very humbly. 'God save you, your reverences,' he said.

The proudest of the three laughed in his face. 'Who do you think you are, old man?' he asked him. 'Why are you all wrapped up in rags, except for your face? Haven't you lived long enough? Isn't it time to die?'

The man looked into his face, and answered him patiently. 'I have walked all over the world, and still I cannot find the person I seek. I have met no one, in town or city or village, who will exchange his youth for my age. So therefore I grow ever more aged, counting off the years that God has willed to me. Death himself refuses to take away my life. So I walk on, a restless wanderer through the world. With my staff I knock upon the earth, calling out "Dear mother, let me in. Open the gate. See how I grow feeble. I am nothing but skin and bones. Dear mother, let these bones rest within you. I would gladly exchange my box of treasures for the comfort of a winding cloth around my corpse." Yet mother earth will not help me, sirs. So you see me standing before you with pale and withered face.

'But, gentlemen, it is not right that you insult me. I have done you no wrong, in word or deed. Have you not read the Holy Book? It is the duty of the young to stand in reverence to the old. White hairs demand respect. Do not injure the old, in case you are harmed when you reach the same age. That is all I have to say to you. God be with you, wherever you may travel. I must go on as before.'

'You are going nowhere, you old fool,' one of the three said to him. 'By Christ's passion you are not getting off so lightly. You just mentioned that false traitor, Death, who has killed all of our friends in the neighbourhood. You have my word on it. If you are spying for him, you will pay for it. Tell me where he is. Otherwise, expect the worst. I swear it on the body and blood of Jesus. You are in league with Death, aren't you, in a conspiracy to slay all of us young people!'

'Young gentlemen,' the old man said, 'if you are in such a hurry to find Death, turn up this crooked path here. You will find him sitting under a tree in an oak grove. I left him there only a minute ago. I assure you that, despite your threats, Death will not run away from you. Do you see that tall oak? He waits there. May Christ, who saved the world, save you!' The old man then went on his way.

So the three wastrels, with loud cries, ran towards the oak tree. And what did they find there? They found piles of gold florins, newly minted, heaped on the ground. They reckoned that there were more than eight bushels of this treasure. They forgot all about Death. He was the last thing on their minds. They thought only of this glittering hoard of coin, so fresh and bright that it dazzled their eyes. The three of them sat down beside it in amazement.

The worst of them spoke first. 'Brothers,' he said, 'listen carefully to what I have to say. I may joke and play about, but I have a good head on my shoulders. I know what I'm talking about. Fortune has granted us this treasure-trove. It is ours to spend as we like, in joy and festivity all life long. Easy come, easy go. Who would have thought, for God's sake, that this would be our lucky day! We must find a way of carrying this gold back to my house – or to yours, of course, we are all in this together. Only then can we be sure of it. But we cannot move it in daylight. We will be accused of theft, and hanged straight away from the nearest tree. No. It has got to be done by night. We have to transport the gold carefully and quietly so that we arouse no suspicions. This is what I suggest. We cut sticks and draw. The one who draws the longest will run back into town, and purchase bread and wine for us. The other two will keep watch over the treasure. As long as he comes back quickly with provisions – and says nothing when he is in town – we will be able to carry home the gold tonight to whatever place we think best. Do you agree?'

Then he picked up three sticks and, bidding them to draw in turn, put them tightly within his fist. The youngest of them chose the longest stick and so, according to the plan, he ran off towards the town as quickly as he could. As soon as he was out of sight the one who had conceived the plan turned to his friend. 'You know that you are my sworn brother,' he said in a low voice. 'So I will tell you something to your advantage. We are alone. He has gone into town. You saw him. There is plenty of gold here to share among the three of us. No doubt about it. But what if I arranged it so that only two of us would benefit? Wouldn't that be a friendly thing to do?'

The other one was puzzled. 'How are you going to do that? He knows that the two of us are guarding the gold until his return. What are we going to do? What are we going to tell him?'

'If you swear to keep this secret,' he whispered, 'I will tell you in a few words what has to be done.'

'I swear. I will never betray you.'

'Listen closely then. Two people are stronger than one. Is that not so? When he comes back, get up as if you were about to play; pretend to wrestle with him, and at the same time I will stab him in the back. You must use your knife on him, too. Then we will be able to share out the gold between us, my dear friend, just you and me. We will be able to indulge ourselves. Why, we will dice all the day long!' So these two scoundrels agreed to kill their friend and newly sworn brother.

The youngest man, who had gone into town, had also been considering the situation. All he could see, and think of, were those glistening piles of coin. 'Lord,' he said to himself, 'if only I could keep all that treasure for myself! No one in God's world would be more pleased and happy.' It was at this point that Satan, the foul enemy of mankind, whispered to him that he should procure poison and feed it to his two friends. When a man is living in such sin as he was, the fiend is permitted to tempt him even further. So he determined, there and then, to purchase poison and do murder without compunction or regret. He went to an apothecary in the town, and told him that he wanted to buy poison to exterminate some rats; he said that he also wanted to get rid of a weasel that killed the chickens in his yard, as well as all the other household vermin that creep out by night.

'Well, sir,' the apothecary replied, 'I have the very thing. I swear to God that this arsenic will kill anything and everything. A creature has only to take a tiny piece, the size of a grain of wheat, and it will die. It begins to work after a few minutes. It is strong and violent. And, as I said, it is always fatal.'

'Excellent. I will take it.' So the apothecary made up a box of the poison for him. The young man went out into the street, and walked into a tavern. Here he ordered three bottles of wine. Into two of them he put the poison, while he left the third for his own use. He intended to spend the entire night in carrying the gold back to his own house. After he had finished preparing the poisoned draughts, he returned to his friends beneath the oak tree.

Do I need to state the obvious? The two of them, just as they had planned, stabbed the young man to death. When they had murdered him, they laughed. 'Let us sit down and drink,' one of them said. 'We deserve a rest. After we have got through this wine, we can think about burying him.' He opened one of the bottles and put it to his lips. 'Chin chin. Open another one.' So they refreshed themselves, or so they thought. They were drinking poison, of course, and soon died.

I don't think any medical expert could describe in detail all of their suffering. It was unutterably horrible. Death had caught them, after all, two murderers and a poisoner.

Oh cursed sinners, filled with malice and wickedness! You have been fattened with gluttony and lapped in luxury. You have thrown the dice for the last time. Blasphemers, your curses against Christ have come back upon you! Your swearing, your pride and folly, have destroyed you. Why is mankind so false to its creator, who purchased its redemption with His own blood?

Now, all you good men and women, learn from me and beware the sin of avarice. Forgive us our trespasses. That is the prayer. So I have come here to pardon you. Just give me your coins, your jewellery and your silver spoons. Here is the papal bull of dispensation. Wives, what will you give me for it? Bales of cloth? Look. I can write down your names now, and ensure that you pass easily into the bliss of paradise. By the high powers granted to me, and for a certain sum, I can absolve you of all your sins. You will be as innocent as the day you were born. The price is worth it. Cash down. And may Christ in His mercy grant you His pardon. May He save your soul. Etcetera. Etcetera.

'And that, fellow pilgrims, is the way I preach. Oh, I forgot one thing. I have plenty of wonder-working relics in my bag, as well as many pardons given to me personally by the pope. If any of you wish to take advantage of these holy writs, offer me some money and kneel down before me. In return for your devotion, I will give you absolution. I can absolve you now, or at any time during the course of our journey. My pardons are always fresh and always renewed – as long as you are able to pay for them, of course. Isn't it a blessing that I am among you? I can wipe away your sins at any time, night or day. I am at your service. It is possible that one of you might fall from his horse and break his neck. You have me as a security. I can absolve you before the soul leaves the body.

'Let me start with our Host here. I am willing to bet that he is the one most enmired in sin. Am I right? Come forth, Harry Bailey, and give me some money. Then I will let you kiss the relics, one by one. Unfasten your purse, sir.'

'I will do no such thing,' our Host replied. 'May Christ curse me if I give you so much as a groat. You would tell me to kiss a pair of your dirty underpants, and swear that the shit came from a saint! By the holy relic of the true cross, I wish I had your greasy balls in my hand rather than your fake papal bulls. Let's cut them off and enshrine them in a hog's turd. That's where they belong.'

The Pardoner was so angry that he could not say a word. He just glowered in silence.

'I really can't be bothered to make fun of you,' our Host said. 'I will have nothing to do with an angry man.'

The Knight saw that everyone was laughing at the Pardoner, and so he rode to the front of the procession. 'Enough of this,' he said. 'No more. Now, sir Pardoner, recover your temper. Smile. And you, sir Host, make amends to our friend here. Kiss him on the cheek in token of amity. And you, Pardoner, respond in kind with the kiss of peace. This will be a love day. We will go on our way as before with good cheer and laughter.' So the Host and Pardoner were reconciled. And the pilgrims went on their way rejoicing.

Heere is ended the Pardoners Tale

The Shipman's Tale

Heere bigynneth the Shipmannes Tale

Once upon a time a merchant dwelled in Saint-Denis, a town just north of Paris; he was rich enough to pass as a wise man, in the world's eyes. He had a beautiful wife, too, who liked good company. She was gay and carefree. That sort of woman costs her husband a great deal of money. He had to spend more than she earned in compliments and admiring glances. She went to every feast and every dance, enjoying those pleasures that pass as swiftly as shadows on the wall. I feel sorry for the man who had to pay for them all. The poor husband has to clothe his wife, wrap her in furs and festoon her with jewels – and all for the sake of his own reputation! Meanwhile, she dances to her own tune. If he decides that he is not going to foot the bill, considering it to be a foolish waste of money, then the wife will just get someone else to pay. Or else she will borrow the money. And that is dangerous.

This good merchant, Peter by name, had a splendid house and welcomed more guests and visitors than he could count. He was generous, and she was beautiful. Do I need to say any more? I will get on with my story. Among these guests, of all types and degrees, there was a monk. He was about thirty years old, at a guess. He was good-looking, fresh-faced and virile. He was always under the merchant's roof. He had been invited there in the first days of their friendship, and was now treated as a familiar companion. I will tell you the reason. This young monk and this merchant had both been born in the same village. Each one claimed the other as a cousin. They proclaimed their common bond all the time, and swore eternal friendship. They said that they were brothers as much as cousins. They were as happy in each other's company as larks on the wing.

This monk, John, was generous to a fault and never failed to reward all of the servants in the house. He was agreeable to everyone, from the meanest serving-boy upwards, and spared no expense. He gave gifts all around. So of course he was always welcomed; the members of the household were as happy to see him as birds welcoming the rising of the sun. I am sure you get the idea.

It so happened one day that the merchant was preparing himself for a journey to Bruges, where he had some business to arrange. He was going to purchase some fine lace, I think. So he sent a message to John, who lived in Paris, inviting him to spend a day or two with him and his wife before he set out for Bruges. 'Come to Saint-Denis,' he said, 'and be entertained.'

So the monk requested leave of his abbot to go on a journey. It was easily granted, since John himself already held the post of bailiff in the monastery. He was used to travelling and supervising the farms and granges of the house.

A day or two later he arrived at Saint-Denis, where he received a great welcome. Who was more cherished than 'our dear cousin, John'? He brought a pitcher of Malmsey wine with him, from the monastery's cellar, and some bottles of white wine. He brought with him, too, a brace of pheasants. So I will leave the merchant and the monk, for a day or two, to their meat and drink.

On the third day the merchant, before travelling to Bruges, was obliged to take stock of his financial affairs. So Peter secluded himself in his counting house to work out the income and expenditure of the last year. He needed to know the amount of his profit. He brought out all of his boxes of money and account books, laying them down carefully on the exchequer board. He was so rich, in coin and credit notes, that he made sure that he locked the inner door before he got down to business. He did not wish to be disturbed by anyone. So he sat there, doing his sums, all morning.

The monk had been awake since dawn, too. He had been walking up and down the garden, muttering the devotions of his morning office. The merchant's wife came softly into the same garden, and greeted him demurely as she had so often done before. She had in her company a young girl who was in her care and under her charge. 'Oh good John,' she said, 'what is the matter with you, rising so early?'

'My dear cousin,' he replied, 'five hours' sleep a night is sufficient. Of course that may not be enough for the old or the infirm, or for those poor married men who lie dozing in bed all day like weary hares who have just escaped from the hounds. But, dear cousin, why do you look so pale? Can it be that your husband has been keeping you busy all night, with one thing or another? You need to rest. I can see that.' Then he laughed out loud. But he also had the good grace to blush at his thoughts.

The merchant's wife shook her head. 'God, who knows everything, knows this. That has nothing to do with it. As God gave me life, I swear that there is not a woman in France who is less interested in that sad game than me. Do you know the old song: "Alas and woe is me I am forlorn/ I curse the day that I was born"? But I dare not tell how things are with me. There are times when I think of leaving the country. Or of killing myself. I am so full of woe and fear.'

The monk stared at her in alarm. 'God forbid, dear niece, that in your grief you should do away with yourself. Tell me everything. I may be able to help or counsel you. Confide in me. I promise never to betray you. I swear on my breviary here that I will never repeat anything you say. I will remain as silent as any stone.'

'I make the same oath,' she replied. She put her hand upon his breviary. 'May I be torn to pieces by wild men. May I be condemned to hell itself. I will never betray your confidence. Not because you are my cousin. But because you are my true and trusted friend.' So they swore their oath, and gave each other the kiss of peace. Then they started to talk.

'Dear cousin,' she began, 'if I had time and opportunity, I would tell you now the story of my married life. I have been a martyr to that man you call your cousin.'

'No, no, you are wrong,' he replied. 'He is no more my cousin than the leaf on that tree. I only called him that so I had an excuse to visit this house. And to see you. I confess to you now that I have loved you from the first moment I saw you. I swear this on my profession as a monk. Explain to me now what you have suffered at his hands. Tell me quickly, before he returns.'

'Oh dear John,' she said, 'my true love. I wish that I could keep all these things secret, but alas –' She brushed a tear from her cheek. 'I cannot stand the sight of him. He is the worst husband in the world. Yet, since I am his wife, I am not supposed to reveal the secrets of our marriage. Or of our marriage bed. God forbid I should do so. I am bound to honour and obey him.' She paused for a moment. 'But I have to tell you this. He isn't worth as much as a fly. And what upsets me more than anything is his stinginess. You know well enough that a woman wants six things. I am no different. She wants a husband to be healthy and wise, wealthy and generous; she wants him to be obedient to his wife, and good in bed. Just those six things. Is that too much to ask? Yet, by Christ who shed His precious blood for our salvation, I have to find one hundred francs by next Sunday. Why? To pay for my new gowns. And I only bought them to bring credit on him! I would rather die than be shamed in public for bad debts. If my husband finds out about it, he will kill me anyway. So please, John, can you lend me the money? Otherwise, I am ruined. If I can borrow the hundred francs from you, I will be forever thankful to you. I will pay you back, of course, on a stated day, but I will also do whatever else you require of me. Anything at all. If I am untrue to my word, take any vengeance you wish. Tear me apart with horses. Burn me alive.'

The monk was very courteous in his reply. 'I have so much pity for you, gentle lady, that I here plight my word to you. I swear that, when your husband has gone to Bruges, I will solve your problem. I will bring you the hundred francs.' Saying that he fondled her thighs and buttocks, embraced her, and kissed her a hundred times. 'Go upon your way,' he said, 'quietly and discreetly. Let us dine soon. I see from this sundial that it is past nine o'clock in the morning. So go now. Be as faithful to me as I am true to you.'

'Of course. God forbid that I should behave in any other way.'

So she sets off as merry as a magpie, and instructs the cooks to prepare a good meal for the master and his guest. Then she went off to see her husband, and knocked boldly on the door of the counting house.

'Who is it?'

'It's me. Don't you think you ought to eat something, Peter? How much time are you going to spend with all your sums and calculations? Let the devil take all these account books! Surely you have enough of God's blessings without having to count them all? Come out. Forget your bags of money for a while. Are you not ashamed that dear John has not had a meal all day? Let us go to mass. And then eat.'

'My wife,' the merchant replied, 'you know nothing about men's business. It is too complicated for you to understand, I suppose. But let me explain this to you. Take a group of twelve merchants. Only two of them will succeed and prosper. Only two will make a good profit in the course of their careers. We put on a brave face, of course, and make ourselves busy in the world. But we have to keep our affairs secret – until we are dead. The only alternative is to go on a pilgrimage. Or just disappear. That is the reason I pore over my books. I have to know how to master the tricks of the world. I am always in dread of failure, bankruptcy, and all the other hazards of business life.

'I am going to Bruges tomorrow, as you know, but I will be

back as soon as I can. While I am away I want you to be modest and courteous with everyone. Look after our property as carefully as you can. Keep the house neat and tidy. You have enough provisions, I am sure of that, so don't overspend. You don't lack meat or wine. You have all the clothes you need. But I'm feeling generous. Here is some silver for your purse.' And with that he closed the door of the counting house and went down with his wife for luncheon. He had done enough work for the day. So they attended a quick mass and, as fast as they could, they sat down to eat. The tables were laid, the dishes come and gone in an instant. No one ate more than the monk.

Then, after the meal was over, John took the merchant to one side and spoke to him very seriously. 'Dear cousin Peter,' he said, 'I know that you are about to take horse and travel to Bruges. God be with you and speed you on your journey. Ride carefully. And be careful of what you eat. Your health may be at risk in this hot weather. Be temperate in all things. What am I saying? There is no need for elaborate courtesies between cousins like ourselves. Farewell. God protect you! That's all I need to say. If there is anything I can do for you, by day or night, just let me know. I am always here to help you.' He was much affected, and put the sleeve of his habit to his eyes. 'Oh. There is one other thing. I have a favour to ask of you before you go. Can you lend me one hundred francs, just for a week or two? I have to purchase some cattle for the monastery. Our stock is getting low. I will repay you promptly. You have my word as a monk on it. But can we keep the matter to ourselves? I have to buy the cattle today, you see, and I don't want to be forestalled. Now farewell again, dear cousin Peter. Thank you for your kindness. And for the hundred francs.'

'That is nothing,' the merchant replied. 'Consider it done. My gold is at your disposal, dear cousin John. In fact everything I have is yours. Take your pick. God forbid that I should deny you anything. I must tell you one thing, however. For us merchants money is the staff of life. We can get credit while our reputation is good. But to be without money – well, that is disastrous. Pay me back any time you like. There is no hurry. I want to help you in any way I can.'

So the merchant takes one hundred francs out of one of his chests, and gives the money secretly to the monk. The only people who knew of the loan were the lender and the borrower. Then they relaxed and enjoyed themselves until it was time for John to return to the monastery.

On the following morning Peter mounted his horse and, in the company of his apprentice, made his way to Bruges. He arrived safely, and at once got down to business. He dealt in cash and credit; he bought and sold. He did not dice. He did not drink or dance. He paid attention only to profit and to loss. He behaved exactly as a merchant should. So I will leave him in the market place.

On the Sunday following the merchant's departure, dear cousin John presented himself at Saint-Denis. He was freshly shaven, smelling of soap; even his tonsure had been clipped. Everyone in the house saw him, and welcomed him. Even the serving-boys greeted him. But who was most pleased to see him? You have guessed. I will come straight to the point. The wife had agreed that, in exchange for the hundred francs, she would spend the night with him. She promised that she would give him value for money; and so she did, throughout the night. The monk was exhausted, but he was happy. He left at dawn, wishing a merry good day to the entire household. No one had the least suspicion of him. So he rode off to the monastery, as free from rumour as any innocent. There we will lose sight of him for the moment.

The merchant, having successfully completed his business at the fair in Bruges, came back home to Saint-Denis. He was greeted fondly by his wife, and together they celebrated his return. He told her that the price of merchandise had been so high that he had been forced to take out a loan of two thousand gold sovereigns; now he was obliged to travel to

Paris in order to raise the money. He had some cash, of course, but he needed to raise the rest from his friends.

When he arrived in Paris, his first thought was of his dear cousin. So in the expectation of good wine and good conversation he called upon John in his monastery. He had no intention of asking him for money. He just wanted to catch up on all the gossip, and make sure that his friend was still in rude health. John welcomed him very warmly, and asked about his affairs. Peter replied that he had done well enough, thanks be to God, and had made a profit. 'There is just one problem,' he said. 'I have to raise two thousand sovereigns by next week. Once I have repaid that, I will be laughing.'

'I am so pleased that you have come back to us in good health,' the monk replied. 'If I were a rich man, I would gladly give you two thousand sovereigns. I haven't forgotten your kindness to me the other day, when you lent me one hundred francs. But I have repaid you. Two days ago I brought back the money and gave it to your wife. I put it down on your counter. She knows all about it. I gave her a double entry.' He coughed. 'Now, if you will excuse me, I have to go. Our abbot is about to leave town, and I have to ride with him. Give your wife my fondest regards, won't you? What a darling! Farewell, dear cousin, until we meet again.'

This merchant was as careful as he was astute. He raised the money and handed the two thousand sovereigns to some Lombard bankers, who gave him a bond in recognition of full payment. Then he rode back as cheerful as a chaffinch. He knew that he had made a profit of a thousand francs on the deal. No wonder he sang and whistled as he returned home.

His wife met him at the gate, as was her custom, and all that night they celebrated their good fortune with some amorous turns in bed. The merchant was out of debt. The merchant was rich. At break of day he embraced her, and began kissing her again. At the same time he fucked her hard.

'No more,' she pleaded with him. 'Haven't you had enough?' Still she played with him for a little longer.

The merchant turned on his side after she had pleased him, and whispered to her. 'Well, wife,' he said, 'I am a bit annoyed with you. I don't want to be, but I am. Do you know why? You have come between myself and my dear cousin. You have sown a little seed of division between me and John.'

'How? Tell me.'

'You never mentioned to me that he had paid back the money I lent to him. He gave you cash in hand, I believe. But he feels aggrieved that I did not know about it. As soon as I started talking about loans and repayments, I realized that there was something wrong. Yet I swear to God that I wasn't referring to him. Do me a favour, dear wife. Always tell me, in future, if I have been repaid in my absence. Otherwise I might start asking debtors for money that they have already given me. Do not be remiss in this.'

The wife was not at all put out by his rebuke, but answered him boldly enough. 'By the holy Mother of God I defy that false monk, that so-called cousin John! I didn't pay any attention to this bond, or repayment, or whatever you call it. I know that he brought some cash to me, but I assumed that he was giving it to me for your sake. I thought that he wanted me to dress up, to entertain and be entertained in your honour. He has been given hospitality here often enough. I thought he wanted to repay me in kind. May God's curse fall upon our dear cousin. But since I see you are displeased with me, I will come to the point. You know well enough that I always pay my debts on time. I pay you your just tribute night after night. I am running out of double entries. Should I ever fall behind in payment, you may chalk it up. I will soon honour the debt. I swear to you that I have spent everything on fine clothes and on hospitality. Not a penny has been wasted. Don't I look a credit to you? So don't be angry. Let us laugh and play. You can play on my body, if you wish. Bed is the best payment of all. Forgive me, my dear husband, and come beneath the sheets. You will not regret it.'

The merchant realized that there was no alternative. It

would have been madness to criticize her any further. What was done was done. 'I forgive you, dear wife,' he said. 'But, in future, try not to overspend. Keep your money in your purse, I beg of you.'

So ends my story. God be with you. And may you always be worthy of credit!

Heere endeth the Shipmannes Tale

Bihoold the murie wordes of the Hoost to the Shipman and to the lady Prioresse

'Well spoken, Shipman,' Harry Bailey said. 'By the body of Christ, I enjoyed that tale. May you sail around the coasts for ever and a day, master mariner! But may that false monk, cousin John, have nothing but bad luck for the rest of his life! Let this story be a lesson to all of us. A monk is nothing but an ape in a man's hood. The monk made a monkey of the merchant, and of the merchant's wife. Never let one of those rogues enter your house.

'Now let us go on. Who is it to be? Who is going to tell the next story?' He rode up to the Prioress and, with as much modesty as a young maid, addressed her. 'My lady Prioress, by your leave – if it doesn't offend you – I wonder if you would be so good as to entertain us all with another tale? Only if you wish to, naturally.'

'Gladly, sir,' she replied.

The Prioress's Prologue

The Prologe of the Prioresses Tale

Domine dominus noster

Oh Lord, oh Lord, how great is thy name! How thy marvels are spread over the world! The wise men of the earth praise you. The little children pray to you. The suckling infants proclaim you and your glory. I will praise you, too, out of my own poor mouth. I am a feeble woman, but I hope to find you in my heart.

I hope to find words in honour of you, Lord, and of the purely white lily, blessed Virgin, who bore you. I will tell my story for her sweet sake. I cannot increase her honour, of course, since she is the root and source of all virtue. She and her blessed Son are the salvation of the world.

Oh Mary, full of grace, the unburned bush burning in the sight of Moses, you who did receive the Holy Ghost descending from the seat of the Lord God. In humility of spirit you found the wisdom of God within you. Your heart was lightened by the weight of the Lord. Oh holy Virgin, help me to tell my story!

Hail holy Mother, no one can express your magnificence or your modesty. Who can number your virtues? Who can measure your bounty? You guide men into the light of the Lord. You anticipate their prayers and plead for them before the throne of the Almighty.

My learning and knowledge are so weak, holy Virgin, that I cannot express your mercy or your love. Your light is too bright for me to bear. I come to you as an infant, scarcely able to speak. Form my broken words uttered in praise of you. Guide my song.

The Prioress's Tale

Heere bigynneth the Prioresses Tale

In a great Asian and Christian city there once stood a Jewish ghetto. It was financed and supervised by a lord of that place, intent upon making as much profit as he could from the vile practice of usury. It is evil money, accursed by Christ and His saints. Yet the ghetto was open. There were no gates, and all the citizens could walk or ride through its main street.

There was a little Christian school at the end of this street, where its young pupils learned the rudiments of their faith. Year after year the children were taught how to read and how to sing, in the way of all small boys and girls. Among these children was a widow's son, some seven years old. He attended school every day.

His mother had taught him to kneel down and say a Hail Mary whenever he came across an image of the Virgin. His mother had told him that he must always pray to the blessed Lady, even in a crowded street. And of course he obeyed her. An innocent child learns quickly. When I think of him I cannot help but recall the image of Saint Nicholas, who, at the same young age, did reverence to Christ.

This little boy was seated on his bench one day, studying his primer, when he heard some other children in the class singing out 'Alma Redemptoris' in praise of the Mother of our Saviour. He drew closer to them, listening very carefully, and after a while he had by heart the words and the notes of the hymn. He could sing the first verse by rote.

He was too young to know what the Latin words meant. But

then he asked a schoolfellow to explain it to him, and to interpret it in simple language. He went down on his knees and
begged him so many times that his young friend eventually
agreed to translate it for him.

Then this fellow explained the hymn. 'I have heard that this
song,' he said, 'was composed in honour of the blessed Virgin.
It is meant to praise her, and to beseech her to come to our aid
when we are about to die. That is all I know about it. I am a
chorister, not a student of grammar.'

'So this hymn was written in honour of the Mother of God?'
the innocent boy asked him. 'I am going to make sure that
I have learned it by heart before the Christmas season. I don't
care if I am scolded for not attending to my lessons. I don't
care if I am beaten three times a day. I am going to learn this
song in honour of Our Lady.'

So his comrade taught him the words, syllable by syllable,
until he could repeat them without any mistakes. He began
with the first verse:

> As I lay upon a night,
> My thought was on a maid so bright
> That men call Mary, full of might,
> Redemptoris mater.

He mastered the notes, and sang out the hymn boldly wherever he went. He sang it when he walked to school in the
morning, and when he came home again in the afternoon. He
was devoted to the praise of the Virgin.

As I have said before, this little boy always made his way
through the ghetto on his way to school. So he sang out 'Alma
Redemptoris' earnestly and brightly as he passed through the
Jewish quarter. He was blissfully unaware of his surroundings.
He simply wanted to honour Our Lady.

But then the enemy of mankind, Satan himself, rose up
among the Jews. He was full of bitter poison. 'Oh people of the
Old Testament!' he called out. 'Is this right? Is this fitting? Can

you allow this child to walk among you uttering blasphemy? It
is against your reverence. It is against your Law.'

So, from that time forward, the Jews of the neighbourhood
conspired against the little boy's life. They hired a murderer,
and told him to wait in a dark alley close to the route of the
child on his way to school. This cursed man seized the boy and
cut his throat; then he buried him in a pit.

It was a cesspit where the Jews were accustomed to squat
and shit. Oh cursed people, children of Herod, what will be
the consequence of your evil deeds? Murder will out. That is
certain enough. The blood of the murdered boy will cry out.
The children of God will hear the voice!

Oh holy Christian martyr, pure virgin child, you will now
sing for ever in the halls of eternity. You will be the companion
of the white celestial Lamb. You will be one of those seen in
visions by the great evangelist Saint John of Patmos. You are
one with the virgin martyrs who sing perpetually.

The poor widow, the mother of the young boy, watched
and waited all that night. But he did not return home. At first
light she left the house and, with pale and careworn face, she
searched the streets for any sign of him. She enquired after him
at the school, and there she learned that he had last been seen
singing in the ghetto.

So the poor woman followed the footsteps of her child and,
half out of her mind with grief, she visited all those places
where she hoped that he might still be found. She called out to
the blessed Virgin and begged her for help. Then she began
to walk among the Jews themselves, asking whether any of
them had seen her small son. Of course they all denied even so
much as glimpsing him.

But the grace of Jesus entered her heart and guided her to the
place where her son had died. She came into the alley where
the cesspit had been dug, in which his little body was buried.

Oh great God, whose praises are sung in the mouths of
the innocent, how great is Thy power! This is what happened.
This jewel of chastity, this emerald of innocence, this ruby of

martyrdom, sat up in his filthy grave and, with his throat cut from ear to ear, began to sing. He sang 'Alma Redemptoris' in a clear strong voice that could be heard throughout the ghetto.

All the Christian people in the neighbourhood gathered together to watch this miracle. They called for the magistrate at once, and he arrived very quickly. He heard the boy singing. He gave thanks to Christ, and to our Saviour's heavenly Mother, before ordering that all the Jews of the quarter should be arrested.

The child was borne on the shoulders of the crowd and carried in procession to the abbey; he sang all the way. His mother was carried, fainting, beside him. No one could persuade her to leave the side of her small son. She was another Rachel, inconsolable for loss of her child.

The magistrate ordained that the Jews with knowledge of the murder should be put to death immediately in the most shameful and terrible way. He could not countenance their unholy crime. Some of them were torn apart by horses. Some were hanged, drawn and quartered. 'Evil shall they have,' he said, 'that evil deserve.'

The little child lay upon a bier before the high altar, where a mass was said for the sake of his soul. After the service was over the abbot and the monks made haste to bury the child in consecrated ground. And, as they sprinkled holy water over the bier, the child once more rose up and sang 'Alma Redemptoris'.

The abbot was a saintly man. The monks were holy, too, or ought to have been. So the reverend father began to question the boy. 'Dear child,' he said to him, 'I beseech you. I call upon you in the name of the blessed Trinity. Why are you singing? *How* can you sing, when your throat is cut from side to side?'

'My throat is cut as deep as my neck bone,' the child replied. 'In the course of nature, I would be long dead. But Jesus Christ has deemed it fit that His power should be known to the world. He has performed this deed in honour of His sacred

Mother, the blessed Virgin. That is why I am able to sing "Alma Redemptoris".

'I have always loved the Virgin above all others. She is, in the light of my faulty understanding, the source of grace and mercy. She appeared before me at the moment of my death, and asked me to sing this hymn in her honour. You heard it. When I had finished singing, it seemed that she placed a small grain of seed upon my tongue.

'Wherefore I sing again, more clearly than before, in praise of Mary. Until this seed is taken from my tongue, I will sing ceaselessly. She has told me everything. "My little child," she said, "I will come for you. When the seed is taken from your tongue, do not be alarmed. I will not forsake you."'

The holy abbot then reached over to the boy, and took the seed from his tongue. Whereupon the child died peacefully. The abbot was so moved by this miracle that the salt tears ran down his cheek. He fell to the ground, upon his face, and did not stir. All of the monks then went down upon their knees, weeping and calling upon the blessed Virgin. Then they rose and with reverent hands took the child from his bier; they placed him in a tomb of marble, in the chapel of Our Lady. He lies there still, thanks be to God.

Oh little Saint Hugh of Lincoln, you were also slain by the Jews. Your death, so short a time ago, is still fresh in our memory. Pray for us sinners now, and at the time of our death. May God have mercy on our souls. Pray for us, Mother of God, so that your grace may descend upon us. Amen.

Heere is ended the Prioresses Tale

Prologue to Sir Thopas

*Bihoold the murye wordes of the
Hoost to Chaucer*

All of the company seemed grave, and reflective, at the end of the Prioress's tale. But then the Host changed the mood by making a joke at my expense. He looked at me, and winked at the others. 'What sort of man are you?' he asked. 'You look as if you are trying to catch a rabbit. All you ever do is stare down at the ground. Come closer to me. That's better. Look up. Smile. Fellow pilgrims, this is a good man. You see the extent of his waist? It's just like mine. He is a big boy. I am sure that some nice young woman would love to embrace him, plump though he is. Yet he is always abstracted. He is always miles away. Come on, man, tell us a funny story. The others have. Now it is your turn.'

'Host,' I said, 'don't take this personally. But I don't know any stories. I can't tell any stories. All I can recall is an old rhyme that I learned in my childhood.'

'That will do,' Harry Bailey replied. 'From the expression on your face, I think it will be an interesting one.'

Sir Thopas

Heere bigynneth Chaucers Tale of Thopas

THE FIRST FIT

Listen carefully, please, to me
And I will tell the company
A funny little story.
At some time in history
There was a knight and gent
Good at battle and at tournament.
What was his name?
Sir Thopas.

He lived in a far, no, *distant* country
Not very near the sea.
He dwelled in a city called Hamelin
Famous for its porcelain.
His father was a rich man, and grand.
In fact he ruled the entire land.
What was *his* name?
I don't know.

Now Sir Thopas was a brave knight.
His hair was black, his face was bright.
His lips were red as a carnation.
But then so was his complexion.
I could have said, red as a rose,
But I will confine that to his nose.

How big was his nose?
Enormous.

His hair was as yellow as mustard paste,
And he wore it right down to his waist.
His shoes were from the Vendôme
And his clothes were made in Rome.
They were so expensive
That his father looked pensive.
How much did they cost?
Thousands.

He could hunt for wild rabbit
And had acquired the habit
Of hawking for game.
He could wrestle and tame
The most ferocious ox.
He could whip the bollocks
Off any contestant.
He was no maiden aunt.

There were many young virgins
Happy to slake his urgings
When they should have been asleep.
But he did not so much as peep
At them. He was chaste as a lily
And stayed so willy-nilly.

So it befell that on one morning
Just as the light was dawning
Sir Thopas rode out on his steed
In hope of doing daring deeds.
He held his lancet like a lord,
And by his side there hung a sword.

He made his way through forests dark
Where wolves howl and wild dogs bark.
He himself was after game,
Which once more I rhyme with tame.
But listen while I tell you more
Of how Sir Thopas almost swore
With vexation.

Around him sprang weeds of every sort,
The flea-bane and the meadow-wort.
Here were the rose and primrose pale,
And nutmeg seeds to put in ale
Whether it be fresh or stale
Or only good as slops in pail.

The birds were singing sweetly enough,
Among the nightingales a chough.
Was that a chaffinch on the wing,
Or was it a dove just chattering?
He heard a swallow sing on high,
And then a parrot perched near by.
What a lot of noise!

And when he heard the birdies sing
He was filled with love longing.
He spurred on his horse
Over briar and gorse
Until the beast was sweating.
It looked like it had been rutting
With a mare.

Thopas himself was exhausted.
He got down from his quadruped
And lay stretched on the ground.
The horse was free at one bound.

It wriggled its arse
And chewed on the grass.
Fodder was solace.

'Woe is me,' Thopas lamented,
'Why am I so demented
For love? I dreamed last night
That I had caught a bright
Elf-queen under the sheets.
What sexual feats
I accomplished!

'If my dreams could come true
What deeds would I do.
I really need a fairy queen,
No mortal girl is worth a bean.
All other women I forsake,
A fairy girl is all I'll take
In country or in town.'

Then up on to his steed
He jumped, in need
Of action with a fairy queen.
He rode along each hill and dale
Looking for that certain female.
Then quite by chance he found
A secret spot of magic ground,
The kingdom of the fairies.
In truth it was a little scary
And wild. And desolate.

He was not surprised to see a giant
Whose name was Oliphiant.
He had a mace
Which he aimed at the face

Of Thopas, saying, 'Get out
Or I will give your horse a clout.
The queen of fairy
Lives in this aery
Abode. It is not for you.
Your horse is unwelcome, too.'

Sir Thopas turned red as rhubarb pie
And said in angry voice 'I defy
You, Oliphiant, and I swear
To aim my lance here where
It hurts. Come out at break of day
And I will show you my way
Of dealing with giants.'
It was a good show of defiance.

Then Thopas rode away quite fast
As Oliphiant prepared to cast
Stones at him from a leather sling.
Yet our fair knight had cause to sing
When all the missiles missed their aim
And were not fit to kill or maim
The valiant warrior.
He was none the sorrier.

THE SECOND FIT

So gather round and hear the rest.
The giant came off second best
And Thopas, of high renown,
Decided to return to town.
He rideth over hill and dale
To reach the ending of my tale.
It will not fail
To amuse you.

His merry men commanded he
To cheer him up with game and glee.
'Let there be a pageant
In which I fight a ferocious giant.
Then let the fairy queen appear
And proclaim herself to be my dear
Paramour.
I ask no more.

'Then let the minstrels blow their trumpets
And the drummers use their drum kits,
And the singers sing their tales
Of kings and queens and noble males
Like me. Of chivalry the flower,
I'll be the hero of the hour.'

They brought him wine, they brought him spices
They brought him cream and several ices,
They brought him gingerbread and mead,
They brought him damson jam on which to feed.
He had a sweet tooth.

Then he decked himself in vestments fair.
Sir Thopas always knew what to wear
In terms of shirts and other finery.
In armour he was inclined to be
Conservative. Just simple chain mail,
With a double brooch and ornamental nail,
Was enough to protect him.

He had a bright helmet,
He had a bright spear,
There was no warrior his peer.
He had a fine shield
To make his enemies yield
And even flee the field.

His legs were cased in leather,
On his helmet was a feather.
It was hard to know whether
He was more handsome than rich
Or, if so, which was which
In his gorgeous display.
He outshone the day.

His spear was made of fine cypress
But it boded war, not peace.
His bridle shone like snow in sun
And as for saddle, there was none
So polished in the world.
His banner was unfurled
To taunt all foes to take him on.
And that is it.
That is the end of the second fit.
If you want to hear more,
I will oblige. No need to implore.

THE THIRD FIT

Now say no more, I will continue
To tell how Thopas and his retinue
Fought against elves and giants
And cannibals and monsters and tyrants.
There is no end.

You have heard of Arthur and of Lancelot
But this knight could prance a lot
Better on his noble steed.
He was a good knight indeed.
Sir Thopas took the lead
In chivalry.

So off he trotted on his charger
This knight looked larger
Than life. Upon his helmet
There rose a lily
Which looked sweet but silly.
The road ahead was hilly
But he continued willy-nilly –

Heere the Hoost stynteth Chaucer of his Tale of Thopas

'For God's sake stop,' the Host said to me. 'That's enough. It is all so stale and old-fashioned. You are giving me a headache with your corny rhymes. Where is the story here? This is nothing but doggerel.'

'I beg your pardon?' I was very dignified. 'Will you please allow me to carry on? You did not interrupt anyone else. In any case, I am doing the best I can. The rhymes are not corny.'

'Forgive me, Mr Chaucer. I must speak my mind. Your story is not worth a shit. What is the point of it? You are doing nothing but waste our time. I have made up my mind. No more versifying, please. Can you not tell us an adventure, or deliver some kind of prose narration which mingles entertainment with instruction?'

'Gladly, sir Host. I will tell you a little story in prose that will entertain you, I think. Unless, that is, you are very hard to please. It is a tale about the moral virtues of a patient and prudent wife. It has been told many times before, and in many ways, but that doesn't bother me. It is still a good story. Let me cite the example of the four gospels. Each one of them describes the passion and crucifixion of Our Saviour. Each of them has a different perspective, but still manages to tell the essential truth of Our Lord's suffering. Some say more, and some say less. Some add details. Others are very brief. You know who I am talking about, of course. I refer to Matthew,

Mark, Luke and John. They have written four separate accounts, but their basic meaning is the same.'

'Please, Mr Chaucer –'

'Therefore, lords and ladies, do not be offended if I tell the story in my own way. I may introduce more proverbs than there are in the original, but I have the best of intentions. I simply wish to increase the power of my message. Don't blame me if I change the language here and there. I will deliver the gist of the story true and entire. Believe me, I have no intention of spoiling the effect of this merry tale. So now please listen to me. And, Mr Bailey, please don't interrupt.'

The Monk's Prologue

The murye wordes of the Hoost to the Monk

'Stop, stop.' Harry Bailey stood up in his saddle. 'If that was the introduction, I hate to think what the rest will be like. And I am tired of stories about patient wives. They do not exist. Take my wife, for instance. Go on. Take her. She is as patient as a mad bull. When I chastise my servants, she comes out with a great wooden stick and urges me on. "Go on," she says. "Beat the shit out of them! Break every bone in their worthless bodies!" If by any chance one of our neighbours fails to greet her in church, or slights her in some other way, she makes me pay for it when we get home. "You fool! You coward!" she shouts at me, all the time waving her fists near my face. "You can't even defend your wife against insults. I should be the man around the house. Here. You can have my distaff and go spin a shift." She can nag me like this all day long. "It is a shame," she says, "that I should have married a milksop rather than a man. You have about as much spine as a worm. Anyone can walk over you. If you cannot stand up for your wife's rights, then you do not stand for anything."

'So it goes on, day after day, unless I choose to make a fight of it. But what's the point? I just leave the house. Otherwise I would work myself into a state of madness. She makes me so wild that – I swear to God – she will make me kill somebody one of these days. I am a dangerous man when I have a knife in my hand. It is true that I run away from her. But she has huge arms, and strong wrists, as anyone who has crossed her will know. Anyway, enough of her.'

Our Host then turned to the Monk. 'My lord,' he said, 'God be with you. It is your turn to tell a story. Look, we are already coming up to Rochester. It is time for you to ride forward and speak. But in truth I don't know your name. What shall I call you? John? Or Thomas? Alban, perhaps? That's a good monkish name. And what house do you come from, sir? Are you from Selby or from Peterborough? Your skin is very fair and very soft. You are not used to hard labour. And you are not likely to be a penitent or a flagellant.

'My guess is that you are an official of your house. You are a sacristan, perhaps, or a cellarer in charge of all the wines. Am I right? I am sure that you are in a position of authority. That is clear from your appearance and your behaviour. You have the manner of one who leads. You are no novice. You look strong and fit, too. You could look after yourself in a fight. What a mistake it was to introduce you to the religious life. You could have been good breeding stock. A big cock among the hens. If you had followed the call of nature, you would have fathered many lusty children. No doubt about it. It is a pity that you wear the cope of office.

'I swear to God that, if I were pope, I would give a dispensation for every strong and lusty monk to take a wife. Otherwise the world will shrink to nothing. The friars and the monasteries are full of good English spunk, and we laymen are nothing but drips in comparison. Frail shoots make a weak harvest. Our wills and our willies are so weak that nothing comes from them; no wonder that wives queue up for the attentions of you monks and friars. You have got Venus on your side. You don't pay in counterfeit coin. You have the genuine article beneath your robes. Don't be cross with me, sir. I am only joking. But of course there's many a truth in a good joke.'

In fact the Monk took the Host's jesting in good part. 'I will play my part in this pilgrimage,' he said, 'by telling you a tale or two. They will be moral tales, of course. That is the mark of my profession. If you like, I can narrate the history of Saint

Edward the Confessor. Or perhaps you would prefer a tragedy? I know hundreds of them. You know what a tragedy is, I suppose? It is a story from an old book. It concerns those who stood in authority, or in prosperity, only to suffer a great fall. They went from high estate to wretchedness and misery. Their stories are sometimes told in verses of six metrical feet known as dactylic hexameters – da da dum dum da da. Homer uses it. But sometimes they are told in other metres. In England we have alliteration. Then again they are often told in plain prose. Have I said enough on that subject?' The Host nodded. 'Now listen, if you wish. I cannot promise that I will tell you these stories – of popes, of emperors, of kings – in chronological order. I will just mention them as I remember them. Forgive my ignorance. My intentions are good.'

So the Monk began.

The Monk's Tale

Heere bigynneth the Monkes Tale

De Casibus Virorum Illustrium

So I will lament, in the manner of tragedy, the fate of those who once stood in high degree. They fell so far that they could not be rescued from the darkness. When the doom of Fortune has been decided, no one can avert its course. Never rely upon prosperity. That is the lesson of these little histories.

Lucifer

I will begin with Lucifer. I know that he is an angel rather than a man, but he is a very good example to us all. Fortune cannot help or harm an angel, of course. Nevertheless he fell from heaven into hell, where he still resides. Oh Lucifer, son of the morning, you can never escape from the flames of the inferno. You have become Satan. How you have fallen!

Adam

Behold Adam, lying in Eden (now known as Damascus). He was not made from human seed, but wrought by God's own finger. He ruled over all of Paradise, with the exception of one tree. No human being has ever been so blessed as Adam. Yet for one bad act he fell from grace. He was consigned to a fallen world of labour and misery.

Sampson

Behold great Sampson, heralded by an angel before his birth, consecrated to Almighty God! While he retained his sight, he was the noblest of all. No one in the world was stronger or more courageous. Yet foolishly he told the secret of his strength to his wife. In doing so, he condemned himself to death.

This mighty champion slew a lion, and tore it to pieces with his bare hands. He was on his way to his own wedding, and he had no weapons. His wife knew how to please him, with her wicked wiles, and could coax all of his confidences out of him. Then she betrayed him to his enemies, and took another man in his place.

In his anger he took up three hundred foxes and bound them together by their tails. Then he set the tails on fire, with a burning torch tied to each one, and with them he set ablaze all the cornfields in the land. He destroyed the olive trees and the vineyards. In his rage he killed a thousand men, although his only weapon was the jawbone of an ass.

After they were slain he was tortured by a thirst so great that he turned to God for help. He prayed Him to send water, or else he would die. Lo and behold, a miracle occurred. From the molar tooth of this dry jawbone there sprang forth a fountain of water, with which Sampson refreshed himself. So God saved him. All this really happened. You can read about it in the Book of Judges.

Then one night in Gaza, despite the presence of all the Philistines in that city, he tore up the entrance gates and carried them on his back. He took them to the top of a hill, where everyone could see them. Oh noble Sampson, fine and courageous warrior, you would have been without equal in the world if you had not whispered your secret to your wife.

Sampson never drank wine or strong liquor. He never cut his hair or shaved himself. What was the reason? He had been told by a divine messenger that all of his strength lay in his hair. He ruled Israel for twenty years. Yet bitter tears would fall down Sampson's cheeks. One woman would lead him to destruction.

He had told Delilah where his strength lay. She sold the secret to his enemies and, while he slept in her arms one night, she took a pair of shears and cut off all his hair. When his enemies burst in upon them, they were able to bind Sampson before putting out his eyes.

When he still had his hair, there was no one in the world who could defeat him. After he was blinded and shorn, he was consigned to a cavernous prison where he was forced to labour at a mill with slaves. Sampson was the strongest of humankind. He was a fearless judge, a wise and noble man. Yet his fate was to weep out of blind eyes, bitterly mourning his wretchedness.

Let me tell you the final chapter of this sad story. His enemies celebrated with a great feast and called Sampson before them to play the part of a jester; the setting was a hall of marble pillars. Here Sampson stood his ground, and took his revenge upon them all. He took hold of two pillars and shook them so violently that the whole building collapsed. He was killed, but so were those who had enslaved him.

The leaders of the country, and three thousand of their followers, were among the dead who lay among the ruins of the hall. I will say no more about Sampson. But remember the moral of this tale. Husbands must never tell their secrets to their wives. Their lives might depend on it.

Hercules

Let us praise famous men, and principal among them mighty Hercules. In his lifetime he was the flower of might. He killed and skinned a lion. He overthrew the Centaurs, part human and part horse. He slew the Harpies, winged spirits of death. He stole the golden apples of the Hesperides. He drove back Cerberus, the hound of hell.

What else? He slew the cruel tyrant, Busirus, and forced his horse to eat him, flesh and bone. He strangled a serpent while he was still in his cradle. He broke off one of the two horns of Achelous. He destroyed Cacus in a cave of stone. He overcame and killed the mighty giant Antheus. He slew the wild boar of Mycenae. He even held the heavens upon his shoulders.

No man in myth or history has killed so many monsters and prodigies as Hercules. His fame spread all over the world; he was renowned for his beauty as much as for his strength. He visited every kingdom and was welcomed everywhere. No man could defeat him. One commentator says that he was able to raise pillars to mark the eastern and western boundaries of the known world.

This noble warrior had a lover. Her name was Deianira, and she was as fresh as the first day of May. The old writers tell us that she was busily employed in knitting him a shirt, as women do. It was bright and colourful, but it had one fault. It was suffused with a fatal poison. Hercules had worn it only for a few hours when the flesh began to fall from his bones.

Some learned men tell us that a man named Nessus was responsible for making this shirt. I do not know. I will not accuse Deianira. I only tell you what I have read. As soon as Hercules had put on the shirt, the flesh on his back began to bake and harden. When he realized that there was no remedy he threw himself into the hot coals of a fire. He did not want to die by poison. It was too undignified.

So died Hercules, a mighty and worthy man. Who can trust the dice that Fortune throws? Anyone who makes his way in the difficult world must know that misfortune and disaster are always at hand. The only remedy is self-knowledge. Beware of Dame Fortune. When she wants to mislead, or to deceive, she chooses the least predictable path.

Nebuchadnezzar

No one can conceive or describe the majesty of this mighty and glorious king. No one can count his wealth or estimate his power. Twice he conquered Jerusalem, and stole all the sacred vessels of the temple. He took them back with him to Babylon, where they were laid down reverently with his other treasures.

He had captured the royal children of Israel and had ordered them to be castrated; then they became his slaves. Daniel was among them, and even then he was judged to be the wisest of all. It was he who could interpret the dreams of the king, when the king's own seers and magicians were baffled by them. Clever boy.

Then Nebuchadnezzar ordered a statue of gold to be fashioned, sixty cubits in height and seven cubits in breadth. He ordered all of his subjects to worship and make sacrifice to this golden image, on pain of death. Anyone who disobeyed his command would be flung in a fiery furnace. Yet Daniel, and two of his young cousins, refused to bow down before it.

The great king was filled with pride and was fully conscious of his might. He believed that God Himself could not challenge him or deprive him of his power. Little did he know. This proud king was humbled suddenly, and reduced to the condition of a beast of the field. He imagined himself to be an ox; he lay with the herd, and ate their food. He walked on all fours and munched on grass.

His hair grew like an eagle's feathers, and his nails became as long as an eagle's talons. After a number of years had passed, God gave him back his reason. With the return of his humanity, Nebuchadnezzar wept. He thanked God, and promised that he would never again trespass into sin. He kept that oath until the day of his death. God be praised for His justice and His mercy.

Belshazzar

The name of his son was Belshazzar, and he reigned over Babylon after his father's death. Yet he did not heed the warning, or the example, of Nebuchadnezzar. He was proud in heart, fierce, and an idolater. He lived in high estate but then, suddenly, Fortune cast him down. There were divisions within his kingdom.

He gave a feast for all the nobles at his court, and bid them all to be of good cheer. He told his servants to bring out the sacred vessels that his father had taken from the temple at Jerusalem. 'We will pour libations to our gods,' he said, 'in honour of my father's victories over the Jews.'

So his wife, his lords and his concubines poured wine into the holy chalices of the Lord and drank their fill. But then Belshazzar happened to look around, gesturing for a servant, when he saw a hand writing very quickly on the wall. There was a hand, and nothing else. No arm. No body. Of course the king was aghast, and shook with fear. He looked with horror upon the words that had been written. Mane. Techel. Phares.

None of the wise men in the kingdom could interpret these three words. Only Daniel knew the secret of the saying. 'Great king,' he said, 'Almighty God gave power and glory to your father. He loaded him with wealth and honour. But your father was proud. He did not fear or venerate the Almighty. So God sent him grief and wretchedness. He took away his kingdom. He took away his reason.

'He was an outcast, lost to human society. His companions

were the beasts of the field. He ate the grass and the hay, exposed to the elements, until the time came when it was revealed to him that Almighty God has dominion over all creatures. Only to Him belong the power and the glory. Out of pity for the poor man, God restored his humanity and gave him back his kingdom.

'You, sir, his son, are also filled with pride. You are following your father's sinful course, and you have become an enemy of God. You drank from the sacred vessels stolen from the temple. You encouraged your wife and your concubines to do the same. You are worse than a blasphemer. You also worship false gods. You will soon feel the force of the true God's wrath.

'You ask about the hand that wrote those three words upon the wall? It was sent by God. Trust me. Your reign is over. You are now less than nothing. Your kingdom shall be divided, given over to the Medes and the Persians.' On that same night Belshazzar was assassinated. Darius ascended the throne, although he had no right or claim to it.

So, fellow pilgrims, learn the moral of this story. Authority on earth is brittle. Power and wealth are transient. When Dame Fortune goes against you, you lose everything. You lose your friends, too. A friend made when Fortune smiles becomes an enemy when Fortune frowns. You know the proverb well enough.

Cenobia

Cenobia, queen of Palmyra in Syria, was renowned throughout the world for her nobility no less than for her skill in arms. No one could match her. She was of royal blood, descended from the kings of Persia. I will not say that she was the most beautiful woman in the world. I will only say that, in appearance, she had no defects at all.

From her childhood she disdained feminine pursuits. She

did not want to stitch or sew. She ran off into the woods and joined the hunt for wild beasts; she liked nothing better than to let the arrows fly. She was faster than the creatures she pursued, and never tired. When she was older she killed lions and leopards. She ripped a bear apart with her 'bear' hands.

She tracked them down. She sought their dens and lairs. She explored the mountains all night and, when she was tired, she slept beneath a bush. She could wrestle any young man to the ground, however strong he was. Nothing could withstand her force. It is needless to say that she was still a virgin. She would lie beneath no man.

But her friends eventually persuaded her to marry. She betrothed herself to a prince of that country, Odenathus by name, although she made him wait a long time for the ceremony. You should realize, too, that he was as fanciful and as wayward as she was. Nevertheless they were happy. They lived in married bliss.

Except for one thing. She insisted that he could have intercourse with her only once. She wanted to have a child. That was all she wished for. If she discovered that she was not pregnant after the first time, Odenathus was allowed to do it again. Just the once, of course.

If she was with child after that, then her husband was not permitted to touch her for forty weeks. Then he would be allowed another go. It did not matter if he complained, or wept, he got nothing more from her. She used to tell him that sex for its own sake was a sin. It was lechery, and a reproach to all women.

She bore two sons, whom she brought up to be virtuous as well as learned. But let me tell you the story. So here we have Cenobia before us, esteemed, wise, generous without being profligate; she was indefatigable in war, and modest in peace. There was no one like her in the wide world.

Her way of life was affluent beyond measure. She was rich in treasures. She was dressed in the finest robes of gold and pearl. She still loved the hunt, but she also strove to learn as many languages as she could. She studied books, earnestly trying to discover the most virtuous form of life.

To cut a long story short, she and her noble husband were so expert in arms that they conquered many kingdoms in the East and occupied many famous cities in lands as far away as Turkey and Egypt. No enemy could escape them, at least while Odenathus lived.

You may read all about their battles against Shapur, king of Persia, and against other monarchs. You can learn about their victories – and of their defeats. Petrarch, my great master, has told the story of Cenobia's downfall in abundant detail. He has described how she was captured and taken.

It had all been going so well. After the death of her husband her strength and courage seemed to be redoubled. She fought so fiercely against her enemies that there was not a king or prince in that region who could withstand her. So they made treaties with her, and exchanged gifts with her. They promised anything if she would only leave them in peace.

The Roman emperor, Claudius, dared not enter the field against her. Neither did his predecessor, Gallienus. The kings of Armenia and of Egypt, of Syria and Arabia, all quailed before her. They were terrified of being slain by her, their armies in flight.

The two sons of Cenobia were always dressed in regal garments, as the legal heirs of their father. Their names were Hermanno and Thymalao. But in fact Cenobia ruled. Yet there came a time when sweet Fortune turned sourly against her. The queen was not mistress of her destiny. She was doomed to fall from sovereign power and to experience sorrow and disgrace.

This is how it happened. When the emperor Aurelianus donned the imperial purple at Rome, he decided to take vengeance upon the queen of Palmyra for all the insults the empire had suffered at her hands. So he marched with his legions into her lands. She fled from him, but eventually he caught up with her and captured her. He put her in chains, together with her two sons, and rode back with them to Rome in triumph.

He carried with him her chariot of gold, richly jewelled, and ordered that it should be driven in his victory procession so that every Roman might see it. Then Cenobia herself was led before the people, wearing her crown but pinioned with chains of gold.

This is the wheel of Fortune. The noble queen, once the terror and the wonder of the world, was now on display to the mob. She who had led her troops in mighty battles, and who had conquered castles and cities, was brought low. She had once borne a sceptre, but now she carried a distaff with which to wind wool.

Peter, king of Spain

Oh worthy Peter, noble king, the glory of Spain! Fortune raised you so high. But now you are remembered only for your miserable death. Your own brother chased you from your realm. And then you were betrayed by your enemies and led into his tent, where he killed you with his own hands. He took over your kingdom and your possessions. He was as black as an eagle in a snow-white field.

Peter, king of Cyprus

Oh noble Peter, worthy king, who won by your mastery the great city of Alexandria. You vanquished many heathens in the course of your career! You were so triumphant that some of your own subjects envied you. They killed you in your bed for no other reason than your nobility. Thus does Dame Fortune turn the wheel, and bring men from glory to distress.

Bernabo of Lombardy

I sing of you, Bernabo Visconti, lord of Milan, scourge of Lombardy, lover of ease and delight. Why should I not recount your misfortunes? You were raised high, only to be brought down by your brother's son. Your nephew cast you into prison, and there you died. I do not know the reason. I do not know the killer.

Ugolino, count of Pisa

Who can relate the suffering of Ugolino, count of Pisa? There was a dark tower, a little way out of the city, to which he was consigned. He was imprisoned there with his three children, the oldest of whom was only five years old. What cruel Fortune shut these little birds within a cage?

He was destined to die in that prison. The bishop of Pisa, Roger Ubaldini, had borne false witness and had stirred up the people against him; so Ugolino was confined, with so little meat and drink that he despaired of his life.

There was a certain time each day when the gaoler brought his food into the cell. Ugolino was waiting for him at that time when, suddenly, he heard the great door of the tower closing. He heard the sound clearly, but he said not a word to his children. But he knew in his heart that they would all now starve to death. 'I wish that I had never been born,' he said to himself. And he wept.

His youngest son, three years old, crept upon his lap. 'Father,' he said, 'why are you crying? When will the gaoler bring us our food? Do you not have any bread for us? I am so hungry that I cannot sleep. I wish that I could sleep for ever. Then I would never be hungry! Please give me bread!'

So the poor child grew weaker and weaker each day. Eventually he climbed into his father's lap and whispered to him, 'Farewell, Father. I must go now.' The little boy kissed him on the cheek, laid down his head, and died. When Ugolino saw that his son was dead he gnawed his arms with grief, lamenting the faithlessness of Fortune. 'I am bound upon the wheel,' he said.

His two surviving children were convinced that he was gnawing on his flesh out of hunger rather than grief. The eldest of them implored him. 'Father,' he said, 'do not eat your own flesh. Eat us, instead. You gave us life. You have the right to take it from us. Our flesh is yours.' Within a day or two, both of the little boys were dead.

In his despair Ugolino also laid down and died. So ended the life of the mighty count of Pisa, drawn down into grief from high estate. If you wish to read more about this tragedy, you will find it in the pages of the great poet of Italy known as Dante. He has written a detailed account of the last days of Ugolino. His words will live for ever.

Nero

The emperor Nero was as great a fiend as any that dwells in hell. Yet, as Suetonius tells us in his *Lives of the Caesars*, he was the master of the world, from east to west and from north to south. His robes were of the purest white silk, and were covered with fine jewels. He delighted in diamonds and in sapphires.

He was prouder, and more pompous, than any emperor before; he was more fastidious than a maid, and would never wear the same robes twice. He used to fish in the Tiber with nets of gold. His caprices were turned into laws. His lusts were always satisfied. Dame Fortune smiled upon him.

He burned Rome to ashes for his entertainment. He killed all of the senators of that city just to hear how they groaned in their death throes. He killed his brother, and slept with his own sister. He made sad work of his mother, too. He cut open her womb so that he could view the place where he was conceived. That is how little he thought of her.

He did not cry at the sight of her ravaged body. He merely observed that she had once been a fine-looking woman. How could he judge of her beauty, when she lay dead before him? Then he called for wine, and drank off a draught. He showed no sign of remorse. When strength is united with cruelty, there breed monstrous offspring.

In his youth Nero had a teacher who tutored him in literature and morals. This man was the very flower of learning, as the old books tell us, and he managed to impart to his pupil all the lessons of civility. Nero then was compliant and obedient. He hid his vices very well.

The teacher's name was Seneca. He ruled over Nero with words rather than deeds. He did not punish him, but he reproved wrongdoing. 'Sir,' he would say, 'a good emperor must love virtue and hate tyranny.' What was his reward? Nero ordered that the wrists of Seneca should be slit as he lay in a bath.

Nero hated any authority placed over him. In particular he always felt a grievance against Seneca. So the philosopher chose to die in the bath, his blood in the water, rather than endure any more grievous punishment. That is the way the emperor slaughtered him.

There came a time, however, when Dame Fortune no longer favoured Nero. She detested his pride. And she knew, even though he was strong, that she was stronger. 'I cannot allow this vicious man to glory in his power and wickedness. I will throw him from the emperor's throne and, when he least expects it, he will suffer a great fall.'

One night the people of Rome rose up against him. When he learned of the revolt he ran out of the palace and looked for allies among his confederates. But their doors were closed to him. He knocked upon their gates, and cried for help, but they did not listen. He knew then that it was over. He stopped crying out, and went on his lonely way.

The uproar of the people continued. There were shouts and oaths resounding through the streets, and Nero could hear them asking one another: 'Where is that false tyrant? Where is Nero?' He was almost out of his mind with fear. He prayed to his heathen gods for help, but of course they could not assist him. He knew that he was about to die, and he ran into a nearby garden to hide himself.

There he found two peasants, sitting around a large bonfire. He begged and pleaded with these two men to kill him and to cut off his head. He did not want to be recognized and shamefully mutilated after his death. Then he killed himself in front of them. He had no choice. Dame Fortune looked down, and laughed at his fate.

Holofernes

Behold Holofernes, the general of Nebuchadnezzar. There was no king's soldier more famous or more victorious. There was no one stronger in battle. There was no one more filled with pride and presumption. Fortune kissed him, fondled him and then led him to a place where his head was cut off. It happened before he knew it.

For the sake of their wealth, and their liberty, men held him in fearful respect; he made his enemies renounce their faith. 'Nebuchadnezzar is your god,' he told them. 'You shall worship no other deity.' No one dared to disobey him – except in one city under siege, Bethulia, where an elder named Joachim was the high priest.

Take heed of the death of mighty Holofernes. One night as he lay drunk among his army outside Bethulia, lying in a tent as spacious as a great barn, he was murdered by a woman. Despite his power and his strength Judith hacked off his head and, unknown to anyone, crept out of the tent and brought the severed head back to the town.

The illustrious king Antiochus

What need is there to describe the sovereign power of this man, proud in intent and evil in deed? There was no one in the world like him. You can read of him in the Book of Maccabees. You can read there, too, all of his vainglorious words. Then you will learn of his ruin and fall, and of his death on a bare hillside.

Dame Fortune had so favoured him that he thought that he could touch the stars with his hand; he believed that he could lift mountains, and command the waves of the sea. Of all the people on the earth he hated God's chosen; he tortured and killed them, believing that their God had no power over him.

When he received the news of the defeat of his generals, Nicanor and Timotheus, he burned with wrath and hatred. He commanded that his chariot be prepared, and swore that he would not leave it until he had come to the gates of Jerusalem, where he would wreak his vengeance. But God forestalled him.

The Almighty smote him with a grievous wound, invisible and incurable, festering in his guts and causing him unendurable pain. Yet it was a fitting vengeance for one who had inflicted suffering on so many others. Even in his agony he pursued his evil purpose.

He ordered his army to prepare for battle. But, as he did so, God crushed his pride. Antiochus was hurled from his chariot by an unseen force, and his body was so badly mangled that the bones protruded through the flesh and skin. He could no longer ride a horse. He could no longer hold the reins. So he was carried everywhere in a chair of state, his body black with bruising.

The vengeance of the Lord was soon complete. His festering wounds had bred maggots beneath the skin and, as the wicked worms crept through the body, his flesh began to stink terribly. None of his attendants could bear the smell of him, sleeping or waking. He fell into despair, weeping all the time, because he knew now that God alone was the lord of creation.

Neither he, nor those around him, could endure the stench any longer. They could not stay in his company. So he was taken to a hillside, where he was left in all his agony. Alone among the rocks he died. So this thief and murderer ended his days with the just reward for all the pain he had caused to others. He was killed by his own pride.

Alexander

Do you know the old song, some talk of Alexander, some talk of Hercules? Well, everyone knows the story of Alexander. It is common throughout the civilized world. He conquered the whole world, too, and every sovereign was eager to make peace with him. He laid low the pride of man and beast, as far as the world's end.

There is no comparison to be made between him and any other general; the seas and continents quaked in fear of him. He was the flower of chivalry and the lord of grace. He was the heir of Fortune's bounty. He was so full of courage that nothing could divert his progress in arms – nothing, that is, except for the charms of wine and women.

He does not need my praise. Why should I repeat his victories over Darius, king of the Persians, and of a hundred thousand other rulers, generals and commanders? As far as any man could ride, or travel, the land belonged to Alexander. He owned the world. There is no more to say.

He was the son of Philip, king of Macedon and the first high ruler of Greece, and he reigned for twelve years. Oh worthy Alexander, then Fortune rolled the dice against you. You lost the game. Your own people poisoned you.

No tears are enough to lament your fall. In you died honour and nobility. You conquered the world, and yet that empire was not large enough for you. Are there words enough to describe false fortune and the horror of poisoning? I don't think so.

Julius Caesar

By dint of labour, of wisdom, and of strength, Caesar rose up from humble beginnings to the highest power. He was the conqueror of the Western world, by force or by treaty. All the nations were tributaries of Rome at the time Caesar became emperor. But then Dame Fortune's wheel turned.

Mighty Caesar fought in Thessaly against his father-in-law, Pompey the Great. Pompey had a vast force, made up of all the Eastern nations as far as the rising of the sun. Yet the valour and strength of Caesar conquered that Eastern army. Only a few soldiers, with Pompey himself, escaped from the battle-field. So Caesar became the object of awe in the East. Fortune was then his friend.

May I take a moment to lament the fate of Pompey himself? He fled the battle, as I said, but one of his men proved to be a foul traitor. He cut off Pompey's head and presented it to Caesar in order to win favour. The conqueror of the East was humiliated in death. Fortune had found another victim.

Caesar returned in triumph to Rome, where wreathed in laurels he led the victory procession. Yet there were two Romans, Brutus and Cassius, who had always envied his high estate; they entered a conspiracy against Caesar, and chose a place where they could easily assassinate him with hidden knives.

Caesar went in procession to the Capitol one morning, as he was wont to do, where he was surrounded by his enemies and struck many times by their blades. He lay there, dying in his own blood, but he did not groan at any of the blows against him – except, perhaps, for one or two from those once closest to him.

Caesar was so proud, and so manly, that he maintained his

honour even in death. He placed his toga over his waist so that no one might see his private parts. As he lay dying, and knew that his fate was drawing near, he would not be shamed.

I recommend that you read this story in Lucan's *Pharsalia*, or else in Suetonius. They will tell you how Dame Fortune first favoured, and then failed, the two great conquerors Caesar and Alexander. You cannot trust her smile. Keep an eye on her. Look what happened to all these heroes.

Croesus

Croesus, once king of Lydia and enemy of Cyrus the Great, was taken up in his pride and carried to the stake where he was to be burned to death; but then there descended a great rain from the heavens that quenched the flames. Croesus escaped, but he did not pay proper respect to Dame Fortune until he was suspended on the gallows.

When he had escaped from the consuming fire he could not wait to return to war. He believed that Fortune, having rescued him with a rainstorm, had also made him invincible against all of his foes. He had a dream one night that increased his confidence and his vainglory.

This was the dream. He was in a tree, and Jupiter there washed his entire body. Then Phoebus brought him a towel with which to dry himself. This was a good omen indeed. He asked his daughter to interpret the dream to him; she was skilled in all manner of prognostication.

'The tree you saw,' she told him, 'signifies the gallows. The washing of Jupiter signifies the rain and the snow. The towel that Phoebus brought you is an image of the sun's warm rays. You are going to be hanged, Father. There is no doubt about it. The rain will wash you, and the sun will dry you.' So did his daughter, whose name was Phania, warn him of his coming fate.

And indeed he was hanged. The proud king ended on the

gallows, where his royal estate could not save him. The tragedies of the proud and the fortunate have the same burden. They are threnodies of grief against the guile of Dame Fortune, who kills where she might cure. When men put their faith in her, she fails them and covers her bright face with a cloud.

Heere stynteth the Knyght the Monk of his tale

The Nun's Priest's Prologue

The prologe of the Nonnes Preestes Tale

'Hey!' the Knight called out. 'That is enough, sir Monk. You have spoken justly, I am sure. It was all very true. But a little sorrow goes a long way. People cannot bear too much tragedy. As for me, I hate hearing about the sudden fall from fortune into sorrow. I prefer to look on the bright side. I like to hear of those poor folk who have attained great riches or happiness, climbing up the ladder from low estate to wealth. That cheers me up. That is the story I wish to hear.'

'I agree with you,' Harry Bailey said. 'One hundred per cent. This Monk has spoken at length about the tragedies of various people. How did he put it? Fortune is covered with a cloud? Something like that. But there is no point in wailing and lamenting. What is done is done. As you said, sir Knight, it is not an exciting subject.'

Our Host then turned to the Monk. 'So, sir, no more, if you please. You are annoying the entire company. Your little homilies are not exactly entertaining. There is no fun in them. Wherefore good Monk – Peter is your name, isn't it? – wherefore, Peter, I beg you to tell us something different. Something amusing. If it were not for the clinking of the bells on your bridle, I would have fallen asleep listening to you. I would have slipped from my horse and sunk in the mud. Who cares about Holofernes? Or Croesus? There is an old saying used by preachers and teachers. "If a man has no audience, he had better stop talking." Of course I am always ready to listen to a well-told tale. Why not a story about hunters and hunting?'

'I'm afraid not,' the Monk replied. 'My heart would not be in it. Let somebody else tell the next story.'

So the Host spoke out boldly and rudely. 'Come towards me, you, the Nun's Priest over there! Tell us something that will lift our spirits. Be merry. Be daring. I see that you are riding on a poor nag of a horse, but that should not stop you. As long as it can carry you, it has my blessing. So. Make us laugh.'

'Willingly, good sir,' the Nun's Priest said. 'I will be as cheerful as you could wish.' So then this sweet Priest began his story to the company of pilgrims.

The Nun's Priest's Tale

Heere bigynneth the Nonnes Preestes Tale of the Cok and Hen, Chauntecleer and Pertelote

Once upon a time a poor widow, somewhat stooped by age, was living in a tiny cottage; it was situated in a valley, and stood within the shadow of a grove of trees. This widow had led a simple existence ever since the death of her husband; she had few cattle, and fewer possessions. She had two daughters and, between them, they owned three large sows, three cows and a sheep called Molly. The walls of her little house were thick with soot, but this is where she ate her simple meals. She had no use for spices or dainty food. Since her modest repast came from the produce of her farm, she was never flatulent from overeating. A temperate diet, physical exercise and a modest life were her only medicines. She was never hopping with the gout, or swimming in the head from apoplexy. She never touched wine, white or red. In fact her board was made up of black and white – black bread and white milk, with the occasional rasher of bacon or new-laid egg. She was a dairywoman, after all.

Her small farmyard was protected by a palisade of sticks, with a ditch dug all around it. Here strutted a cock called Chanticleer. There was no cock in the country that crowed louder than this bird. His voice was more impassioned than the organ that is played on mass days in church. His crow was better timed, and more accurate, than the clock on the abbey tower. By natural instinct he knew the movements of the sun; whenever it covered fifteen degrees across the sky, he began to crow as mightily as he was able. His comb was redder than the coral of the sea, and it had more notches than a castle battle-ment; his legs and toes were a beautiful shade of azure, just like lapis lazuli, and his nails were as white as the lily flower. His feathers were the colour of burnished gold.

Chanticleer had seven hens in his household. They were his companions and his concubines, devoted to his pleasure; they were as brightly coloured as he was, and the brightest of them was a hen called Pertelote. What a gentle, kind and attentive bird she was! She carried herself so nobly, and was so affec-tionate, that Chanticleer had loved her ever since she was seven days old. He could not get enough of her. You should have heard them crowing together at dawn, harmonizing on the words 'my love has left me'. In those days, of course, the birds and the animals could all speak and sing.

So it happened that, one morning at dawn, Chanticleer sat on his perch among his seven wives; beside him was sitting Pertelote. Suddenly he began to groan and moan, just like eone who is having a bad dream. When she heard him, she ıme alarmed. 'Dear heart,' she asked him, 'what is trou-g you? Why are you crying out in this way? You are asleep, ɔpose. Please wake up.'

hanticleer opened one eye. 'Ma dame,' he replied, 'don't be med. God knows I have just had a frightful dream. My ·t is still fluttering beneath my feathers. I hope everything ......s out for the best. I hope that my dream does not prove prophetic.'

'Tell me.'

'I dreamed that I was walking up and down the yard here, when I saw a savage beast very much like a wolfhound. It was about to take me in its jaws and swallow me. It was a tawny colour, somewhere between orange and red, but its tail and ears were black. It had a horrible little snout, and its eyes glowed like burning coals. It gave me such a fright, I can tell you. That must have been the reason I was groaning.'

'Shame on you,' Pertelote replied. 'What happened to your courage? Now you have forfeited all my love and respect. I cannot love a coward, for God's sake. Whatever we women may say, we all want husbands who are generous and courageous – and discreet, too, of course. We don't want to marry misers or fools or men who are afraid of their own shadow. And we don't like boasters. How dare you say, to your wife and paramour, that you are afraid of anything? Do you have a man's beard without a man's heart? For shame! And why are you afraid of dreams? They mean nothing. They are smoke and mist. They come from bad digestion or from an overflow of bile. I am sure that this dream you describe is a direct result of your bilious stomach, which leads people to dream of flaming arrows, of orange flames, and of tawny beasts that threaten them. Bile is the red humour, after all. It stirs up images of strife and of yelping dogs, just as the melancholy humour provokes the sleeping man to cry out about black bulls and black bears and black devils. I could give you a list of the other humours, and their effects, but I will forbear.

'Suffice to say what Cato said. That wise man declared that there was no truth in dreams. So, husband, when we fly down from our perch, remember to take a laxative. I swear on my life that you need to purge yourself of all these bad humours. You must shit out your bile and your melancholy as soon as possible. I know that there is no apothecary in the town, but I will teach you what medicinal herbs to chew. We can find them in the farmyard here, and they will cleanse you below and above.

'You are choleric by complexion, of course, with your red crest and comb. Beware that the midday sun does not find you full of hot properties. If it does, you will fall into a fever or a chafing sickness that will kill you. I know it. So let us find some worms to aid your digestion. They can be followed by spurge laurel, centaury and fumitory. Why are you making that face? I can pick you some nice hellebore and some euphorbia. I know for a fact that ground ivy grows in the garden. Just take a stroll there and eat some of it. Stay cheerful, husband, I beg you. There is nothing to fear from a silly dream. I can say no more.'

'Ma dame,' Chanticleer said, 'thank you for your advice. Can I bring up the subject of Cato? You are right to say that he was of great renown as a teacher and that he did dismiss the importance of dreams. But there are other authorities, all of them mentioned in the old books, who are even more learned than Cato. They take quite the opposite position. They have proved by experience that dreams are intimations of the joys and woes that people will suffer in this existence. There can be no argument about it. It is a fact of life.

'One of the greatest authors tells the following story. Two young men had gone on pilgrimage, in sincere devotion, when they came into a town so full of fellow pilgrims that they could not find an inn for the night. There was not a bed to be had for either of them. So they decided to split up, and separately find whatever accommodation there was. One of them ended up for the night in a cattle-stall, surrounded by oxen, while the other had more luck and secured reasonable lodgings. That is what luck does. It favours one over another. It is the way of humankind.

'So the more fortunate of them was sleeping in bed when he was visited by a bad dream. He dreamed that his companion was calling out to him in distress. "I will be murdered," he cried, "in an ox-stall! It will happen to me tonight! Come and help me, friend, before it is too late!" The sleeper woke with a start and sat up in bed; but, when he was fully awake, he turned back to sleep again. It was just a dream, after all. But then he had the same nightmare again. It was followed by a third vision, when his friend appeared before him covered in blood. "I am slain," he said. "Behold the wide and deep wounds that cover me. Arise at dawn tomorrow and walk down to the west gate of the town. You will find there a cart-load of dung. My corpse is hidden there. Be bold. Arrest the carter at once. I was murdered for my gold, you see." Then the apparition, with pale face and sorrowful eyes, told the whole story of his killing in the cattle-stall. This was no false dream, I can assure you.

'On the very next morning the man went down to the cattle-stall and called for his companion. The carter came up to him and told him that his fellow had already left town. He had gone at dawn. Of course the young pilgrim was suspicious, having in mind the dream of the night before. So he went at once to the west gate of the town and there, just as he had been informed in his dream, he found the cart-load of dung ready to manure the land. Then he cried out "Harrow!" and "Vengeance!" He told the townsmen that the body of his friend and companion lay buried here, having been foully murdered. He called out for justice. He demanded that the authorities of the town take action. "There has been a murder! The corpse of my friend lies here!" What do I need to say? The people tipped the cart on to its side and there, among the shit, was the body of the dead man.' Chanticleer ruffled his feathers, with a little shiver of disgust, before going on.

'Oh God in heaven, You are just and true. See how You have revealed the truth. "Murder will out." That is the saying. Murder is so abominable a crime that God will not allow it to be concealed. It may take a year, or two, or three, but eventually it will be revealed and seen for what it is. The authorities took the carter and tortured him until he confessed; then he was hanged and his corpse cut down from the scaffold.

'So you see, dear Pertelote, the real meaning of dreams. In the same book – in the very next chapter – there was another true story. Two men were about to pass over the ocean to a distant country, but the wind was against them. So they decided to stay in the city beside the harbour. Then, on the following day, in the evening, the wind had become favourable. The two men went to their beds in good spirits, in full expectation of being able to sail the next day.

'But listen. One of these men had a strange dream. He thought he saw a man standing beside his bed, telling him to stay behind and not to sail. "If you leave tomorrow," he said, "you will be drowned. There is no more to say." The man woke and, rousing his companion, told him what he had seen and heard. He begged him to postpone the journey. But the fellow laughed and made fun of him. "I will never allow a dream," he said, "to dictate my life. You must be joking. Dreams mean nothing at all. Men may dream of owls and apes and monstrous things. Men dream of events that have never been and never will be. But since I can see that you are determined to stay here and lose the tide, I must leave you. God knows I will miss your company, but so it must be. Farewell."

'So he took his leave, and went his way. Then it happened. I do not know how or why. Midway across the ocean the ship's hull was breached, the crew and passengers drowned. There were other ships sailing with them, having left on the same tide, but they were undamaged. Therefore Pertelote, dear chick, from such examples you may learn that there is truth in dreams. I advise you not to ignore them. You do so at your peril.

'I was reading the life of Saint Kenelm the other day. He was the son of Kenelphus, the king of Mercia in times gone by. Shortly before he was murdered Kenelm dreamed that he was about to be killed. He told his nurse about the dream, and she advised him to be careful and to watch out for traitors. But he was only seven years old; he was too young and too innocent to pay much regard to his dreams. But all came to pass. He was murdered by his own sister. It is a most terrible story, which I advise you to read.

'Dame Pertelote my love, listen to what I have to say. The honourable Macrobius wrote a commentary on Cicero's *Dream of Scipio*, in which he declared that dreams can foretell the future. Not all of them – I grant you that – but some of them. Then, if you wish, dip into the Old Testament and see what is written in the Book of Daniel about the subject. You can read about Joseph, and about his dreams of the sheaves and of the sun. What about the pharaoh of Egypt? Ask his butler and his cook whether dreams mean anything. They were rightly interpreted by Joseph, for good or ill. Wherever there are true histories of mankind, there are reports of dreams and omens. Remember the king of Lydia, Croesus, who dreamed that he was sitting in a tree. Of course he was soon hanging on a gallows. And there was Andromache, the wife of Hector, who dreamed that on the following day her husband would be slain in battle. She tried to persuade him to avoid the field, but of course the dream came true. Hector was slain by Achilles outside the walls of Troy. It is a long story. It is almost dawn. I will say only this. I know from my dream that I will suffer some kind of misfortune. In any case, I do not need laxatives. I hate them. I distrust them. They are poison.

'So, my dear, let us speak of merry things. God has given me one great blessing. It is you, my chick. Whenever I see your lovely face, with your beautiful red eyes and your gorgeous beak, I am happy. My fears dissolve. I know it has been written that woman is man's ruin, but I prefer the other saying. "Woman is man's delight and bliss." When I feel your soft feathers at night – I can't fuck you, of course, because our perch is too narrow – I feel safe and relaxed. I am so full of joy that I defy all the dreams in the world.'

And, with that, he flew down from his perch into the yard. It was dawn. With a crow and a cluck he woke up all of his wives, to feast on the corn scattered on the ground. He was manly. He was king of the yard. He put his wings around Pertelote, and fucked her, at least twenty times before the sun had risen much higher. He looked as strong as a lion. He did not strut in the yard like a common bird. He walked on tiptoe, as if he were about to rise in the air. Whenever he spied some more corn he clucked some more, and all his wives came running over. I will leave you with this picture of Chanticleer, monarch of all he surveys, and carry on with the story.

It was the beginning of May – 3 May, to be exact. Chanticleer was strutting up and down the yard, with his seven wives by his side. He glanced up at the sky, and saw that the sun had entered the sign of the bull; by instinct, and nothing else, he realized that it was coming up to nine o'clock. So he crowed his heart out. 'The sun,' he said to Pertelote, 'has

climbed forty degrees by my reckoning. No. I tell a lie. Forty-
one degrees. My dear chick, listen to the singing of your sister
birds. Just look at the bright flowers bursting into bloom.
My heart is full!' Yet in a moment ill fortune would befall him.
The end of joy is always woe. God knows that happiness in
this world is fleeting. If there was a proper poet to hand, he
could write all this down in a book as a sovereign truth. But
you must listen to me and learn. I swear to you that this story
is as true as the adventures of Sir Lancelot, fervently believed
by all good women. I will continue.

There was a fox, tipped with black from head to toe, who
was a very model of slyness and iniquity. He had dwelled in a
forest, near the old woman's cottage, for three years. The previous night, as high fortune had dictated, the fox burst through
the hedge that protected the yard where Chanticleer and his
wives were accustomed to take the air. He lay concealed in a
bed of cabbages until the following morning, ready to seize the
proud cock at the first opportunity. That is what assassins
do, when they are waiting for their prey. They hide, and they
plot. Oh false murderer, lying among the cabbages! You are no
better than Judas Iscariot. You are worse than Genylon, who
betrayed brave Roland. You false traitor. You are another
Synon, who caused the wooden horse to be brought into Troy.
Oh Chanticleer you will curse the morning when you flew
down from your perch. You were forewarned in your dreams
that this day would be hurtful to you, but you spread your
wings none the less. Well, as some wise clerks say, what will
be will be. God has made it so. There is much debate and
argument on the point, among the schoolmen. Thousands of
them have disputed on the claims of free will and necessity. I
really don't have the wit to solve the conundrum. Augustine
has tried. Boethius has tried. Thomas Bradwardyn has tried.
Remember him? There are those who believe that all is predes-
tined and prejudged in the fathomless mind of God. But there
are others who distinguish between providence and destiny. It
is not necessary that things happen because they have been

ordained but, rather, things that do happen have indeed been ordained. It is too much for me. I am telling a tale of a cock and a fox. That is all. I am relating the sad story of a bird that was persuaded by his wife to ignore his dream and to strut around the farmyard.

The advice of women is often fatal. It was a woman's advice that led to all our woe. I am talking about Eve, who advised Adam out of Paradise. He had been happy there. If I have offended anyone among you, dear pilgrims, take it in good spirit. I am only joking. Consult the authors who know about such things. Read what they have written about women. In any case these are the words of the cock. They are not mine. I mean no harm to any female.

Dame Pertelote and her sister birds were all merrily scratching in the sand, and taking a dust-bath in the sunshine, and joyous Chanticleer was singing more sweetly than the mermaids of the sea (Theobaldus in his *Bestiary* reveals the sweetness and the purity of the mermaids' song). He was watching a butterfly fluttering idly among the cabbages, when suddenly he became aware of the fox lying among the stalks. He was not inclined to crow any more. Instead he cried out 'Cok! Cok!' and started up in abject terror. An animal desires to flee from its natural enemy, even if he has not seen one of them before. It is instinctive.

So Chanticleer was about to run away, in fear of his life, but the fox began to talk to him in a mild and well-mannered way. 'Gentle sir,' he said, 'dear oh dear, where are you going? Are you afraid of your friend? May I be damned to hell if I harm a feather on your back! I have not come here to spy on you. I have been lying here so that I could hear you sing. Truly you have a marvellous voice, more melodious than that of any angel in heaven. You have more grasp of song than Boethius, who wrote a book on the subject. I remember well when your father, an excellent fellow, and your dear mother honoured my poor house with their presence. I would be pleased to invite you there also. As for singing, my ears do not deceive me.

Apart from your good self, your father had the best crow I have ever heard. His morning call was delicious. He sang from the heart. He used to strengthen his voice by standing on tiptoe and stretching out his neck as far as it would go. He tried so hard that he became cross-eyed with the effort. He was so expert in the art that there was no other bird in the region who could match him. He was the greatest songster. I have read that book about the ass, Burnellus, in which a cock gets his revenge upon a young man. As a boy he had broken the leg of the bird; on the day of the man's ordination the cock refuses to crow, and the man sleeps through the ceremony. Yet there can be no comparison with the wisdom and subtlety of your father. As I said, he had no rival. Will you sing for me now, good sir? Will you prove to me that you are your father's son?'

So Chanticleer rose up and beat his wings. He allowed flattery to overturn his judgement. He did not see an enemy, but an audience. Oh lords and ladies, there will be many flatterers and time-servers in your retinues; they will please you more than those who tell the truth, but take care. Read Ecclesiastes. There may be treachery at court.

So Chanticleer stood up on tiptoe, stretched his neck, and closed his eyes before beginning his song. That was the moment that the fox jumped from the cabbage patch and seized the cock by the throat; then he ran off into the wood, with no one in pursuit. Destiny cannot be averted. Fate will have its way – if only Chanticleer had not flown down from his perch, if only Pertelote had taken her husband's dream more seriously. All this happened on a Friday, by the way. It is well known to be an unlucky day. Oh Venus, goddess of love, this cock was your most fervent devotee. He did everything in his power to serve you. He did it all for pleasure, not to fill the world with more birds. How can you allow him to die?

I wish that I had the eloquence of Geoffrey of Vinsauf, who wrote a famous elegy when his sovereign, Richard of the Lion Heart, was killed by an arrow. Why do I not have the words, and the learning, to lament this woeful Friday? Why cannot I express my grief for the demise of the cock?

In the hen-run itself there was such a wail of sorrow, louder than the plaint the ladies of Troy made when their city was taken. The poor birds made more noise than Hecuba, on seeing the death of her husband at the hands of Pyrrhus. When Chanticleer was taken off, they screamed. And what of Pertelote? She was beside herself. She was frantic with grief, in more agony than the wife of Hasdrubal, who was killed as Carthage was destroyed in flame. She was so full of torment and of rage that she hopped on to a bonfire and burned herself to death. Unhappy birds! You cried as much as the wives of Rome when Nero burned down the city. They watched their husbands perish in the flames. They were guiltless of any crime, but they were condemned to death.

Let me return to the story. When the poor widow and her two daughters heard the crying and confusion of the hens, they rushed into the yard. They were just in time to see the fox racing back to the wood with Chanticleer in his grip. So they called out: 'Harrow! Harrow! The fox! The fox! Havoc! Havoc!' They ran after him, and they were joined in the pursuit by the whole village. There was Talbot and Garland and Malkyn, still with her distaff in her hand. The dog, Colin, sprinted beside them with his tail up. The cows and the calves, even the pigs, were roused by all the shouting and all the barking. They were all running as if their hearts would break. They were yelling as loudly as the fiends in hell. The ducks were quacking up a storm. The geese flew backwards and forwards. The bees came out of the hive in a wild swarm. The noise was so great that no London mob or riot over the price of wheat could equal it. They screamed after the fox. They blew their trumpets and beat their drums. They sounded their horns. They shrieked and whooped. They made so much din that it seemed that the heavens might fall.

Now, good pilgrims, I ask you to pay attention. See how Dame Fortune can ruin the hopes and expectations of her enemies. Chanticleer, caught in the jaws of the fox, trembling with fear, spoke out. 'If I were you, sir,' he said to his captor, 'I would turn upon my pursuers now and taunt them. I would tell them to go back from where they had come. For good measure, I would damn them to hell. I would tell them that you are safely on the margins of the wood, and that I will never escape from your jaws. I would tell them that I am dead meat.'

'That's a very good idea,' the fox replied. And at that moment, as soon as he had opened his mouth, Chanticleer leaped out and flew up into a tree.

'Alas,' the fox cried, looking up at him. 'Alas, dear Chanticleer. I am embarrassed. I am afraid that I have given you the wrong impression. I must have frightened you when I grabbed you and ran out of the yard. But I had the best intentions. I meant you no harm. Come down from that tree, and we can talk about it. I will tell you the truth and nothing but the truth.'

'You must be joking,' the cock replied. 'I'll be damned if I am fooled again. Your flattery won't work any more. I am not going to close my eyes and sing for you. He who keeps his eyes shut deserves his misfortunes. That is the lesson I have learned.'

'There is another lesson,' the fox said. 'Bad luck will come to one who opens his big mouth at the wrong moment.'

So this is the moral. Do not be careless, or impetuous. Do not trust flatterers.

Some of you may think this is a cock-and-hen story, a piece of foolishness. But learn the moral, at least. As Saint Paul says, you ought to be able to sift the wheat from the chaff. That is good advice. I will leave it there, lords and ladies. May we all lead good lives and go to heaven!

Heere is ended the Nonnes Preestes Tale

The Epilogue to the Nun's Priest's Tale

'Well, sir,' our Host said to the Nun's Priest. 'Blessed be your bum and balls! That story about Chanticleer was one of the funniest I have heard. If you were a secular, I bet you would be a bit of a cock yourself. You would be thrusting with the best of them. Seven would not be enough for you, would it? What about seven times seven? Or seven times seventeen? You could keep going. Look at him, fellow pilgrims. Look at his muscles. Observe that brawny neck, and noble chest. With his bright eyes, he reminds me of a sparrowhawk. There is no need for him to dye his hair with red powders. He has that brilliant colour naturally. Thank you, sir, for an outstanding story. And God be with you!'

Then our Host turned to another pilgrim, the Second Nun, and in gentle voice invited her to tell her tale.

The Second Nun's Prologue

The prologe of the Seconde Nonnes Tale

I speak of that nurse and mistress of all the vices, known in English as idleness, that gate to sin and hell – we must avoid it at all costs and instead cultivate a busy and useful life. We ought to concentrate on work, rather than on pleasure, or else the devil may take us unawares.

Satan has a thousand snares and traps ready to entice us; if he sees an idle man, he creeps up with his net. In an instant the man, not realizing the danger, is caught and damned. So I beg all of you to work hard and to avoid the sin of sloth.

And even if we have no fear of death, and the world to come, reason itself teaches us that idleness is the rotten soil from which no harvest can be gathered. Laziness is a laggard, prepared only for sleeping and eating and drinking. It consumes the goods of the world, the fruit of others' labour.

I am about to tell you a story that illustrates the foulness and folly of idleness, the source of so much harm to all of us. I am about to relate to you the glorious life and death of the holy blissful virgin whose wreath is crowned with rose and lily flower – the maid and martyr, Saint Cecilia.

Invocacio ad Mariam

Oh blessed Mary, the flower of all virgins, I call upon you first to guide my pen. You are the comfort of all sinners on the earth. Help me to tell the story of the maiden's death, and how through her martyrdom she won eternal life in the mansions of heaven.

Hail holy Mother of God, well of mercy, balm of sinful souls, in whom our Saviour chose to dwell for the sake of all mankind. Your humility has exalted you. You have so sanctified our nature that God Himself chose to take on flesh and blood.

Within the blessed temple of your body the threefold God, the centre of eternal love and peace, took human form. All creation sends up unceasing prayer and praise to Father, Son and Holy Ghost. You are the spotless Virgin who carried in your womb the creator of the world.

You are the spring of mercy, pity, peace and love. You are the source of virtue and of bliss. You come to the aid of those who pray to you, but out of your benignity you help others before they beseech you for comfort in distress. You go before, and heal their sorrow.

So help me now, blessed maid, in the valley of the shadow of death. Think of the woman from Canaan, who told your blessed Son that even the dogs eat the crumbs that fall from the tables of their masters. I know that I am a sinful and unworthy daughter of Eve, but please accept my faithful prayer.

Faith is dead without good deeds. Allow me the time and place to perform works in your honour, and thus avoid the darkness of hell. Hail Mary, full of grace. I beg you to speak a word for me in the abode of bliss where there is eternal song. Daughter of Anna, blessed one, Mother of Christ, hosanna!

Send your light to me in the darkness of the prison of this world; lift from me the burden and contagion of the flesh; save me from lust and all false affections. You are the haven of refuge, the solace and the comfort of all those in distress. Assist me now in my appointed task.

I ask that all those who hear, and read, this story will forgive my lack of grace. I have no skill or subtlety in narration. I am relying upon the words of one who so revered the saint that he wrote down her story. It is to be found in the book known as

The Golden Legend. Please pardon any of my faults for the sake of the holy martyr herself.

I will first interpret the name of Cecilia, and expound its meanings in terms of her life. It means, in English, 'the lily of heaven', alluding to her virginal chastity. It also refers to the whiteness of her honesty, the evergreen stalk of her conscience, and the sweet savour of her reputation. Thus she is called 'lily'.

Cecilia may also mean in Latin *caecis via*, or 'the path for the blind'. This refers to her teaching and her example. We also arrive at her name by conjoining 'heaven' and 'Lia', *caelo et lya*; heaven here means holiness and Lia is the name of the active life in the world.

Cecilia may also be construed as 'lack of blindness', or *caecitate carens*. The meaning is easy to understand. The holy saint is filled with the great light of wisdom and of virtue. Then again her name may be the conjunction of 'heaven' and 'leos' or people – *coelo et leos* – and she is indeed the heaven of the people.

Just as we may look up at the night sky and see the moon and the planets and the wandering stars, so when we observe the heavenly maid we see the shining paths of faith and of wisdom as well as the bright constellations of virtue and of good works.

The philosophers tell us the seven spheres of heaven revolve quickly through the firmament, sending out great heat, so Cecilia was always swift and busy in her good works; she was as perfect in form as the celestial spheres, and she burned continually with the fire of grace. So I expound her name.

The Second Nun's Tale

*Heere bigynneth the Second Nonnes Tale of
the lyf of Seinte Cecile*

This holy maid, Cecilia, came from Rome. She was of noble family, and from her cradle she was brought up in the religion of Christ. She studied the gospels faithfully, and all the time prayed that Almighty God might preserve her virginity.

Yet it was deemed necessary for her to wed. Her bridegroom, Valerian, was a young man of noble descent. When the day came for their marriage, she retained all of her humility and piety. Beneath her golden wedding gown she wore a hair shirt next to her tender flesh.

While the organ played, and the music filled the church, Cecilia sang a secret song in her heart to God. 'Oh Lord,' she prayed, 'preserve me undefiled in body and in soul.' For the love she bore to Christ she vowed to fast on every second and third day, spending those hours in prayer.

Night fell, and the time came for bed. She must lie with her husband, according to custom, but before this took place she whispered to him, 'My sweet and beloved husband, I have something to say to you in confidence. If I tell you this secret, will you promise never to betray it?'

He made the promise, of course, and swore an oath that he would never reveal what she said to him. So she told him. 'I have an angel that so loves me that he protects me night and day. He stands guard over my body.

'Believe what I say. If he should see you touching me, for the purposes of love or of lust, he will kill you at once. You are still a youth, but you will be slain. But if you love and respect me in a clean and virginal way, then he in turn will love and honour you. He will demonstrate his joy to you.'

Valerian, guided by the grace of God, spoke softly to her. 'If I am fully to believe you, dearest wife, let me see this angel for myself in all his brightness. If he is truly an angel, then I will accede to your wish. But if this is a trick – if you love another man – you can be sure that I will kill you both with this sword.'

Cecilia answered him at once. 'The angel will appear to you, as you wish. But first you must embrace the faith of Christ and be baptized. Go to the Appian Way, just three miles beyond the city. Speak to the poor people who dwell there, and repeat what I am about to tell you.

'Tell them that I have sent you to them so that they might take you to the secret abode of old and saintly Urban, where you are to have private conference with him for the good of your own soul. When you come face to face with this holy pope, repeat to him the confidence I have already imparted to you. When he has absolved you from your sins, then you will see the angel.'

Valerian followed her instructions faithfully, and travelled to the Appian Way. There, within the catacombs, he was brought into the presence of the saintly Urban. He told him Cecilia's words, and at once the old man lifted up his arms in wonder.

He cried for joy, and prayed through his tears. 'Almighty God,' Urban said, 'Jesus our Saviour, the shepherd of the world and the begetter of all virtue. You have sown the seed of chastity in the body of the beloved maiden Cecilia. She obeys You in everything and works unceasingly for the greater glory of Your name. She has recently taken as her husband a young man as proud and fiery as a lion. But he stands before me now with the meekness of a lamb.'

There was a short pause after these words, but then there

appeared before Valerian the figure of an old man dressed in robes of brightness; in his hands he was carrying a book printed with words of gold.

At the sight of this Valerian fell down in fear. But the apparition lifted him to his feet, and began to read to him from the book. 'One Lord. One faith. One God. One Christendom. One father who rules over heaven and earth.' These were the words of gold.

When he had finished reading this text, the old man asked Valerian a question. 'Do you believe these words to be true? Yes or no?'

'I do believe,' Valerian answered. 'There are no words more true and blessed. They are the hope of humankind.'

Then the old man vanished from sight and, on the spot, Pope Urban baptized Valerian. When the Roman returned home he found Saint Cecilia, his wife, in the company of an angel. The angel had two coronets in his hand, one made up of lily and one of roses; he gave the first of them to Cecilia and, according to the old books, he gave the second one to Valerian.

'Keep these coronets inviolate, with a pure body and mind,' the angel told them. 'I have brought them from paradise. They will never wither or die; their perfume will never fade. The sinners of this world will not be able to see them. Only those who are chaste and innocent will have sight of them. And you, Valerian, who trusted the word of God so readily and so fully, ask what you wish of me. I will grant your favour.'

'I have a brother,' he replied. 'There is no man I love more. I pray that you grant my brother the grace to know the truth that has been revealed to me.'

'God is happy to fulfil your request,' the angel said. 'Both of you will win the palm of martyrdom. One day you will both partake of the blessed feast.' At this moment Valerian's brother, Tiburce, arrived at the mansion. He smelled the sweet savour of the lily and the rose, and he was bewildered.

'I wonder,' he said, 'how, at this time of year, the rose and the lily can be in bloom? Their perfume is so strong and deep that I might be holding them in my hands – it has touched my heart, and I feel reborn.'

Then Valerian came up to him and welcomed him. 'We have two coronets,' he told him, 'lily white and rose red, shining brightly. They are invisible to you as yet but, through my prayers, you are able to sense their presence. You will be able to see them, dear brother, as soon as you embrace the true faith.'

'Are you saying this to me, brother, or am I dreaming?'

'We have been dreaming all our lives. Now we must wake and know the truth.'

'How do you know this? How can you be sure?'

'I will tell you,' Valerian replied. 'An angel from heaven has taught me the truth. You will know it, as soon as you renounce the false idols of heathen worship.'

Saint Ambrose has written about the miracle of these coronets of flowers, in the preface to his mass for Saint Cecilia's Day. That wise father of the Church has declared that Saint Cecilia received the palm of martyrdom when she renounced the world and the flesh. She was thereby filled with the grace of God. 'Witness the conversion of Valerian and Tiburce,' he writes, 'as a token of her holiness. That is why the angel brought down two sweet crowns from heaven. This virgin has brought bliss to both these men. The world will know the worth of truth and chastity in love.' Then Cecilia showed to Tiburce the folly of worshipping false idols; they are made of stone and wood; they are deaf and dumb; they are to be shunned.

'Who does not believe this,' Tiburce told her, 'is as dumb as wood and deaf as stone. This is the truth I now know.' On hearing these words Cecilia kissed his breast in token of their kinship. 'I now take you as my faithful friend,' the blessed maid said. 'Just as the love of Christ made me your brother's wife,' she added, 'so now for the same love I take you as my kinsman and dear relation. Now that you have forsaken your false gods, go with your brother and be baptized. Cleanse your soul. Then you will see the face of the angel.'

Tiburce turned to Valerian. 'Will you tell me, brother, where are we going? Who will baptize me?'

'There is a man,' he replied. 'Come with me now in good heart and spirit. I will take you to Pope Urban.'

'To Urban? Are you taking me to see him? That would be strange. That would be wonderful. Are we talking about the Urban who has so often been condemned to death? About the man who is in perpetual hiding, and dare not show himself? If he were found, or seen, he would be consigned to the flames. We also would keep him company in the fire. While we are looking for the divine world, concealed by the light of heaven, on earth our bodies will burn. Is that the truth of it?'

Cecilia replied to him calmly. 'If life on earth were the only life, my dear brother, then you would be right to fear death. But it is not the only life. There is a better life in another place that will last eternally. Fear nothing. Jesus Christ has made a promise to us. God the Father has created all things in heaven and earth. He has given reason to mortals. God the Holy Ghost has, through grace, imparted to us the soul. God the Son, when He took on human form in the world, declared that there was another life to be won elsewhere.'

'Dear sister,' Tiburce said, 'I don't understand. You have told me just now that there is only one living God. Now you speak to me of three.'

'I will explain it to you now,' she replied. 'You know that man has three faculties of the mind, namely, memory, imagination and judgement. So in the divine being there are three persons distinct and equal.' Then she began to preach to Tiburce about the coming of Christ and told him of his passion and crucifixion. She explained that Christ came to earth in order to save mankind, and to lift the burden of sin and woe derived from the original fault of Eve. When she had explained these things to her brother in faith, Tiburce was happy to accompany Valerian into the presence of Pope Urban.

Urban gave thanks to God for their conversion, and gladly taught Tiburce the principles of the Christian faith before baptizing him. He had become a knight of God. He was filled with such grace that he saw the angel, too, each day. Whatever he prayed for, he was granted.

It would be impossible to say how many miracles Christ wrought for them. Yet there came a day when the bailiff of Rome found them and arrested them. Then he brought them before the prefect of the city, Almachius, who was well known to be an enemy of all Christians. He soon divined their faith, and ordered them to go and worship at the temple of Jupiter.

He turned to his officers. 'I order you,' he said, 'to take off the head of anyone who does not bow down before the image of the god.' One of these officers, Maximus, bound the two martyrs and then, weeping with pity, he led them through the city of Rome.

Maximus heard the teaching of Valerian and Tiburce, and was moved by it. He was given leave by the other officers to take them to his own house, where the two saints preached to him and to his family. All the officers were present, too, and all were converted to the true faith by the holy words of the gospel.

Cecilia herself came to the house late that night, accompanied by priests who baptized all those assembled there. Afterwards, at break of day, she spoke to them in a clear calm voice. 'You are all now warriors of Christ Jesus our Saviour. Renounce the works of darkness. Put on the bright armour of righteousness. You have fought a battle against the devil, and you have won it. Your course is almost done, and you have preserved your faith. Now take up the crown of eternal life. God Almighty will place it on your heads, as the reward you deserve.' When she had finished, some officers of the court arrived to take Valerian and Tiburce to the temple of Jupiter.

When they were led before the image of the god they refused to make any sacrifice to it. They declined to bow down before it or offer incense to the idol. Instead they fell to their knees and prayed to the true God. So they were beheaded on the spot, and their souls rose into heaven.

Maximus was present at their execution, and afterwards related that he had seen the souls of the two saints ascending to paradise in the company of bright angels. He wept many times as he told this story to others, but his tears converted them all to the true faith. When he heard of this, Almachius ordered that he should be whipped to death with cords of lead.

Saint Cecilia then took up his body and buried it beside the graves of Valerian and Tiburce, where they shared a simple stone. But then Almachius struck. He ordered that the virgin should herself be taken to the temple of Jupiter, where she would be obliged to venerate the idol with incense.

But the officers of his court had been converted by her preaching. They wept aloud, and proclaimed their belief in the Christian faith. 'We believe that Christ is the son of God,' they told him. 'We believe that He was God in human form. We know this to be true. The holy maid is His servant. We swear to this, even if we are condemned to death.'

When the prefect of the city heard of these things, he ordered that Cecilia should be brought before him. He asked her first about her rank and degree. 'I was born and raised a gentle-woman,' she told him.

'Now let me know this,' Almachius replied. 'What religion do you espouse? What are your beliefs?'

'That is a foolish question, sir. You are asking me two things at once. That's silly.'

'Why are you so impudent to me?' Almachius asked her.

'Why? Because I have a clear conscience. Because I have come here in good faith.'

'Do you have no respect for my power?'

'Your power is very small. The authority of any man is no more than a bladder filled with wind. The point of a pin will puncture it. Then there is nothing.'

'You began in the wrong tone. Now you are being offensive.

Do you not know that the rulers of the land have ordained that all Christians will be arrested and punished. But, if they renounce their so-called faith, they will escape any penalty?'

'Your rulers are mistaken. You and the other nobles are also wrong. You make us guilty by passing a foolish law. You know very well that we are innocent of any crime. We are Christians, who honour the name of Christ. That is all. Where is our offence? We will never renounce the cause that we know to be true and just.'

'You have a choice,' Almachius replied. 'Renounce your faith or suffer death. There is no other way.'

When she heard this, Cecilia began to laugh. 'Oh, sir, you are a simpleton. Do you think that I would renounce my innocence in order to become a sinner? Do you not see that you are making a fool of yourself? You stamp and stare. You rage at me as if you had lost your mind.'

'Foolish woman! You do not know the extent of my power. The rulers of this land have given me the power of life and death, over you and everyone else. How dare you speak to me like that? You are puffed up with pride!'

'I speak nothing but the truth. I am not proud. We have been taught as Christians to hate the sin of pride. And if you want to hear another truth, then I will tell you this. You have lied. You have said that our rulers have granted you the power of life and death. You can take away only the mortal life. You have no other jurisdiction. So you can be the minister of death. But that is all.'

'Enough of your impudence,' he said. 'Make sacrifice to Jupiter. Then be on your way. I do not care what you say about me. I can endure that like a philosopher. But there is one thing I will not permit. I cannot allow you to speak ill of our native gods.'

'Oh foolish man,' she replied. 'You have said nothing to me that has not been vain and ill-considered. You are an incompetent officer and a presumptuous judge. You might as well be blind, for all the good your eyes are. Can't you tell that this idol is made of stone? You have announced that a piece of granite is a god. Put your hand on it. If you cannot see it, taste it. Can't you tell? It is made of stone. It is a shame that all the people will be laughing at you for your foolishness. It is known that the Lord God is in the heavens. Anyone can tell that these stone images are of no use or value. Do you not see that they have no purpose? They are cold. They are lifeless.'

Her words enraged Almachius. He ordered his officers to take her back to her house, and there burn her to death. 'Bathe her in flame,' he said. 'Clean her.' They followed his orders literally. They placed her in a bath, pinioned her, and then lit great fires beneath her that were fed with logs night and day.

All that night, and for most of the next day, she felt no pain; she remained quite cool, and did not burn. There was not a drop of sweat upon her forehead. Yet she was still destined to die in that bath. Almachius, frustrated of his purpose, sent one of his servants to slay her as she lay there.

He took out his sword and three times he tried to behead her. But this torturer did not succeed. He could not take the head from the body. It was forbidden by law to aim a fourth stroke at a victim, and so with drawn sword he hesitated. He dared not break the law.

So he left her in the bath half dead, her neck badly mangled, and went on his way. The Christian followers of Cecilia then flocked to her house. They brought sheets and towels with them to staunch the flow of her blood. She endured this torment for three days, during which time she spoke and preached to them all.

She bestowed her worldly goods upon them, and blessed them. She left them in the keeping of Pope Urban himself, to whom she spoke these words. 'I have asked this of God Almighty. I have begged Him to give me three days so that I might commend the souls of these people to your care. And I ask you to turn my house into a church.' Then she died.

Pope Urban removed the body under cover of darkness and buried it at night in the catacombs with the other saints. Then he consecrated her house, baptizing it as the Church of Saint Cecilia. It stands to this day, a holy place devoted to the honour of Christ and of the saint herself.

Heere is ended the Seconde Nonnes Tale

The Canon's Yeoman's Prologue

The Prologe of the Chanouns Yemannes Tale

We had ridden scarcely five miles after we had heard the tale of Saint Cecilia when we came to the hamlet of Blean, a few miles from Canterbury. Just as we entered the forest there we were overtaken by a man dressed in black, with a white surplice showing beneath his gown. His mount, a dapple grey, was so soaked in sweat that we could scarcely credit it. It was clear that he had been riding hard for some miles. The poor horse could hardly go any further; its collar was dripping wet, and its flanks were flecked with foam. His rider travelled light, however, with only a bag of two pouches fastened to his saddle. It was a warm spring, after all. I wondered who this man in black might be, until I noticed that his hood and cloak were sewn together. I knew at once that he was a canon of the Church. His hat hung down his back, from a cord, and he had put a burdock leaf under his hood to keep his head cool and to prevent the sweat from running down his face. He had galloped fast and furiously. It was extraordinary to see the sweat on him; he held as much liquid as a distillery.

When he came up to us he cried out in a loud voice, 'God save you all! I have come all this way for your sake. I rode as fast as I could to catch up with you. Do you mind if I join you?'

His servant now rode up behind him. 'Gentlemen,' he said, 'I saw you leave the inn early this morning, and I told my master here all about you. You seemed such a jolly crowd. So he was determined to ride with you. He likes a bit of fun.'

'I'm glad you told him,' the Host replied to the boy. 'It looks as if your master is a clever man. Witty, too. And I bet he has a few stories to keep us all amused. Am I right?'

'Stories? He has got a million of them. He is very entertaining, if you know what I mean. I will tell you something else. He is skilled in many ways. He has many talents. He has undertaken work of great importance, too, which no one else could manage. Unless they learned from him how to do it. He may look ordinary enough, but it will profit you to get to know him. I bet you anything that you will gain from acquaintance with him. He is a very wise man. He is one of the best.'

'Tell me this. Is he a priest or a scholar? What kind of man is he?'

'He is more than just a priest, sir. I will tell you, in a few words, what kind of art he practises. I cannot let you know everything, even though I do work as his assistant. But I can tell you this about his business. He is a man of such subtlety and skill that he could turn all this ground on which we are riding – the whole route, from Southwark to Canterbury – into gold and silver. I am not exaggerating.'

'Good God!' Harry Bailey was astounded. 'That is a marvel, to be sure. But since your master is such a wise man, and so worthy of honour, can you explain why he is wearing such a tatty old gown? It is dirty and full of holes. It isn't worth a penny. Where is his self-respect? According to you, he is worth a lot of money. If he can turn this road to gold and silver, why does he not buy a better gown? Tell me the answer.'

'Why are you asking me that, sir? As God is my witness, he will never prosper. Don't mention this to anyone, by the way. It is a secret between you and me. The problem is that he is too clever for his own good. When you have too much of a good thing, you can overreach yourself. That is his case, I believe. My master has misused his great gifts. It is a cause of grief to me, I can assure you. God help him. That is all I can say.'

'Never mind that,' Harry replied. 'Tell me more about this

work of his. Since you know all about him, you must also know his secrets. I assume that he is shrewd as well as wily. So tell me everything. Where do you both live?'

'We dwell beyond the walls of a town, in an area full of cellars and blind alleys. It is the haunt of thieves and robbers who must conceal themselves. It is a place for those who dare not show their face by day. That is where we live.'

'Tell me another thing,' our Host asked him. 'Why is your face so discoloured?'

'God has not favoured it, I admit. I am so used to blowing into the fire that the flames have changed my colour, I suppose. I am not one to preen myself in front of a mirror. I get on with my work, and try my hand at alchemy. But we are always making mistakes. We miscalculate the amount of heat, for example. We can never get to the end of the experiment, and fail somewhere along the way. But that's no problem. There are plenty of gullible people who will give us a pound of gold – or ten pounds, or twelve pounds – on the understanding that we will be able to double the amount. I know that this may be a false promise, but we still have faith in the technique. We still have hope. The trouble is that the science is so difficult to master. Although we have sworn the contrary to our customers – our patrons, I should say – we never get it quite right. I would not be at all surprised if we became beggars.'

While this young Yeoman was talking, his master came close and listened carefully to everything he said. This Canon, dressed in black, was wary and distrustful of others. Cato has taught us that the guilty man always believes that he is the object of suspicion. That is why the master drew so close to the servant. He wanted to hear everything. Then he interrupted the boy. 'Shut your mouth,' he said. 'Don't say another word. Otherwise, you will regret it. How dare you slander me in the company of these strangers, and blab all my secrets?'

'Carry on, young man,' Harry Bailey said. 'Don't pay any attention to him or his threats.'

'Don't worry,' the boy replied, 'I don't intend to.'

When the Canon realized that all his threats were useless, he fled in sorrow and in shame.

'Ah,' his Yeoman said, 'now we can have some fun. I will tell you everything I know. He has run away, has he? I hope he goes to the devil. I don't want to have anything else to do with him, I can promise you that. Not for all the money in the world. He was the one who led me into the false game. Yet I never thought of it as a game. I was deadly serious, believe me, in its pursuit. I laboured. I sweated. I worried. I cried. Yet, for all that, I could never leave it alone. I wish to God that I had the brains to tell you everything there is to know about alchemy. I can only explain a small part of the art. Now that my master has gone, I will do my best. So . . .'

Heere endeth the Prologe of the Chanounes Yemannes Tale

The Canon's Yeoman's Tale

Heere bigynneth the Chanouns Yeman his Tale

PART ONE

I have lived with this Canon for seven years, but I am nowhere near to understanding the secret. I have lost everything I owned, as have many others. Once upon a time I was clean, cheerful and well dressed. Can you believe it? I now use an old sock as my hat! I used to be plump and ruddy-cheeked. Now I am thin and sallow. I am losing my eyesight through all the hard work. Stay away from alchemy at all costs. Where is the benefit in trying to transmute metals? The sliding science has left me penniless and in despair. Nothing good has come of it. I have borrowed so much gold that I will never be able to repay my debts. Let me stand as a warning to everyone else, like a wolf's head. If anyone were foolish enough to practise alchemy, it will prove to be his undoing. He will not succeed. He will empty his purse. He will addle his wits. But there is worse. As soon as he has lost all of his money, through his stupidity, he will try to persuade others to follow his example and try their hand at the black art. 'Misery loves company.' That is the proverb, is it not? Well, enough said. Now I will tell you all about our work.

When we practise in our laboratory we look very wise and learned; we use high terms and rarefied phrases to explain our mysterious labours. Then I blow upon the coals until there is no breath left in my body. Is there any need to explain the exact proportions of the dark materials that we use? There is always the silver, of course. We would normally put in five or six ounces of it. We compound this with arsenic, with burned bones and iron filings. Then we grind the mixture to a powder, and put it in a little earthenware pot. Add a little salt, and some paper. Place a sheet of glass over the pot, sealing glass and vessel with some clay so that no air will escape from it. We can change and moderate the fire at will. Then begins the hard labour, the watching and the calculating. We are supposed to purify, to blend and to disperse all of the ingredients. We use quicksilver, too, which is the name for unrefined mercury. But for all our tricks and devices we never got anywhere. We used lead and arsenic, ground together with a marble pestle in a marble mortar. It made no difference. There was no result. We boiled volatile spirits – again to no effect. We experimented with the residue left at the bottom of the flask. But it did no good. Our labour was in vain. All the money we spent was lost, too.

There are many other aspects of the art of alchemy. I cannot tell you them in the correct order – I am not that learned – but I will mention them as they come to me. I will not be able to put them in their proper categories, of course. Let me see. There is red clay known as Armenian clay, although it does not come from Armenia. There are green verdigris and white borax. Then there are the various vessels that we use for our distillation and purification, some made of clay and some made of glass. We have flasks and retorts, phials and tubes, crucibles and alembics. There is no need to mention all of them. They were expensive enough, but they were all useless. Have I mentioned the red waters or the gallstones of a bull? Then there is sal ammoniac. And the arsenic. And the brimstone. Do you find it confusing? I could go on all day about the various herbs we use. There is agrimony, which smells so sweet; there is valerian, and there is moonwort.

So we toiled over the coals and crucibles all day and all night, with the lamps burning around us. The furnace was at full blast, and we heated the liquids to their various boiling points. We used unslaked lime as a caustic, as well as chalk and the whites of eggs; we had powder ground out of ashes and dog shit, piss and clay; we made fires out of wood and out of charcoal; we sprinkled purified salt and vitriol, and then mixed in alum and brewer's yeast, the hairs of men and of horses, the grease of a sow and the sweat of a red-haired child. Sometimes the amalgam turned yellow, and sometimes silver white. We would fuse and ferment, diffuse and distil.

Let me explain to you the nature of the four spirits and the seven bodies, as my master taught them to me. The first spirit is mercury or quicksilver and the second is orpiment of golden hue; the third spirit is sal ammoniac, the moisture of volcanoes, and the fourth is brimstone. The seven bodies are as follows. The sun is gold, and silver is the moon; Mars is iron and Mercury, of course, is quicksilver; Saturn is lead and Jupiter is tin. The seventh, Venus herself, is copper.

Whoever practises this cursed art is doomed to failure and ruin. He will sell all his goods and come to no good. There can be no doubt that he will lose everything. So come forward, budding alchemists, and try your luck. If you have money to burn, then stoke up the chemical fires. Do you think that it is an easy craft to learn? Not so. You can be a priest or canon, monk or friar – I promise that you will not have scholarship enough. You can study all the texts, night and day, and still go nowhere. The mystery is too deep. For a layman, it is impossible to unravel. It makes no difference whether he is learned or not, he will fail in either case. Alchemy is too difficult.

Oh, I forgot to mention the acids we use, with the metals and oils. They help in the hardening or softening of the materials. They can also be used to cleanse and purify – you need more than a book to understand these things. No more words now. I have named things that should not be named. I have said enough to raise a fiend, the ugliest in hell.

The object of our quest is the philosopher's stone, the magic elixir. If we possessed that, we would be safe from sorrow. But our labours have proved worthless. I swear to God that, for all our craft and care, the stone will not come to us. The loss of time and money has brought us close to madness. But still there is that hope, that yearning, which keeps us searching for the key. If we have that, we have everything. So you see that the craving can never be satisfied. It is a sharp spur, always pressing us onward. We will never let go, we will never slacken. The quest is lifelong. In hope of future glory, we are willing to forsake everything else. We can never turn our backs on the metals and the crucibles. Although we may only have a torn sheet to cover us at night, and a rough coat to wear by day, we will still spend everything we have on the pursuit of the elixir.

These alchemists smell of sulphur and of brimstone. Wherever they go, they stink like goats. Their odour is so hot and rancid that you can spot them from a mile away. So you can always recognize them from their smell and from their threadbare clothes. If anyone asks them privately why they look so shabby, they have a simple reply. If anyone knew our identities, they say, we would be killed for our secrets. Hush hush. So they deceive the innocent.

Well, enough of this. I will get on with my story. Before we place the pot upon the fire, my master tempers the various metals. Only he can do this – now that he has gone, I can speak freely – and only he knows all the virtues of the lead and silver. He has a fine reputation among the cognoscenti, believe me, although there have been many times when he has come to grief. How does that happen? There are occasions, for example, when the pot explodes or falls to pieces. These metals are so volatile and violent that they can pierce the walls. We have to strengthen the stones with lime and mortar. They sink through the floorboards, or they fly up to the ceiling. Sometimes they just lie scattered on the floor. The expense is terrible. I have never seen the devil, but I am sure that he is somewhere in that room with us. There could not be more violence, or anger, or strife, or sorrow, in hell itself.

When the pot exploded everyone blamed everyone else.

Everyone started to fight. Some said that the pot was left on the fire for too long. Some said that the bellows were not strong enough. Then everyone looked at me, because that is my department. 'Not true,' said a third. 'The metals were not mixed correctly.' 'Bollocks,' said a fourth. 'Stop squabbling and listen to me. The fire should have been kindled from logs of beech, not logs of oak. That is the reason.' I could never tell who was right or wrong. I only know that the argument went on and on.

'Enough,' said our master. 'What is past cure is past care. I will be more vigilant next time. I am sure that the pot was cracked. That was the cause of the trouble. Well, let it go. Don't get depressed about it. Cheer up. It's not the end of the world, is it?'

Then all the debris was swept up in a heap. We put some canvas sheeting on the floor, and piled the debris on to it. Then we picked through the pieces of metal and chemicals, looking for anything we might retrieve. 'Look,' one of our number said, 'there is some of the metal. It is not intact, but we can still use it again. Things may have turned out badly this time, but we will succeed in the end. We have to trust our luck. No merchant is prosperous all the time. There will be occasions when he loses his cargo at sea, and there will be occasions when he sees it safely landed.'

'All right,' our master said, 'you have made your point. I will make sure that everything is done properly next time. If I am wrong, then lay the blame on me. There was something the matter, I know that much.'

Then the argument began again. One man said that the fire was too hot, for example. Hot or cold, it never worked. We never got the desired result, however hard we tried. Still we carried on with the madness. We were lunatic with greed and desire. When we were all together, we looked on one another as Solomon the Wise. Have you heard this proverb – 'All that glisters is not gold'? Not every apple is good for eating, however sweet it looks. So it was with us. The greatest fool among us was deemed to be the wisest. The most honest and honoured was in fact the biggest thief. You will learn the truth of this before I leave your company. Just listen to my tale.

PART TWO

There is a canon – do you know the man I mean? – who would infect with his presence a town the size of Nineveh or Rome. No one would be able to describe his infinite tricks and subtleties. You could live a thousand years and not be able to fathom all of his craft. No one is his equal in falsehood. He is so sly in his use of words, so slippery in his language, that he can make a fool of anyone he talks to. He could beguile the devil, even though he is one himself. He has duped many people, and will carry on deceiving them as long as he lives. Yet this is the curious thing. Men travel for miles to consult and converse with him; little do they realize that he is a swindler in disguise. If you like, I can explain it to you.

My story is of a canon, as I said, but I beg other canons not to believe that I am slandering their brotherhood. There is a rotten apple in every barrel. God forbid that a whole order should be tarnished by one man's sins. It is not my intention to defame you, good sirs, only to chastise one of your number. I address my story to everyone, not just to you. You remember well enough that among the twelve apostles there was only one traitor, Judas by name. Why should the other holy men have shared his guilt? Only he was culpable. But I will say this. If there is a Judas in your house, get rid of him at once. It will save you shame and embarrassment later. So do not be angry with me for telling my story. Just listen.

There had lived in London for many years a chantry priest, who earned his living by saying masses for the dead. He was so sweet and – how can I put it? – serviceable to his landlady that she would not hear of him paying anything for his board and lodging. She even bought his fine clothes for him. So he had plenty of ready money to spend. There was gold in his purse. Let me now explain to you how that gold fell into the hands of the malicious canon.

The canon came one day to the priest's lodging, and asked to borrow some money. 'Can you lend me a gold mark?' he asked him. 'I only need it for three days. Then I will repay you. If I let you down, I give you leave to hang me from the nearest tree!'

The priest took the coin from his purse straight away, and gave it to him; the canon pocketed it, thanked him, and went on his way. Three days later he promptly returned the money, much to the surprise and delight of the priest. 'Well, really,' the priest said to him, 'I don't mind lending you money, good sir, if you repay it so readily. You are true to your word. That is clear enough. How can I refuse you anything in the future?'

'What? You never thought I would trick you, did you? Please. Honesty is my middle name. I will always keep my word, to the day I die. God forbid that I should ever lie to you or deceive you. It just won't happen. Believe me when I say that I have always paid my debts. I have never let anyone down. There is not a false bone in my body.' He lowered his voice a little. 'Since you have been so good to me, I will let you in on a little secret. You have been kind to me, and I will be kind in return. I am willing to teach you, if you are willing to learn, the secrets of my work as an alchemist. If you watch carefully, I can assure you that you will see a wonder.'

'Is that right?' the priest replied. 'Go ahead, for God's sake.'

'I will do it if you wish. For no other cause but to please you.'

'Of course.'

Do you see how this villain lured his prey? He granted the priest a favour the priest had not asked for. That kind of favour bodes no good. I will prove that to you in a moment. And so this false canon, this root of iniquity, took great pleasure in betraying good Christian people. The devil planted wickedness in his heart. God give us the grace to withstand his wiles!

The poor priest had no idea, of course. He never saw the trap being laid for him. Oh silly innocent man! You will soon be blinded by avarice. Unfortunate priest, you have lost your way. All unawares, you are falling into the clutches of a fox who will trick you and deceive you. Let me hurry on now to the conclusion – and to your confusion. I will display your folly and stupidity. And I will reveal, as far as I am able, the wickedness of the man who led you forward.

Do you think I am talking about my master? Not at all. I am talking about another canon, a hundred times more skilful than the man I serve. He has betrayed more people than you can imagine. It is impossible to describe all of his falsehoods. Whenever I talk about him, my cheeks grow red with shame. Well, they would grow red if they could. I know well enough that I have no colour left in my face. The glow left my cheeks when I first began working among the stinks and fumes. Anyway, listen to the false canon.

'Sir,' he said to the priest, 'get your servant to buy some quicksilver. Tell him to hurry. Two or three ounces of the stuff will suffice. When he comes back with it, I will show you a miracle. Something you have never seen before.'

'Of course,' replied the priest. 'Right away.' So he ordered his servant to go to the apothecary, and purchase three ounces of quicksilver. The boy rushed off, and returned very quickly with the material. He gave it to the canon, who laid it down carefully. The canon then asked the servant to bring some coals, and to start a fire. This was promptly done.

Once the coals had started burning the canon took a crucible from the folds of his cloak. He showed it to the priest. 'Take hold of it,' he said. 'I want you to do this for yourself. Pour into this crucible an ounce of the quicksilver. In the name of Christ, we will make an alchemist of you yet. There are very few people to whom I would confide my secrets. I will show you how to harden this quicksilver. In front of your eyes I will make it as fine and as durable as the silver in your purse. You can test it with your teeth, if you like. If you prove me wrong, then you can reveal me as a liar and a fraud to the whole world. I have a powder here, in my pocket, that will do all. It cost me a lot of money, but it is worth it. It is the agent of all my work, as you shall soon see. Tell your boy to leave the room, by the way, and shut the door behind him. No one else must learn our secrets.'

So the silly priest obeyed him, got rid of the servant, and closed the door. Then they set to work. At the bidding of the false canon he put the crucible on the burning coals, and blew upon the fire with all his might. Then the canon sprinkled some white powder into the crucible. I don't know what it was – chalk, powdered glass, something like that. Whatever it was, it was worthless. It was only there to fool the priest. The canon told him to pile up the coals. 'In token of the great love I bear you,' he said, 'I will show you how your own two hands can work the miracle.'

'God save you! A thousand thanks!' replied the priest, who was now busily stoking up the fire.

While he was occupied, the false canon – this foul wretch, this servant of the devil – took out from his sleeve a piece of charcoal made of beechwood. A little hole had been drilled in the side of this coal, which the canon had filled up with metal filings; he had then sealed the hole with wax, so that none of the silver could escape. He had made this device a few hours before, and had brought it with him. I will tell you later what other tools he carried with him to deceive his victim. He wanted to rob the priest of everything before he left him. It angers me when I talk about him. I want to catch him. I want to trap him. But he is here and there and everywhere. He is so various. He is as fluid as quicksilver itself.

Now listen carefully to what followed. He hid the hollow coal in his hand while the priest was bent over the fire. 'Dear friend,' he said, 'you are doing this wrong. Let me have a go. I do feel sorry for you, too, sweating like a pig. Here. Take my handkerchief. Dry your face.' While the priest was wiping his eyes, the canon quickly slipped the coal into the middle of the crucible. It was soon burning away merrily, just like all the others.

'Let us stop for a drink,' the canon said. 'We deserve it. All will be well now, I know it. Sit down for a moment and rest.' When the hollow coal was ablaze, of course, the silver filings blended together and flowed into the bottom of the crucible. The priest knew nothing of the trick, and assumed that all the coals were alike. He could not see the deception the canon had practised on him. Now the alchemist saw his opportunity. 'Come over here, sir,' he said, 'and stand by me. I know very well that you do not have a mould for the metal. Can you go outside, and find or purchase a block of chalk. I will carve it into the proper shape. At the same time can you bring with you a bowl or pan of cold water? Then you will witness the wonderful workings of the art. I know you trust me but, to be doubly sure, I will not leave your sight. I will accompany you everywhere you go.'

So they left the chamber, carefully locking it behind them. They found the materials and, to make a long story short, the canon carved the chalk into the shape of an oblong mould. How did he know how to mould it? When the priest was not looking he took a bar of silver from the sleeve of his gown and fashioned the mould around it; then he concealed the silver in his sleeve once more. It weighed no more than an ounce. You will hear more about this bar later on.

For his next trick the canon poured the material from the fire into the mould, and then plunged it into cold water. He turned to the priest, and asked him to feel the interior of the mould. 'You will find silver there, I believe.' Of course he did. These were the silver filings hidden in the coal of beech, now fired into one ingot. What else could they be? So the priest did as he was requested. Lo and behold, he brings out a rod of fine silver.

'God's love be yours,' he told the canon. 'Mary, Mother of God, and all the saints bless you! Let their curse strike me if I do not become your servant and assistant. Teach me the subtleties of this noble craft. I will be your man for ever.'

'Hold on, sir priest. Let us try this a second time. Once you have learned the details, you will be able to repeat the experiment on your own. Why don't you take another ounce of quicksilver and cast it in the pan with the silver bar? Do what you did before. Quickly.'

So the priest poured in the quicksilver, scattered the powder over it, and set the pan over the fire. Then he blew into the flames, on the instruction of the canon, and waited for the outcome he desired.

In the meantime the canon was getting ready to fool the priest again. He took out from his pocket a hollow stick, in the end of which he had secreted an ounce of silver filings. He had secured the end with some sealing wax, just as he had done with the piece of coal. While the priest was busy with the fire, the canon once again sprinkled some more powder into the crucible and stood waiting expectantly. You have seen the measure of his falsehood, have you not? May the devil flay his skin! May God desert him in his last hours! Then he took the stick and began stirring the coals. Of course all fell out as before. By which I mean, the filings of the silver fell out. As soon as the wax melted they ran out of the crucible and soon became liquid metal.

What do you think happened, gentlemen? The priest was fooled by the same trick twice. The idiot was so pleased by the sight of the silver that I scarcely have the words to describe his delight. He was delirious. He gave himself up, body and soul, to the deceiver. 'Yes,' the canon said, 'I may be poor, but I have a certain wisdom. And I prophesy this. There is more silver to come. Do you have any copper in the house?'

'Of course. I know where to find some.'

'Well, sir, hurry up and get it.'

So the priest went off, found the copper, and brought it back to the canon. As soon as he had it in his hands, the canon carefully weighed out an ounce. No pen can describe, no tongue can tell of, his wickedness and false seeming. He was the minister of lies and deception. He seemed friendly enough to those who did not know him, but in thought and deed he was a fiend. It wearies me to list his crimes, but I do it only to put you on your guard against him and others like him.

This is what he did. He put the ounce of copper into the crucible, and placed it upon the burning coals. Once more he cast in his white powder. Once more he asked the silly priest to blow upon the fire. It was all a trick, of course, a piece of showmanship to fool the gullible. Then he poured the molten copper into a mould, and plunged it into cold water. There was a hiss. Steam arose. At that moment the canon quickly took out from his sleeve the silver ingot he had made before and put it in the water, whereupon it sank to the bottom of the pan. As the water trembled to and fro, he was able to remove the copper and conceal it. The priest, intent upon the fire, had seen nothing. The canon now took him by the arm. 'Well, sir,' he said. 'If this hasn't worked, then I blame you. I need your help here. Put your hand in the water, and see if you can find anything. Go on.'

So the priest plunged his hand into the pan and, of course, retrieved the ingot of silver. Hey presto! The canon smiled at him and said, 'Well, brother, let us take these silver ingots to the nearest goldsmith and get them assayed. I am sure they are the genuine article, but I want to have them tested all the same.' So they visited the local goldsmith and laid their silver on his counter; he tested the three ingots with fire and hammer. They were silver all right. Of course they were.

Who could have been happier than the foolish priest? No nightingale in May, no bird upon the wing, could be so blithe. No young girl could have been more ready to dance and sing. No knight could have been more lusty or fearless. The priest was now desperate to learn the secret of transmutation. 'How much will it cost me,' he asked the canon, 'to learn the formula? I must have it. For God's sake, tell me.'

'I must warn you,' the canon replied, 'it is not cheap. There are only two people in England who know the secret. One of them is a friar in Oxford. The other one is me. No one else.'

'I don't care how much it costs. Just tell me.'

'It is expensive, as I said. I can let you have the formula for forty pounds. At that price, it is a bargain. If you were not such a dear friend of mine, I would be charging you much more.'

So the priest went back to his chamber, and took out his strongbox. He counted out forty pounds, and brought the money back to the canon in exchange for the secret recipe. It was a great deal to pay for a fraud and a delusion.

'Sir priest,' the canon said, 'I don't want any great fame. In fact I prefer to remain unknown. So I beg you. Let this be a secret between us. If other people knew of my gift, why, I would be the object of hatred and of envy. I would be a dead man.'

'God forbid! You don't need to tell me that. I would rather lose all the money in my possession – I would rather go mad – than betray you.'

'Thank you. Thank you from the bottom of my heart. Now I must bid you farewell, sir. Goodbye! Good luck!' The canon gave the priest the kiss of peace, and left him. The priest never saw him again. He soon discovered that the so-called formula was useless; every experiment failed, and every session ended in tears. He had been completely fooled. The canon was a master of the black art of treachery.

Consider, gentlemen, how people in every walk of life strive for gold. There is so great a desire for it that it has become scarce. I could not count the numbers involved in alchemy, for example. They are led astray by philosophers who speak in misty terms. They never understand a word of their jargon. Their minds are addled. They chatter nonsense like magpies. They never achieve anything. If a man has enough money, he will easily learn how to turn his wealth to nothing.

This is the only transmutation that takes place. Mirth is replaced by sorrow. Full purses are changed into empty purses. The hopes and happiness of those who have lent money are turned into curses and bitterness. They ought to be ashamed.

Those who have been burned should flee the fire. I have one message for those of you who dabble in the false art. Abandon it. Leave it before you are ruined. Better late than never. If you lose everything, I am afraid that it will be too late. Seek, but you will not find. You will be like blind Bayard, blundering everywhere, not seeing the snares and traps in front of him. Can he stay on the high road? Of course not. He crashes into rocks and hedges. That is the way of alchemy, too. If you cannot see with your eyes, try to use your inner sight. Try to be guided by reason and judgement rather than staring wildly around for any portent. You may think you are wide awake, but you are sleepwalking to disaster. So put out the fire. Smother the coals. Give up the pursuit. If you don't believe me, believe the writings of the true alchemists themselves.

You have heard of Arnaldus of Villanova? In his treatise on alchemy, the *Rosarium Philosophorum*, or rose-garden of the philosophers, he makes this statement. 'No man,' he writes, 'can mortify mercury without the help of its brother, sulphur.' The father of alchemy, Hermes Trismegistus, put the same point. He taught that the dragon could be slain only by the death of its brother. By the dragon, he meant mercury. The dragon's brother is also known as sulphur. Both of them issue from the influence of the sun and the moon, from gold and from silver. 'And therefore,' he wrote in warning, 'let no unlearned man attempt to practise this art. If he has not understood the words of the philosophers, he is not fit to experiment. He is a fool and a charlatan. The work of the alchemist is the great secret of the world, the mystery of mysteries.'

One of Plato's disciples once asked him a pertinent question. It is recorded in the *Theatrum Chemicum*, if you care to look it up. 'Tell me, sir,' the disciple asked him, 'the name of the secret stone?'

'You must take up,' Plato replied, 'the stone known to humankind as Titan.'

'What is that?'

'It is also called Magnasia.'

'I am afraid, sir, that I am not following you. These terms are unknown to me. Can you tell me the nature of this Magnasia?'

'It is a liquid made out of the four elements.'

'Can you tell me the source of this liquid? Can you tell me its root?'

'No. Certainly not. The true philosophers have sworn never to divulge the secret, in speech or in writing. It is so dear to Christ that He has forbidden us to reveal it to anyone. He will only allow it to be told to those whom He holds most dear. It is a form of holy revelation. That is all I have to say.'

So I conclude from this that God Himself guards the secret of the stone. What is the point, therefore, in persisting? Abandon your quest. You may alchemize all of your life, and still end your days in suffering. Whoever makes God his enemy will pay dearly for it. If he goes against God's will, he merits severe punishment. At that point I must stop. Farewell to you all. May God send every true man comfort and consolation!

Heere is ended the Chanouns Yemannes Tale

The Manciple's Prologue

Heere folweth the Prologe of the Maunciples Tale

Do you know the village of Harbledown, called by everyone Bob-up-and-down? It is on the outskirts of Blean forest, about two miles from Canterbury itself. This was the spot where our Host began to play the fool. 'Dobbin is in the mire,' he said. 'Help me pull him out. Have you ever played that game? Is there any one of you who can rouse that fellow at the back? I will pay good money to see his eyes open. A thief could rob him and tie him up, without him noticing. He is fast asleep. Look at him. He is close to falling off his horse. He is the Cook from London, isn't he? Roger. That is his name. Roger of Ware. Can somebody please go and wake him up? I insist that he tells us all a story. It may not be worth much, but it is a good penance for him.' Our Host rode up to him. 'Wake up, Roger! God help you! What is the matter with you? Why are you dozing in the daylight? Were you bitten by fleas all night? Were you dead drunk? Were you lying with some whore? Whatever you did, you did too much of it.'

The Cook then tried to rouse himself. He was pale-faced and puffy-eyed. 'I swear to God,' he replied, 'that I was suddenly filled with utter tiredness. I would rather sleep than drink a barrel of the best wine from Vintry.'

The Manciple then rode forward. 'If it helps,' he told the Cook, 'I am quite ready to tell a story in your place. If our fellow pilgrims don't mind, and if our good Host permits it, I can begin at once. I don't think you are in a fit state. Your face is pale. You look dazed. And, if I may say so, your breath smells horrible. You really are not well.' The Manciple turned towards the rest of us. 'You can be certain, sirs, that I will not flatter him. Just look at the way he is yawning. Look at that gaping mouth of his, as if he were about to swallow us all! Close your mouth, man. Your foul breath will infect the whole company. Have you got the devil's hoof in there? You stink. What a fine fellow you are! Do you fancy a quick joust or wrestling match? I don't think so. You are too drunk to fart.'

This little speech enraged the Cook. He shook his head, he gnawed his lip, he stared hard at the Manciple. But he was too drunk to say anything. Words failed him. Then he fell off his horse. He lay helpless in the mud, as some of the pilgrims tried to lift him up. There was much shoving and pushing, much tugging and heaving, before they got him back into his saddle. He may have looked as pale as a ghost, but he was heavy enough. If only he had kept hold of his ladle, and never uncorked a bottle. He would have been a better horseman, that's for sure.

Harry Bailey came up to the Manciple. 'You can see for yourself how drunk he is. He could no more tell a story than my horse. I don't know whether he has been drinking wine or ale, but the effect is the same. He talks through his nose. And did you hear that sneeze? He has a bad cold as well. I don't suppose he can keep on his saddle and talk at the same time. He can hardly ride a straight line. If he falls from his horse a second time, it will be very difficult to hoist him up again. So, sir, please take his place. Tell us a story. I must mention one thing, though, before you begin. I think you were unwise to criticize him so publicly. One of these days he may pay you back, and lay some small charge against you. He may find fault with your accounts, for example, or with your expenses. I know that he has dealings with you. Trifles can sometimes cause a lot of trouble.'

'God forbid that should happen. As you say, it is not difficult to point out small mistakes. I would rather pay for his horse than get into a legal tangle with him. I didn't mean to upset him. Honestly. It was a joke. And do you know what? I know how to calm him down. Here in my satchel I have a flask of good Rhenish wine. Shall we have a bit of fun? Roger of Ware will gulp this down in a second. Just see if I'm wrong. He cannot refuse a drink.'

The Manciple was not wrong. The Cook took up the flask, and drained it in a moment. He really did not need the wine, of course. He had drunk more than enough already. Then he returned the flask and, as far as he was able, thanked the Manciple. 'Thashwasgood.'

Our Host laughed out loud. 'I am convinced now,' he said, 'that we will have to take strong liquor with us wherever we go. It is a sovereign remedy for strife. It turns fights and arguments into love-feasts. Blessed is thy name, Bacchus, god of wine. You can make the greatest enemies the best of friends. I will worship you from this time forward! Now, sir Manciple, we turn to you. Will you tell us your tale?'

'I will. With pleasure.'

The Manciple's Tale

*Heere bigynneth the Maunciples Tale of
the Crowe*

When Phoebus lived upon the earth, as the old books tell us, he was the most gallant knight and most lively bachelor of all. He was also the most skilful archer. He killed the serpent Python as the great snake lay sleeping in the sun. He accomplished other great deeds with his bow. You can read about them in those old books I mentioned.

He was also an expert musician, capable of playing any instrument. His voice was so exquisitely beautiful that it ravished the ear. Amphion, the famous king of Thebes, whose singing raised up the stone walls of his city, could not rival him. He was also the most handsome man that ever was, or ever will be, in the world. What need is there to dwell on the details of his beauty? It is enough to say that he was matchless. He was also a very gentle, worthy knight of peerless renown. That is why this flower of honour, this Phoebus, always carried with him his bow. It was a token of his victory over Python, but he was also looking out for sport and adventure.

Now in his house he had a crow. He kept it in a cage. This bird was as white as a swan, by the way. It was whiter than snow or the fleece of a lamb. Phoebus fostered it, and taught it to speak so well that it could mimic the voice of any man or woman it heard. And it sang so sweetly, too, more melodiously than the nightingale. It was a joy to hear its notes.

At this time Phoebus had a wife, whom he loved more dearly than life itself. Night and day he did his best to please her and delight her. He had only one fault – he was a jealous husband

and, if he could, he would have kept her under lock and key. He was afraid of being cuckolded, as would be any man in that position. But all precautions are useless. A good wife, innocent in thought and deed, should not be watched or doubted; if the wife is not so good, you cannot hold her down. I take it as a law that you cannot restrain a woman who wants to roam. Every writer concurs on that subject.

Back to my story. So Phoebus does all he can to please her, hoping that all his attentions and all his affection will stop her from chasing after any other man. But God knows that you cannot thwart the course of nature. You cannot crush the force of instinct. Put any wild bird in a cage. You can feed it, give it water, hang little bells from the bars, attend to it in every possible way, it will make no difference. It will still wish to be free. The cage might be made out of gold. The bird would still prefer to be in a wild wood, feeding off worms and dirt. It will try as hard as it can to escape. It desires only its liberty.

I give you the example of the cat. You can feed it with the choicest meats, and the richest milk. You can make a bed for it with the finest silks. As soon as it sees a mouse, it forgets all about its creature comforts. It is not interested in cuts of ham or beef. It wants only to eat the mouse. Nature holds dominion. Need knows no law. Think of the she-wolf. When desire moves her, she wishes to mate with the foulest wolf she can find. That is her appetite. I have cited these examples to prove the faithlessness of the male, not of the female. We all know that men lust after the lowest of the low. Their wives may be beautiful and noble and loving. It makes no difference. They want fresh meat. They delight in novelty. They sicken at the thought of their virtuous wives.

Phoebus Apollo was different, of course. But for all his innocence he was deceived. His wife had fallen for another man. He was of low reputation, and far beneath Phoebus in every respect. It is the kind of situation that happens all the time, and is always a cause of grief and misery.

So whenever Phoebus was away from home, his wife invited

this man to come and fuck her. Fuck her? Sorry. That is vulgar. I suppose I should apologize. But it is the truth. Plato said that the word should always fit the deed. If I am going to tell my story properly, I need to use the appropriate terms. I am a plain man of plain speaking. And there really isn't any difference between a common woman and a lady of high degree if she is free with her body. They are both steeped in sin. Oh, there is one difference. The high-born lady is deemed to be a 'lover', while the common woman is called a 'slut'. In truth, of course, one lies as low as the other. They are both on their backs.

In the same way there is no difference between a usurping tyrant and a thief or outlaw. They are exactly the same. Alexander the Great was once told that a tyrant who burns down homes, slaughters his enemies and destroys land is acclaimed as a great general and leader; a small-time thief who does not have armies, and who can only rob a few houses without doing much damage, is damned as a rogue and criminal. But I am not a great expert in such things. I cannot quote you chapter and verse.

So, anyway, the wife of Phoebus stripped this man and fondled him. You can imagine the rest. All the time the white crow was sitting in its cage and watching the whole thing. It did not even chirrup. But as soon as Phoebus returned home it sang out, 'Cukoo! Cockoh! Cuckold!'

'What is that song?' Phoebus came over to the cage. 'I have never heard you sing so loudly before. It does my heart good to see you so cheerful. But what is the song?'

'It is a true one, Phoebus, I know that much. For all your virtue – for all your beauty – for all your faithfulness and honesty – for all your music –'

'Get on with it, bird.'

'You have been deluded and deceived. A man of very little reputation – a man who cannot be compared to you in any respect – a man with the worth of a gnat –'

'Go on.'

'Has been fucking your wife. I saw him with my own two eyes.'

What more need I say? The crow told him what had happened in great detail. It told him how his wife had betrayed him time and time again. Phoebus turned away, struck with grief, thinking that his heart was about to break. He took up his bow and plucked an arrow from its sheath; with that, he killed her on the spot. There is no more to say.

Then he fell into a frenzy. He smashed all of his instruments – his harp, his lute, his gitern – and then he broke his bow and arrows. When he had finished, he turned once more to the crow in the cage.

'Traitor!' he screamed at it. 'With the tongue of a scorpion, not of a bird, you have destroyed my happiness! Damned is the day when I was born. I wish I were dead. And my dear wife? You were the source of all my bliss. You were always true and faithful to me, I am sure of that. Now you are lying here dead in front of me. You were innocent, weren't you? How could I have been so blind, so stupid? How could I have committed such a crime against an innocent and virtuous woman? What was I thinking? My senseless anger has struck down a blameless victim. Distrust has destroyed us both. Every man, beware of haste. Believe nothing without strong evidence. Do not strike before you know the truth. Consider very carefully what you are doing. Anger and suspicion are not enough. They lead you into the dark. That is why I, Phoebus Apollo, now wish to kill myself.'

Then he turned to the crow. 'Villain! False bird! You used to sing sweeter than a nightingale. You will never sing again. These fine white feathers will turn to black. You will be dumb, unable to speak, for the whole span of your life. That is how traitors are punished. You and your offspring will be black for ever. Your breed will be silent, except when you croak in warning of a storm. Your cry will remind the world of wind and rain. That is your punishment for the death of my wife.'

Phoebus reached into the cage and pulled out all of the bird's white feathers one by one. Then he struck it dumb, depriving it of speech and song, before he drove it out of the house. May the fiend take the bird. And that is why, ladies and gentlemen, all crows are black.

So take heed of this story and remember to think before you speak. Guard your tongue. Never tell a man that his wife has been unfaithful to him. Whether you are right or wrong, he will hate you for it. According to eminent scholars, Solomon had learned discretion at an early age. But, as I said, I am not a learned man. My mother is my real teacher. Once she said to me, 'Son, for God's sake think of the crow. Curb your tongue and keep your friends. A loose tongue is more destructive than the devil. You can cross yourself to ward off the foul fiend.

'God has given you teeth and lips to restrain the tongue. Use them. And use your head, too. Think before you speak. The loud mouth often comes to grief. No one has ever been punished for saying too little. Do not hold forth, except of course in praise of God and His saints. What was I saying? Yes, restraint is the first virtue. That is what small children are taught every day. That was the lesson I learned, too. Too many words are bad for you. What is a rash tongue? It is a sword that wounds and kills. Just as a knife can cut off an arm, so can a tongue sever a friendship. God hates a jangler. Read the wise sayings of Solomon. Read the psalms of David. Read Seneca. They will all tell you the same. Do not speak. Just nod your head and stay silent. Pretend that you are deaf, even, if some gossip tries to spread rumours. The Flemings have a saying: "The less chatter, the more cheer." If you have not said a wicked word, my son, then you have nothing to fear. If you say something wrong or foolish, you will never be able to take it back again. What is said is said. It flies into the air, and cannot be caught. You will become a victim of your own verbosity.

Spread no news, and start no gossip. Whatever company you keep, high or low, restrain your tongue and think about the crow. Have I said enough?'

Heere is ended the Maunciples Tale of the Crowe

The Parson's Prologue

Here folweth the myrie words of the Parsoun

By the time that the Manciple had finished his story, the sun was low in the sky. It was by my calculation no more than twenty-nine degrees in height, and my shadow stood out before me. It was four o'clock, and a spring evening was about to descend upon us travellers. We were riding through the outskirts of a village when the Host reined in his horse and addressed us.

'Good lords and ladies,' he said, 'our work is almost done. We lack only one tale, according to my reckoning. We have heard from every class, and every degree, in the course of our journey. My ordinance has almost been fulfilled. There is only one person left to entertain us. I hope he does it well.' He turned to the Parson, who rode a little behind him. 'Sir priest,' he asked him, 'are you a vicar or a parson? Do you have your own church or do you serve another? Speak the truth, please. It doesn't matter what rank you hold, as long as you can tell a good story. You are the last. Open up. Sing for your supper. Let us see what you are made of. I can tell by your appearance, and your expression, that you are good at this kind of thing. Tell us a good old-fashioned fable, will you?'

'You will get no fable from me, Mr Bailey,' the Parson replied. 'Do you not recall the words of Paul to Timothy? He condemns those who stray from the path of truth and who invent lies or fantasies. Why should I give you chaff when I can offer you good wheat? So if you wish to hear morality and virtuous matter, I am your man. If you are willing to give me an audience I will do my best to mix instruction with delight. But I am a man of the south. I cannot call a lady "a bonny wee thing" or tell you something "canny". I cannot lay claim to being much of a poet, either, so I will tell you something pleasing and suitable in prose. Now, at the end of our journey, I will bring matters to a conclusion. May the Saviour guide me and inspire me to lead you to Jerusalem. Our pilgrimage on earth is an image of the glorious pilgrimage to the celestial city. With your permission I will now begin my story. What is your opinion?

'There is one other thing. I am no scholar. I am sure that there are some among you who are more learned and able than I am. I can offer you only the substance, the essential meaning, and I am perfectly willing to be corrected.'

We all agreed to this. It seemed good to us that we should end our journey with some virtuous text. We were happy to hear the Parson's soft voice at the end of the day. So we asked our Host to entreat him to continue.

'Sir priest,' he said, 'God be with you. Give us the fruit of your contemplations. But you must hurry. The sun is sinking in the sky. Give us much matter in a short space. May God help you in your task, good man. Now please begin.'

So the Parson rode before us, and began his story. We had entered a forest. 'Our sweet Lord God of heaven, who wills that all men have full knowledge of His godhead and live in the sweet bliss of eternity, admonishes us with the wise words of the prophet Jeremiah. Stand upon the old paths and find from old scriptures the right way which is the good way, on this pilgrimage upon the earth . . .'

I held my horse back as the pilgrims made their way among the trees. The evening fell and the birds of the forest were silent. I could still hear him speaking of 'the right way to Jerusalem the Celestial' when I dismounted and walked into a small grove. There I went down on my knees and prayed.

Chaucer's Retractions

Here taketh the makere of this book his leve

'I make this request to all of those who hear or read this little treatise. If there be anything here that pleases them, they should thank our Lord Jesus Christ from whom proceeds all virtue and all wisdom. If there be anything here they dislike I beg them to ascribe the fault to my ignorance and not to my will. I would have written better if I possessed the gift of eloquence. The Bible tells us that words must be used to instruct us. That has always been my intention.

'So I beseech you, for the mercy of God, to pray for me to Christ our Saviour. Plead with Him to forgive my sins, and especially my transgressions in the writing and translation of books of worldly vanity. I now revoke and condemn these books: *Troilus and Criseyde*, *The Book of Fame*, *The Legend of Good Women*, *The Book of the Duchess*, *The Parliament of Fowls*, and those stories of *The Canterbury Tales* that may be construed as sinful. I also recant *The Book of the Lion* and, if I could remember them, many other books. I renounce the songs and lecherous lays that I have written down, in the hope that Christ will forgive my trespasses. Grant me mercy, oh Lord. But for the translation of *The Consolation* of Boethius, for all the saints' lives, for all the homilies and moral tales that tend to virtue – for all these I thank Christ and His blessed Mother, beseeching them and all the saints of heaven to pray for me now and at the hour of my death. Send me grace so that I may repent my sins and save my soul. Grant me true penitence, confession and absolution. In the merciful name of our Saviour,

Jesus Christ, king of kings and priest of priests, who redeemed the world with His precious blood, may I be one of those saved on the day of doom. *Qui cum Patre et Spiritu Sancto vivit et regnat Deus per omnia secula. Amen.*'

I rose to my feet, and walked back to my horse.

Heere is ended the book of the tales of Canterbury, compiled by Geoffrey Chaucer, of whos soule Jhesu Crist have mercy. Amen.